Books by *April Alisa Marquette*:

Fiction

~The Cohort Trilogy
Absolution
Progression
Iniquities

~The Cohorts, Generation Next
Improbable

~The Sea Isles Series - A Trilogy
Exodus
Affinity
To Be Announced

Turnabout

~A Tranquility Tale
Rebuke

*

Non-Fiction
Co-Authored with Jessica Janna

~The Relinquish & Reap Series
Seedling
Sowing
Yielding

**Ask for them ... at your local Barnes & Noble,
or Books-A-Million bookstore!**

I thank all the men—gay, and not, who aided me to pen this tale.

Special thanks to *Marcel Dion* for your candor, humor, and input.

For those who struggle, it gets better.

Iniquities

Gross injustice; wicked act …

The Cohort Trilogy

Book III

by

April Alisa Marquette

April Rain Publications

Books that captivate

Visit the author at www.aprilalisamarquette.net
Library of Congress Catalog Card No.: On File

Publisher's note:
    The novel *Iniquities* is a work of fiction – for adults, only.

Prologue

BACK then, young Beau would have been overjoyed to hear it, but now he was miserable, especially when he found out 'the solo' forced him to spend additional time with pot-bellied, florid-faced Mr. McCuddy. The man had smelly coffee and cigarette breath.

Beau also hated that when he and Mr. McCuddy were alone, the teacher inappropriately touched him.

Becoming emboldened with each next attempt, slimy McCuddy rubbed his fat belly against Beau because no one else saw.

Sick of all the pawing, young Beau wanted to confide in Mireya. Then then again, he didn't, because what if she changed toward him? What if his same-aged best friend began eyeing him with disgust, the way Mr. McCuddy did?

Not wanting that, Beau opted for silence.

He did think about telling his aunt, though. Feisty and round, Nell Moore would put a stop to Mr. McCuddy's mess; Uncle Brantley would too. Unc might even kick the man's flimsy behind because nothing angered Beau's uncle more than men trying to misuse his nephew.

Yet to keep the peace and keep his secret from being splashed all over school, Beau kept quiet.

Until McCuddy tried to out *him*…

Iniquities

You will again have compassion on us; you will tread our sins underfoot

and hurl all our iniquities into the depths of the sea.

Micah 7:19 (NIV)

Chapter 1

Tall and lanky, the thirteen-year-old wanted to ask the man and woman something; yet he backed away from their improperly closed door, after hearing their voices. The kid had seen the couple in their cozy boudoir. He had also heard the man whom he thought of as his father.

"You know he's not like other boys, right?"

The woman, buxom and brown, lay facing her husband, the boy's uncle. "I know." The boy's aunt sighed, and her large breasts heaved and fell against her little nightie. "It's why you're doing all you can, Brant. I love and thank you for it. One day *he* may even thank you too."

"I don't want the boy's thanks; I just want him to be ok." The big man searched for words. "I want him to...*be* somebody, ya know? I want him to become a *man*, one he can be proud of, his preference aside."

"He will," Beau's aunt assured. "You'll see."

However, adult Beauregard DeVeaux reflected, *his uncle never did see.* When Beau recalled his uncle's early demise, Beau felt anger and sadness. He thought it was such an iniquity, a gross injustice!

Beau also thought about his first cousin. How old had she been when they'd lost her father? Perhaps eighteen or nineteen—too young for such a tragedy, in Beau's opinion anyway. He had been thirteen or fourteen, even younger. He had taken Uncle Brantley's death hard, much harder than he had his mother's leaving.

When Beau had been eight, his mother had up 'n left without a word. Nevertheless, she had been a witch, of the first magnitude, so by disappearing, she had done her small son a favor. Not long afterward, Beau had been taken in by his aunt and uncle, such a blessing.

Yet, as an adult, looking back, Beau wondered. What would his life have been like had his mother disappeared when he'd been a toddler? Since she had always despised him, had she bounced sooner, maybe he would be different. Lord knew his likes and dislikes would be different.

He would probably have fewer nightmares. Had Mother's monkey-ass left before all the damage, he might even have been 'normal.'

Thirty-something, with shades on, and sea breezes wafting over him, Beau recalled what he had been told. Not long after his mother took him, again, from Emmett, his father died. Prostate cancer. Then his aunt hired a PI. She hounded the man too, until he located her brother's boy. Then from the investigative report, Nell learned. Her nephew was living with an older man, because the child's druggie mama had run off. The bitch had left the child, in a nasty apartment, alone; an eight year old!

As an adult, Beau recalled seeing that report. His aunt still had it after all these years. Beau didn't know why. All he knew was that as a boy, he'd felt his world had been turned upside down when the older man, his downstairs neighbor, had said, 'Boy, you gotta leave.' Beau hadn't been afraid of his aunt back then, but he'd trembled upon re-encountering her husband, because previously it had been *men* who had done vile things to him. Only his father and his older neighbor had not violated him. Therefore, facing Uncle Brantley, who had been as tall as he had been wide, had been traumatic. The man's booming voice, and his hands, the size of hams, had nearly caused Beau, the kid, to hyperventilate.

"Young man," Brantley had thundered, "you'll want to do whatever your aunt says. That way, we'll have some peace around here. Oh, and you'll have chores. You'll get an allowance too; if you pull your weight. Don't, and there'll be consequences."

Most miserable, Beau had not known what that last word meant, but he hadn't liked it. When his uncle had backed out, closing the door, Beau realized. He was shaking, so much so that he hadn't noticed. He had his own room, for the first time since... he could not remember. Yet despite his all-consuming fear, one day, and then the next rolled away. Soon Beau could not imagine his life without the love of a good man.

He and his uncle hadn't had long, though, only six years. As an adult, Beau realized, those years had been his uncle's investment –in him.

Wildly successful as an actor, a filmmaker, and the lead singer in a quasi-renowned band called *Infusion*, Beau eyed his long outstretched limbs and slowly rose. He found his sea legs and grasped the gleaming deck rail. The actor pushed his designer sunglasses higher on his nose and thought about how he loved sailing. He enjoyed the way his luxury vessel skimmed the Mediterranean. He liked the peacefulness, which enabled him to think. However, he did *not* want to keep thinking sad things. He was on vacation, for crying aloud. He was in *le Midi*, the South of France, where all was beautiful, and where, so far, he had well spent his days off. In the heart of Paris, he'd visited the *Sacré Coeur*, a Roman Catholic Basilica. At *The Louvre* he'd toured exhibition rooms and galleries. He'd strolled the *Jardin des Tuileries*, the garden located near the *Place de la Concorde*. Beau planned to check out *Caveau de la Sunset*. He would do so one evening because he'd heard about that club. There, it was said, anything could happen, when the sun went down. That and more Beau would do during his time away.

Then he would go back to the states and buckle down. At home, he would edit his new documentary. He would see where they were on the film project that he would also bring to life. He had to compile tracks too, for his band's new album, among other essential things.

Suddenly Beau leaned over the deck rail. The actor told himself to breathe, to concentrate on the vista. He fought to catch his breath. When he did, he knew one thing. He had to stop *thinking*.

No longer feeling like he hyperventilated, Beau stood upright. He raised his binoculars. Standing on the yacht's polished wood, he zeroed in on structures long ago erected in the lush countryside. Chateaux dotted the riverbank. Their architecture ranged from the Roman to the Renaissance periods.

Again, Beau became aware of the glorious weather. Vaguely, he heard music, and the conversation of those he had invited to share this trip with him. Allowing his binoculars to dangle from the cord around his neck, Beau gazed at the water, dazzling in the sunlight. However, he thought about his life, again. What an unbelievable ride, up until now.

Turning, he faced his guests. While doing so, Beau made himself ponder dinner. He also thought about where he might want to party come evening, because it was simple. The tall buff man wanted no more jaunts down memory lane. Mostly, Beau wanted no more thoughts of his uncle because Beau needed to face facts. The man was gone, and Unc had been, for more than two decades now.

Chapter 2

Kismet called. Beau was apprised of it when he returned to his enormous decadent suite at *La Résidence*. Dang, he thought, he almost wished his first cousin and her mom were present. It would be fun to watch his aunt amble about the hotel. She would place a hand at her ample chest. The little round woman would also murmur, 'Oh my,' because the tranquil haven on the *Cote d'Azur* was most prestigious. On a private beach, the hotel was beautiful, and its service unsurpassed.

About to receive a massage, Beau vowed to call both his aunt and his first cousin later. Face down; he lay on the masseuse's table. With a pristine sheet draped over his buttocks, the actor found himself wondering what Kismet was doing. As heated smooth stones were placed on his back, Beau bet his cousin was fussing over her twins. Boy, how time flew, he mused, because the twins were now five years old.

Expert hands applied gentle pressure, and Beau sighed. He recalled the twin's mother. His cousin and her husband had purchased a home in the town of Winter Creek, New York. They'd done so, not long after Beau and his cousin had lost a beloved friend.

Pushing that from mind, Beau thought about his cousin's culinary skills. Maybe she was currently in her huge country kitchen. Cuz was probably cooking. Or maybe Kismet was seated in another room, thinking. Beau *had* asked something of her, and it was big.

Back in the winter, the actor hadn't really asked. He and his first cousin had been brainstorming, and things had taken shape from there. Feeling his muscles loosen, Beau realized. He had been knotted up. The knots had begun with that conversation. He'd requested something that could be considered an enormous imposition. Even now while thinking about it, Beau's heart raced beneath the masseuse's capable hands. Beau wondered. *What if Kiss wouldn't accommodate him?* Then he'd have to find another way. He would need someone else, but the woman that the fam called Kiss was his first choice. There was no one he trusted more.

Well, Beau would trust his *aunt* with his life, and he trusted his uncle's daughter, the one who had been born outside his aunt and uncle's relationship; however, neither of those women could help. Beau's aunt was too old, and her stepdaughter was way too busy.

As he felt heat from the topmost massive stone, and the pressure of the masseuse's hands, Beau recalled a different winter day. It was then that he had told Kismet that they needed to call things off...

Standing in her den before a cozy fire, Beau had sounded disappointed. "It was just a dream, Kiss, but we can't do it."

Aproned, she stared in disbelief. "Why're you saying this?" She'd been gung-ho. "I told you I'd discuss it with my husband. I said I'd help, so why're you backing out, now? You've wanted this for –forever."

"Don't you see," Beau moaned. "You 'n I can't do it! We're first cousins." He swore. "Never thought I'd say it, but being family sucks."

"It doesn't," she insisted. "Some of your DNA can still be instilled."

"It can't, Kiss. Your mother and my father are siblings. Inbreeding isn't a myth. It's disgusting, and I don't want my kid to wind up loco."

With her just-beginning-to-brown biscuit-colored skin, curvaceous waved, like there was no problem. "You got a man, right?"

Sort of, he did. Wearing a turtleneck, Beau plunked onto his cousin's comfy sofa. It wasn't official, but he and 'his man' had known each other for years. They spoke often; hung out, and took trips. They had the most amazing sex, shattering all Beau's preconceived notions about how it could be, with the same person, many years in. Dismissing all of that, Beau wanted his cousin to forget questions. He wanted her to go into her large beautiful kitchen and check her homemade stroganoff. Maybe then he could pull himself together, before her kids barreled in from the snow. Sure, he was crazy about 'the four monsters,' but he needed to absorb the dissolution of his dream. Beautiful Beau just wanted to stand before the blazing fire a moment, alone.

Yet Kismet remained, a forty-something brick house. With hands on ample hips, she inquired,"Diddley, what about your man?"

"What about him?" Beau asked through clenched teeth. His heart hurt, and he just wanted quiet. Now that 'it' was never going to happen.

"*Your man* can do this –*for* you," Kismet said looking up like nothing was amiss. "Of course, we'll need a clean bill of health, and—"

Just that fast, the tall man was excited again. He almost missed it when his cousin said, "If he'll sign stipulations, then it'll be on."

Beau realized. He was yet in France, in the springtime. The masseuse began to remove the now-cooler stones from his back. But back in the winter, he'd thought his cousin was crazy. While he had eaten with her, the monsters, and the hubby, he'd considered her words. *He could use a donor.* They were often medical students, and he could pick the one he wanted, with the IQ, looks, and genetic makeup he desired!

Since it appeared his cousin would insist on using her eggs, Beau's child would still receive his family DNA, from her!

Beau rose from the masseuse's table, thanking the woman. He descended the decadent French spa's marble steps. In the warm roiling waters of the indoor pool, the actor felt buoyant.

Beau remembered being at another iconic hotel. In LA, he had gotten off The Ten, his superfast luxury plane. Getting in a limo, he'd pondered his and Kismet's scheme as he had pecked his date on the cheek.

The ebony-skinned actress looked stunning in a slim navy column.

Nevertheless, the actor's mind drifted. However, at the fundraiser held at a luxurious Beverly Hills Hotel, Beau remembered to compliment the actress. He did so while escorting her beneath a coffered ceiling. Glimpsing a multi-tiered chandelier, his mind went back to 'it.'

Beau barely noticed the elegantly patterned marble floor or floral displays. Handsome in his tux, Beau did manage to make conversation and chuckle, but only because it was expected. At the glitzy affair, the actor/producer drank, donated, and danced on the chilly rooftop terrace. In a mental fog, he reminded himself to be more attentive. Still, he'd mechanically moved through the affair that was all old Hollywood glam. Looking back, Beau did not know how he'd managed to appear gracious, but attendees said he had.

In France, in the spa pool, he recalled agreeing that he and Kismet would discuss things with the fam, because in a way, they'd be involved.

Exiting the warm, salt-water pool, Beau gave an excited little shimmy, because *just maybe...* his and Kismet's far-out scheme really could *work*!

Chapter 3

HAVING completed his morning massage and swim, he went back to his fabulous French suite. There Beau drank coffee and recalled *that* winter conversation. To the only man who could vaguely even be considered his man, Beau mentioned his desire.

Appearing nonchalant, the optician said he knew. When Beau stared, the other man, five foot eleven, with sunlit hair, and skin the color of sand, grinned, "I did. I already knew you wanted that."

Beau chuckled and said he should not have been surprised that Saavion was aware of his deepest desire. That was because Beau found it easy to talk to the optician. For that reason, Beau cited 'the offer.'

"Wow." Seated in Beau's home office, Saavion appeared impressed. "That's beyond generous, on your cousin's part. She really loves you."

Beau nodded, because indeed she did, and he her; "But we've still got a problem."

"*You* can't do it," the optician stated.

Beau swiveled in his plush leather office chair. "How'd you know?"

"Du-uh; you and Kiss are first cousins, Beau. I wouldn't think you'd chance it; not when you can use a *donor* and get a healthy baby."

"I don't want just anybody though," Beau mused aloud. Over time, he had warmed to the idea, "However, picking the right man could be fun."

The optician noted the light in the tall, buff, brown, filmmaker's eyes. That light meant Beau was thinking, about his future. The optician wanted to be part of that future. True enough, he had never pondered having kids. As a gay man, Saavion Kennings had not thought of the possibility. He had simply felt like certain things—kids included—he would never have. It had not bothered him.

Saavion mentored kids and had a heap of Godchildren. Beau's friend, Valeria, also an optician, had bequeathed Saavion all her offspring. Therefore as a Godfather, Saavion had never longed for a child. However, *Beau* did. Thus, an opportunity had presented itself, and before he was aware, Saavion said, "I'll be your donor."

Beau shook his head, "Nah, I couldn't accept, but thanks."

Saavion frowned, "What's wrong with *me*? Am I not good enough?"

"Yes, but a friend doesn't ask *this* of a friend. It strains things."

"You're not asking," the optician pointed out, "and I'm offering."

Beau's hand crept up. Through his tee, he felt for his dog tags, the ones his uncle had worn while in the Korean War. "Why?" Beau asked, unable to comprehend. "You've never wanted kids. Why this, now?"

"I don't necessarily need kids," Saavion admitted. "I see them almost every day, but I could do this." He shrugged, "For you. You want this, so I'd do it because..." The optician whispered to give his statement emphasis, "It's within my power to do so. Provided it's ok with Kiss."

Beau felt like ice water coursed through his veins. He rubbed his chilled arms as he spoke. "You know there'd be testing and such—*if* we let you do this. You'd need to show Kiss a clean bill of health, too."

The optician's eyes twinkled. "And you wouldn't need to see it?"

Beau chuckled, "Now, you're funny." The actor said so because he and the other man slept together. They periodically traded doctor's notes. Returning to the previous topic, Beau said, "Kiss will need your documents because the donor's sperm will enter *her* body. She and the doctors will need your complete medical and mental history."

The light-skinned man shrugged. "Done, and I don't want pay." Saavion said so because what would he do with *more* money? Years back, he had happened upon a fortune. He'd invested in a company that created a video game based on a mythological Greek warrior-god. He had not known that in the testing phase, the game would hit. Nor had it been foreseen that at tradeshows, the game would become all the rage. Going in, Saavion had not known that the first game would spawn others, or that 'suits' would get involved. Without Saavion's knowledge, some of those executives had even approached *Beau* to voice the main character. What a kick! Back then, it hadn't crossed either man's mind that the games would spin off into blockbuster movies, but they had. Both had profited enormously. From that time forth, Saavion had made other lucrative investments, because it seemed, he had the Midas Touch.

Aware that the other man's financial foundation was sound, Beau still argued. "Saav, you've gotta accept something, because this won't be a cakewalk. I mean, if Kiss and I agree, there'll be doctors, physical as well as psychological. There'll be scheduling, legal documents, and more. So I insist because I'd compensate any other donor."

"OK. Listen," Saavion began. "I've got a list of charities. You can pick one, *and* let me be the Godfather." The optician smiled. "Granted, your baby's mother would have to agree, but I am a great influence; just ask your pal, Val."

Beau gazed out at the snowy landscape. OMG! He thought, *I could actually become a father*! Stunned, the actor turned back to the man whom a former roommate had also found attractive. Years ago, the all-female, sassy, butter-yellow Ronni had threatened, 'Beau, if you don't get with Saavion, *I* will.' She had known the optician was openly gay. 'Still, I'll turn him out, leaving no chance for your team, ever again.'

Beau recalled laughing with Ronni. Suddenly his heart ached because damn did he miss her! He and pal Valeria had roomed with Ronni for nearly three years. Allowing bittersweet memories to fade, Beau addressed the optician. "You'd do this, despite the legalities, just to be my child's Godfather?"

"No." Saavion told the truth. "Your charitable donation would be my payment, but I want to be your child's Godfather, so I can be part of their life. You know, since I *will* have had a hand in producing him or her. Get it?" Saavion grinned, "I'd have 'a hand' in it."

"I get it." Beau motioned below his waist as though he were pulling on his wanker. "Seriously though, I still don't get why you'd do this."

"I'd do it *for you*. Dammit, Beau! You're dense. I've known you for ten years. To be a dad was always your dream. And you'd be the best."

Again, Beau felt chilled because his cousin had said the same thing.

The man with the sunlit hair admitted there were other reasons he was willing to help, yet he revealed just one. Love. "I love you, Beau. I have for a long time. That's why I'd do this, and more. So talk to Kiss, and get back to me. Lemme know when to see the fancy doctors." Saavion smirked. "Gotta get set to dry-dog it, ya know? In a room where somebody *will* be watching."

Beau moaned as though in pain. He used the endearment, "Nugga…you gotta use lotion, at least, when you choke the chicken."

The optician stood and touched his lips to Beau's. "Baby, when it's you in the mind flick, I don't need lubricant."

Feeling a surge of desire, Beau palmed the other man's head. Opening his mouth, he wielded his tongue. When the two came up for air, Beau huskily asked, "You feel like showing me?"

Saavion played coy. "Showing you what?"

"That mind flick business, and no missionary—"

"None of that 'girl' stuff, I know," Saavion Kennings nodded, aware that Beau hated that particular position. To the actor, it too closely resembled those he often assumed onscreen early in his career. Beau had done so while shooting love scenes, with women.

However, Saavion also knew there were times when Beau didn't mind 'assuming the position.' Those times Saavion lay back, with his legs raised and the soles of his feet in the air. With pillows and hands beneath Saavion, Beau would tilt the optician's bottom upward, until he could nudge into the tight little anal opening.

With that erotic image in mind, Saavion peeled off clothing as he winked. "Man, I got a *few* things I wanna show you. I was just waiting for you to ask."

Chapter 4

FORGETTING that erotic winter scene, Beau's mother came to mind. Damn! He didn't want to think about that ol' hag, but how could he not? His sexual preference was most likely due to her and her evil.

Neither would Beau forget being tossed down the steps, when his father, a tailor, was not home; one of his earliest memories…

Ophelia had known the three-year old's father would disapprove, but so what? Emmett was working. Therefore, Beau's mother screamed she would knock the devil out of her small son, "Wit' your lil faggot-ass!"

Ophelia had been angered because her child had run from the man in his father's bed, the man with whom she had so recently romped. Ophelia had stood her stupid boy before the man whose eyes had traveled appraisingly over him. Then the kid had run, and hid.

As an adult, Beau realized his mistake. As a kid, he had reappeared just as the man was leaving. Glad to see the back of that man, small Beau stood on the steps beside Ophelia as she yelled about money. Salty about being gypped, she turned her ire on her boy. The little scaredy cat. It was *his* fault that she had lost money, she thought; running off like he had. Therefore, using her eagle-like talons, Ophelia had quickly grabbed the child. Viciously, she'd hurled him to the concrete.

Afterward, when his father found him bruised and sprained, Ophelia lied. Jittery and profusely scratching, she claimed the boy had simply tripped. Disbelieving and angry, Emmett grilled his wife. However, sick of him and accusations, Ophelia locked herself in the bathroom. From there, she hollered, "Kids *fall*, Emmett! Beau fell! That's all!"

That was the beginning, Beau the adult dispassionately recalled. While sipping his morning brew, he eyed the lightening sky. Had his father known the extent of things, Emmett would have seriously hurt Ophelia, or worse. That knowledge comforted Beau, somewhat, as did his daily affirmations. One was particularly soothing.

Some things that happened to me in the past were NOT my fault.

Beau had to remind himself that Ophelia had put him in harm's way, often, for her own selfish gain. She had even shoved him at another man, another time, while greedily sniffing white powder. With a wave, she'd advised the man, "Use him, but lea' me alone!"

Beau reminded himself that he could forgive Ophelia. He only had to be willing, and he was. Sure, the witch was dead, and sure, she could no longer hurt him. He just wanted to get to the day when he could recall her without bitterness. The actor knew it could be done because when he remembered the most precious gift the woman had ever given him, for a few moments, Beau did not hate her. When he thought about his brother, Thomas, Beau felt joy. Beau had not known the boy-man until Thomas was nearly grown. Beau met his brother for the first time, upon meeting Ophelia again, after nearly two decades of abandonment.

When the brothers met, the old sea hag had Thomas slinging shit for her, so she could profit, such little that it had been. It had only been a moment before Beau realized his brother was selling drugs and wanted out. Then Beau knew that like him, his brother had also suffered at Ophelia's hands.

Nowadays, though, Thom was doing okay. True, he was getting cozy with some woman, a nurse, Beau believed, but he guessed Thom needed a life too.

Forgetting those things, Beau recalled that upon 'reuniting,' with Ophelia, the old moneygrubber had started making demands. Then she had progressed to issuing threats. That had been when Beau's brother had made a choice. Due to that choice, Beau and his brother had finally become family, despite their trifling mother.

Now Beau was looking to expand his family. Wouldn't his brother be surprised and excited? When Thomas found out he might become an uncle, the stocky younger man would be pleased. He loved family, especially since while growing up he had only had objectionable Ophelia.

Beau realized he too would be excited, when things finally progressed from the planning stage to that of reality. However, now, all of that seemed a long way off.

Chapter 5

ON a spring Saturday, Kismet Staar, Director of Global Accounts, and her software engineer husband stood in their multi-functional kitchen. In the room that looked like something out of a décor magazine, she had started breakfast. She had also sent their children outside, due to adult undercurrents.

On the flagstone terrace just off the kitchen, Kismet saw her girls. Beneath an awning, at a table, the youngest, a twin, eagerly bounced as her thirteen-year-old sister meticulously dressed a doll. As she beat eggs, The Momma noticed the day lady. Ms. Fannie had helped ever since the twins had been born. Kismet watched her two boys, as did Ms. Fannie. Wildly they ran in the spring sunshine. Soon, one of them, perhaps the boy twin, would wind up crying and tattling.

Kismet chanced a glance at her husband. In the kitchen with her, he had his long locs drawn back into a ponytail as quietly, he sat at the table, across from maple cabinetry.

Repairing his big sexy woman's laptop, Lyle didn't see splashes of cream or refreshing Granny Smith Apple green. All he could see was red. That was because his woman was determined to do this artificial insemination business of hers—and Beau's, despite *his* wishes.

Sure, a few months back, Kismet and her cousin had discussed things. They'd moved forward with lawyers, contracts, doctors, and trips to shrinks, even though as Kismet's husband, Lyle announced he had misgivings. However, as her spouse, he *had* given written consent.

Lyle wondered why everybody couldn't just forget the whole sordid deal. Yeah, and why couldn't this be an ordinary Spring Saturday? The kids would still be in their pjs, and he and Kiss would be naked. He glanced at the clock. 8:37 a.m. They would still be in their comfy rumpled bed. There, he'd have been making love to her, sucking on her huge pretty tits. He could see it now. With the soles of her feet on the bed, she'd have tried to get more of him while listening out for the kids. She would have run her hands down his dark brown back too, while whispering, "Harder, baby."

But no, they weren't doing of that, because she'd changed the rules. For her punk-assed cousin.

"Lyle," Kismet called in passing. "Do you have to do that on this table? Mama 'n them will be here soon and I want them to sit there."

Lyle knew Mama Nell would not care. Mom-in-law's husband, Deac, a church deacon, would care less.

Kismet spoke again, while feeling like lately, Lyle ignored everything she said. She vowed not to let him get on her nerves as she reminded him that their family of friends gathered once a month. He knew it was a rotating affair, held at different homes, and this was their Saturday to host. Yet, Kismet mused as she brewed coffee; her dark man with the chiseled features probably wasn't moving his doohickeys because he knew that today she had only invited family. Paring fruit, she recalled the subject she wanted to discuss. She'd do so with Beau's blessing, but she couldn't forget that she didn't have Lyle's, because he wouldn't let her.

BUXOM older Nell poured coffee for her husband, retired New York police officer Claude Bevere. "OK now, Deac?"

The chunky, gray-haired man in the polo shirt nodded as Kismet, the mother of four cleared her throat.

Facing her adult family members as they sampled this and that, she spoke loudly. "You all know Beau and I are journeying toward a baby for him, but we've nixed using his sperm and someone else's egg."

In the sun-splashed kitchen, all conversation ceased and Kismet's husband stiffened, because how dare she do this? Lyle knew his wife hadn't invited her longtime sister-friend Valeria René, or Val's husband and kids. Kiss hadn't even invited the older, pink-cheeked, brunette Amy. Last month, she and Dr. Foster had hosted this silly breakfast thingy. Beau wasn't present either, Lyle noted, and neither were his hangers-on. So why, Kismet's husband wondered, was she doing this? Yeah, she had probably already explained, but likely, he'd ignored her.

"Recently," she said, "the doctors and I have worked to use *my* eggs, and the sperm of a donor. For obvious reasons."

Lyle could have gone ballistic, but he remained cool, outside.

Farai, the female founding editor of a well-known fashion magazine looked up. Sounding like a grown-up Valley girl, she asked her sister, "Kiss-met, weren't you and Beau going with an *unknown* egg donor?"

"Fa-WRY," Kismet began while handling a tray, "I told you, Beau and I changed our minds." When Lyle stood to take her laptop from the kitchen, the younger sister glanced at her husband.

Upon his return, Nell admonished Lyle to sit. Aware that her son-in-law had not yet wrapped his mind around things, the older woman patted Lyle's shoulder. "I've started a plate for you, honey."

Kismet's half-sister asked, "Kiss-met, why're you using your eggs?"

Buttering blueberry muffins for the kids, The Momma shrugged. "My husband caused me to do so."

Head jerking up from the steaming plate he'd just received, Lyle had questions. "Me? I caused this? What have *I* got to do with anything?"

Realizing he had sounded sardonic, Lyle's wife faced her sister. These days, it was easier to talk to the magazine publisher. "Farai, the other week, Lyle asked what if something happens to Beau," whom the family called Diddley. Sure, Lyle had been trying to win an argument, Kismet knew, but, "He caused me to think when he asked who'd take care of Beau's child?"

Farai, whose Southern African name meant *rejoice* in Shona, shuddered. "God forbid, but we all would."

Kismet nodded. "You'd think so, right? But while researching, I found out that if Diddley marries, *his partner* might wind up with custody of his child. But …what if that partner would only want the child's entitlements?"

"You mean Beau's *money*," the Deacon clarified. "Like all those people who surfaced when," King of Pop, "Michael Jackson passed."

"Exactly," Kismet nodded. "We all know people already want stuff from Diddley. Later, a partner might want to drain his estate, through his child."

Buxom, gray-haired Nell topped off her and the Deacon's coffee. "You're right, Kiss, some king already asked Beau for millions."

Kismet grabbed the reins of the runaway conversation. "Yes. Well, it's those types of things we can avoid if *I* carry Diddley's child."

"By starting with your own eggs," the Deacon again interjected.

"Yes." Kismet eyed her mother and sister. "I thought: with all these women in our family, Diddley shouldn't have to search for a surrogate."

"No," the media titan put forth, "but I can't do it."

Kismet nodded, "I know Farai. You're too busy. And Mama's uh—"

"Too old; go on 'n say it sugar," Nell smirked. "Never again will another baby come from these old hips."

When the laughter dissipated, Kismet noticed. Her husband hadn't cracked a smile. Still, she forged ahead. "Therefore, in pondering those things, I realized: *I'm it.* I also volunteered because, in some states, a surrogate has rights to the child she carried. If she doesn't, that can spell disaster –if the custodial parent passes before the child comes of age."

"But in *this* case," the Deacon surmised, "with *you* as the surrogate, that could *dispel* or avert disaster. I'm wit'cha now, girlie."

Kismet nodded. "I thought, this way, we the family, and *I*, The Momma, could have some say. Ultimately, Diddley's will would supersede all, but I'd have some control, should he leave us."

"Assuming you're alive, girlie. And you'll need supporting documents."

"Deac," Farai faced him. "Beau's partner may also have to agree."

Kismet spoke to her sister. "So, you understand."

"Of course," Farai stated. "Beau's child could return to you because you used your eggs."

"Yes, but only in the event of a disaster. Otherwise, the baby will remain with Beau. She'll be his responsibility."

"Or *he* will be Beau's responsibility," the Deacon put in.

Seated aside, Nell tapped on the heavy wooden table. "Diddley's mate *will* be granted ample time with the child, right KissGirl?"

"Of course." Nell's daughter revealed that as a mother, she could not see cutting the biological father out. "That's why Diddley and I are trying to make things right for everyone involved."

Farai sipped her mimosa. "Another baby would be nice."

Lyle had to give it to his Kismet Staar. An admirable businesswoman, she could make anything sound plausible. Still, he abhorred the prospect of a baby—that was not his—entering the world through his wife. And even though he was hating on her first cousin right now, Lyle despised talk of Beau's possible demise.

As a software engineer who had founded his own company, Lyle didn't care for hypothetical court cases or custody battles. Truthfully, he detested everything associated with this stupid shit that could so easily go sideways. He just wanted simple, and to him, all of this sounded, ironically, like too much *engineering.*

Tuning back in, Lyle heard his sister-in-law say, "Kiss-met, Diddley and I were speaking last week and he said that for his child, he wants the same type of environment that Mama and Daddy provided for us."

Kismet's mother thought of Brantley, her beloved first husband. He sure would have been proud of what their young'uns had become.

Stunned by the words, "You know Kiss-met, people will say you're doing this for the money," buxom older Nell forgot first husband Brantley, to gape at his daughter.

Kismet also stared at the woman who had been born to maternal affluence. Calmly, she spoke to her half-sister, the sophisticate who had single-handedly increased her maternal family holdings. "Farai, you know I don't care what outsiders might say. I would do this for Diddley even if he had a regular job." Daring to look at her husband, Kismet continued. "I just want what's best for him, his child, and us as a family."

All of that was fine and good, Lyle angrily mused, but what *he* wanted was for this little pow-wow to end. He wanted everyone to get the eff outta his house! *And* he needed a drink. Lyle just didn't want his in-laws to know. They'd think it was too early for hard liquor.

Lyle glanced at the beefy gray-haired Deacon, who turned to him. "All of this sounds reasonable to me," Nell's husband said, "but you're the man who needs to agree, and you've been mighty quiet, son."

When Lyle feigned keen interest in the pattern on his plate, the Deacon turned away. "Well, Ms. Kiss, since it appears I was just talking to myself, I'll tell *you*. You and your man need to take each other's feelings into account."

Kismet nodded. That she had tried to do, but Lyle had repeatedly made it clear. He disapproved, and he wasn't willing to compromise.

Seated aside, Lyle forked up frittata. As man of the house, he *had* to do something. But what? A thought struck and he grinned.

Narrowing her eyes, Kismet wondered. Why did her man appear uncharacteristically smug, now, when he'd been sullen. What was up?

Aware that his wife watched, Lyle Manfred regulated his expression. He knew that independent and stubborn, Kiss had undertaken insemination, so likely, she would not change her mind. Therefore, the husband nearly shrugged; his wife had forced his hand. Now there was only one thing to do. He would just have to whip out his big black dick. *He* would have to get Kismet pregnant... provided she wasn't, already.

Chapter 6

DAYS later, lounging in his fabulous French suite, Beau forgot tripping down memory lane to contemplate the time. It was roughly about 6 p.m. Central European Time. Therefore, he could return his first cousin's call. In the states, it would be noon, he hoped.

Following pleasantries, Kismet told Beau, "I feel like running away. I do, because how can one family accumulate so much laundry in one week?" Kismet also said her thirteen-year-old was acting up, again. "She feels our plans will cause her to be displaced." Kismet sounded aggrieved, "But I've told her, several times, she was my first baby."

The Momma told her cousin and longtime confidant that recently, over brunch she'd mentioned her daughter's antics. Her forty-something girlfriends said she should be grateful that Déja wasn't boy crazy. "Val even claimed if Déja *wasn't* expressing her feelings, I'd need to worry."

Beau understood. Kismet's two older children were adopted, so it was natural for one or both to feel threatened as the family dynamic changed.

Feeling trepidation, Beau ventured to ask about Lyle.

Kismet sighed. "My husband is another story."

"He's still opposed?" Beau asked because the business owner had recently begun acting as though his being straight was a badge of honor. It was surprising to Beau because Lyle had been cool. Before.

While listening to his cousin, Beau fingered his dog tags. He did so whenever he became upset.

"My husband claims he's glad I discussed things with him before I made my decision. He *says* he's not pissed, but he is. Why else would he use his acerbic tongue to lash me, anytime he draws me into some petty argument. When he used to use his tongue to—"

"Kiss," Beau loudly cut in. "I – do – *not* – want – to know."

She laughed. "Okay, but lemme tell you this. Lyle asked why I wouldn't just go screw somebody to get this new kid. Isn't that mean?"

In his plush suite, Beau was flabbergasted. "Is he drinking –more?"

For a moment, the mother of four remained silent. Then wearily, she admitted, "That, dear cousin, has picked up a bit, but such is life."

Inaudibly Beau sighed and felt relief. It was selfish, but he was glad that his forty-something cousin, who faced daunting odds, wasn't backing out. He was grateful, and so he said.

"Diddley, you've thanked me a thousand times, but you'd do this for me, if you could. I'm just glad we can talk because who else would understand?"

"Well, Sugar Momma," Beau stated, about to ring off, "just let me know what—if anything—I can do."

"If you could do more, *you'd* be going to the doctors. *You'd* be getting poked and prodded. Quit worrying. Just keep letting me bounce things off you." Since I can't do so with my *husband*, Kismet thought but did not say. "Just know this, Diddley, when you've got your baby, we are going to celebrate."

"Yes, we are cuz, in a major way."

THAT evening when he stepped out onto this luxe hotel balcony, Beau noticed the sky. Peach, gold, and glorious, it announced an imminent sunset. Sipping *Beaujolais*, Beau thought about going out. He wondered if doing so would take his mind off things back home.

Again, he pondered the trouble his cousin was having. Maybe he should not have asked her. Perhaps he should have asked one of the other women in his life. There was one, in particular, he could have asked...

She had milk chocolate skin and big, fluffy, natural curls. While they'd lived together, she had often tried to straighten her hair. She had almond-shaped eyes that were some color, gray or green. With lovely mocha skin, the woman possessed a magnetic inner beauty.

Thinking about her, Beau knew that were she to be his surrogate, his offspring would be beautiful, inside and out. With her too, he could use his own sperm. That is, if her husband agreed. However, girlfriend was a no-go because she was currently with child.

Smirking, Beau remembered. His lovely little friend liked to screw, perhaps as much as he did. Actually, right now, she was probably lying spread-eagle, her wrists tied to the bedposts, while her husband worked her over, with his massive stick. Nightstick was what she called it.

With the sky darkening, Beau swirled mahogany liquid and realized he wasn't hating. He had even said so when he dissuaded his former roommate from describing private encounters. He had said, "Val, I don't need the visual." But what she didn't know was that he actually had a visual of her man's member. Some years back, at her parent's fortieth wedding anniversary, Beau and Valeria's husband had stood at adjacent urinals. Beau's eye had involuntarily fallen on Fabian's member, and good-googa-mooga! Even resting, the man's piece had been formidable. Beau had then understood why his former roommate kept turning up pregnant. She couldn't get enough of the pipe.

Heck, he couldn't get enough of it either. Like his former roommate, Beau loved to indulge. There wasn't a person alive who enjoyed a good stick-n-a-lick more than he did. That, his Uncle had spoken to him about. Uncle Brantley had said, "Son, your business shouldn't become everybody's business." By that mantra, Beau tried to live.

Perhaps, Beau thought while swirling *Beaujolais*, he recalled his Uncle because earlier in the day, he had seen someone from back home. In France, of all places, he had run into the R & B singer Luscious. The shorter man whose given name was Lucian had asked if he could appear at Beau's hotel suite. Politely, Beau refused. Then the singer who falsely advertised, the man who packaged his piece to appear larger than it really was, pressed. Beau rebuffed, because never would Beau forget the singer, the self-proclaimed ladies man's revelation. "I like to take meat in the back." Back in the day, Lucian had admitted that while doing so, he loved to be choked too until his eyes bulged.

Turning to get dressed for his evening out, Beau recalled the first time he'd met Lucian. Early in their careers, they'd met at a photoshoot. Afterward, they'd gotten together, and Lucian told Beau, "You need to know one thing. I'm a total top." Beau knew Lucian had said so because while on tour, the singer often slept with women. At the time, Lucian was still holding to the notion that he was straight, with a twist. What stupidity.

Lucian had also mentioned his need to ride bareback, something that Beau would have none of, and he realized; Lucian had a few deviant tendencies. The singer had also been a bit too talkative for Beau's taste, evidenced by something he'd let slip, some years into their acquaintance.

Over drinks, Lucian had said, in that sandpapery voice of his, that he didn't go in for too much of that 'faggot-y stuff.' From that one statement, Beau had known. The raspy-voiced crooner was deep in the closet. Beau had known then that he and Lucian would never share much, because Beau wasn't into hiding.

Checking himself in the mirror, Beau forgot Lucian, who was now more out than in. Beau guessed time changed things. Time, and a tabloid tale which had alleged that the crooner had severely beaten a man. The article had also mentioned a shared hotel room and attempted sodomy.

Beau recalled the singer's shock at having the story hit the airwaves. Then when Lucian had stopped acting as if it was all a misunderstanding, he'd showed Beau photographs.

Staring at a man with a black eye, Beau had felt considerable shock. Realizing he was looking at the man who had gone to the tabloids on Luscious, the singer, Beau had also felt disgusted because who, but the mob beat someone and then took photos of their handiwork?

Angered, Beau had found himself looming over the shorter, but more powerfully built Lucian. Menacingly, Beau asked the singer if he had shown the photos because he was proud of what he'd done. "Or," Beau continued, "did you show me those because you're thinking to threaten or intimidate me?"

Wordlessly, Lucian's silly little grin let Beau know he'd hit the nail on the head. However, in an attempt to appear nonchalant, Lucian shrugged. "I can't understand why you're so upset, man."

"Well, let me explain." Forcing calm, Beau admitted, "I'm angry because I know you. I know your type."

Lucian's grin had then resembled a grimace. "You know my type…"

Beau nodded. "Yes. You have an exaggerated sense of self. You step on people because you're a recording artist, because you're considered a 'celebrity.' But that's not right." Placing a hand at his head, Beau had added, "Now that I think about it, I hope you *did* show me those photos for some twisted reason." Into its opposite palm, he pounded a giant fist. With anger rising, reminiscent of his days as an abused child, Beau nodded, "Because then I will beat your muthafuckin' ass, right here, right now." Beau indicated the incriminating photos. "I will bust you up, just like you did that poor guy."

Noticing the simmering rage just beneath Beau's seemingly calm façade, Lucian recognized he was out of his depth. It had been unsettling to realize; he did not know what to expect from the tall brown young man who seemed so easy-going. Suddenly, Lucian recalled that at times, he *had* glimpsed Beau's alter ego. Therefore, placating the hot young actor whose rise critics deemed meteoric, Lucian claimed the black-eye man was nothing.

"*Nothing*? A *person*, nothing?" Beau had asked, aware that hurriedly he needed to leave. There was venom churning within him, but it was due to old hurts. Periodically, Beau knew, the past reared its ugly head. It was why he had to be careful. He had been boxing since the age of fifteen. His hands were lethal weapons. Therefore, he'd bounced.

As he stood before the ornate mirror in his posh hotel suite, he no longer saw himself as a man in his late thirties. He did not see all that was luxe laid out behind him. He only saw that night, many years ago. The night when a twenty-something male had been tremendously angry.

In the mirror, Beau saw the boy-man whose mother had viewed *him* as nothing; therefore, she had repeatedly allowed unspeakable evils to be visited upon him. Many times while he was raped and violated, his no good mother had been sprawled nearby, most times in a drug-induced stupor. Other times, she had been laser-focused on heating a pipe filled with crack so she could chase the genie.

Forgetting his past, as he stood before the mirror, Beau remembered that long ago evening. Slowly, he had strolled from Lucian's room. As he did, how he'd wished the shorter man would have tried him.

As a thirty-something, now Beau knew. That night was why he and the other man, who was still a jerk, had never had dealings afterward. The successful actor, filmmaker, and bandleader, also realized why earlier in the day he had refused Lucian's offer.

Beauregard DeVeaux had done so because although he had been called many things in his life, he was a man of integrity. Beau held to certain principles, one of which was: a man did not treat other people *as though they were nothing*. That man did not step on others, even if they would allow it. Also, a man did not hang out with men with whom he had nothing in common. A real man remained true to himself, and *never* did he seek the company of men he could not abide.

Those things Beau had learned long ago, from a *prince* among men... his Uncle. Brantley.

Chapter 7

AT home, Kismet checked on her sleeping children. Since her husband had not come up to bed, she knew he was still angry. She only hoped he wasn't downstairs drinking. That made him mean, evidenced by things he did, things she had not mentioned to anyone.

Seated in her bedroom, she recalled the morning she'd made the family breakfast. After the adults left, Lyle disappeared. Then that night, he'd returned to kiss and caress her. It had been nice, because ever since her surrogacy and the psychologist's survey, her husband had withheld affection despite knowing her 'appetite.' However, in his arms, she had become cognizant of why he was amorous. Kismet had eased away before Lyle could get her thoroughly aroused, and he had hit the ceiling!

With her feet on a damask fringed hassock, the curvaceous woman stared beyond the open heavy drapes. Facing the truth had hurt. Knowing Lyle had been crafty had stung, but softly Kismet had told him her truth.

"I know what you're doing Lyle, and it won't work."

Lyle had then acknowledged that IVF was nothing like just doing it to get pregnant. "The regular way," he'd angrily stated, "You just threw your big leg up and bam! Babies. Now with in vitro, wow Kiss, you don't even need a man—well, not a *real* one, anyway."

DAWN broke, in Paris, and like his cousin, Beau too sat remembering things...

Laying eyes on the boy, the man knew he was different. Yet big Brantley Moore had simply said, "Well, you're not a fairy—no flitting about 'n such. Still, you and I both know you're...*yourself*."

Uncle Brantley raised a large hand. "Now, don't go feeling bad, son, just listen. Ain't a thing wrong with being different; I tell the girls that all the time. Farai and Kismet understand. Still, with you, you'll have to learn how to handle *others*. I say so because you'll meet people who won't know how to react once they realize what your different is."

Beau placed his coffee cup on the balcony's heavy table and recalled. Not long after that conversation, his uncle started teaching him what the large man called the game of life.

Brantley had searched for just the right mitt and balls. He had also opined that in life, someone was always trying to tag another out.

"Still, if you've got skills, you can slide right past anybody trying to do you in." This Uncle Brantley had said after teaching Beau to catch.

Patiently he'd explained. "Diddley, you've got to see the ball. Keep your eye on it. Now get up under it. Catch it—and hold onto it. Yeah!"

Beau had done that reasonably well, but pitching had been another story. "No. Not like that." Beau recalled the big man striding to the mound, while nearby, other kids learned from their person.

"Face the plate." Uncle Brantley tossed out instructions as he demonstrated. "Mimic me. Come from down low. That's it. Come high—yep. Now throw!" Ducking, he heartily laughed.

After a few tries, he yelled, "Hey, boy! You got it!"

On the way home, the big man stopped at the Far Rockaway Carvel. Motioning for Beau to exit on the car's passenger side, the big man said, "Guess you deserve a treat, son."

When Beau and his Uncle stood at the creamery window, about to order, Beau inhaled. It was then that he fell in love with the smell of soft-serve ice cream. That summer evening, beneath a sky full of stars, young Beau licked sprinkles from a dripping cone.

Using a bear paw, Brantley grabbed his nephew's neck and playfully jostled the boy. "You're gonna be a fine player, son. You'll see. It'll be soon too. Ya just need a bit more practice." Brantley tapped Beau's baseball cap. "Then, no more throwing like a girl for you, huh?"

Beau recalled laughing because he had been happy. Ice cream had slid down his chin as the moon rose higher in the sky. And the pre-teen had known; his uncle loved him; the man would never belittle or hurt him. Big Brantley Moore had only wanted the best for his nephew.

Now grown and successful, Beau realized he was so, partially because of his aunt and his uncle. With his eyes on bougainvillea, he smelled morning baking and coffee, and his heart ached. How he missed his uncle. The actor wondered if one day some youngster would think fondly of *him*. Would that young person remember him the way he did the man who had taught him to face any pitch life tossed his way?

Then Beau asked himself two questions.

Why did he now feel like he faced a ninety-mile-an-hour curveball? And for the first time in a long time, why did he feel like he had no bat?

Chapter 8

BEAU wondered why he careened down memory lane. Why was he re-living things? Was his and Kismet Staar's 'project' the reason he felt like getting his house in order? Sure, his life was changing, and Beau often wondered if he was ready. Could he could handle what was to come without effing it up? He honestly didn't know. This he admitted while seated at a famed restaurant located at the end of St-Tropez harbor. Yet he knew he had to go for it, give this next phase of life his all.

Looking up, Beau noticed the server whose accent he loved.

"Sir, would you like *café crème, café dècafféné*, or a *café léger*?"

Beau chuckled. "But *non*, I'd prefer café nwah-zette."

"Ah," the young man nodded. "*Café noisette*, it is."

Beau often shunned sweets. However, he was on vacation. In addition to the French version of the macchiato he ordered something with *sucre*. Later, he glanced down at the delectable *Cointreau*-laced creation. He noticed that while he'd been seated beneath the restaurant canopy, time had elapsed. Yet Beau had barely tasted his dessert soufflé. He hadn't seen fashionable singles or lovers stroll by. He hadn't noticed exiting patrons, nor had he heard background music or conversation. He had been thinking, again. Continuing to do so, he rested his fork and recalled the first time he'd met *her*. With her cinnamon-hued skin, *she* was *another* woman he could have asked to carry his baby...

Long ago, they had been in middle school together. She had been big-boned and feisty, sort of like his cousin Kismet Staar. Yet Mireya had been more like him. Beau remembered being young, self-absorbed, and silly. He and Mireya had both been typical junior high school kids.

Each day, they'd entered their wood-paneled homeroom. Thumping her books down, Mireya had slid beside Beau. In the nineteen-eighties, she'd smelled like bubble gum and grape body spray. Her hair hadn't been sleek either, because her edgy cut hadn't come until high school.

The two had laughed a lot. In science class, Mireya had been squeamish. Outside that class, she had been fearless. She had always had 'news' too, so between them, Beau and Mireya had known most everything that went on in the learning institution that was their second home.

In Springfield Gardens, New York, they'd lived just streets apart, so they rode the bus together. Wearing tight jeans and sneakers superbly coordinated with her colorful tops, Mireya Nickel, the only child of an attractive single mother, had often waited for Beau. Whatever the season, they rode, studied, and lunched together, and in time, Beau could not wait to see the wide-faced pretty brown girl with the bubbly personality.

Wanting only to share and laugh with her, his best friend, Beau began to rise early, no longer needing to be roused by his aunt. Often he sing-sang her name, "Me-RAY-ah, I met a girl named Mireya." Then after showering, he'd slam through the Moore family's back door. With half an apple in his mouth, he'd wave at Mireya who'd be at the front gate.

Backing her car out, Beau's aunt would call, "Be good learners!"

Beau, who could sing, wound up in glee club. Mireya wound up in Home Economics. Glee and Cooking alone separated them. Thus, their peers and teachers considered them a tweenaged couple. Yet the friends knew better. Their relationship was less, but then again, so much more.

Mireya's mother worked and it was lonely at the Nickel house. Therefore, early evenings, the kids did homework in the Moore's kitchen. The pair often called out to Beau's aunt, who bustled in to start dinner after a long day of work.

But never would Beau forget sitting in glee club, minus Mireya. Very artistic, one day, he doodled, and a nude male appeared. Before he knew it, Mr. McCuddy, the glee instructor, stood eyeing the drawing. McCuddy's chubby face pinked up, and hastily Beau covered the paper.

Yet Mr. McCuddy had seen the male genitalia thrice enlarged.

Beau wound up in detention, and the instructor never treated him the same again. The man became snide and picked on Beau unnecessarily. Therefore, Beau told classmates he would transfer out of Glee.

Yet one day, McCuddy caught him, alone. "Hey Mister—or should I say, Miss? I hear you wanna jump ship. Well, DeVeaux, you will not."

Beau tried to wrench free, but McCuddy held him fast. "Spring contest is looming, and this year I intend to win, with you as soloist."

Months prior, Beau would have been overjoyed to hear it, but now he was miserable, especially when he found out that the solo forced him to spend additional time with pot-bellied, florid-faced Mr. McCuddy. The man had smellycoffee and cigarette breath, but even more than that, Beau hated having to be alone with the teacher. Then the man inappropriately touched Beau. Becoming emboldened with each next attempt because no one else saw, slimy McNutty—as some of the kids called the instructor—also rubbed his fat belly against Beau.

Sick of it, Beau wanted to confide in Mireya; then again, he didn't, because what if *she* changed toward him? What if she, his same aged best friend, began eyeing him with disgust, the way Mr. McCuddy did? Not wanting that, Beau opted for silence. He thought about telling his aunt, though. Feisty and round, Nell Moore would stop McCuddy's mess; Uncle Brantley would, too. He might even kick the man's flimsy ass because nothing angered Brantley Moore more than some man trying to misuse his nephew.

Yet to keep the peace and to keep his secret from being splashed all over school, Beau kept quiet, until McCuddy tried to out *him*.

In the auditorium of Queens College, on chorale competition night, Beau scanned the sea of faces. Excited, he watched people call to others. Under recessed lights, many stood or sat talking, while all waited.

When things got underway, glee clubs made their way to the stage. Some gave it their all, incorporating dance moves, while others lacked pizazz. However, Beau's middle school was a hit! They received two standing ovations, and *he* received more. He could not remember ever feeling so elated in his life!

Dancing around, Mireya was there, as were Beau's aunt, his uncle, his cousin Kiss, and her half-sister, cousin Farai. Their neighbors, and Pa Fulton, and Grandma Lacey were there; she had nicknamed Beau. All were fairly bursting with joy, for *him*! And McCuddy chose to act out.

The tallies were read, and all heard that Beau's club had not won. They had been awarded *second* place. Yet the glee club members were ecstatic. Mrs. Jewelyn, the pianist, was all smiles. But Mr. McCuddy was upset. Placating him, the gray-haired pianist reminded sweaty Mr. McCuddy that their club had never before won a thing.

Still, the instructor churlishly whined; he'd wanted *first* prize. Then as Beau and others watched, another chorus triumphantly raced onto the stage, and surly, McCuddy blamed 'his loss' on his club's soloist.

"This is what I get," he snarled loud enough for his singers and Mrs. Jewelyn to hear, "for sending a freakin' *girl* to do a *boy's* job!"

Before all gathered, the fat man jabbed a finger at Beau. Sweaty, sickening McCuddy also exaggeratedly dropped his wrist in parody. Girlishly he tossed his head before, utterly disgusted, he rolled his eyes.

A few glee club members laughed and whispered, while others stared, and for Beau, the night was ruined. Beau felt sick to his stomach because how *could* McCrummy? While packing up, other kids forgot the incident, but Beau could not. He wanted to die. People had laughed at him, when he had given his all. He had endured weeks of McCuddy's inappropriate actions, only to have everything end on the wrong note.

Beau knew he wasn't a girl; he didn't even act like one, unlike his friend Jervais. However, Beau had always known he was different, somehow. Now, because of a stupid drawing, McCruddy knew it too, and the sour-smelling man had tried to make that knowledge public!

On the ride home, in the rear of the family's gray station wagon, Mireya asked why wasn't Beau happy, why hadn't he touched his favorite, White Castle burgers, with onion rings and a shake?

Choked with hurt, Beau could not reply. In the idling car, before her darkened house, quickly Mireya kissed his cheek. Smelling like grape and bubblegum, she scooted over Kismet and Farai. Exiting the car, Mireya called, "Bye, Grandma Lacey. Thanks for the ride, Mr. Moore!"

That weekend, both Beau's aunt and uncle tried to get him to talk, to say why he was dejected. However, refusing to utter a word, the boy ate very little and wondered *how* on earth could he tell? He decided not to chance it, or they'd become different too. Beau didn't want to be loved less, *or* for his family to send him to live with Heaven only knew whom.

Therefore, after a weekend fraught with turmoil, Monday morning arrived. On the house front, Beau met Mireya. Putting polished purple fingernails on his sleeve, she looked up at him. "Beau Diddley, I know something's wrong, and until you say what it is, we're not leaving."

He knew she meant it. Yet, he began to walk, pulling her along.

Mireya spoke as she popped gum. "You'd better talk to me."

Passing tulips and budding trees, tall and gangly, Beau spoke because he couldn't hold back any longer. Quickly he told Mireya everything.

His friend simply nodded as up lumbered a nearly crowded MTA bus. "Okay." Without judging, the very thing that Beau had been afraid of, Mireya stated, "I'll get fat Fuddy Duddy."

Beau flashed his bus pass and followed her into the morning throng. Jostling into place beside her, he advised, "Say nothing, Reya. You'll only make things worse."

April Alisa Marquette

"How can I?" she asked. She was bent and rummaging through her patched denim bag. The crowded carriage heaved and swerved. Glancing up, she said, "I got you." She touched her chest. "Friends for life. Okay?"

"Okay, but Reya..." While looking out of the Q4 bus window, Beau held to the overhead railing as he spoke. "Just forget I said anything."

"Nope. And you'll thank me," she said, her broad face innocent.

When they neared the school, big-boned Mireya jumped off the bus. In the sunshine, she blew bubbles and moved quickly, pushing kids aside. Beau watched her deviate from their pattern, zooming off in the wrong direction. He called after her, but heedless, she raced away.

At lunch, there was an incredible buzz. In passing, a few football team members grinned at Beau. Pubescent girls offered him sly come-hither looks as they licked shiny lips. Then scrawny Marty with the thick glasses raced up, "Congrats, Deh-VO!"

Beauregard DeVeaux felt prickles of alarm, "Congrats for...what?"

"You must've have screwed Mireya good," the pip-squeak nodded.

Beau did and did not want to know. "What're you saying, Mart?"

"I'm saying, why else would a girl do what she did, for you?"

Beau immediately grew cold. "What—did Reya—do?"

"You don't know?!" With eyes wide behind his glasses, scrawny Marty jubilantly crowed. "Mireya *knifed* cruddy McNutty!" The small boy squeaked, "In his pregnant belly! EMT's took smelly away on a stretcher—but he is refusing to press charges. He said something about Mireya being a 'troubled youth.' Security held her, though, while she screamed her head off! She kicked and said she would kill cruddy McDuddy, *for you*! She's suspended. Her mother was called and—"

Beau heard no more. He could only think: that morning, Mireya had searched her purse for her *knife*! She said she always kept it with her. Grabbing his backpack, Beau spilled his drink and forgot his chips.

He tore out running.

Scrawny with the thick glasses watched. Then eagerly, Marty turned to another, to finish his tale.

Chapter 9

KISMET knew she had come too far to turn back now. Sure, she felt fear, but she and her cousin had begun a tedious and exciting process. It was something her heart bade her do, despite the difficulty, the arranging, re-arranging, scheduling, and re-scheduling. Those things were relatively easy to handle in contrast to what loomed…getting her marriage back on track.

Her cell rang. "Hey, Diddley. You checking on me?" Hearing that he was, she told him the latest; her daughter had sassed her. "You know I had to regulate her lil behind, right?" Kismet mentioned having told the girl about acting ugly. However, The Momma knew how her daughter felt. "Diddley, she believes that since *I* didn't bring her into the world, I'll love a child that I bring in more than I love her. I asked how she could think such a thing. I asked, doesn't she see that I love her, her brother, *and* the twins," the biological babies "all the same? I asked, why would anything change now?"

Knowing the last question was rhetorical, his cousin's way of processing, Beau kept quiet, aware that he was a sounding board.

"I mean, why would I love Déja any less? For crying out loud," Kismet tossed a bunch of socks into the bin with the whites. "She was my first baby. I learned everything with her."

Aware that it was true, yet Beau asked, "Kiss, did you tell her that?"

"I did. You know I've always told her that *she and I* were together, alone, against the world, before there was anyone else." It had certainly seemed that way when the child's biological mother had repeatedly attempted to confiscate her. "Beau," Kismet called, "I keep telling Déja that she and her brother were my greatest gifts."

Aware that the thirteen-year old's worries were probably magnified by the arguments she heard, Kismet moaned. "Before all of this, my first girl seemed okay, but lately she's become so fearful."

Beau felt like Deja's fears had likely been heightened by *Lyle's* foolishness. But Beau kept his mouth shut and his thoughts to himself. No sense talking about his cousin's husband.

Across the globe, he disengaged from the call. Beau pulled at his non-existent goatee. Sure, he knew what he wanted, and he was grateful that, in a way, his cousin wanted the same thing. However, he had to wonder. Could their plans have a lasting negative effect on her family? Beau hated to concede to such thinking, but what if it were true? Heck, it already seemed as though his and Kismet's little plan was fraying her marriage a bit more each day. Beau shook his head because he did not tear up families. Heck, as far back as he could remember, he had tried to keep his together. He had done so knowing family was important. He had also done so to honor a promise he'd made...

Uncle Brantley went to the hospital. When he came back, he was throwing up. Beau heard him in the bathroom. So standing in the doorway, the lanky fourteen-year-old timidly asked, "Unc, you okay?"

Wearily, Brantley hauled himself up off the lavatory's cool blue and white tiles. Running water, Brantley rinsed his mouth before he truthfully answered. "No, son, this cancer is wearing me out."

"But you're gonna be okay." Beau needed to believe it. "Right?"

"No, Beauregard." Brantley dried his mouth, "I'm not gon lie to you."

Turning to walk with the man who slowly dragged himself down the narrow hallway, Beau got under his uncle's arm. He did so, wanting to aid the man who had always helped him. With his heart beating fast, Beau prayed his uncle would get well. He prayed that life would remain the way it had been since he'd been engrafted into the Moore family.

Brantley Moore spoke as he and his nephew shuffled along. "I told you before, son. Every person enters this world to die—some sooner than others. That is why I am going to need you to do something for me. Look after my Nellie, okay? You'll do that for me, won't you, son?"

Beau nodded, hating the thought. "Yes, Uncle Brant. I will."

Brantley, who had once been all brawn, dropped onto the bed that he shared with his buxom wife. Unnaturally thin, with clothes hanging loosely on his large frame, the man closed his eyes. Lying listlessly on top of the quilt, he was too worn to slide beneath it. Yet he reached for Beau's hand. "You'll be the man around here, soon. Then it'll be your job to watch over the ladies. You'll watch over your aunt, your cousin Kiss, and her sister," from another mother, "won't you?"

With tears blurring his vision, Beau grasped the large hand that had been reduced to mostly bone. "Yes, sir." Again he promised to take care of the family females. Yet Beau prayed he would never have to; why, he was just a *kid* and a weird one at that! He couldn't take care of a thing.

Pocketing his dinner receipt, the adult Beau stood and realized that he was still on vacation, in France. As he made his way from the elegant restaurant, with near-invisible security trailing him, he painfully recalled his uncle's transition, and that afterward he had tried to do as instructed.

Indeed, he had looked after Uncle Brantley's ladies. Beau had done so down through the years until Farai; his uncle's eldest daughter had married an African diplomat. Beau had then watched over Kismet, his first cousin until she'd married Lyle, a software engineer. That had left Beau's sweet round aunt, Nell, the love of Uncle Brantley's life.

Having moved from the East to the West Coast, she had continued to work in juvenile corrections. Then after umpteen years, in California, she finally retired. Nell had then returned to New York for a visit, and she'd surprised everyone by agreeing to marry a former police officer. At nearly seventy years of age, Kismet's mother, Beau's aunt, had wed the man who was also a deacon at the huge church their family attended.

Walking the balmy night in the City of Lights, Beau sighed and knew he had done his best. With people reveling all around, in the city that dazzled and glittered like well-turned-out *prostituée*, Beau knew he had carried out his uncle's wishes. Beau had been there until the family ladies had chosen men who could take them further.

Of that, Beau's uncle would be proud.

Looking away from strolling lovers, and others, Beau had one thought. Other things—personal things—he truly hoped his uncle had no knowledge of, up there wherever he was. Or Uncle Brantley might not be so proud of his nephew.

Chapter 10

BEAU met Jervais. Although they had been in elementary school together, they had not known each other well. Jervais [Jer-VAYZ] had attended the school since kindergarten. Years later, Beau had been the new kid. Having attended numerous schools before, Beau hadn't wanted to befriend the switchie, the girlish boy, who was one of the few in dance club. Keeping to himself, Beau hadn't liked any other kids either. Yet Jervais, with the fluttering hands, kept bothering Beau, the introvert.

Secretly curious, Beau watched the other boy. He realized why Jervais was girlish; in his house, there was no man. There was Ms. Lillian, Jervais' mother; her sister; and Jervais' older sisters. The dancing boy had a baby sister, Barbara, called Bibi, but there was no man.

Sensing that he and Beau were both different, the shorter boy kept attempting to befriend Beau. However, hearing other boys call Jervais derogatory names, Beau simply wanted to be left alone, after all the trouble he had already had. Therefore, he made his stance clear. He did so by kicking and punching kids. Getting the picture, most steered clear of him, but not the boy who often walked on his toes.

Beau didn't understand, but somehow he wound up out-of-school friends with Jervais anyway. Maybe it was because Beau's aunt and Jervais' mother both played bingo. Occasionally, Ms. Lillie even left Jervais and his baby sister at Nell's home when the two ladies went, but only when Ms. Lillie's sister was busy. Sister helped, Jervais had whispered, because his father and a lady neighbor had 'gone missing.'

Despite the missing man, there was laughter and love at Ms. Lillie's house, and her two older girls were fun. They wore large hoop earrings and showed Jervais, Bibi, and Beau, the latest moves from the high school parties they attended.

Beau loved dancing with those willowy girl-women. Like them, he did so with abandon. Those times, Beau, an elementary school kid, felt free. He popped, locked, and flowed to the beat. On occasion, music just seemed to swell and bubble up in his soul. Those times he could not control himself. Beau just had to sing, and sing he did.

The girls and Jervais would halt to listen. Once, tiny Bibi's face was upturned as she'd lisped, "Beau, you thound like an *angel*!"

"She's right, Bo-dacious," Jervais said and looked like he really saw Beau for the first time. The older girls, with their pretty hair and perfume-oiled skin, had agreed. However, when the spell was broken, they called out, "Homework, Vay. Get your books! Beau, you too."

Beau liked that the girl-women were smart, but they knew the latest slang. They often snapped their fingers to emphasize a point. Jervais did the same, and Beau realized; the shorter boy had become like them. However, Beau didn't want to become a singing-dancing girly-boy, so despite Ms. Lillie's welcome, he didn't often visit her inviting home.

In middle school, there was no Jervais. Due to his superior intellect, the little dancer had been moved up two grades. However, in high school, angry, moody, and missing his deceased uncle something fierce, Beau again fell in with Jervais.

By that time, Beau could care less who knew that he and the other young man were friends, or that they were different. However, Beau did hide a few things from Mireya who was possessive. As an only child, she had never really learned to share. For that reason, Beau was grateful that she was a cheerleader and that Jervais went to a different Manhattan high school. Jervais' school nurtured artistic youths.

Beau liked that when Mireya was occupied with her pom-poms, he and Jervais could hang out. Sure, Beau should have been studying, doing something constructive, yet he told himself he was young. The atmosphere at the Moore house was morose too. No one had really gotten over the loss of Uncle Brantley. Beau hated that his aunt worked so hard and that his girl cousins were away at college. Therefore, clutching excuses, Beau stayed in the streets, sometimes hitting hot spots with Jervais, other times Beau just got into trouble. Realizing the little dancer was nearly all he had, the tall, slim but muscular Beau wondered how he had ever been ashamed of Jervais. Having become a formidable boxer, Beau found himself only wanting to defend his petite friend.

Beau remembered. His aunt had urged him to take up boxing. She had not said it would be therapeutic, yet she had secretly hoped it would. Her work in juvenile corrections had enabled her to see that her nephew had issues. He needed an outlet for anger and other emotions.

Unaware of why he had been encouraged to take up the sport, Beau believed no one knew he silently brooded, or that he wondered what was wrong with him. He wondered because his mother had not loved him. He also wanted to know why Ophelia had allowed him to be repeatedly violated, when she could have left him with his father.

Beset by questions, often late at night Beau stifled sobs. Then he told himself to quit being a baby, to be strong, because he was the man of the house, now. But he didn't feel manly, at all. How could he, when every so often he woke, cold and sweaty, having clawed his way out of a nightmare? One in which he'd re-lived things that had been done to him.

Other times, he questioned God. He asked why the ruler of Heaven had taken his uncle. For what? Just to make his aunt sad? On the cusp of manhood, Beau wondered if Nell would ever recover. Would she ever become the feisty little round woman she had once been?

All of those things, coupled with his budding sexuality, caused the young male to feel like mythological Atlas, carrying the weight of the world on his shoulders. Beau also wondered why his sinewy body betrayed him. His penis lengthened and thickened when he saw certain males. Wasn't that supposed to happen when he saw females? He really wanted to find teenaged girls and women appealing, but he didn't.

Struggling under his cumbersome burdens, one day, Beau unwittingly mentioned them to Jervais. Surprisingly, the sashaying boy-man understood. Scheduled to graduate high school before time, Jervais divulged, "You ain't the only one quizzing, Dacious. I do it too..."

Beau was curious. As he lit the lone cigarette he had bought that morning, he asked, "What kind of questions you got, Vay?"

Jervais averted his eyes. "Well, I wonder...why I'm like this." He smacked on spearmint gum. "Why don't I like girls?" Unable to look at Beau, Jervais asked, "Why'd my father leave, was he ashamed of *me*?"

When Jervais fell silent, Beau traded him a truth for a truth. "My mother disappeared, like your father, but before that, she let men..." Beau spoke softly, "get at me." Blowing smoke rings, Beau waited for Jervais to appear surprised. When the dancer did not, Beau continued. "I didn't ask for what they did to me, but as I get older, I wonder if I'm messed up. I do, because I see certain men, and I feel...well, not angry, but *you know*."

"I know, Bodacious. I see certain guys, and I want them too."

"But I wouldn't *be* this way," Beau blurted, "if that bitch hadn't let shit happen to me!"

"Then *we* probably wouldn't be friends," Jervais philosophically replied. "If things had been good, you wouldn't live with your aunt."

Jervais had a point, and Beau nodded, flicking his loosie aside.

"My father just ran off," the dancer vehemently voiced, "and Bibi wasn't even a year old! Hell! What kind of man leaves a baby, and his family, while destroying another one in the process?"

Following Jervais' outburst, teenaged Beau asked if Jervais' mom ever heard from her ex. "I mean, he does pay child support—right?"

"Nope, but the girl next door—the one whose mama ran with my dad—said those skunks live in Jersey, just across the bridge!" Jervais sighed, "Lotta good that does my mother. They stole *her* car! She needed it for work. What's worse is Bibi doesn't even know our dad. Rat bastard could visit *her*." Jervais hugged himself. "He ain't gotta see *me*."

Seeming to digress, Jervais exhaled and mentioned that he would get into a dance company, preferably Alvin Ailey, when he graduated.

"I've already been accepted into one of Manhattan's premier arts colleges, but I need to become a core dancer. Bodacious you know dancing is my life, and I do it all; Ballet, Modern, Hip Hop, Social, Ballroom, Bounce, Tap, Latin, whatever—and I'm hella good!"

Beau laughed along with Jervais. Afterward, the dancer solemnly announced, "I've got to set my mom up for life. You know why."

"I don't know," Beau admitted. "Why do you just have to do this?"

The shorter young man looked away, "Because my dad's gone, and because of my *lifestyle*."

Back then, teenaged Beau had marveled at Jervais' candor. Then Beau had found Jervais' singleness of purpose admirable. Many days following school, Beau visited the studio. There he watched Jervais, who often danced until he dropped, from sweat and exhaustion. Other times, Beau felt horror and pity because Jervais' toes bled, because they took such a beating. Yet Jervais rose *on pointe* to fine-tune ballet moves. In Hip Hop, he did the Toe Drag. In Tap, he did the Stamp Step Toe Heel Turn. Frankly, Beau was amazed at his little friend. Sure, the dancer suffered injuries, but he always painstakingly worked his way back. Grimacing through physical therapy, the dancer never complained. Wearing what looked like tights and legwarmers, Jervais said that without pain, he would not gain.

Watching Jervais, who began each session at the *barre* with a series of *plies* meant to prepare his body for the grueling follow-up, Beau recognized, the shorter male's only option was to make it.

Then Beau vowed to make something of himself too. Jervais had inspired Beau. Therefore, Beau and Jervais pinky swore. Beau even whispered that he would make his sad little aunt proud. Beau vowed that one day the woman who'd become a real mother to him would long for nothing.

He would give Nell Moore everything. Well, every single thing *but* her husband. Sadly, neither he nor she could get his uncle back.

Chapter 11

BEAU, the successful adult, forgot Jervais' pledge to take care of his mother, Ms. Lillie. The actor, filmmaker, and bandleader forgot pinky swearing with the tiny dancer. Beau simply stopped thinking and started talking, to himself. While getting dressed, he vowed to go take in the lights, the sights, and the sounds of French nightlife.

Then his phone rang. Turning from the mirror, he answered. The concierge said his car would be on the curved drive at the resort front within minutes. Ringing off, Beau realized he actually felt naughty, and like he needed to drink and dance. He might even get into a lil something—or some*one*, later, he mused, if the night permitted.

Hours later, after drinks with friends at one place and dinner at another, Beau wound up at *Caveau de la Sunset*, the club where it was said anything could happen, after dark. Outside, seated in the rear of a luxury vehicle, Beau liked that it was a nice night. For the moment, he people-watched, a favorite pastime. Beau did so as Boulder, once special forces turned bodyguard, and others, dissuaded autograph seekers. From his vantage point, Beau watched an African-American male and his entourage. Beau realized that abroad, Americans were always easy to spot. They were just so out, and curious about everything.

Beau found it amusing the way the stocky male strode about with his peops dogging his every step. Suddenly the man whirled and waved muscular arms. Was he yelling, at the club's bouncer? Why, Beau inwardly asked, did it seem like the man wanted the attention of those waiting in line while hoping to get in the club's door?

Beau thought it all show, on the man's part. He felt it was pretentious, to say the least. Squinting, Beau leaned forward. Then he recoiled because that was *Lucian*. Realization caused Beau to shake his head. It was apparent; the singer had not grown any. Somewhat older than in years past, it was evident; the man still needed pomp and circumstance. He still needed to be surrounded by those who hung on his every word.

Looking away, Beau guessed the crooner still had not become comfortable in his own skin. Beau also noticed the moment that Lucian recognized Boulder. Oh, damn.

Beau sighed, because Lucian, a.k.a. Luscious, the singer, knew Boulder had been Beau's bodyguard for years.

With his entourage in tow, the short, stocky crooner headed toward the shiny parked vehicle.

Watching him approach, Beau groaned.

Huge, bi-racial Boulder blocked the singer, while Beau nearly wished he had not been gawking through the open window. How simple of him! Yet he signaled that it was okay.

Stepping slowly aside, Boulder remained ready to lunge. Flexing, he wordlessly let Lucian know: he was a dog that could still snap his chain.

Glancing up at the rock face that remained impassive, Lucian seemed to comically inflate, causing some in his entourage to nervously giggle. However, carefully sidestepping the bodyguard, Lucian began his third act. He greeted Beau as though they were old friends, for the benefit of others. Quickly forgetting those that Beau's team backed down, Lucian asked if the filmmaker was planning to enter the club.

Not awaiting an answer, Lucian announced, "I got VIP booked." Further puffing up, he nodded. "Got champagne, and girls too." He shrugged, to indicate it was all blasé. "Why 'on't you come hang out? Later, maybe you and I—"

"No." Beau heard nothing more, because he'd made a split-second decision. Sure, he had a few days of vacation left, but he would return home. In the states, he had a life, and a bevy of things to oversee and do. What he did *not* have time for was insipid games and hookin' up.

Succinctly he said, "Nah man. We out." Beau signaled his team.

Yet Lucian cajoled and whined, producing nothing. Stridently then, he called out to his entourage who again fell in step behind him.

Watching the stocky singer, Beau called off his dawgs as he realized; he was not about to sleep with anybody. The truth was: he had too much waiting for him at home. Therefore, the actor guessed, his days of getting with somebody, just for the sake of doing so, were over. Perhaps he was older and wiser, or maybe seeing cocky Lucian had helped him recognize. What he shared with his optician was the closest thing he had ever had to real. That, Beau would not jeopardize. Texting his assistant, he asked that his plane be readied. The tall man did so because it was time to get down to business, time to pick up the threads of his life and move on.

Chapter 12

BEAU was flying into MacArthur. His time away was over, and work was calling. Sure, he was on hiatus from the movies. Well, really from acting in the big-budget flicks he'd become known for, but other projects warranted his attention. The actor leaned forward. From his window, he saw trees, with their lovely new green leaves. He noticed the colorful flags mounted on the airport sign below. All blew in the wind. Sure, the day was gray, typical early spring weather on Long Island, but boy, was he glad to be home!

Well, he wasn't there exactly, but he would be, soon. In minutes, Beau would be ensconced in a town car, headed toward the point. He would be driven to his lovely abode located between the airport and Montauk. Yet as his plane circled, readying for the dip to the runway, Beau remembered something.

He'd gotten kicked out of Sal & Lu's—the Pietro brother's gym...

"No more boxing for you, kid, not here."

One of the owners said it before closing the glass and metal door.

Shocked, Beau stood on the sidewalk as the hefty man's wrist flicked and the lock clicked. Angry, Beau turned, as big Sal called out.

"Come back—when you wanna fly right!"

Beau knew why the giant Italian had barred him from the gym that the Pietro brothers ran. In the haven for troubled youths of all backgrounds, Sal and Lu had spoken to him numerous times.

"Sure," big Sal had said, his Brooklyn accent apparent, "you're a great boxer Beau, and you been here a while. Ya got talent, kid, but you got too much going on. Ya head ain't here."

"Ya know?" Luigi had bitten down on his ever-present cigar. "You know what we're saying?" Salvatore's shorter brother had inquired while chomping cigar. He'd nodded. "Sure, ya do."

"Get your head right," big Sal continued. "Then, we'll see."

"*Capiche*?" short Lu stood, a signal that there would be no more talk. Lu's eyes narrowed because he was sure the tall kid had forayed into the forbidden. Drugs. Neither Luigi or his younger brother Sal, who had been a two-time golden glove winner in his division, needed that shit. Narcotics would bring heat, and the Pietro brothers needed no heat. In avoiding that, and the flames of a burning hell, the brothers had given their lives to Jesus, in atonement for their many sins and heinous crimes.

Now they prayed for their family members who remained in sin. Now the Pietro brothers ran a gym for young men who needed guidance. However, if a youngster thought he could do things *his* way, then Sal and Lu cut that kid loose. They had to, but they made it clear, the same way the door locked, it could unlock. They could allow a kid back in, but that kid had to do things their way, the Pietro brother's way.

Luigi dialed Ms. Moore from juvenile corrections. Before she'd sent her nephew, she'd sent many kids. When the nephew appeared, he'd been fourteen maybe, Lu recalled. The kid had just lost his father figure. Lu thought the kid was uninterested, but Ms. Moore said the kid was grieved and had a host of issues. Now the kid was seventeen, and a good boxer, but he thought he was invincible. Sheesh; youth. Luigi told Ms. Moore her kid was no different from most. They knew it all. They thought. Therefore, Luigi spelled it out for efficient Ms. Moore. Her nephew could not stay, but he could return, after he got his head right.

On the busy street, Beau skirted outdoor bins at a farmers market. Beneath the noisy elevated train, he wanted to push the Filipino woman holding odd fruit. Beau wanted to shove the Jamaican lady with yucca in the basket over her arm. Instead, he sucked his teeth and glared at the Latinx trio walking behind a kid on a colorful tricycle.

Sometimes Beau hated Brooklyn, the steaming cauldron of all nationalities. He hated the jarring neon signs, the foot and motor traffic, and the noisy trains. He hated the fake department stores. Opened by new immigrants, everything was sold, a hodge-podge of items, batteries, bedspreads, detergent, tinned meats, flip-flops, and winter coats.

Sauntering by a West Indian food joint, Beau's mouth watered at the scent of roti and rice 'n peas. Yet he kept his head down, his hood pulled forward. He didn't want anyone to get a clear look at the face he couldn't bear to notice nowadays—his lovely face—his aunt said.

Beau barely heard the screeching train overhead. He'd miss that one. Crossing in traffic, he only knew that Uncle Brantley would be ashamed of him. Now. Crossing another street teeming with people going his way and opposite, Beau knew that Sal & Lu were disappointed too, now.

Suddenly within, Beau felt venom rise. He really should have kicked Luigi's ass! Beau could have taken the shorter man because Lu wasn't made of muscle like the taller, solidly built Sal. Lu looked hard, but he was just solid fat. Still, had Beau jumped Lu and beat the spaghetti out of him, big Sal would have made mincemeat out of Beau. This Beau knew.

Angrily moseying along, Beau was aware, down past the anger, that those two had only been there for him. He also knew he needed to do as they said. *And* he needed to avoid them clowns on Linden Boulevard.

Hovering in doorways, 'the clowns' had appealed to the lonely, angry, lost place inside him. Wearing velvet Pumas, pricey footgear, and dark denim, one dude claimed he had what Beau needed. He'd said, "Just try it." Walking away, Dude hadn't seemed to care if Beau did or not.

That was how they had gotten him. Then they'd given him weed, no charge. Although Beau had wanted to, he hadn't mentioned it to Jervais, who was so damn clean. Well, not really, but the only thing Jervais put in his body, other than rabbit food, yogurt, and water, were dicks, of every size and color. Therefore, Beau forgot the dancer.

With this new bag of weed, probably his thousandth—that he'd had to pay for, no more freebies—Beau thought of Mireya. He could go to her cold empty house. Her mother was always working, so they would have the place to themselves. But Mireya would want to mimic her mother who constantly bent over for men. 'Supplementing her income' was what Ms. Lana called it. So nope. Beau ascended the concrete steps two at a time. He knew he and Mireya could not share a joint. She'd get stupid. He knew from previous puff-puff binges, she would want to kiss, breathe hard, and use her hands to roam his body.

Pushing through the turnstile, Beau needed someone else to get high with. Waiting for the train, he stood too near the platform edge. Wishing the train would race through, he knew its velocity and centrifugal force would knock him to the tracks and thereby end his misery.

When the train moseyed up, he got on it. Yet alive, he slouched in a corner to ignore the noise, metal on metal, whenever the motorman braked. Beau ignored conversations and jostling silly, junior high school kids who still needed the attention of strangers. Disregarding a beggar, Beau remembered. *Kieran*! Now there was a perfect get high partner.

HE sat in Kieran's cramped apartment. Finally, Beau felt hazy and good. He was almost too hot, though, because he still wore his hoodie. However, he was nearly there, all floaty and mellow. His lower half was nude. Beau could not remember when Kieran, his sometime lover, had deftly removed his jeans and boxer shorts.

Pulling on his own man-piece, Beau knew Kieran's roommates weren't due back for a while, so they could get it on. But before that, he wanted Kieran's mouth on his throbbing flagrant erection.

He watched Kieran, who danced and sang with Irene Kara. "*Baby look at me, and tell me what you see...*" Beau also wagged his stiffened pole, seductively, he hoped. Doing so, he realized one thing. He hated the theme song from 'Fame,' perhaps because the way he was going fame would never be his. Beau desperately wanted it, though, and to act on the big screen. Yet, all he did lately was act *out*, which had gotten him booted from school's drama club. And that setting he had really enjoyed!

Forgetting those things, Beau watched Kieran drop clothing. Beau felt his temperature rise too as Kieran's cute booty wiggled. Every gyration of Kieran's, designed to make Beau lose his mind, caused desire to scramble forward. Therefore, watching the sexy dance, the sinewy brown body, and those slender fingers that trailed over that long inviting neck and over those pebbled nipples, Beau licked his lips. He also caught Kieran's wrist, when with lithe fingertips, Kieran reached out to fondle the balls that Beau thought would burst with longing.

Beau pulled, and Kieran landed on his lap. He felt Kieran's firm warm glutes. The peach-soft skin slid over his aching hardened member.

"Not yet, baby," the five-foot slim-goody teased, and slid to the floor. Nestling himself between Beau's gaping thighs, Kieran wrapped his fingers around the throbbing staff that he could not wait to taste. Opening his mouth, Kieran felt powerful when he made Beau moan.

Sliding forward on the loveseat, Beau sheathed himself in the softness. Then with hands on either side of the other boy-man's head, Beau set the pace. Unable to help himself, he began to thrust deeply, attempting to touch Kieran's tonsils. Feeling incredible, Beau raised his pelvis each time he forcefully lowered Kieran's head. Withdrawing, all the way out and feeling cool air, Beau thrust again, wishing it could last.

However, Kieran had other ideas and jolted Beau when Kieran wrenched free. He drew his tongue, flat and wide, over Beau's ballsac.

Shivering with delight, Beau hoisted the other man onto him.

"Wait," Kieran breathed. "Ms. Kiera has something for you."

Beau's part-time lover stood and squeezed a tube of lubricant. He started high at the cleft of his own buttocks as greedily Beau eyed the free-flowing liquid. Down it ran, between those glorious butt cheeks. Unable to think, because he only wanted to feel, Beau pulled.

Facing away from Beau, Kieran was down on Beau's big needy erection. Beau made sure the shorter man was seated firmly on him. Then with one foot, Beau spread Kieran's legs. Using the muscles in his thighs and pelvis, Beau forced himself higher, up into the small tight anal opening.

Breathing raggedly because he was so excited, Beau thought he might convulse...but not...yet, the taller young man told himself. He had to make the feeling last.

Therefore, Beau tried to pace himself, to give Kieran one good hard ride.

He occasionally bit Kieran's nape and back, while his large fingers gripped Kieran's tiny waist, locking buttocks to groin. Beau proceeded to rocket to the stratosphere...before grim reality pulled him back down again, into despair.

Chapter 13

FOR some reason, Kismet Staar re-lived insemination day, through a dream...

Returned from his vacation abroad, Beau had driven her to the appointment. Good thing, because she had been too shaky to drive. On that spring morning, she'd cried too because Nell, her precious mother, stood in the waiting room. Beside Nell had been the older woman's friend, perky, pink-cheeked, brunette Amy. She'd stood with open arms.

Following the procedure, Kismet exited the sterile room and had again burst into tears. Although she had never really been a crybaby, the sight of mocha-skinned Valeria René, complete with rounded belly and toddler on her hip, had tipped the scales. Valeria and Kismet had gone to college together. They had been sister-friends ever since. Also present were two other women, Kismet's dear friends, Abigail and Jade.

Tearfully Kismet had hugged each woman, her mother, and Amy included. Inwardly, she had tried to pull herself together, to remember that she had not needed her husband after all, since Lyle had made it clear. He wanted no part of the shenanigans.

When they left the facility, all the other women had gone out to eat, but Kismet had begged off. She had only wanted the quiet of her own home, because that was how she had set things up. Feeling beat, she was grateful too that her cousin drove in silence. She was thankful that once she got home, she would be able to get into her comfortable bed, with no one other than herself to look after, for once.

Really, Kismet could not thank Deac enough. Her mother's husband had agreed to retrieve her four kids from school and ferry them back to his and Nell's house. There, the kiddies would spend the night. The Momma thought about her children as her cousin pulled onto her driveway.

In her large maple and cream kitchen, Kismet was surprised to find Ms. Fannie, who helped with the kids. But they were elsewhere...

Seeing the perplexed look, the day lady explained. "While you were out, Mr. Beau purchased groceries." Then per his instructions, Ms. Fannie had prepared homemade chicken soup, with warm flaky biscuits.

"Beau said I was to make sure you're comfortable," the plump woman announced, reminding Kismet, as she often did, of a little bird.

While making tea, Ms. Fannie divulged that Beau had said the kids would be elsewhere. "Still, he gave me recipes from your mother's friend. She got them from Zola Mae. I think this Zola made up the recipes?" The older dovelike woman frowned, not fully understanding, but Kismet did, and she was touched.

Her mother's friend Amy had shared recipes dear to her, those long ago handed down from her loving, southern, black caregiver.

Leaving Ms. Fannie to bustle about, Kismet entered her bedroom. Yet she did not see the soothing oyster colored walls or the lovely old crown moulding. She paid no attention to the sweeping archway leading to the alcove where her big poster bed sat. Pride of place, it rested on a lovely rug, between two windows. Kismet did not see wall sconces or the pedestal table displaying fresh flowers.

As she walked creaky polished wood, she didn't see the massive fireplace, traditional décor, or the heavy drapes that pooled prettily beneath each window. Kismet did not see the fringed hassock upon which she often put her feet. She simply entered the *en suite* bathroom.

Again in her bedroom, Kismet didn't notice lamps, or silk shades. She saw no silver-framed photos of her children, or the comfy seating area where she sometimes read. Instead, with her heart heavy, she donned a soft, warm nightgown and its matching robe.

Yet she remembered to make the appropriate noises upon accepting a tray of food. She did so because both her cousin and Ms. Fannie had taken the time to care. Unlike her husband.

When the dovelike little woman closed Kismet's bedroom door, after promising she'd look back in, The Momma allowed herself to feel. Hurt washed over her in waves. Allowing it to do so, Kismet did not so much as swipe or dab at the tears that rolled steadily down her cheeks.

Fresh off his cell phone, Beau knocked. Then entering his cousin's sweet retreat, he remarked on how good the food smelled.

Kismet agreed. With a watery smile for Beau who had gone to such trouble for her, she even attempted to eat. She soon gave up, though.

Concerned, Kismet's cousin asked if she ached. Wanting to be helpful, he also dashed around the inviting room, gathering silk and satin throw pillows. These he pooled behind her. "You need to lie back," he said, grasping her ankle and attempting to put her socked feet on the bed.

Despite disappointment and tears, Kismet chuckled. "I'm okay, Diddley." She knew he wanted to help, to do anything that would make things better, but he could not. Therefore, she told the truth. "I've got a few cramps, but really, it's my *heart* that aches."

The very thought caused her to burst into tears.

Then as he often did, Beau felt for his beloved dog tags, while looking quizzically down at the woman propped up in the big poster bed. Unaware of what to do, he instinctively did what his aunt had, for as far back as he could remember. Seating himself beside Kismet, he gathered her in his muscled arms. Without words, he held her, and let her cry. He also wished to get her lout of a husband in the boxing ring, just once. He'd beat the stew out of the man.

When the sobs subsided, Beau couldn't help but ask, "You regret it?"

"Nooo, never." With averted eyes, Kismet divulged, "You smell good, Diddley. You always do." Suddenly she changed tracks. "I know it's silly for me to be upset because he said he didn't want anything to do with this…"

Lyle, Beau thought. His cousin's husband.

"But," she continued, "I kind of thought; well, I'd hoped—" She could not finish the sentiment due to tears.

"Kismet Staar, you hoped that *as your man,*" Beau acknowledged for her, "Lyle would change his mind. You wanted support. Kiss, that's nothing to be ashamed of."

"I guess I know it, but I still feel hurt, and I feel silly for feeling that way."

Beau nodded, because how many times had he too felt the same way?

HOURS later, she woke from a very real-seeming dream, quite possibly with the beginnings of the baby that Beau wanted, in her belly. But, she thought with tears on her lashes, she had no husband in her bed.

In her darkened bedroom, Kismet reached for a tissue, and with her house as silent as a tomb, she went back to sleep, only to be awakened a little while later, by the creak of a floorboard.

Groggy from her earlier crying jag, for a moment she wondered if she imagined the figure that made to get into bed with her. However, when she felt the familiar weight, as her husband sat on the mattress, she knew he was no figment of her imagination.

With her voice sounding hollow, she spoke. "Lyle, I'm not telling you to leave this house, but I am telling you that tonight, in this bed, you are not wanted."

In the moonlight, he turned to face her. He appeared stunned. "What are you saying, Kismet?"

Lyle's breath smelled of liquor, and it sickened her. She also felt a mite scared, because each day, this new man proved she did not know him, at all. As his wife, she hated to admit that she had no idea anymore what he was capable of, yet she held her ground.

"Since you've made it clear that you don't want to be with me, right along in this period, *I* feel the same. Right now, *I* don't want *you* here." *And especially not in this bed*, she thought but did not say.

However, the words, unsaid, hung in the air between them.

When, Lyle dejectedly sighed, Kismet furtively glanced over.

Lyle took his time about getting up. He also made a project of gathering a few things.

Finally, he left the bedroom and Kismet allowed herself to lie back down. On the stairs, she heard her husband's downward tread. Then in the dark, with slivers of pale moonlight slipping through the drawn drapes, she pressed her face deep into a pillow. Hoping the sound was muffled, she let herself cry, this time as though her heart would break.

She promised herself it would be the last time she would do so.

Afterward, Kismet roused herself. Patting her puffy eyes, she threw back the cover, because enough of that; she needed to check on her children.

However, before her feet touched the floor, The Momma realized… Like their father, the kiddos were not present.

Chapter 14

BEAU had nearly forgotten the happenings of so many years prior. He'd had to, to finish editing his latest documentary about Afro-Caribbean Rhythms and World Music. He had also found out where the team stood in procuring the money needed to turn his highly anticipated screenplay—now done, into a movie.

Each day, sometimes, through his assistant, he spoke with his people. He touched base with his manager. He talked to Jayé, [Jah-YAY] his agent. The tiny barracuda had been with him so long, that she well knew him. Thus, she often made all the right things happen. Beau collaborated with his publicist too.

He made it a point to keep up with Gypsy, and Kendu, his band's drummer and backup. Both men were like younger brothers to him.

Whenever Beau felt himself easing down memory lane, he told himself no. He had promos and appearances to make. There was an awards show to present at, and songs to co-write. He had Malay tracks to check out, rehearsals to attend, and a few major upcoming gigs. Then before long, he and a scout team that included his cinematographer, lead investigator, and his DP—his director of photography—would jet down to a gorgeous island. There, they would check out settings with April Alisa, the author of a book he wanted to bring to the big screen. So he literally had no more time for jaunts down memory lane.

Yet Beau could not forget that late in high school, his grades had suffered. He had wasted too much time with the college sophomore Kieran, whose grade point average had been commendable.

Beau recalled that back then, he had also progressed in his choice of recreational drugs. He had moved on to what he'd called heron. He'd shot the liquid into his veins for an indelible high.

Looking back, Beau wondered. Had the drug already been in his system? The truth was his mother had pursued substance every single day of his young life. So had he been more like her than he knew?

Never though, Beau recalled, had he pierced the flesh of his arms, like his mother had. That would have been too obvious he felt, because he had seen track marks on Ophelia. However, he had squeezed his calf muscles and shot up in his legs. A bit painful it had been, just before the pleasurable rush of his high, that never lasted. After a few tries, Beau had even learned to hit the sweet spot, the one that sent momentary bliss winging through his veins, but Beau hadn't believed he was an addict.

At least that's what he had told himself as he ran little 'errands' for his dealer. Those he was paid for, but stupidly, he turned right around and handed the money back over for more of 'the bird,' so he could fly.

While shooting up, Beau had often wondered if he would become like his mother. Chasing highs, she had cared about little else.

Just before he flew, young Beau would sometimes hazily wonder if he were any better than the woman who had lost all regard for everyone, even those who should have been closest to her.

The adult Beau remembered that during that time, one evening, he and Jervais had hurried along.

Jervais had been worried about 'long drink of water,' and inconspicuously, the little dancer glanced over. Again, he noticed. His friend appeared as he often did, like Beau no longer cared—about much of anything. Although he was naturally good-looking, the tall, brown, slender but muscular Beau wore the same type of drab hoodie, jeans, and scuffed sneakers he'd worn every day for the past two years.

Jervais remembered when his friend had taken pride in presenting himself. Now, no more. He never carried books either.

"Yo, what's up with you?" the dancer asked, one cold February evening when Beau met him outside the high school for those in the arts. "Where are your books? And why you got that same shit on again, with that hood hiding your face?" Disgusted, Jervais did not hold back. "You smell like you slept all day. What, you Dracula now?"

"Yo, who are *you*—my fuckin' mother?" Beau asked, hunching into his puffed, pseudo-down jacket.

"You ain't *got* a mother," Jervais quipped, reminding Beau that although smaller and feminine, the dancer was still nobody's pushover.

"Yo, let's just start again," Beau grumbled, his way of apologizing.

"Yes, let's, because if you wanna jump down somebody's th'oat you should've stayed away, like you been doing. Yeah," Jervais mumbled, somewhat jealous, "or you should've gone to the queen of the fairies." He sneered while saying the name, "Kieran."

Beau smirked, as they hurried down Amsterdam Avenue, bustling with foot and vehicular traffic. "What you got against Ms. Kiera?"

"I got nothing," Jervais promised as the wind cut and stung. "Say his name right too—or better yet, don't say it at all, because I don't like who you've become since you've been hanging out with…that—*thing*."

Beau stiffened, shoving cold fists deeper into his pockets. He really didn't need a lecture, not when he had so recently received a severe dressing down from his aunt…

As he walked, he didn't tell Jervais, but short buxom Nell had walked into her house. She had seen her nephew taking the last glass from the cabinet. She'd exploded. "Why are all my dishes in the sink?!" Nell looked around her cooking space, usually kept spotless. "And why is this garbage not out? It stinks."

With her coat on, Nell bent to knot the plastic bag. "Isn't this one of your chores, Diddley?" She also huffed about working sixteen-hour days, to keep all hail 'n hearty—whatever that meant. "So Beauregard, you know what *I'm* doing, but I don't know what *you're* doing. I only know you're flunking out of school, and out of life, it seems. Oh, and I know Salvatore and Luigi don't want you at their gym anymore. Not 'til you straighten up." Nell angrily flung the bag toward the back door.

With cans and trash inside, the thin plastic burst when it hit the floor. Smelly beans and other debris skittered over the linoleum, and Beau's aunt screamed. High-pitched, her wail was like that of a wounded animal. Nell also pulled at her head of thick hair, its curls brushed back from her forehead.

"Beauregard DeVeaux!" Unbelievably frustrated, the short round woman kicked a can. "Why aren't you doing what you're supposed to?"

Throwing up her hands, she fell onto a kitchen chair. Staring at the table, she sounded like she had no fight left in her. "Puppy, I've done all I can with you."

Those words, and the fact that she had called him by the nickname she'd given him when she rescued him from ever having to fear his mother again, rocked Beau to the core. He recalled that Nell had also taken him to the pound to pick a pet. She had given him his beloved dog tags then. Thus, he could only stare as his aunt sadly intoned that *his only job* was to get good grades, "While I do everything else.·

"You work summers, but that can't be too much," Nell said, "because I break my back to support all of y'all. I buy clothes and food. I only ask that you three make something of yourselves, and stay out of trouble." Wearily Beau's aunt asked, "So why aren't you doing that?" With all joy and light long gone from her countenance, she queried, "Are you even going to graduate—on time? Forget about college, for you, now." Nell couldn't bear to think of it. "Here I am, slaving away like a dang pack mule, since Brantley went and left me to do this alone, and—"

Nell's face reddened, and it hurt Beau to see her sitting there so still, while in two hands, she twisted the ends of her wool scarf. Watching her, he could not have known that again she thought about her husband who had left money for his interment, and for the three kids' college. Brantley had even managed to pay off the house, but the cyclical bills kept coming, and other things were always needed.

Every time Nell turned around, another expensive book was required for college-aged Kismet Staar, who attended Clarke-Atlanta University, although they bought some of the books in 'used' condition. The house boiler had needed fixing, as had a portion of the roof, and Nell had recently had her transmission flushed. None of it had been cheap.

Nell bit her lip when she saw how insurance ate up her earnings. Now Beau and Kiss had to be on her plan, because Brantley was gone. Twisting her scarf ends, Nell momentarily forgot her nephew, to think of how she wanted to remove her coat, and her clothing, especially her bra; raggedy thing. But she hadn't the strength to move. And the truth was she needed all new underpinnings. Yet she could not afford them!

Nell wanted to get comfortable too, but that would mean lying in her man's arms while he watched basketball. But that would never happen again, she thought, as a tear trickled down her cheek. Guess she would never also make love again, either. Wow. She was going to wind up a nun... Sure, men found her bustling personality and her big tits enticing, but she wanted Brantley. Her brawny, robust, healthy Brantley.

Nell's nephew watched as tears cascaded down her cheeks.

With a sigh, she voiced that she could be grateful for one thing. Brantley's older daughter was taken care of, "Because that child's mama is richer than Zeus. Good thing, because I could never afford insurance for Farai too. Shoot," Nell swore, her equivalent of cussing. "All *that* I got to deal with, including them bad-behind kids down at juvie, and here *you* are—my boy, cutting up, for no good reason."

Well, with what he had been through, Nell thought but did not say, the youngster had reason, but, "Your antics," she stated, "I do *not* need."

Sure, her nephew was on the cusp of becoming a black man in America, Nell cogitated, twisting her scarf. She understood; he lived in a society that many times begrudged men like him their very existence. On top of that, her boy was gay. Oh, he thought nobody knew, yet *he* knew, and he was having a hard time accepting it.

Wearily, Nell spoke. "Child, I have no earthly idea of how to help you. I'm nobody's man, for crying out loud, and I sure as heck don't know the first thing about raising one." That took them back to what she faced every day. "Brantley was supposed to be here, but now he's not!"

"How," Nell plaintively asked with her face in her hands, "am I supposed to get this right, on my own?" She faltered as Beau just stood there, staring at her. "Here I am, trying to abide by my man's wishes, but sometimes I just wanna fall into the bed he and I shared, and I never wanna get up again. I just want to sleep on away from here."

Raising tear-filled eyes, she looked at Beau. "I'm doing the best I can, Puppy," Nell eked. Her red nose began to run as she became swamped with hurt. Nell felt utterly worn, *and* she was so angry she could erupt.

She was also embarrassed, because what kid needed a blubbering adult in a filthy kitchen? "Oh, God!" Nell squealed and quickly dropped her head to her folded arms.

Beau watched as her shoulders began to shake. He felt stunned, and realized what he hadn't before. Although his aunt seemed so, she was *not* indomitable. Suddenly, to the teenager, Nell looked like what she was, a short, stout woman who'd had as much as she could take. She had grown tired of being everybody's go-to, when she had no go-to.

As he and Jervais walked, Beau recalled how he had stood, rooted to the spot, unable to say a word, and unable to rub his little aunt's back. He'd felt like such a cad. Recalling that awful scene while hastening down ridiculously-lit New York streets in the nighttime, Beau remembered breaking down.

Keeping pace with his oldest friend, Beau was glad Jervais did not need to constantly make conversation. The dancer occasionally got lost in projections for his future. That was good because Beau didn't know if he could have spoken right then, not with memories assailing him. Beau realized that at the Springfield Gardens house, he had not seen the proverbial table turning. Yet in the kitchen, with garbage strewn and dishes piled in the sink, his little aunt's arms had surrounded him.

When had she risen from her chair, smelling faintly like lavender? Beau wondered, as soothingly, she'd rubbed his back. She'd noticed him crying, and she'd pressed his face to the shoulder of her coat. Forcing words through her own subsiding sobs, Nell showed that she cared about Beau's hurt as repeatedly she said, "I know, baby."

Now…as a fully functioning adult, looking back, Beau knew that all along his aunt had known. Her nephew felt like the rug had been jerked from beneath him. Nell had known that, because she too had been hurt, and grieving the untimely loss of her loved one.

Beau remembered that when he had ceased to cling, Nell wet a dishtowel and urged it on him, something she would never have done otherwise. "Dab your eyes," she advised, "and let's both do something."

Beau could not look at the woman who had slaved and sacrificed so much more for him than his biological mother ever would have. "What's that?" he managed with the cool cloth feeling great on his puffy eyes.

"Let's make my Brant proud, you and I." Nell took the towel, ran cold water on it, and dabbed her face. Laying it aside for laundering, she made a vow. "Puppy, I *will* find happy again, but you gotta find you."

Released from reflections, Beau, the youngster stood outside the brick building where Jervais would spend hours bruising and torturing his body, urging it to submit to his whim and will. Beau no longer felt the bristling cold. He barely saw other dancers hurrying inside. He only remembered locking eyes with his aunt as in her kitchen, he'd forced out one word. "Okay." With that word, he had been promising to do better, to become a man, of whom his aunt *and* his uncle could be proud.

As Jervais pulled on the heavy metal door that would take him into the world of those who soared and made magic, their every move accompanied by music, Beau caught the dancer's coat. Glancing back, the shorter male announced, "I gotta get inside."

Beau felt sheepish as a group of jovial teenaged girls passed. "I know," he said, "but…I wanted to tell you something, Vay."

Standing on his toes, Jervais seemed a little impatient. "What?"

Beau spoke quickly, so his friend would not wind up late. "I haven't forgotten—our promise… I just got a little off track for a minute."

"But you're back now?" Expectantly, Jervais looked up at his childhood friend.

Beau nodded. When the dancer squeezed his fingertips, Beau felt warm all over.

"I'm glad, Bodacious. I really am, because I was starting to miss my *friend*."

Chapter 15

KISMET Staar sat in her study, staring into the barren fireplace. Raising her eyes, she gazed at her Elizabeth Catlett painting. Over the mantel, it depicted women in vibrant red dresses. With the seemingly independent beings, Kismet had always felt kinship. However, lately, she did not. Swiveling in her leather chair, she stared out of the multi-paned window. Her tree-dotted lawn in all its autumn regalia reminded her that summer was gone and that she'd again undergone the process. A new egg had been fertilized. Now there was monitoring to see if it would become viable. She sure hoped it would, and that this baby held.

Kismet sighed and felt like she had been run over by a bus. Not because the procedure had been tedious, but more because she didn't want a third attempt. Sure, she'd read that it often took several tries, sometimes even six or more, for a viable pregnancy. Yet there was nothing wrong with her, not anything physical, and she was mentally okay. She was just tired. All the machinations—as Lyle called it—were foreign, not to mention the expense! However, the cost, her cousin was handling.

So said Lyle, "Your punk-ass cousin can purchase anything, right? Anything but the baby that you might deliver."

Re-focusing, Kismet was grateful, she supposed, that Lyle had taken their children to the movies. With him, their sullen thirteen-year-old, and the mischievous younger kids out of the house, The Momma had a little me-time. In the quiet, she thought. True, she wanted this baby for her cousin. Yet part of her felt selfish. That part didn't want to give up Beau's baby.

Seated at her beautiful carved wood desk, a gift from her cousin, Kismet placed her head in her hands. The whole situation reminded her of one years back. Her dear friend Valeria René had been trying to have a baby after suffering miscarriages. Therefore wanting to aid her, Val's sister had volunteered to become her surrogate. But it became apparent, Val's sister wanted the baby for herself.

Kismet had thought that was foul. Now, however, she sometimes found herself feeling the same way. She wanted to scream. No, she wanted to punch Lyle, because he was the reason she was all twisted up. He was uncooperative, and he always had something snide to say. As her husband, wasn't he supposed to be supportive? Where was *that* man, her paragon of strength? He was gone. In his place was Mr. Surly.

In her daughter's place was the same type of teenager. With attitude, the thirteen-year-old had said she didn't know why her mother was doing things to tear the family apart.

Since Déja had sounded like Lyle, Kismet questioned the grown-behind girl. Déja refused to speak. The Momma reminded the girl that she would always be loved, "But Manfred children aren't allowed to give parents the silent treatment. Not when the parents go above and beyond for those children," Kismet stated. Forgetting how she'd wanted to slap the girl, Kismet vowed to pray, because slapping would change nothing.

Lyle's question popped up and Kismet tried to push it from mind.

What will you tell that new kid when he or she asks why you kept four *other children, but not him or her?*

Seated in her study, Kismet realized that in giving Beau what he wanted, there were things that she wanted too. They were things that her cousin, with all his money, could not give her. Heck, to tell the truth, one of the things she wanted was her husband. Kismet wanted Lyle like he had been, before. She wanted his manly frame on her, as it had not been, in forever. She wanted to kiss and laugh. The new Lyle they could discard, along with his mistress...drink.

Kismet wanted understanding too. Lyle didn't necessarily have to agree with her decision, but why not acknowledge its validity? Sure, he was her man, but it was *her* body. She was free to do with it as she chose, as long as she did not hurt herself, him, or their children.

Sick of turmoil, Kismet sighed. Suddenly she longed to take her twins, the round-faced boy, and girl, into her arms. As she sat in the big old house that was currently quiet, save for the occasional gong of a clock, she remembered sweating to push the twins forth. She would do the same with the new baby. Kismet recalled nursing the twins, inducing burps, and singing lullabies. That, she would not get to do with this new baby; the one she hoped would continue to grow inside her. The thought saddened her.

Kismet recalled patting all her children's backs and reading silly stories to them. She taught, scolded, tickled, and fed all of them. Often when they'd been mere months old, she'd made love with their father, as they'd lain in a bassinet aside. None of that would she do with the new baby. Yet that child would reside in her heart, ever one of her children.

Kismet scoffed because psychological tests had agreed, she was ready. However, even now, in the fall, at this late date, she needed to do what Lyle suggested. She had to ask herself one question, and answer truthfully. *Could she let a child of hers go*, even to her cousin?

Kismet needed music. She selected one of her favorite gospel songs by the Georgia Mass Women's Choir. The piano introduction began, and she realized *Order My Steps* had become her prayer. When the soprano sang, *teach me your will... while you are working, help me be still*, Kismet felt so full. Listening, she was transported back to the services of her youth. About to cry, Kismet inwardly pled to be supernaturally led.

Snatching a tissue, she realized, if she was to do this, with grace, she needed the peace of the Holy Spirit.

As the song built to an exuberant crescendo, Kismet crumpled the tissue and noticed. She felt...calm, as she reached for the ringing phone.

"KissGirl." The voice was rich and soothing. "How are you, sugar?"

"Mama..." Tears sprang to Kismet's eyes. "I don't know."

Nell's voice remained soft, "You wanna talk about it?"

With hope suspended by a thread, the younger woman asked, "May I come over?"

"Sugar pie," Nell sounded near to chuckling, "you come right now."

LEAVING her sweet man propped comfortably atop their bed, Nell turned to go. Yet she turned back, "You alright, Deac?"

With a football game on, the gray-haired, thick-bodied man in the long-sleeved polo shirt caught his wife's hand. "Yes, my love."

Squeezing the deacon's thick fingers, Nell nodded. "Okay. Well, I'll be up front, with KissGirl." Nell ambled from the bedroom with its pale striped walls. In her small galley kitchen, she strapped on an apron. So what, her clothes were ancient? She still didn't want them soiled.

Softly Nell hummed as she prepared a tea tray. She laid out cake slices. Then at the knock, she called, "Come in. I'm in the kitchen."

Enfolded in a meaningful hug, one that threatened to start her crying again, Kismet sighed, grateful for the quiet house, her mother's lavender scent and warm body—all thoroughly soothing.

"I love you so much, KissGirl..." Nell cooed, as she often did not.

"I know," Kismet stated, sounding muffled. "I wuv you too."

Nell laughed and released the younger woman. As she folded napkins and poured cream, Kismet watched. Her mother's thick, graying bob was held back on the sides with tortoiseshell combs, and Nell wore her birthstone earrings. A member of the generation that never failed to do so, Nell had powdered her face. Her nails were, as always, a rose color. The older woman also wore her wedding band, but not her diamond, because she did not want to roon, as she often said, ruin her sparkle.

Kismet noted the taupe, sturdy knit pants—bet they had an elastic waistband—and the eggshell-colored cable-knit sweater, beneath an apron. She saw the whimsical socks and sateen ballerina slippers.

"Bring that KissGirl; we're going in here."

The daughter obeyed, setting the tray on the charming dining room table. With its neutral palette, there was a porthole window on one of the bungalow's walls. Seeing it, Kismet thought what she always did. How cute. She glanced at a framed lithograph called *Ushers of the Church*. Artist, Leroy Campbell's women in white walked up a serene, green, country road. Seeing them reminded Kismet of times long past.

At the table, adorned with antique lace, Nell poured from a gold-rimmed teapot. Her daughter lifted a matching dessert plate of moist delicious cake. Beneath her small chandelier, Nell could see that her daughter had been crying. Thus, she coaxed, "Talk to me, sugar..."

With downcast eyes, Kismet sighed. "Where do I start?"

Not one to beat around the bush, Nell said, "Kismet Staar, I asked you before. Now again I ask. Can you carr' this baby, and let him go?"

Not caring that her daughter's eyes were averted, Nell continued. "Are you positive you even wanna do this? I mean do you b'lieve you can give a baby up, after you've carried him or her to term? You know, that baby's not gonna be under your roof. So, do you b'lieve you can live with him or her elsewhere? KissGirl, look at me. I ask these questions because you, my darling, usually need to have things your way."

Kismet softly spoke. "I can live with all of what you just said, Mama... but only because it's Diddley."

With her cup at her lips, Nell remained silent.

April Alisa Marquette

"For a while now, Ma, I've been soul-searching. I know it'll be hard...to release the baby, but this baby is not mine, not fully. I also understand this would all be harder if I weren't the one doing it."

"You mean if Beau had a different surrogate."

"Yes. Knowing how much he wants a child, I'd regret not being involved."

Nell sighed and sipped her tea. "I understand."

"No, Mama, you don't. You can't possibly." Kismet met her mother's eyes. "I may have mentioned a few things, but I don't think I've said anything about my children, or about how Lyle would step up if anything happened to me. His family would step in. You would too, Mama, as would Farai. That's all I want...for Diddley; no outsiders swooping in to confiscate his child or his money. We don't need outside complications.

"This, I've explained to Lyle many times. I've said that for me, this isn't about monetary compensation, because Lyle and I have been so blessed. I'm doing this for the preservation of family. That's all."

"Well, KissGirl," Nell nodded, "I'll tell you what. Initially, I didn't see all those angles, but I now I understand, and I'm with you."

Nell set her coffee cup down. "KissGirl, when you were a toddler, Brantley and I knew you were smart. But all these years later, I'm still in awe of you."

"How so, Mama?"

"Well, sugar, I just happen to use common sense, but *you*, baby; you see every angle. Then on top of that, you've got the best heart."

Placing an elegant hand at her chest, Kismet loudly exhaled. "Thanks for saying that, Mama, but right here, I feel sad and hurt."

Nell leaned forward. "Your heart hurts? That needs checking."

"It's not that kind of hurt, Ma."

"Oh." Nell blinked. "Your *soul* feels wounded...right?"

Aloud, Kismet wondered how her mother knew.

"I know," Nell acknowledged, "because I'm a mother too; I've been one for a long time. I know too because had I been forced to give your cousin Beau or your father's daughter Farai up, I could not have done it, and I didn't birth either of them. To let them go would've broken my heart. To let *you* go, would have killed me, after all that perspiring to get you here. So, I understand. I believe in this that you're doing."

"Mama, I'm grateful for your support. But...I need that from Lyle too. I need Heaven to intervene. You know?"

Nell nodded. "Well, we'll pray, and your man will survive."

"Yeah, but will my *marriage*?" Kismet wondered.

Her mother remained silent, because that question, Nell could not answer.

Chapter 16

BEAU'S stomach growled, and he glanced at his watch. No wonder. It was 9 PM. In his office, he noticed, all was cloaked in shadow. It was time to call it a day. He heard more growling. He actually hadn't eaten since…breakfast. No, his bad, he'd downed green tea at ten a.m.

Rising, Beau tidied up because he would get out and get some vittles. At home, his little Siamese cat JaMocha and his big dog would be waiting. Quickly labeling a few things, he longed to see his fur babies. He replied to two email queries and quickly shut down. Pocketing his thumb drive, he grabbed his jacket.

He passed *Jumping for Joy*, a painting. It depicted lithe African-American dancers in a lush green garden. It caused him to think, as he often did, of his first friend, Jervais. Thoughts of the real-life dancer had initially prompted Beau to purchase and hang the artwork in his space.

In the outer office, Beau spoke to his assistant. He asked Tatum, the kid from the Midwest, "Didn't I tell you to go home hours ago?" Shaking his head, Beau told carrot-top, who'd left the town where he'd grown up, "Leave. Soon. I mean it, Tate. Come in late tomorrow."

Beau waved and recalled that when asked to speak about himself during his interview, the kid of Irish descent had said that 'back home,' everybody knew everybody else's business, including the fact that he was gay. The undergrad revealed his desire to live someplace where things could remain private. Tatum had also mumbled about not knowing why people had to drag other people's business into the street.

Unbeknownst, Beau had immediately found Tatum's privacy concept endearing. The entertainer had hired the kid on the spot. He had never regretted choosing the kid whom he called Tate, for short. Sometimes Tatum got overzealous, but he never erred for lack of trying. That Beau liked, and rewarded.

Beau passed young brown male employees. Diligently they worked on different sections of film. Beau bid them good night. Striding toward the elevator, he recalled when he too had been a very young man…

Outside, he expertly wheeled his sporty, midnight blue coupe and realized he was getting up there. He thought it because back in high school, he and cinnamon-skinned Mireya had believed that only old men drove luxury cars, but now he felt his ride was pretty sweet.

How far he'd come, Beau mused, accelerating. With exquisite sound surrounding him, he remembered mornings and the subway. While traveling to his and Mireya's Manhattan high school, they'd hopped three trains, one after the other, never once pondering car ownership.

Evenings, however, Mireya's cheerleading duties precluded their riding home together. So Beau and his lady-boy friend, Jervais, often went dancing, at Savage or the Garage. Those two New York clubs they'd called, respectively, Sa-vaj and the Gay-raj because they'd gone on gay night. Often they had used fake IDs too, until they were older.

While driving along, Beau, the adult, realized his past pursuits had gotten him into a world of trouble.

Naturally curious, he had often found himself in what many called the T-rooms. There he had learned, firsthand, about cruising. Back then, the NYC subway system had housed an underworld where some of the hot spots were restrooms. Referred to as clubhouses or cornhole palaces, Beau had ogled many, and there he'd had numerous sexcapades.

Maneuvering onto the highway, he remembered that all sorts of things had happened in the 'penile colonies.' On the regular, he had seen dapper businessmen in custom-tailored workwear, getting the stuffing pounded out of them. Tourists had willingly done so too. Often, they had engaged with banshee boys who had the largest cocks Beau had ever seen. Bent over, the receivers would ecstatically moan. Afterward, they'd re-adjust their expensive attire and exit. Above ground, they would act as though they had never laid eyes on any ethnic b-boy, until the next episode.

Sexy, virile, and nearing forty, Beau couldn't remember just when the city had legislated to close the T-rooms. He only knew it had been back in the days of Mayor Koch. At that time, a few angry citizens and Daily News editors had hissed and written about 'those dens of iniquity.' They claimed druggies, trollops, and harpies perpetrated evil there.

Yet Beau hadn't seen it that way. Those palaces of cornucopia were where he had gotten an education. He had learned things in Greenwich Village too, and down at Chelsea Piers, now a historic site on Manhattan's West Side. Nowadays, he wouldn't do what he had, back in the day; the practice had been too kamikaze. However, he did not regret the experiences. Nor did he regret having met his friend Brett back in that netherworld.

April Alisa Marquette

Driving along, Beau suddenly remembered his childhood friend Jervais. Vay had changed, drastically. The dancer had become wildly extroverted, a T-room queen, and Beau tried not to think about why.

Instead, he thought about his then-new friend. Brett. Dark-skinned and slender with curly hair, Brett had been a bit of a wallflower. However, in time, Beau began to understand the new young man, the one who believed he was a natural-born woman, on the inside.

This Beau knew because one day, Brett revealed his deepest secret. He had been born with both male and female organs. "I was called a hermaphrodite," Brett stated. "But people like me prefer the term transgender. It doesn't imply any specific sexual orientation."

Beau understood. He said sometimes conventional labels didn't fully apply to the rainbow nation. "As LGBTQ, we're more than our sexuality."

Brett agreed and admitted he hated that word, hermaphrodite. To him it sounded stigmatizing. "In my mind it conjures up an ugly image."

With his dark skin beautifully unblemished, Brett gazed up at Beau. "Did you know that in the scientific and medical fields, some people call people like me *intersex* persons?"

Beau said he hadn't been aware, just before Brett announced he didn't like that term either; "Not when the truth is: I just want to be *me*."

Beau traversed the Long Island Expressway in his sporty coupe. Driving, he remembered Brett gushing, "Beau, you're just perfect! I can see why Vay calls you Bo-dacious. Did you know you're only the second person I didn't have to convince I'm not alien? Jervais was the first."

Beau appeared confused. "Come again?"

"Well," Brett began, "I usually wind up explaining myself, like I just did, but despite it, most people don't understand, or they decide they can't deal. Then the relationship or the friendship ends." Brett snapped his fingers. Just like that."

Shaking his head, Beau asked, "Why? I mean, how narrow-minded is that? Heck, you had nothing to do with the way you were born."

At that moment, slender Brett decided, Beau was a keeper, and their friendship blossomed. Until Beau introduced Brett to Mireya....

Feeling threatened, the cinnamon-skinned high school senior's claws came out. Never had she wanted to share Beau, and she especially couldn't see sharing him with a male who—to her—seemed too female.

However, believing it might soothe tensions, Beau let Mireya in on slender Brett's secret. Beau said they were both girls, inside.

Then the curvy cheerleader who had known Beau since middle school dismissively waved. Sounding unconcerned, and catty, she said, "Brett, if that's your real name, I just hope you'll one day become okay with yourself—as a him, a her—or whatever."

Mireya fiercely also hoped, although she didn't say it, that Brett would do so *away* from Beau.

Feeling as though Mireya did not understand or want to, one day Brett mentioned his thoughts to Beau.

Tall, buff, and brown, Beau didn't say much. Yet he knew Brett had spoken the truth. Beau also wished he had never introduced his two friends because the three-way friendship was a pain.

Leaving memories of tense interactions behind, Beau wheeled his 'old man car.' While doing so, he admitted one thing. Pertaining to the three-way friendship, many days, he *still* felt the strain.

Chapter 17

KISMET asked her husband, "Why are we still on this?" For crying aloud, she was three months along! With the fertility specialist, she'd had numerous consultations, and back in the spring, the biological father had signed off on all his documents. Before her first insemination, she had asked Lyle to accompany her. The native of Belize had declined. Thank God, her family of friends had cared enough to show up. Now in chilly mid-autumn, Kismet forgot those things as she and Lyle left the shopper's club. In the growing dark, with his SUV in sight, she recalled that before her first insemination, she'd had basic screenings, as had the biological father. As Lyle pushed the heavy cart filled with supplies for home, Kismet recalled having kept quiet about the observation of her ovarian reserve. The purpose had been to determine her egg quality. Kismet had kept all talk of psychiatrist visits mum, yet they were to ensure she was a viable surrogacy candidate.

However, Lyle knew about the self-administered steroid injections. They were the prerequisites to the fertilized egg that Kismet would carry. Nonetheless, she had not mentioned the extensive research she had done before embarking on the journey that she found both scary and wonderful. By the time of her second insemination, she knew so much, she could have written a book, she felt. In that book, she would not have failed to point out what her husband had made clear.

He did not care to know all she had been through.

That hurt. Sure, Lyle Manfred had signed consent forms, but he'd done so grudgingly. Glancing over at him, Kismet wondered how long her spouse would continue in this vein. And how long would he drink?

The man who used to imbibe occasionally, and only socially, spoke. "He's not even *there* yet, Kiss." Lyle placed fabric softener in the boot of his SUV.

Sliding onto the front passenger seat, curvaceous Kismet knew her husband spoke of her first cousin. How sick she was, of Lyle's irascibility, even as he asked her a question.

"Don't you think y'all are jumping the gun here?"

With a sigh, Kismet wondered, why did Lyke keep upsetting himself, and her? Lord knew that since July, when she'd undergone the process again, she had stopped mentioning anything about the baby. Kismet kept quiet because she didn't need Lyle getting all bent. Therefore, closing the passenger door, she tossed over her shoulder, "My cousin *is* there. And one day he may even get married."

"Oh come on! Don't call it marriage, Kiss," Lyle scowled as he continued to stow groceries. "That's between a man and a woman. Just say he'll wind up unionized, or something, with somebody."

Holding a thirty-six pack of eggs, Kismet felt incredulity, and anger. She really could not believe Lyle! And she turned. "Where's this straight-laced discriminatory stuff coming from?"

With narrowed eyes, she realized. After years of marriage, Lyle could yet surprise her, but lately, not in a good way. "Wow, I honestly thought you liked Beau. Before. I didn't know you had a problem with him."

Lyle stowed the last package, as mid-autumn winds cut and stung. "He's okay. I guess. My problem happens to be *my wife.* Suddenly, she's got a new career, giving away babies."

"That's not fair. You know I have a career. You know my firm agreed I could work from home. Oh, and no one said anything about babies, plural. I'm carrying one." Soon to enter her second trimester, Kismet reminded her husband, "And I'm not negligently *giving* this one away."

"I forgot. You're getting paid," Lyle scoffed. "Ah, and your dear loaded cousin is footing the bill for everything, even the extras."

"Its business, Lyle, like an adoption, so it has to be legal, and with the money I've received so far, I've padded our kids' college fund."

"Then that makes this all okay. Right, Kiss? Except, this *isn't* an adoption!" Slamming the rear door, Lyle shoved the shopping cart into its post. He realized he could use a drink, although he had already had one. Yep, before he and Kismet Staar had come out. He had sneaked a nip while she pulled on her coat. As she'd lovingly instructed their kids, and the lady who kept them, he'd hurriedly tossed back a second drink.

Now, sliding behind the wheel, Lyle forgot stolen drinks to preempt his wife. He did not need her further getting on his nerves. "Look, Kiss, just—be quiet, because I'm sick of discussions."

She stared out at pools of light and recalled that were it a few years back, she'd have punched Lyle in the face. But since she had prayed and meditated, all to subdue her temper, she would let things go. Nevertheless, on this evening with leaves fluttering, Kismet spoke softly, knowing she was throwing fuel on a flame.

April Alisa Marquette
71

"Don't speak to *me* about being sick, and do not tell me to be quiet. Heck, marriage may be what Beau wants. It may be what he'll have, too, whenever he gets to it. And since he wants a baby, *I* happen to be the one carrying it for him—end of story, because that's what *I* want. Oh, and as your wife, I want your support. That would be nice, for a change."

Lyle pulled into traffic. "*He* wants, and *you* want. That's all I ever hear, but who hears what *I* want?"

Kismet's eyes narrowed because throughout their marriage, she had sometimes heard that question. Now, however, there was no sincerity, only craftiness. Yet she humored Lyle by asking, "What do you want?"

Kismet's husband pressed hard on the gas. "Forget it."

"Tell me –and yellow lights don't mean speed up."

Who are you? She wondered. *Now?*

As Lyle switched lanes, his tone warned her. "Leave it alone, Kiss."

"No," she insisted. Since she wanted peace with what they were in the midst of, she asked, "What are you not saying?" *Because you sure as hell are hiding things; things like all them drinks you think I don't know about. And your drinking is making you mean.*

Hurriedly, Lyle pulled over and huffed, "They don't last long."

Noticing the lighted package store, his wife asked, "Who?"

"Them friggin' flighty *fairies*," Lyle nearly yelled. "Then, what'll happen to the kid?"

Kismet felt like she had been slapped, even as she pushed from mind the fact that Lyle was frequenting the liquor store a little too much. "Let's say you're right," she testily began, "for the sake of argument. Does the fact that a couple may not wind up together for all eternity mean they shouldn't experience full lives?"

She raised a hand. "No. Don't interrupt. Let's forget Beau. Let's concentrate on us. Using your theory, then maybe *we* shouldn't have certain things, because 'statistics' say people like u*s* don't stay together."

"You know I ain't talking 'bout us," Lyle huffed because why'd she have to take shit so far? "You know most gays fall apart, Kiss, or one dies, unnaturally."

Kismet knew she should just let the subject drop; she was getting angry, which was no good for her or the baby. It would spike her blood pressure. Still, she asked, "Says who—the moral majority? Narrow-minded politically correct, hypercritical people? Those who do dirt in the dark, but wear stiff white in the light?"

Lyle's lips twisted as he thought of the drink that he would soon imbibe. He would welcome the burn, the numb, mellow way it would make him feel as it slipped down his throat and into his bloodstream.

"What if *we* don't remain together," he heard his wife ask. Really, Lyle wished she'd shut the fudge up, especially when she said, "God knows it feels like that's inevitable. *Or*," she went for the jugular, "what if one of *us* dies, unnaturally, maybe from …cirrhosis of the liver?"

Lyle flung his door wide. "Quit trying me, Kiss."

"Well," she tried not to yell. "Don't make light of my cousin's life! Stop trying to fit him—and me—into restrictive boxes, just because what we want doesn't suit *you*!"

"I'm going in here." Lyle's booted foot was on the ground.

Outside the vehicle, the wind howled as his wife waved. "Go. Run away." She taunted the man who had been a tyrant. "Some say that's what African-American men do; when things get rough, they bail…"

With anger etched on his chiseled dark face, Lyle swung his long, locked hair behind him. "You know that's a lie. And you forget, Kismet Staar, *I'm* from Belize."

"How can I forget?" Kismet asked, "When our girl twin was named for your homeland. And where you're from doesn't matter," Kismet spat, "because, slave poachers dragged *us all* from *Africa*. They just deposited us in different places afterward."

Re-seating himself and closing his door, Lyle jerked his wife to face him. "You've always got something to say. Well, I do too."

The man's voice became deadly low. "I told you I didn't want this. I said your cousin's friend—that chesty Marina—could have done this."

Her name is Meh-RAY-uh," Mireya.

"Whatever. Kiss, you acted like no one else was capable of doing this baby shit. Now, *I* look like a fool!"

"You? How do *you* look like a fool? This was not done to harm you. Beau had a desire, one I could fulfill. Thus, the situation."

Lyle thrust his wife's wrist from him. "I'm sick of hearing about your cousin; he ain't your husband. I am. What *I* want should mean more to you than what he wants."

Kismet stared and softly swore. "Damn it, Lyle. Why are we always fighting?" She simply wanted to make love, and talk, and be heard. Watching a man pass outside her window, she quietly asked, "You think we'll ever get past this? You know, be able to converse, without anger?"

April Alisa Marquette

"I've *been* talking to you." Opening his SUV door again, Lyle's brown eyes searched his wife's. "I've said, that baby," he pointed at her unchanged midsection, "is yours—and *mine* too, because you, *all of you*, your eggs included, belong to me. But you don't hear me."

Lyle's eyes fell then, to caress Kismet's lips. "You were mine, Kiss, the night I met you at that club. You were mine when I became Déja's father, and that time you caught the flu, and I took care of her. You have been mine since we got her brother, and since I adopted both of them. You've been mine since you became pregnant with the twins. You've been mine since Belize and Bonaire were born. If you've forgotten, you *gave yourself – to – me* the day you married me..."

Lyle looked lost and hurt. "So, Mrs. Manfred, I'll say it again. Since that baby will be *ours*, in a way, I can't see us not raising him or her. That is all I've been saying, but you haven't heard me. You can only hear your cousin, not your man."

Tears sprang to Kismet's eyes, and softly she said, "I hear you, Lyle, and I understand, better than you think." The Momma turned away, aware that although they had four children, her husband could not see her bringing another one into the world if they would not care for it.

She almost felt the same way, but she and her husband had not made love to conceive this child. It was why she clutched Lyle's hand and attempted to explain, again. "Babe, this infant *isn't* ours. I am, in essence, now an incubator, a host."

Lyle's eyes searched his wife's, "But you used your eggs."

So...despite all his pretending, he *had* heard. "I did," she acknowledged, feeling defeated. She also knew she didn't have the fortitude to explain again, why she'd used her own eggs.

Feeling bereft, Lyle got out of the vehicle. He stood with wind racing all around. "Then that baby *is* yours. In a way," *therefore it is mine too,* he thought, *in a way.* "He or she will have your DNA, Kiss."

Lyle sadly shook his head. "I cannot imagine what you're gonna say to him or her—because one day they're gonna ask; that child will want to know why you gave them up, when you and I kept four other children. And I'll want no part of this mess."

Slamming his door, Lyle yelled. "Think about it, Momma!" Then he went to again purchase the liquor that would drown the pain. When he drank, Lyle believed he could pretend he had his wife back. Lyle could act like his life was the way it had been, before all *this*. Before Beau.

Chapter 18

UNLIKE Beau's childhood friend Jervais, slender, dark-skinned Brett had *not* been a T-room queen. Brett had been an observer, while Jervais, the dancer, had become wildly extroverted. Beau hated to think about it, or about afterward, but...Jervais had decided to go all out.

After high school, he attended Dance College for a year and a half, during that time Jervais suffered *another* injury, this one heart-wrenching. The injury had sentenced and sidelined Jervais, forever.

The sports medicine doctor had quietly said it was no one's fault; it was just the way things sometimes went. He echoed what another physician had said not long before, "Brittle bones you've got."

Jervais hadn't wanted to hear that, not again, and he certainly hadn't wanted to hear the rest. *He would never ever dance professionally again.*

Jervais had been stunned because, in addition to coming back from the many breaks he'd suffered, a toe included, he had also recovered from a busted hamstring and torn articular cartilage in his left knee. That surgery had left him diminished, but not destroyed. However, this last time he had broken his left ankle and tore cartilage in his previously injured left knee. Still, Jervais had been unable to face that he would never become a member of the elite Alvin Ailey dance core.

"I was supposed to take classes, a summer intensive, in France during my season abroad!" A canvas for pain and disappointment, his face appeared monstrous and distorted as he yelled, "I – want – my – *chance* to be further developed for the company!"

When Beau, the high school senior, stood in the hospital room, unable to say a thing, Jervais shouted, "I've *got* to keep my role as soloist!"

Jervais ranted about things of which Beau had had very little prior knowledge. Jervais said that as far back as he could remember he'd walked on his toes; he even got out of bed that way. He spoke of how he'd *suffered* to become a professional dancer. "Everybody thinks this shit is glamorous. It's not! They think if you've got talent, that's all you need, when the truth is: talent is only the beginning!" He'd yelled that the life of an artist like him was one of unpredictability and low pay. Jervais mentioned working on contract. It was only for a particular number of weeks at a specific pay rate, and the benefits stunk. They were usually not equivalent to those received by an office worker. "But I chose this life! I could handle it. I worked my ass off. I *worked* up to soloist!"

Jervais said he had been promoted due to his relentless pursuit of perfection. As a result, his pay and exposure had increased, along with rivalries. Dancing was pretty on stage, but the underbelly, backstage, was cutthroat and ugly. Yet he loved it. It was his world.

"I was supposed to become a *principal dancer*! I was at the door!" Jervais further ranted, his face contorted, and in his neck, veins angrily stood out. "My money was finally getting right." He had been scheduled to go overseas, because during the interim, before his next contract began, Jervais had been good enough, at last, to work with other dance companies. "I was finally getting to the place where I could start to live in some kind of comfort—and now *this*! I can't believe it! I can't!"

As Beau repeatedly visited Jervais, Beau became aware that his friend felt severely dejected. Deeply depressed, Jervais no longer had spunk or sass. He just stared out of the window and hissed that he didn't want any more surgeries. He wanted no more scars to add to those crisscrossing his body. He despised painful physical therapy, and he did not want to wear a brace, although it would guard against further twisting.

With fists flailing and his face grotesquely contorted, Jervais railed at Beau, and at his mother, Ms. Lillie. As Jervais howled about the injustice of it all, Beau, the high school senior, realized something. Dance, to Jervais, was what *heroin* had been to him! When the shorter male danced, he flew. Like an addict, dance was all Jervais knew to pursue.

Jervais was also unwilling to change all that surrounded him. He didn't want to stop frequenting the places that fostered his former lifestyle. He did not want new friends, lesser mortals who didn't seek to fly. He wanted the life he had known, and angrily he inquired, "If I can't have that, what the fuck will I do? Dancing is all I know *how* to do!"

However, after the denial stage, following extreme anger, and phases of depression, Jervais sullenly acknowledged that his lifelong dream was gone. With hollows beneath his eyes, he faced away from Beau and moaned that it was no use, furthering his education.

He also dissed a small academy. Jervais said he didn't want their position after college, teaching the *pas de deux* to children.

When he was able to hobble from the hospital, Jervais Krig chose. He *would* become well known in what many referred to as Scrotland.

Since his dream was gone, he would become the scrotum king. He knew how to do that.

Aware of the new direction his friend sought, Beau, disapproved. He believed the lost dream, coupled with the devastating end of Jervais' relationship with a fellow dancer, had pushed Jervais over the edge.

Beau hated to recall it, but his friend's so-called man, Danté, had done Jervais so wrong. Danté moved another dancer into his and Jervais' shared one-bedroom apartment. Danté knew the other dancer had long vied for Jervais' soloist spot. Yet Danté did his dirt, with no opposition, while Jervais lay writhing in pain at the hospital. Then despite his protests upon arriving home, Jervais was told that he had to vacate.

"Sorry," devilish Danté shrugged, "but your spot in our bed, *and* at the dance academy, has been filled."

As he watched the now-gaunt-looking angry little man limp along on his stylish walking stick, Beau wished none of it had happened.

Glancing up at the young man he thought of as 'long drink of water,' Jervais spoke. "Bodacious, quit looking like that. I'll find a place." Dismissively, Jervais waved, "Until I do, though, I ain't taking that rat's nest or any of those others. Since she begged, I'll stay with Mom for a while; give her a break you know, by watching Bibi, sometimes."

The dancer also announced that he had finally learned something.

"What's that, Vay?"

"I now know the meaning of a song I've danced to a gazillion times."

Beau asked, "What song is that?"

"*God Bless the Child.* I now realize," the shorter male stated, his eyes not containing any of their old mischievous sparkle, "that song means God blesses those who have their own. So quit worryin' Dacious, I'll survive. I know what I gotta do. I'll keep my end of our pinky swear too, even though, for me, the game has changed."

Beau wondered what that meant. However, it was not long before he and his friend Brett fully understood.

Jervais willingly became a *plaything*...for moneyed men.

Chapter 19

To Beau, it did not seem as though two decades had passed. Yet while driving, he recalled even more strange scenarios. He nearly burst out laughing. Yes, because back in the eighties, his slender, curly-haired friend Brett had had a *girlfriend*.

What had that child's name been? Beau squinted; Mar-something. Oh. *Mar-la*! And boy had Marla been crazy about Brett. Back then, Brett had seemed to be a slim young man. Still, Brett had explained to Beau that he allowed Marla to hang around because he needed a cover girl.

Having low self-esteem because she deemed herself overweight, Marla unwittingly aided Brett to conceal his true nature. With chubby, cute Marla on his arm, Brett attempted assimilation. Brett thought he appeared to be a young man who dated a bona fide young woman. Until one summer evening when all came to a screeching halt.

In the inky night, with red taillights before him, thirty-something Beau navigated the expressway and clearly remembered...

Brett called, sounding shaky. "Beau, I need you. Now. Please. I need you to get me away from here."

"Why are you whispering?" Beau had asked, "And where are you?"

Brett kept his voice low. "I'm at Marla's, well really at her neighbor's."

Having heard the tears in his friend's voice, Beau admitted he had to find his cousin, borrow her car. "But don't get your hopes up until I call you back," he advised.

"No," Kismet had said, thrown across her bed with the window a/c humming. "Have you forgotten? You don't have a license—yet."

"I've got a permit, and *you*," the seventeen-year-old pointed, "are my licensed driver. So come with me."

Kismet blew on her outstretched hands. "Nope, I've got cramps. I'm tired, my nails are wet, and I have work in the morning."

Beau felt like smudging her manicure, as he announced, "Kiss, your summer job does not mean more to me than my friend."

"Well," she gestured toward the door. "Go, because my video, *Lick You Up N Down*," by the R&B group *Silk*, "just started."

"Really?" Beau asked, unable to believe she had given in so quickly. From the hallway, he also yelled, "That song's called *Freak Me Baby*."

"Whatever!" Kismet called out, "Don't tell Mama." Jumping up, Kismet stood in the doorway. "No accidents—you hear?!"

In his cousin's hooptie, Beau rolled all the windows down and left Queens via the Cross Island Expressway. Despite its sputtering, he pushed Kismet's rinky-dink car. Merging onto the Southern State parkway, he arrived in Hempstead in time to pull Brett from a nasty fray.

OUTSIDE her mother's Long Island home, Brett's girlfriend paced. She wore a tank top and shorts. With bra straps cutting into her plump shoulders, she also yelled and cried, beneath the starlit sky.

Joining Marla, her identical twin, Darla, attempted to hit and punch slender Brett because earlier, Brett had taken Marla's car.

"How would you like if somebody did that to you?" the twins spat, chubby fists raised, as perspiration pebbled on their pecan brown skin.

From what Beau could gather, Brett had taken tank top Marla's vehicle without her consent. When she'd paged him, he'd ignored her.

Driving, the filmmaker laughed, because life had been a trip, back before cell phones! Beau also remembered that Marla admitted she'd grown increasingly concerned. She'd then resorted to calling Brett's mother. Getting the answering machine, Marla had left one last message.

"Brett Webster, I will call the cops! You call me back in five minutes, or I will report my car stolen." Marla and her twin had yelled into the receiver, "Then you will go to jail!"

Marla had angrily added, "Then criminals will turn yo' ass out."

Upon hearing the answering machine threats, Brett stormed from his mother's home. Soon after, he appeared at the red brick ranch.

"Who is *he*?" Marla asked, jabbing at the man in her front passenger seat. She also asked, "Where'd you go, in my car, that *I* couldn't go?"

Noticing that Darla, the twin eyed his towering male friend, quietly Brett spoke, because it was time. "Marla, I never meant to hurt you…"

Feeling a spark of *frisson* caused by the soft words, the chubby girl-woman opened her arms. "Forget it, Brett. Let's just kiss and make up."

Brett refused. Yet he took Marla's hands. "I can't do this anymore."

When Beau arrived, he watched Brett admit to having thought about things. "I know you'll probably race up the block," to church on the hill where they met. "There," Brett said, "Marla, I know you'll talk bad about me," at the parish that his mother attended. "But I don't care anymore."

Brett felt a twinge of sadness for the woman who had rescued him from Foster Care. He knew that she who had adopted him would be embarrassed by tonight's news, but Brett shrugged. It could not be helped. He would never go back to that church, or to the house where he'd felt oppressed.

Jerking her hands free, Marla shouted. "Speak English, boy!"

Calmly Brett shrugged. "I'm not a boy—not really. It's what I've been telling you. I'm tired of pretending. I want to be my real self. Now."

"Gibberish!" Darla, the twin, yelled, as Marla in the tank top stared.

Standing in the glow of the street lantern, Beau watched as without inflection, slender Brett said, "Marla, I'm sorry. This is hurtful, but..." He thumbed, indicating the male who'd ridden shotgun. "You see him?"

Marla's eyes slid over and back.

"Big dude was at my mom's with me," while mom was at bible study. "I was having sex," in adopted mother's hot little home, "with *him*."

"Oooh!" Darla, the twin yelped, and her fat fist shot out. However, tank top Marla chose not to understand. She spoke in a little girl's voice. "Stop playing, Brett. Get rid of him, so we can talk."

Beau watched as feeling panicked, Brett whined, "No... No more talking." Brett simply wanted off the woebegone carousel. "This is it," Brett insisted. "We're done, Marla." To prove it, Brett brought the hem of his t-shirt up. As Beau, big dude, the twins, and others who had gathered, watched, beneath the stars, Brett knotted his shirt between his pectorals.

Tall Beau eyed Marla, who stared at Brett standing before her with his navel showing. Marla gasped when slender Brett turned down the waistband of his button-fly jeans, exposing a bit of his pelvis. "Wh-what you doing?" she stammered, her eyes darting between Brett and 'friend.'

"I'm showing you who I am," Brett announced. He then sashayed toward big dude. Palming the man's head, Brett tongued the man down.

Marla screamed, and Darla, the twin, squalled too, just before both young women raced forward, intending to tear Brett limb from limb.

"Did you screw this trash in my car?" Marla yowled as wildly she thrashed. Beau blocked her windmilling arms, until she ran out of steam.

"You—with the baby dick," she huffed, "probably gave me AIDS!"

Not caring that neighbors inched closer, tank top Marla sobbed and recalled a recent diagnosis. *Bacterial vaginosis.* She remembered other STD's, and that this last time the doctor had told her straight up.

"BV is often the result of fecal matter. It sometimes lingers in the fold of a man's penis, circumcised or not, if he has anal intercourse with another. Then during vaginal intercourse, that bacteria is transferred. So Marla, if you engage in anal penetration, advise your young man to thoroughly cleanse before vaginal entry."

Wanting to throw up, as madly she swung a heavy arm, Marla now knew why the fecal bacteria! *She* and Brett had not engaged in anal sex. Yet, he had obviously done so with *men*! Now she knew why she had been smelly and infected. Now she knew why the gross discharge.

Feeling rage, the likes of which she'd not previously known, she wanted to kill Brett. Suddenly she shoved beanpole Beau aside and flung herself, heaving and crying, up her mother's front steps. In the darkened kitchen, she felt around, because her mother, a night nurse, had often told her and Darla about the horrible cases she saw. Now she, Marla, could become one of those cases, because of girlish Brett and his carelessness!

Pounding back down into the balmy night, Marla didn't care that more people had gathered. Hoisting her knife high, she charged, intending to hack Brett—him, her, or whatever he was, to death…

Yet driving his luxury coupe, the adult Beau remembered how his teenage self had felt upon seeing Marla dash into the house. He had not liked the escalating emotions or the sense of unpredictability. Neither had a neighbor who had called Marla's mom, on duty at the hospital.

When Marla returned, wild-eyed, wielding a butcher knife, Beau had hustled slender Brett off what was usually a tranquil, sycamore-lined street. He did not do so soon enough. However, finally, with his foot nearly on the floor, he forced his cousin's hooptie back to the parkway and back to Queens. During the tense ride, no one spoke. Beau let big dude out at Hillside Avenue. "The F train's here," Beau called and pulled into traffic. Not long afterward, he stopped before a friend's home.

Beau saw golden light spilling onto the front walk. He knew that flamboyant Jervais, the former dancer, would be present. Earlier, they had spoken, and Jervais had announced he would sit with Bibi. Jervais had also stage-whispered to his best friend, "Lil' sis has *raisins* now, and she wears a training bra."

"Stop telling my business!" Jervais youngest sister had wailed.

Hearing her, Beau acknowledged, "Lil Bibi's growing up."

"I know—getting titties, can you believe it? And mom's got a *date*."

"Stop telling our business!" Bibi again yowled.

Beau forgot that. He pulled Brett from the car. It was nearly eleven p.m. He glanced at Jervais' sporty little ride, a gift from a 'sponsor.' Ascending the front steps with Brett in tow, Beau was taken back to all the times that he, an elementary school kid, had frequented this house. Back then, sassy Jervais had become his first friend, even before Mireya. Ms. Lillie, Jervais' mother, had become his second mother, behind Aunt Nell. Therefore, it was natural for Beau to show up there. He rang the doorbell, and fond memories flooded back as the lock clicked. Then surprised, he fell into Ms. Lillie's arms. "Ms. Lil, you're here!"

"Well, it *is* a school night for Bibi, so I couldn't stay out." She grinned. "I know chatty Jervais told you about my date. Come inside."

"Ms. Lillie," Beau spoke, "meet Brett. Brett, you know Jervais, but you never met his mom, my second mom. This is lovely Ms. Lillian."

"Hey Bo-Dacious." Jervais descended the stairs with the aid of his stylish walking stick. He was showy in tight jeans and a shiny shirt. Standing on French manicured toes, he said, "Brett, you're a sight!"

The foursome sat at the kitchen table. While Beau and Jervais nursed red kool-aid, like old times, all listened. With a glance at Ms. Lillie's bathrobe, Brett explained. He mentioned his birth and the pressure his parents faced with choosing his sex. Raised as a boy, he'd never felt right. All of that had led up to him having a girlfriend, and the happenings earlier in the evening. Brett concluded by saying he could no longer pretend. With averted eyes, he said his soul died a little each time he acted the man's part, because really, he was a woman, inside. With tears flowing, Brett blurted that when he was with a man, he felt right. But when he was with a woman, sexually, he felt lesbianic. Brett said he'd felt that way with Marla, because he was heterosexual.

Beau said nothing, and Ms. Lillie looked pensive.

"I get it," Jervais piped up, patting his salon waved hair. He touched Brett. "You feel that way because you're really a *girl* inside."

Aware that he didn't want to see a doctor, Ms. Lillie bathed Brett's chest, neck, and cheek. She dabbed ointment on a long nasty cut and bandaged other non-life-threatening wounds. "It's sad though that you hurt *her*, young Marla."

"I feel *so* bad about that," Brett disclosed, "because she didn't deserve this, but I just couldn't pretend anymore, and Marla wouldn't listen! Ms. Lillie, I tried to tell her, I swear. I even stayed away, to let her get me out of her system, but she wouldn't." Brett sniffled. "Dang, and I really liked both those girls."

Beau acknowledged that Marla and Darla *were* cute chubby things.

"They're so funny too." Brett's face crinkled as he swiped at a tear. "I would love to be friends with them, if I wasn't...me, you know? We could shop and gossip. Now," Brett sniffled, unable to believe it was over, "I'll never see them again." He looked at Ms. Lillie. "Right?"

"Maybe not, hon, but tell you what. Why not let some time pass? Then send one or both of them a card. Apologize and ask forgiveness for the hurt you caused."

Ms. Lillie looked at those gathered around her table.

Turning into his exclusive gated community, Beau, the formidable man, recalled his second mom's words. They had remained with him ever since that night long ago.

"I want you three to remember one thing. Life holds inequities, things that are unequal or unfair. It presents *iniquities*, too, things that are wicked and unjust. Unfortunately, unjust things will be done to you, and you will do them to others—hopefully not intentionally." Ms. Lillie waved, "Whatever. You will all learn that some things can never be undone. It's why you must remember this; *although you can't do a thing about how others treat you, you can be aware of how you treat others.*"

Ms. Lillie squeezed Brett's hand. "My bed is calling; I've got work tomorrow, and you all have summer jobs. So home you go."

"Oh, Brett," Ms. Lillie called, turning. "I just remembered what you said about your home. So stay here tonight." Again she turned. "Vay, make up Trish and Fawn's old room. Beau, my love, remind Nellie: Friday, Bingo."

"Yes Ma'am." Beau stood and hugged Ms. Lillie. "Good night." Afterward, he realized he was exhausted due to all the excitement. "See ya, Vay." Beau addressed slender Brett as he walked to the door. "I'll page you tomorrow. Oh and Brett, from now on, we'll refer to you, girl, as you are, inside."

"Yeah, why not?" Jervais agreed, looking from Beau to slender Brett.

"Would you?" Brett asked and burst into tears, because finally, someone cared enough...to understand.

Chapter 20

HE passed through the manned gates of Icebury Court. Beneath weeping willows, he disappeared around a darkened bend. Up a hill, Beau made a series of turns and zoomed onto the lengthy curved drive. In the multi-car garage, he heard excited barking.

In his palatial home, he caught the huge front paws. "Hey Frost," he cooed and ruffled silver fur. Passing through the elegant butler's pantry, he scooped his Siamese cat off granite, where she did not belong. "Bad girl." In his custom kitchen, he swiped a large hunk of warm dark bread. He left the rest folded its linen napkin. Entering the master suite, followed by his dog, Beau stripped and configured his digital shower.

Back in the kitchen, he wore sweats. He attacked fresh green beans, pearl onions, and new potatoes. Casting his eyes upward, he savored the garlic-crusted porterhouse. Man! Did JeRell, his houseman/chef, have skillz. While eating, Beau recalled dialing home. He'd told JeRell not to wait up. "Leave me some vittles though, because I'm hungry as a hog."

"When have I not?" JeRell had testily inquired. The chef was touchy but damn good. It was why Beau kept him on, and because they were friends. They had been, since the December day that Beau found out he was nominated for a SAG award. Feeling jaunty, he had whistled while entering Sal 'n Lu's. In the gym, a big man had said something snide. Forgetting his Screen Actors Guild nomination, Beau, the pugilist, had turned. "Yo, you talking to me?"

Big & Bald had become sarcastic, and Beau suggested they meet in the ring. There, he had bloodied biggie's nose, and biggie cuffed him over the eye. With mutual respect, they'd wound up sparring partners.

Later, Beau found out that biggie, a sous chef, sought work. Therefore, he made an offer. He and JeRell had been rolling ever since. However, Beau forgot meeting JeRell to recall nearing graduation...

Back then, he had been so ready to bounce. Young Beau realized he would soon leave high school. He'd gotten his grades up, with his aunt's help. She had also gone with him when he'd spoken with Sal and Lu. Before they went, she told him, "I'm not saying anything, this is all you."

The Pietro brothers accepted his apology. They also worked out a way for Beau to spend part of the winter at Sal's upstate cabin. There, under strict supervision, the youngster wound up sweating, shivering, and believing he would die, to get clean. Afterward, Cinzia, Sal's girlfriend, treated him to her old-world Italian cuisine. What a treat! Heartily Beau ate, at last, as Cinzia and Sal's small son watched.

In the spring, Beau again rode the train with Mireya, a rarity. Hanging out, choppin' it up, talking about the familiar, felt like old times. Nevertheless, Beau wanted to forget community college in the fall. As the E train clacked along, he only wanted to think about the coming summer. Glancing aside, he knew Mireya was not thinking about the prestigious four-year to which she had been accepted. With that smirk, Beau knew she thought of prom. She spoke incessantly of it, and the guys who'd asked her because, like a flower, she had blossomed. He wished she'd go with somebody because he was undecided.

Beau's aunt had been encouraging. She had said, "You should go, Puppy because, to graduate, you've overcome a lot." She had even become emotional. "My Brant would be so proud..."

Beau felt an inkling of anger because his uncle should have been there! Yet the thought he kept to himself; no sense hurting his aunt, not when the loss was never far from mind, although it had been three years. Not committing to prom, Beau said he would think about it. He'd told Mireya the same, but confident that he would attend, she made plans.

At last, Mireya thought, she would have the buff, brown Beau. Other girls wanted him, she knew, because he was tall, athletic, smart, and strong. Still, Mireya let all them skanks know; she and Beau would attend together. She told anyone who would listen, about afterward.

Yep, because now she was sexy. Now her buff, brown friend would not be able to resist her. She had stretched out. Now her figure resembled an hourglass. True, she only had a few female friends, but who cared? The guys were on her—but she had chosen Beau. His indifference baffled her, though. Well, he *had* been up at that cabin, doing Lord knew what, in the mountains with that Rocky Balboa-looking boxer and his pixie faced girlfriend. Therefore, pondering Beau's nonchalance, Mireya complained to her twice-divorced mother.

Readying herself for a man who belonged to another, Lana replied. "Reya, boys usually aren't smart or swift."

April Alisa Marquette
85

Lana's daughter forgot innocuous words. Mireya refused to believe Beau would not want her. Standing before her bedroom mirror, she pushed her breasts higher and remembered Daffy's. On Fifth and 18th, the department store didn't seem to carry the latest fashions. However, she'd found the sweetest outfit! Then at Lingerie's, she'd even given Beau a preview of coming attractions. After begging him to accompany her, Mireya had asked if he liked her one-piece. Blandly, he'd said it was nice. At home, she stared at herself in the lace confection. She knew when he saw it *on* her, he'd devour her. That was what she wanted.

PROM night came, and Mireya double-checked. She had brown liquor for the limo ride. She had mints and money, so time to scram.

Her mother appeared. Slinky in a shiny, spaghetti-strapped catsuit, Lana took Polaroids. Scanning with the camera lens, she looked away from shapely Mireya. Lana ogled the tasty cannoli, yummy brown outside and creamy rich, she knew, inside. Boy, would she eat Beau up! *If* she could ever pry him loose from her daughter. All too soon, Lana heard noises about it being dusk, time to go. She kissed Mireya, so she could kiss Beau, on those luscious teenaged lips.

In high heels, Mireya provocatively sashayed down the outside steps as Lana brushed barely-concealed breasts against Beau's back. "You're legal now," she whispered, "so visit me." Acting like he hadn't heard, Beau kept moving, and Lana hissed, "We'll do naughty wet stuff."

In the limo, Mireya drank to get the party started. On the sofa, easily seen through the living room window, Lana wriggled from her jumpsuit. With curtains wide, she splayed bare legs. Envisioning her daughter's date, slowly the mother pleasured herself, for anyone passing to see.

While riding, Mireya offered brown liquor, but Beau waved it aside.

At prom, on the dance floor, Mireya gave Beau what she thought was a taste of things to come. He nearly regretted attending. Beau noticed others who couldn't keep their eyes off his curvaceous date. Feeling slow and awkward, he felt like people were distant. Not seeming to notice, with her hair piled stylishly high, and wearing stilettos and a mini, Mireya shook and sizzled. Looking like a brown pin-up girl, she liked that her bazooms attempted to burst from her bandeau top.

Then Beau realized. Mireya's moves angered the girls, while her gyrating left their guys ga-ga. Shaking his head, Beau felt ready to go.

When it was time, he all but carried his inebriated date from the dance floor. He fended off wolves too, those who wanted to 'help' with her.

A big burden, Mireya purred, "I want you to do me."

"Afterparty!" Someone screeched as Beau hauled his date from the building. Loudly she sang, "Got our own partay, me 'n my baybay!"

Beau folded Mireya into the limo, while at home, Lana bent over for the alderman. She did so to 'pay for' her daughter's ride.

In the limo, Mireya crossed bare legs. Seated across from her, Beau heard her breathing heavily. Annoyed, his eyes flicked to the window. He didn't want to see her breasts that kept trying to jump from her tube-like top. Yet his eyes strayed back, and watching the shapely girl-woman, he knew. Something was *wrong*—with him. He did not feel aroused. He guessed he should have, but he only felt disgusted.

Again, Mireya shoved her bottle at Beau. "Loosen up." She then touched her body, arching it; "So you can get you some of *this*."

Beau set the bottle aside. To clear misconceptions, he turned —and felt as though he had been attacked! Mireya grabbed his head. She wrapped her legs around him. With a high heel she pressed his derriere. *Ouch.* She shimmied and got her tiny top to her waist, just before she flipped herself and Beau. Seated astride her date, she saw the driver who strained to see. Ah yeah, Mireya grinned and ground her core onto Beau. Baffled, she found him neither eager nor hard.

He was surprised she had so much strength. He found his hands on her breasts and he squirmed. Bending his fingers, Mireya caused him to pull down her lace underthing, so not appealing. To Beau, her fleshy mounds felt like water balloons, and her nipples mirrored staring eyes.

Yeesh, she'd opened her mouth, on his! Beau gagged because her breath was rank from drink and no food. He needed her to stop flicking her tongue too, snake-like, against his mouth. Lurching up, Beau deposited his date on the seat, while hoping his new pants weren't soiled.

"Squeeze," she ordered, trying to again affix Beau's hands to her breasts. Attempting to lock her legs around him, Mireya clung, monkey-style. Yet Beau extricated himself because he'd had enough!

He didn't recall them getting out of the limo, but they were in Lana's darkened basement that smelled of mildew. There, Mireya nearly knocked him to the floor. Gently, however, Beau untangled himself, even as Mireya tore at his clothing and her own. Eager to show him her one-piece lace set-him-off, she jerked on his zipper, "Lessee what we got!"

April Alisa Marquette

Beau was stunned because who was this ravenous beast? Not Mireya, his confidante since sixth grade. Nearly ripping his shorts, she grabbed his member and furiously rubbed, while breathing loudly.

"Hey!" Beau yowled because who was she—TV's MacGyver, trying to ignite a stick at a campfire? "That burns," he reprimanded. Beau jerked too when her mouth covered his limp flesh, but Mireya took the lurching to mean Beau enjoyed, although he still had not hardened.

Believing she'd 'bring him to life,' Mireya reached to finger her crotch. In the semi-dank basement, Beau smelled chicken—or tuna.

However, knowing he would find it tantalizing, Mireya 'moisturized' Beau's lips with her fingertips. Oh, *shit*! He tried to turn, but she held him fast, smearing his lips with her juices. Gagging, Beau repeatedly wiped his face on his sleeve. *Dis-gust-ing*! He thought, not for the first time that evening.

Unable to take more of the kangarooing, the wrestling, or any more of her overpowering grape scent, Beau bucked Mireya off him.

Folding into herself, she began to cry, something she never did. "I don't know what to do," she moaned, as standing, Beau hastily repaired his clothing. He offered meaningless words. Yet Mireya whined. "I try to make you want me, but you don't." Wrapping her knees with her arms, she looked pitiful, nearly curled into a ball. "I'll lose weight, okay?"

Beau wanted to clasp her hands, but again, he did not, as he bent to say, "No, Reya, you're perfect," *when you're not crawling all over me.*

"Then what's *wrong*?" She asked as rivulets of dark makeup ran down her cheeks. Other guys broke her off right. They wanted her, they called and paged, often. Yet the male that she wanted seemed wary.

Wearily then, Beau faced that there could be no more hiding. He owed himself, and Mireya, the truth. He needed to *say* it, aloud.

"Reya, you and I have been through many things." Therefore, perhaps, this, they could get through together, as well; although in the far reaches of his mind, he thought not. "Reya, I want you to know, this isn't about you. I'm just not into this. I'm sure you know why, but I have to say it." He felt like a heel because he *wanted* to want her! She was sexy and smart. She looked so cute when she did homework with glasses perched on her nose. And she could dance circles around him, when he too had moves. They had such fun together, but the wanting part? It wasn't there. He wasn't a red-blooded all American male. Beau didn't stare at female pin-ups. He preferred bodies without curves, those more like his. "The truth is," he forced out, "I prefer…men." He dreamed of them, woke up stiff as a flagpole. The female form did nothing for him.

"Nooo, Beau," Mireya moaned, although she had known since middle school. Yet she'd dreaded it, and figured they could ignore it, then *poof*, that truth would disappear. "Beau, you just have to try harder…"

"I've tried, harder than you'll ever know, Reya," Beau divulged. feeling as though he had disappointed her and himself. He whispered, "Believe me, if I could be with any female, it would be you."

"No…" she blubbered, her makeup running, "You can't be gay."

Beau nearly laughed, because he'd often told himself the same thing.

Mireya folded her arms. "We should have gone slowly."

Beau spoke softly and bent to touch his friend's lovely coiffure. "Slow, fast, it would not have mattered." He said it then, so she would understand, and so *he'd* get used to saying it, "The truth is: I want men."

"You ever *had* a man?" Mireya became indignant. "I don't mean your mama's ol' dirty bastards who forced you when you were little."

Beau was candid; he'd had a few. One waited for him right then.

Mireya's eyes slowly widened. "Then why'd you go to prom with *me* if you were going to ditch me after?" Her eyes narrowed, and she felt like her best friend, the boy-man she'd wanted for her lover, the one she'd wanted forever, had betrayed her. Thus she hissed, "Who is he?"

He heard, *let sleeping dogs lie*, yet he said, "He works on the Ave."

"Where?" Mireya demanded. "Where does this person work?"

Beau felt she had a right to know, "At the African store."

"The Jamaica Avenue candle place?" Mireya became derisive, "That boy don't want you. *I've* had him, a couple of times, in that back room. I sucked his dick better than you ever could. He gave me candles."

Beau turned to leave. "We can talk later, Reya."

"No," she spat and got up, her nudity apparent. Mireya spoke, as from the bottom up, she shimmied into her clingy top. "If you leave without us doing anything…" She averted her eyes, "We can *never* talk again."

Beau pivoted, and Mireya bolted forward. "Gay-Bob! We're done!"

Beau's heart stuttered because he had never dreamed it would come to *this*. As he climbed the stairs, Mireya repeatedly beat on his back.

Friends for life, huh? Well, so much for that. Beau stepped into the night and realized. He'd hurt Mireya. However, she had hurt *him*, too. She had wounded him deeply.

Chapter 21

BEAU'S Aunt said, "Reya from 'round the corner stopped by." Finished labeling things she'd ship to California, Nell announced, "She left her number; asked you to call. Maybe she misses you, Puppy."

"Maybe so," Beau said and felt joy, as well as pain.

Nell gazed up and asked, "What's wrong?"

"You talk about Reya missing me, but I'm going to miss *you*."

"Oh pish-posh," Nell scoffed. "Big man like you, you should be glad this old gal's moving—getting out of town and out of your hair."

"You've never been a bother, A'nt Nell." Beau forced words through the love that threatened to keep him from speaking. "You rescued me," he reminded her. "When you could have easily forgotten me after my dad died. I remember your fights with Ophelia. I remember that she never really wanted me, but you did. You spent your money on me, and on that investigator, to find me. Unc told me. Then you gave me a *home*, a real one with Christmas, birthday parties, baseball, everything."

Beau swallowed. "I never had that, not before you. You even gave Pa Fulton back to me," the old neighbor who'd fed and housed him as a kid. "A'nt Nell, you taught me things, you and Unc. Then we lost *him*…"

"I know, baby," a tear escaped Nell's eye.

Beau knew that losing her best friend, her husband and her lover, had hurt beyond words. Still, "You hung in there," Beau whispered. "You could've bundled yourself in grief and let me, Kiss, and Farai, go to the devil, but nope. You cooked, cleaned, and you worked like a slave."

"With them bad-behind kids down at juvie," Nell chuckled.

Beau smiled. "You mothered them too, all your Department of Corrections juvenile delinquents. It wasn't easy, but you did all those things. So yes, I'll miss you." He would miss her tenacity, too.

The older woman waved. "Stop it, Puppy," she said, knowing that mothering was a calling. She was aware that she had been called to care for those whose families had given up on them, and she cared for others who had never known love. She made a difference. Nell had seen it over the years. As adults, many of her kids returned, just to tell her how she'd changed their lives. They showed her job IDs and graduation photos.

They introduced her to spouses and her 'grandkids.' Proud of her kids-turned-adults, Nell knew they had only needed her prayers, a few hugs, and some tough love. It was why she told her nephew, "Oh, go on now."

"Nope," Beau grinned, "I gotta say this before you leave this week. I want you to *make a life* out in San Diego. I want you to be happy. Enjoy the sunshine. The girls and I," Kismet and Farai, "know you need to do this. So call us—not every day, and we'll try not to be heathens."

Nell grabbed her nephew and held him tightly. Taller than she, he rested his chin atop her head, until she did not clutch him, as if for life.

The young man was intuitive, perhaps from living with women; therefore, he knew his aunt had become worn. He knew she had been lonely and that Bingo no longer held any joy for her. She'd never said it, but he knew she had only continued going for Jervais' mom, Ms. Lillie.

Beau knew his aunt cooked, made a big spread on holidays, and invited people because it was expected. Yet she'd never cut the turkey, or put up lights outside, because those things her husband had done, and Beau realized. When one created a good life, it was hard to let go. So he had taken over some of his uncle's duties. Beau had watched his aunt and he'd become aware. Although she seemed unafraid, Arnell Moore sometimes was, yet she kept moving. Now she was moving, for real, clean across the country. Beau was happy for her, and so he said.

Red-eyed, Nell blew her nose. Then summoning her usual dignified mien, she whispered, "Thank you, Puppy." She looked around and admitted, "Everybody knows I wanted to go. After Brantley passed, Lillian said I looked like I wanted to tear out running, but you kids needed me. We were all hurt, but I was the adult, so I hunkered down and stayed, here, in this house." Nell walked the carpeted living room's length that held only boxes to be picked up the next day. Touching freshly painted walls warmed by sunshine, she sighed. "With memories of my man here, all around and breaking my heart, I stayed." She smiled up at Beau, "But honey-pie, now you, the last of my young' uns, happens to be in your second semester of *college*! You're doing well. So I can go, at last." Nell stared from a bare window, its curtains now folded and tagged in a consignment shop. "You understand, don't you, Puppy?"

Tall, toned, and young, Beau said, "I understand," because she had indirectly asked. "I know that you are *not abandoning* me."

With a curt nod, Nell patted her nephew's hand. "Good, then."

"Go," Beau admonished, "get you some joy, this side of Jordan."

April Alisa Marquette

Nell laughed. The boy had used her words. Gathering packing tape and a magic marker, she realized. Her brother's boy had become a fine young man. He was the same child she had started calling 'Puppy,' when truthfully; she had informed him that his mama was no good. Nell had told her then-introverted nephew not to worry; that should his mother ever darken her doorway, she, Arnell Moore, would tear the skin from Ophelia's bones. Nell recalled tucking her nephew in. She had rubbed the skinny child's back, although, at the time, he had not been used to being touched, the right way. Nell remembered whispering, "Sleep now, baby, because Mama Bitch is here. She protects all her little puppies." That was when her brother's child had become Nell's sweet 'Puppy.'

As she held packing paraphernalia, the memory faded. Standing near, her nephew recalled the same thing, but Nell was unaware. Turning, with hope in her heart, she spoke over a shoulder. "Puppy, don't forget to call Reya. Y'all missed a few years, but don't lose any more."

Not long afterward, Beau dialed. At first, the conversation felt stilted and awkward because he and Mireya felt tentative. After all, years had passed, with no word from either. Yet, she managed to make him laugh, like always, and once again, they were back on—even though so many things had taken place while they had been apart.

Mireya announced that she had briefly been married. She now had a daughter. She was also pursuing her Master's Degree. She and her toddler lived with an older woman, one who wanted to be Mireya's life partner. "I wound up with Ann," the young mother revealed, "because I was putting my life back together after my divorce. Ann has worked at the college forever. Beau, our situation really is complicated. I love Ann, in a way, and she loves me—differently." Mireya acknowledged that for her, "Ann started off as a mother figure." The stout gray-haired woman was there after the divorce. "I thought I was through with men, so I let her talk me into moving in with her. I did because Lana—good ole mother, wouldn't allow me back home, not even for a few months, to regroup. So I let Ann ease in on me because she helped. Now, I want a *man*. Beau, I want my own place too, but Ann keeps saying no; she claims she doesn't care if I get me some dick, just as long as she and I stay together. She says we're building something, and we are. We've started a business. Anyway, with AR-Lees," Arlise, "my baby, and everything else, it's just easier to stay put right now—although trying to eat pussy, old pussy, is so *not* for me!"

Beau snorted with unexpected laughter and spewed cola. Trust Mireya to keep it real, he thought, just like when they had been kids.

"So due to all of that, Lana and I have an on-again, off-again thing," Mireya announced. "But I try with her because I want Arlise to know her grandmother. Still, you know Mother, difficult is her middle name."

Suddenly Mireya jubilantly announced, "Beau, I didn't tell you what Ann and my business is; it's internet-based and mail order. We sell women's sex items, and so much more. Really, we sell confidence."

"How's that going?" Beau asked, genuinely interested.

"It's promising, so much so that we've checked out office space. We have to get the administrative end out of the house. We're looking too because the college will dismiss Ann when they get wind of what we sell, and I want our dining room back."

Mireya wound down, and Beau revealed that soon he would receive his Associate's Degree in Business Management. But, he divulged, he hadn't abandoned his dream of becoming an actor. Toward that end, he was a temp who went on many auditions. "I choose when I work."

The nephew mentioned his aunt and her move to California.

Looking back, Beau recalled that days later, he had moved into an efficiency apartment, and Mireya had stopped by. While spiffing up the tiny bathroom, he'd admitted, "This is nice, you helping me out."

His doorbell rang, and Mireya asked, "Want me to get that?"

"I've got it," Beau called. "Hey Brett." He had thought she—now living fully as a woman—would have arrived later. Forgetting that, Beau introduced her to Mireya and wondered why both women acted stank.

Noticing his confusion, Mireya dismissively announced, "I remember him. I mean her. You introduced us back in the day. He, well, she—now, had a story about multiple sex organs." Cinnamon-skinned Mireya turned then and did her best to exclude slender Brett from the goings-on.

Wanting to shake Mireya, Beau recalled her irrational jealousy. He knew that was why she had suddenly become catty and ugly. Like when they had been teenagers, back when he had initially introduced Brett.

Sometime later, Mireya grabbed her things. Jangling her car keys, she air-kissed Beau while haughtily divulging, "I gotta go get my baby." Leaning in so that only Beau could hear, she hissed. "I hate that he— well, *she*, had years with you, the ones that *I* missed."

Beau was speechless because whose fault was that? Indeed, not his, or Brett's. Heck, on prom night, Mireya had sent *him* packing!

April Alisa Marquette

When Mireya left, slender Brett rolled her eyes. "I see your friend's the same, still trying to make everything about her. She still trying to make life a competition."

"What makes you say that?" Beau asked, wanting to remain neutral.

"Why else would she pompously mention her kid? She wanted me to know she has one, and I don't."

Beau knew Brett wanted kids, yet she would never have her own. Still, Beau said he didn't think Mireya had been mean on purpose.

Later, when she called, however, Beau realized. Mireya had been intentionally mean, evidenced by her words.

"Beau, don't let me find out that you and—that *thing* are a couple..."

SEATED in his home office, Beau drank a glass of Shiraz. Alcohol was fattening, he knew, but he was on hiatus. Also, it was one glass, one time, he told himself. Seated at his large, traditional, glossy wood desk, with his feet, he massaged his dog. He thought about San Diego. Not long after his aunt had settled there, his New York efficiency apartment had started to feel cramped. So he'd moved into a big apartment with his cousin's two former college dorm mates, Valeria René and Ronni.

Mireya visited him at what he and his roommates, his *Cohorts*, had called 'The Cohort Quarters.' Mireya vibed with his IndiAfricAmerican roomie Valeria. However, she disliked Veronica, the other one. "I can't stand that Ronni bitch," Mireya said, "even if her name *is* on the lease."

Beau waited for his computer to boot up. He glanced at the color-saturated painting over his desk, a Meisha Card original. He recalled that he and his butter-yellow roommate, Ronni, had wound up in a melee. Over a man. Amid the madness, he'd called Mireya, and she'd begged him to leave. "Come stay with Ann and me," she'd pled. Then she'd stared at her phone. Beau had hung up, after hurriedly saying, "Call you later, Kiss is here." Back then, Mireya had only hoped Beau's cousin would keep him from killing his roommate, that mouthy yellow Ronni.

Opening an electronic copy of a screenplay, Beau recalled that just days after that fiasco, Mireya admonished him to make up with Ronni. "Ain't a man worth losing a friend over," the young mother had sagely stated. "Nobody knows that better than you and I. Anyway," Mireya continued, "if your guy slept with your roommate—a *female*, then he's a double-dipper. He ain't gay and you shouldn't want his ass anyway."

"That may be," Beau had sulked, "but I still feel betrayed..."

He recalled that long ago winter day. Scheduled to see a potential new home, he'd grumbled. "Thought you didn't like former roomie."

"That doesn't mean I can't see that she's your friend." Mireya switched to mama mode. "Arlise, sit down. Put that seat belt back on."

"Ronni is *not* my friend," Beau mumbled as the young mother pulled up before a swanky bank of co-op apartments; "because," Beau verbally pointed out, "what friend would steal another friend's man?"

"Um, *had* that guy *been* your man," Mireya absently stated, seeking parking, "ol' girl could not have stolen him. Look, there's your agent." Mireya grabbed her purse. She also collected her toddler, "No whining, Arlise. We'll stop at McD's, after we go with Uncle Beau. Okay?"

Sweetly the kid had said, "No," as Mireya hoisted her onto a hip.

At his desk, sipping his aromatic red, Beau remembered moving into that co-op shortly after his career took off. He'd got the supporting role in his first catch-me-if-you-can pyrotechnic thriller. His life had not been all joy, though. He'd received terrible news about his former roommate.

Looking back, Beau couldn't believe how many things had happened that year, and in the ones to follow. Some of them had been great, while others had been devastating, to say the least.

Every single thing he had discussed with April, his author friend. Through their collaborations, they'd published two books. Entitled *Absolution* and *Progression* they were about his life, no holds barred.

Beau took another sip of sherry and guessed he'd have a heap of things to tell April soon. He and she were scheduled to tackle a new book, and *another* project, about which he was super excited.

As his eyes moved over the words on his monitor, Beau thought about his uncle. Beau was grateful that the man had taught him, early on, to make time for those he loved. It didn't matter that Beau was busy or that millions of people considered him 'a star.' Beau knew he would always look out for family and friends.

Determined to get a bit of work done, the actor/producer vowed to lose himself in his electronic screenplay. He vowed, no more jaunts down memory lane. Ah, but he would first text his cousin, see how she was doing. Hopefully, all was going well. Hopefully too, this little venture of theirs wasn't taking a toll on her and her family— Well, no more than it already had.

Chapter 22

A few evenings later, when he still had not reached her, Beau began to worry because when he called, Kismet normally answered. During the day, he rang her cell. Evenings, he rang the house phone. If she didn't answer, Kismet would text, or leave voicemail that she was amid something. Whatever the case, the cousins usually spoke within hours.

Beau hoped Kismet wasn't fighting with Lyle. Again. Beau hoped his cousin was occupied with the kids, or just working from home, as his aunt had suggested. Still, the actor knew he would not feel less worried until he heard from Kismet, because she was carrying his baby.

Heck, he had a good mind to get in his car and show up at her home. He decided against it, though, only because to do so might cause an ugly scene, with the way Kismet's husband was acting lately. Beau didn't want to have to kick Lyle's ass in front of his family. So, Beau decided. If he didn't speak with Kiss in the morning, he and bodyguard Boulder would take a little trip. They would pass denuded trees and fallen autumn foliage. Then he would see what was really going on.

Beau thought about going to bed, but being a night owl, and further, having his cousin on his mind, he knew he would never sleep.

Suddenly he wondered, again. Had he done right, asking her?

Sure, everything they had done up until now signaled a new beginning for him, but hopefully, those things didn't signal the end for her. Beau wanted Kismet happy. He wanted her kids happy. Since his cousin wanted her marriage, Beau wanted that for her too.

In addition, Beau wanted to stop feeling like he had bitten off too much. Sometimes, he wasn't so sure he was ready for all that might soon come. He knew the procedure been a success and that in Kismet's uterus, the fertilized egg had rooted. It had begun to grow. He and she had been ecstatic. She especially because she had not wanted any more 'finagling.' Yet the younger cousin wondered, would the growth continue? If it did, would the ensuing baby be a boy, a girl, or twins—God forbid.

Again, it hit Beau. He was *going to be* a father! The notion was exciting. Yet since he'd found out, he had not opened the nursery door. He felt it was too soon. Daily passing the suite before workouts, he told himself he didn't want paint or decorations. He would not buy or even look at baby furniture or anything of the sort, not until birthing time neared. Beau was superstitious. He didn't want to get cocky or jinx things. He didn't want to want this too badly. He only wanted nature to have her perfect course, now that science had done its thing.

However, what if he became the papa of twins or triplets? Beau fingered his dog tags, Uncle Brantley's old tags from the Korean War. Beau remembered, he was no Ricky Martin. All he wanted was one healthy baby. Wiping damp palms on his sweats, he told himself to stop thinking, or he would hyperventilate. It was something he often found himself on the verge of nowadays. How stupid. Picking up his phone, he did not hesitate. He simply called and asked *him* to come.

When the other man appeared, Beau didn't feel like talking. He wanted no words, music, liquor, or opiates—the latter no longer had any place in his life. He didn't want to posture or jockey for position either. He didn't want to wonder who would be the top or the bottom. He wanted none of the alpha male mess he had incurred with others in the past. He only wanted to screw, relentlessly, without word or thought.

This the optician sensed from Beau's intense kiss the moment they entered Beau's master suite. There, Saavion felt like he had stepped into another world... Although the room was enormous, somehow it felt cozy, perhaps because other than the fireplace's golden flicker, there were no lights. Logs busily crackled while flames leaped, and Saavion noted the massive four-poster bed with its gleaming, rich, dark wood. He noticed luxurious bedding, invitingly piled in shades of burgundy and gold jacquard. Near the bed, in the richly appointed seating section, perfect for lounging or reading, the burgundy drapes, with their peeking gold underskirts, veiled the darkness out of doors.

Stepping onto the plush, hand-tufted wool rug, Saavion quickly stripped. Then he laid out his 'tools' just before he dropped to his knees. Wrapping his fingers around Beau's veined shaft, he reverently held it. With one fluid motion, Saavion slipped a cock ring onto Beau, before he took the engorged head into his mouth.

When Saavion expertly slid his tongue over Beau's balls, Beau moaned. Saavion smiled up because he knew what Beau liked. That was why he turned to employ electrical shock implements. Then again, he sucked, and fondled, until Beau wanted to emit in his mouth.

"Your turn," Beau managed as he pulled the light-skinned man up to lie on the massive bed...

That erotic segue had the optician rising afterward, to bend over. He knew he looked enticing as he arched his sinewy back. He also clenched and unclenched his well-formed buns. He spread his hair-spattered legs, displaying defined muscles, and he remembered. He hated to work out. Yet, there were times when he was grateful for the gruel. Those were times like now, when he found cause to display his lean sexiness.

Lubricated, he received the filmmaker's shaft, and instinctively Saavion knew. There were many things Beau needed to pound out. Therefore, accommodating, Saavion took every inch, every crush, every grind, and enjoyed every moment...

He awoke later, noting it was still dark outside. Nude, Beau was sprawled beside him. Quietly the optician maneuvered to straddle the homeowner. Facing Beau and balancing on his hands, Saavion repeatedly slid his balls and the cleft of his buttocks over Beau's growing erection. Then massaging Beau with a warming liquid, Saavion felt empowered, because again, he was the one to bring Beau to life.

Buff and brown, the filmmaker woke and arranged himself so that he and Saavion were each head to groin. As they grasped, pulled, pumped, and sucked, he recalled why he loved 69. Then it was again time for Beau to insert his male member into the puckered opening.

Moaning in ecstasy, the optician received all, but too soon, he noticed. The hazy light of dawn peeked through the drapes. Saavion had to go. Therefore, in the shower, he used anal glass beads, but afterward, he, the longtime friend with fringe benefits, packed up.

Needing to get home and ready himself for work, he quickly donned his tee and jeans. Grabbing his keys, he descended the sweeping wooden back staircase. Its light-colored paisley runner muffled his footfall. At the door, he turned and opened his mouth on Beau's.

Then as he drove near-empty streets chilled with dew, Saavion realized. For Beau, he had done all he could.

LAST night had been outstanding. That, Beau remembered before he recalled that he still needed to catch up with his cousin. He was finally able to speak with her and she assured him she was fine. Groggily, she also whispered, "Talk...later." Disjointedly, she said she needed a few more z's before she got the kiddiewinks ready for school.

Feeling relieved, Beau rang *her*. Lounging in the sunken, great room at the rear of his home, he realized. He wanted to call the other her too, but the two women would just bicker. It was what they did. Although *initially*, they had simply put up with one another for his sake, now the women genuinely cared about each other. Now, years later, Mireya and slender Brett had forged a fragile bond. Beau suspected it had to do with Mireya's child. With Brett, Mireya sometimes shared her child. Beau knew he was over-simplifying things. It wasn't like Mireya and Brett were still girls and Mireya's daughter was a precious doll. However, sometimes it seemed that way when Mireya allowed Brett to care for the now seven-year-old.

Beau forgot the jealous rivalry that kept him in the middle. He forgot Brett's tedious journey to fully becoming. He forgot that throughout, Mireya had been judgmental. He didn't want to recall how she had bluntly asked how Brett could want parts removed, "To complete some transformation?" Having had enough, Brett had huffed, "You don't have to get it, Mireya. *I'm* the only one who has to—and I want my inside and outside to match!"

Forgetting the tenuous relationship that he would never fully understand, Beau realized he needed Mireya. Although he had a ton of work, the filmmaker didn't quite feel up to it. Earlier, he'd told his agent they'd speak later. An hour ago, the actor had descended his back staircase. He'd passed editing and billiard rooms; he'd passed the theater and had entered his young assistant's office. With Tatum, he'd discussed the few things that couldn't wait. Then admitting he'd laze about for a bit, something he rarely did, Beau went back upstairs and called Mireya.

Waiting, he knew she would take his mind off things. Sure, she'd huffed that he was pulling her from business accounts for The Kitten Heel, Incorporated, and away from monitoring customer service calls. However, Beau knew she would mention some new drama in which she had gotten herself embroiled. Mireya's mess was just the kind of distraction Beau currently needed because in his life, there were things he wanted to forget, if only for a little while.

Chapter 23

IN Beau's glorious great room, they sat on the sofa. Listening to Groove Theory, Mireya stroked the 'lady of the house.' In a silly voice, she cooed, "Hi furry kitty. Hi Mocha, you beautiful girl."

In Beau's stunning New York home, located in the exclusive neighborhood of Icebury Court, there were large windows. These allowed natural light to flood the interior. Throughout, four fireplaces gave the abode a convivial feel.

Beau's meteoric rise to stardom had enabled him to purchase several homes, and though she liked the others, Icebury Court was Mireya's favorite. She adored its dramatic front entrance, seldom used, and its massive main hall that extended to the rear of the home. When she stood in the front, Mireya liked seeing the living room to the right, and the formal dining room on the left. She liked glimpsing the room where she now sat, located at the very end of a lengthy marble hallway. The room could be reached from the house front if she kept walking, but before she reached it, she passed Beau's spacious office, behind the living room. On the left she glimpsed the library and a lovely powder room.

The left wing housed a hearth room, and Beau's kitchen, the heart of the home. In that semi-modern, inviting space, his guests gathered. However, on this day, Mireya and Beau sat in the massive sunken great room at the rear of his home. They faced colossal atrium windows that could be seen from the front entrance. Mireya glanced back. Beneath the vaulted ceiling was a winding staircase and a balcony that faced the atrium. From those stairs, one could access the home's second level.

Lounging on Beau's comfy leather sectional, Mireya gazed through two-story windows at the snowy courtyard beyond. She loved the built-in bookcases that flanked the hearth. They held Beau's family photos, awards, and keepsakes. Mireya liked the grouping of leather club chairs that faced the fireplace. However, there was one thing; the room was enormous. That Beau loved, probably because he was claustrophobic— due to all the time spent locked in closets as a child. Yet Mireya loved that despite its size, Beau had managed to make the room cozy.

Mireya forgot Beau's upmarket home. On that early winter day, she forgot guest suites on the main to announce, "I'm sick."

"Uh-oh." The actor didn't look at her, "You pregnant?"

Cradling Beau's cat, Mireya looked into the blue eyes. "I was talking to you, Mocha. I was about to say I'm sick—of Ainsley Fielding."

Again Mireya thought, what kind of name was *Ainsley* anyway? It sounded like the man should have lived in a moldy castle in a distant land, and like he should have stridden across wind-ravaged moors wearing riding breeches and a flowing poet's shirt. Ainsely. Please. The nickname 'Gypsy' fit him better, because the man was a wanderer.

Beau's longtime friend and drummer was also a beguiler of women. He didn't do it on purpose; actually, he didn't *do* a thing. Yet Gypsy wound up adding to his harem daily, Mireya's reason for being sick.

"Yep, and this time," she told Beau, "I'm putting put my foot down. If Gypsy calls, talking all soft," as was his way, "or if he shows up, with sadness in them light brown eyes, I'll still cut him loose."

Checking his palm planner, Beau looked askance.

"Don't eye me like that," Mireya griped. "I can do this."

Beau shrugged because he and Mireya both knew, if his drummer called, she'd rush to him, quickly flinging her panties aside as she went.

"Quit laughing, Beau, this time will be different."

He smirked. "We'll see. When you remember Gyp's charm, and that he doesn't ask for much, *and* when you remember his uh, *thing*—"

"Hush," Mireya mumbled because, indeed, Gypsy's charm was the problem. He simply spoke, and women wound up spellbound. Gypsy didn't ask for much. That too was a problem, because the man truly didn't seem to want much. And his *thing*, as Beau called it, was the *biggest* problem. Well, the real problem, Mireya realized, was that she, Gypsy's sex slave, couldn't seem to get enough of him. Neither could other women. There was the rub. "B, I'm sorry you introduced us."

Incredulous, he looked at the internet-based businesswoman, the purveyor of sex toys, and reminded her, "I did because you begged."

Ignoring the music, smooth in the background, Mireya sharply retorted. "Do you do everything I ask?"

Aware that she was referring to his refusals, the way he'd turned her down, beginning that fateful night of prom, Beau said nothing.

"Forget you," the sultry woman grumbled. Then lounging beside the multi-faceted entertainer, she smirked and eyed his jersey tee. "By the way, friend, I like that splash of color on you. You look so gay today."

Beau preened because indeed he thought so too. "Don't I, dahling?"

"Yep, displaying designer muscles; you just need your YMCA/Village People high-heeled boots on."

"Bitch." Beau winked. "Look, since you're never gonna let me rest, I guess I should ask. What did Gypsy do now?"

Mireya hated that Beau appeared amused. "Wipe that stupid grin off your face because I happen to be hooked on Gypsy, and it's your fault."

Beau was taken aback, "My fault, how?"

"He's your boy 'n all, but if you'd said he wasn't good for me, from the get-go, at that club—or, if *you'd* wanted me…"

They had been over it so many times until Beau sounded annoyed. "Reya, you know my situation. And I did tell you. I said Gyp only goes three places, to gigs, to church, and home."

"But you didn't say his home was wherever he laid his head!"

Recalling that line from the Temptations hit, Beau raised his glass water bottle. "I warned you." Indeed, he'd cautioned his female friend about the man he affably called the wandering Gypsy, the younger man who often called him Pops. "Remember, you stood drooling over my drummer, and I let you know." Over the noise in the club, Beau whispered, "Just be aware," the man they sometimes called 'Stix,' would always need a ride. Beau admitted Ainsley Fielding was nice, but he seemed to really only love his drums.

Beau was right;, Mireya found out. Gypsy wasn't mean or malicious. He didn't seem capable of either, but he didn't seem capable of genuinely loving either. He went where the wind blew and was content.

"Beau you didn't make it plain," she moaned. "How was I to know, back then, that Gypsy would always need someone to ride him around? *Or* that he would always need someone to ride *him*?" Although that part she didn't so much mind—if she was the only woman riding. "And how was I to know he would fondle his drums like most men fondle tits? You should've made that plain."

"How? When I don't understand the first thing about touching tits."

"Funny." Mireya continued, "You could've said he'd show up, at three A.M. with his sticks 'n other stuff in a book bag on his back!"

Beau chuckled and stroked the cat that had abandoned his friend. "I didn't know all of that, not before you. And Gyp carries a *backpack*."

Mireya waved. "Book bag. You also didn't say he'd want to drag his drum set into my house, every single time. Ann doesn't like it."

"I'm sure she doesn't like a lot of things."

"She's the one who keeps begging *me* to stay," Mireya shrugged. "She says she'll share me—*if* the alternative is to live without me."

"Yeah, but when Gyp makes you moan, under the same roof where your woman resides, I know she'd like to kill him, and you too."

"Ann's not really my woman, and I tell her to see other people, but she claims she doesn't want an open relationship. So I keep it quiet with Gypsy. Your drummer is the problem, not Ann."

Beau sighed. "I told you what I knew; what his groupies said."

"Well," Mireya sighed, "all of that aside, I'm through."

"You're cutting him off?" Beau asked, stroking furry JaMocha Kitty.

"I'm gonna try to, again."

Beau watched the woman who gnawed her lip. "Okay, this is the deal," she said and turned to him.

Atta girl, Beau thought, because he had known there would be one.

"Beau, there's some female whose been hanging around. You've seen her. She wears white, and lately, she's showed up to all you guy's gigs."

Beau remembered. "Matter of fact, *I* told *you* about her."

Mireya rolled her eyes. "She met Gypsy at church. Now she's infatuated. The fact that he slept with her only complicates things."

Beau said it was strange, "But in the last couple of months, everywhere local that we've played, there that round girl has been."

"She's no girl," Mireya sulked. "She looks older than I do."

In thinking aloud, Beau mumbled, "Gyp must have really put it on her..." Realizing what he'd just said, he apologized. "However, that leads me to a question. Reya, is sex why *you* can't cut Gyp loose?"

The woman moaned. "My body loves him, what he does to me."

"Well," Beau made a face, "there's your problem," primarily because, Beau stated, "In some circles, you, Mireya Nickel, are now considered...a lesbian."

Chapter 24

THAT night as Beau slept, he struggled to wake. He desperately wanted out. The man didn't want to be caught in the dream—well rather, the nightmare—again. It was the one where he was on his mother's awful plaid sofa. Semi-aware that none of it was real, that he re-lived it via a dream, didn't make it any less frightening...

He had been a single-digit kid, six or seven, and he was scared. His heart beat so fast it hurt. His neck ached too because the hairy man's big fingers closed around his nape. The man held him—the small dream Beau—down, even though the kid tried to fight, to get away.

Why didn't his mother help him? Frightened, small Beau wondered. Why didn't Ophelia make the scarred man leave him alone?

Suddenly Beau couldn't breathe! The big man flung him, face-first, onto the lumpy sofa. Wildly Beau flailed as panic built, because biggie in the dingy tank top, short black socks, and tighty-whities punched him, and held him down! Beau's face was mercilessly mashed into the sofa seat. Unable to breathe, he felt the man fumble around behind him.

No! The man scratched Beau's butt cheek in the effort to hurriedly rid the kid of his superman underpants. Then the eight-year-old felt like he was being ripped open. He screamed! Tears rolled from his eyes as his open mouth was further mashed into the filthy sofa. The little boy cried and screamed because it hurt so badly and because the man repeatedly punched him in the back. But no one other than his mother heard as fire-hot pain spread from his little anus to his tender spine. The heinous ache radiated outward, even to the kid's fingertips and toes. His kidney hurt too from the punches, yet the man kept ramming something hard, *himself*, into Beau's small body!

Exhausted from fighting, but to no avail, Beau went limp. He would soon pass out. He couldn't get much air, and the pain was too much. Yet the man continued to grunt, laboring over him. "Yeah, that's better," the pedophile rasped when the kid no longer fought. However, the foul male liked it when kids screamed and thrashed. The pedophile liked it because then he could hurt the kids even more as he told them, "Just take it."

As the scarred man continued to rut, handling small Beau like he was a ragdoll, the kid escaped, and the pain-causer had no idea. He simply tried to inflict damage, but in his mind, the boy curled into a fetal ball.

There, Beau almost did not feel the pain, as his mother, who should have protected him, sat drugged out and nodding. Slowly, with shaking fingers and glazed eyes, she lit a cigarette, as he was torn asunder.

All of this, adult Beau saw from the place where he'd drifted. Aware that he was stuck a while longer in the recurring dream, he managed to escape his small body. It was a REM—Rapid Eye Movement—dream-state trick. It was an adult thing that he employed. It made terrible dreams tolerable until the man Beau could work his way free.

Now little Beau hovered somewhere above, perhaps near the ceiling. Weightless, he looked down on the dream scene. He saw the man with the fat hairy back, pumping the daylights out of the kid's—*his*—near lifeless body. Beau saw Ophelia too, friggin' she-devil. She smoked, and the smell was faint, but it reached him, up high, where he hovered.

The acrid smell dragged him back! Damn that smoking cunt! Now he was in his small body again. Exhausted, it ached. Now he had to hurriedly claw his way into a mental corner. There, he hugged his knees and let his mind go blank. He forgot the money that his mother took, payment for the man's use of his small body, even as the smoke curling from Ophelia's cigarette tried to again reach him...

The adult who slept gasped, from remembered smoke. Suddenly, he bolted up. Breathing hard, he was out of the dream. Those scenes, he reminded himself, were no longer his reality. Slowly, he glanced around. Okay. He was Beauregard DeVeaux, the *adult*, and he was free.

BEAU managed to calm down. He intentionally slowed his breathing. Yet shaken and angry, he clasped his dog tags. Rubbing the smooth metal between his fingers, he remembered. He was no longer that defenseless kid. Amid the rumpled covers of his massive bed, positioned across from one of four fireplaces in his home, he remembered. Ophelia had contacted him, back in the day when she realized he'd become successful, a man of means. Her foul ass had seen him on a weekly TV show. The gritty crime scene drama was now seen the world over, in syndication. But back then, Ophelia noticed he'd directed episodes. Then she'd managed to get through his tangle of handlers. With him, she'd pulled the mama card with the hope of shaking him down. From the beginning, Beau had known what she wanted. However, he had given her the benefit of the doubt. Back then he'd let Ophelia talk, because he had hoped, against hope, that she had changed. However, she had not. Still, Beau found out something he had not known. He had a *brother*!

Sitting in the dark of his bedroom, Beau remembered how he'd felt upon finding out. He'd been shocked, pleased, and angry, all at the same time. He'd hated O for not letting him know. Ophelia had known that whenever she ran, her sister-in-law Nell had always found Beau. O also knew that Nell had lived in the same place, with the same listed landline for more than twenty years. So there was no reason for Beau not to have known out about Thomas until Thomas was grown.

Leaning against the headboard, Beau remembered finding out that Ophelia had also caused his brother pain. Heck, when he and Thomas met, Ophelia had Thomas slinging shit for her. Beau had wanted to wring her neck. That drug addict should have sold her own stuff.

Tossing back the silk sheet and comforter, Beau reminded himself that nowadays, Thomas was okay. True, he was getting cozy with some nurse. Yet Beau remembered, his brother needed a life too.

Feeling around, Beau found the tee that he'd earlier discarded. Pulling it on, he remembered. When he'd learned about Thomas, Ophelia had started making monetary demands, and his brother had seemingly stood idly by. When Beau didn't meet O's demands, she'd issued threats.

That had been when something in her younger son had snapped.

Pulling on sweat pants, Beau remembered that his brother was considered slow. Still, Thomas had started what had become Ophelia's demise. Nowadays, Beau often assured his brother that he had done nothing wrong. Beau repeatedly said, "Really Thom, it was *Ophelia's iniquities* that did her in, not you."

In his darkened palatial home, Beau used his toes to rummage for his slip-ons. He could never locate them, nor could he stop thinking.

He remembered that Ophelia had suffered. In the hospital, in a morphine-induced haze, she'd begged him to kill her.

While staring impassively down at her he'd wondered, how the fuck could she think that *he* of all people would aid *her*? Heck, for him, there hadn't been that much forgiveness in the world. Not after all the pain, she had inflicted on him. Back then, Beau had thought it poetic justice.

Beau scrubbed a hand over his stubbly jaw and remembered things best forgotten…things like the yeast infection he had once suffered—in the *throat*—for crying out loud because his *mother* had tirelessly pimped him out, a little trusting boy. He forgot the knotted rope that burned and chaffed his neck when she'd tied him up, for hours, like an abused pet.

Beau pressed a big fist to his eye, to block out unwanted memories. He was an adult now. The actor reminded himself. He was no longer subject to Ophelia's whims. When his cat jumped onto his bed, he ran a hand over her. "Hey JaMocha," he cooed and sounded choked up.

Beau wanted to forget that many years back, he had been compelled to return, each day, to Kings County Hospital in Brooklyn. There, he'd watched Ophelia suffer. She had done the same to him, all those years ago when she had taken him from his dad; so Beau thought it only fair.

After watching her suffer, as her next of kin, he'd had her cremated.

Beau stepped off expensive yarn and onto polished wood. He told himself to forget the past. If he didn't, the thing he wasn't proud of would surface... But he'd had to get rid of Ophelia's ashes.

Wriggling into a sweatshirt over his tee, he wondered why memories haunted him now, more than they ever had before. With the paisley runner warm beneath his feet, he descended the back stairs. In the multi-functional kitchen that was more JeRell's than his, Beau made coffee. Under dimmed recessed lights, Beau remembered what he'd told his then-roommate, mouthy butter-yellow Ronni Brown. When *he* became a parent, he would always protect his child. He would never be negligent, or evil, as his mother had been. That was what he'd said.

Beau placed treats in his husky's bowl, and did the same for the lady of the house, his Siamese cat. He washed his hands. Grasping a mug, he realized. All this dreaming and thinking was about to drive him insane!

Wanting to forget his past and only look to the future, Beau sweetened his creamy coffee. He stepped out on his deck that was wet with dew. Facing east, he saw that the sky had begun to lighten. He forgot the chilled bare soles of his feet. Birds began their morning song, and in the distance, he heard a sports car bullet down a street.

Seating himself on a plump, striped cushion, the tall man attempted to forget fear and retribution. Having heard something other than his dog's pawing to get out, Beau turned. "JeRell," he said, as from the side nearest the carriage house, the robust man appeared.

"Saw the kitchen lights," the gruff-voiced chef admitted. Wearing a hoodie and padded nylon jogging pants, JeRell had left his quarters over the multi-car garage, "Because I knew you'd make coffee." He opened the kitchen's heavy glass sliding door, and Frost, the husky, ran free.

Inside, JeRell helped himself to the Arabica brew. He brought the pot out of doors and gestured. "Top you off, boss?"

With morning air nipping at his bare toes, Beau raised his mug. He watched his dog race exuberantly around. Moments later, he blinked when JeRell returned with a tray of fat tasty pastries and napkins. Noticing they'd been warmed, Beau asked, "Where were those?"

"Bread box. Made 'em yesterday." The chef waved Frost away, "And before you say it, boss, I know you don't often eat sweets—you 'n your Hollywood physique. Still, have one. You're between flicks."

Not the least bit offended, Beau, quipped, "So you wanna be funny."

Having known each other for years, the two men sat in companionable silence. Each drank and ate. Aware that the other man went the extra mile for him, Beau handled his rubbed-smooth dog tags and asked why. "Why do you do it, 'Rell? Why do you look out for me?"

His henchman replied, "You go all out for others." Seated, the chef gestured at the house and acreage. "You ain't let any of this go to your head." The fifty-something bald man further pondered his friend. Beau's abode was in a long island town so exclusive that one never saw a 'for sale' sign outside any home. The magnificent structures that housed hedge fund operators, surgeons, hoteliers, sports stars, and lawyers were snatched up within days of availability.

JeRell remembered that Beau owned other, equally as sought after properties, as well as enviable automobiles. An astute businessman, Beauregard DeVeaux, employed many, yet, the things that gave him the greatest joy were simple. He loved his family and his friends. He was generous, sometimes to a fault, and he held his charities dear. He didn't just write checks. He took an active interest in his beneficiaries. Kids knew him too. Many wrote to him. They sent photos and drawings. Their parents forwarded report cards and college transcripts. Thus, on the lower level, Beau had whole walls of mementos. The teenagers at Sal & Lu's idolized him because he often sparred or chatted with them. He told them his story, and that he too had had to find his way—just like them.

Actually, JeRell remembered, the Pietro brothers' gym was where he and Beau had met. There, they'd punched each other silly; but not stopping at his charities, JeRell recalled, some years back, Beau began a coalition that built affordable homes. A few homes Beau had personally furnished, while the homeowner tagged along, boohooing. The man was even a stand-in dad for Mireya's kid.

Most likely, JeRell cogitated; Beau did those things because, as a kid, before his aunt and uncle found him again, Beau really hadn't had a home. Not with his mother playing her stupid elude-him-if-you-can game with Beau's dad.

"You're just a big deal," the powerfully-built surly chef easily admitted. "But what gets me is you really care about other people. That's something, because sheeeit," JeRell scoffed, "if *I* had your money, I don't think I'd be so noble."

Beau chuckled and glanced over. "What d'you mean?"

"Hell, if I had bank like you, I wouldn't be thinking about other people. I'd just carry a knot on each hip." JeRell nodded. "Man, my pockets would be so full, they'd ha' the *mumps*!"

Beau laughed before he used an endearment, "Nugga...you cray."

"Maybe so," JeRell held out the pastry tray. "Have another."

Beau refused, then recanted. He broke off a piece and tossed it. "I had another of them dreams, he divulged as Frost lunged and gulped.

"I wish you'd stop," the chef stated, his mouth full.

Beau tossed another piece of pastry. "You wish I'd stop what?"

"Giving that dog the fruit of my labor. Oh, and quit dreaming too—at least when you're not on location."

"If I quit, you wouldn't have to do what, Rell?" Listening, Beau knew what was coming, because they had been over it before, several times.

"I wouldn't have to get up at dawn, to babysit yo' ass."

Heartily Beau laughed, and so did the loner, the crusty but indulgent chef whom very few people understood.

Chapter 25

WHILE working out, Beau pondered many things, his brother and that new nurse included. Doing reps, he was unaware that Gina—Beau thought that was her name—was headed to work...

As she traveled, Gina recalled feeling uneasy when 'that man' had appeared. Yet because the medical professional had been in her own home, she had been smart enough not to show fear. Gina had offered a hand and her name. "Come on in," she had also said. "Got a few things that need doing." On faux wood, she'd passed minimalist dark furniture and tall metal vases filled with branches. "It's man's work, you know?"

Gina showed 'that man' Thomas his task. She said she'd be nearby. Un-huh, with her phone, she didn't say, should he try anything.

Aware that she watched from the dining room, Thomas lined his tools neatly on the floor. The measurements taken, he jotted on a pad.

"Well, he's meticulous," Gina told her friend when she checked in. "Yes," she promised, "I'll call every fifteen minutes." Afterward, she made tea and asked the good-sized man if he would like a cup.

He surprised her by admitting he'd never had tea, "Not hot," he said. He drank coffee. "It's what my new family drinks."

Gina didn't allow her expression to divulge her curiosity, but new family, huh? She sneaked a peek: no wedding band or band tan.

Easily, the man spoke of Nell, and Kiss, whom Gina guessed was a cousin. It seemed those two made coffee. "My b-brother drinks it too."

As he sipped, Thomas admitted he liked Gina's hot tea. He also said he had to tell the truth. The Kiss woman wasn't his real cousin. That wasn't even her real name. She was Kismet, and she was his *half-brother's* cousin. Thomas said he and his brother had different fathers. Thomas divulged that although his brother had known his father, Thomas had never known his. Thomas only knew that his mother, who was dead, had been married to his older brother's father. But she'd ditched the man. Then Mother had 'lost' the older brother. Before Thomas had even been thought of, all this happened.

Gina's head reeled, but she kept listening, and Thomas admitted what druggie Mother had not. Mother had actually *abandoned* his older brother. Yet Thomas' mother found his brother again when brother was grown. Mother got excited because she had seen brother on TV. Mother had even found a way to hook up with brother, "But that didn't really work out." Still, Thomas said, he and his brother became close.

"Brother loves me," Thomas revealed and sounded like a child with a man's voice. He appeared proud when he announced, "My brother would do anything for me."

On a different day, when Thomas arrived at her house for another task, Gina again listened. She knew Thomas was a little slow. Yet, she thought, studying him; he certainly was capable, evidenced by his excellent work. Besides, he cleaned up behind himself. Whoever heard of a carpenter who willingly left any place as he'd found it?

Gina realized she rather liked easy-going Thomas. He didn't need to talk all the time, especially not when he was working, and he did other work near his assigned projects. That pleasantly surprised her.

"You don't have to pay me for that," he said, beaming with pride. "I mean, we didn't discuss me doing the other stuff." Thomas nodded. "I usually charge for everything I do, but y-you are nice. You gave me a hot drink. It wasn't strong like c-coffee, but it was c-cute, just like y-you, Ms. Gina." The big man turned away then. "I'm gonna p-pack up now."

Inconspicuously, Gina retrieved and handed over bills from her bra.

Walking ahead of her, Thomas said, "My m-money smells nice."

At her front door, Gina announced, "While we're being truthful, I must say I checked you out." Gina said she knew Thomas had a record. When he faced her, she felt nervous, perhaps because he was large and very male. She wanted to forget that although he'd been working, she could still smell the soap from his shower. She made herself look away from his neatly barbered hair; there'd be no touching it. So what, it looked soft, like the rest of him looked hard, and stupendously male.

"Everybody knows I got a record," Thomas stated. "It's p-public knowledge. Anyway, I learned, from b-being stupid. It don't m-make me a bad person, but if you're sc-scared and don't want me anymore," he glanced around. "Y-you c-can call somebody who's c-clean."

He exited her front door. "Lock up tight, Ms. Gina," Thomas called. "Um, and d-don't give everybody that n-nice hot drink of y-yours."

Chapter 26

BEAU and his band had a mid-week gig in Soho. Even he had to admit, he had been in rare form; singing 'n strutting like it was the last thing he would ever do. Afterward, Beau had been gracious, as fans thronged him. Although they made it damn hard for security, he loved all the love and attention. He always had. He was living his dream.

When people said that on stage, he reminded them of Al Green or Teddy Pendergrass; when audience members said they liked his band's cool vibe, it gave Beau a type of high. He floated when audiences screamed out lyrics over guitar licks reminiscent of those recorded by Jimi Hendrix. When Beau began a number that fused contemporary jazz with sizzling, hard-edged rock, he and the audience went wild. But what he loved most were the intimate venues. He loved to look out and see people grooving to the kick-ass beat. When he heard the booming bass lifted straight from hip-hop, he remembered why he'd named the band *Infusion*. Each member offered their own unique flavor, but as a whole, infused together, the band offered an incredible dose of neo-soul.

Therefore, unlike other artists who held the microphone out to the audience as a signal that *they* should sing, Beau couldn't see doing so. People paid hard-earned money to see *him*, so he gave them a show; he gave his all, and then some. And if they chose to sing along, then great.

Therefore, exhausted, but feeling accomplished, Beau turned out the light in his master bath and sleepily stumbled in the dark. Falling into bed, he closed his eyes, after he'd noted the time. 3:47 AM.

Was that his phone? He thought it minutes later. No. It couldn't be, he hazily mused, as again he heard the familiar ringtone. No, no, no. Not when he had *just* sunk into the best sleep he'd had in…forever.

Feeling around, he managed to still the noise. "Hey," he rasped, wanting to strangle somebody. "Talk, now."

"Beau," she whispered, "lemme come over."

"Reya." Was she crazy? His sleep-fogged brain registered her voice, as succinctly he said, "Tired—worked last night, call back. Later."

"No, let me come over. *Now.*"

Beau dragged his eyes open. Squinting, he growled. "Reya, I will kick your pesky butt. It's four-something; need sleep. Call back."

"No. I will see you in a little bit, and get that crusty houseman of yours up. Tell him to make coffee, or better yet, breakfast."

Beau would have laughed had he not been so worn. Heck, if he woke JeRell with that mess, the chef would pound him like a steak.

"Get up, Beau, and let me in," Mireya ordered. "Be there in a bit."

Dropping the phone, Beau wanted to lie back down. Yet he forced himself up because if he didn't, in seconds, he'd be asleep. Heavy-footed, and missing his slippers, he trudged to the kitchen. Canine nails clicked on the floor behind him. The only good thing about being up at such a gad-awful hour, Beau thought was, he hadn't had enough time to have a nightmare. In the hearth room adjacent to the kitchen, he fell across a much-loved sofa. Curling beneath a cozy throw, he made himself text the pain in the neck. '**Drv rnd, past da garage.**'

She did, and found the deck door open. She smelled coffee too and was unaware that Beau, not JeRell, had made it. The homeowner had done so while groggily thinking, the things he did for friends and family!

Tucking her legs beneath her, Mireya pulled up her own plush throw. Then clasping a mug, she said, "Gypsy called," after one AM. Softly he'd pled, 'Come get me...' Mireya said she'd groaned, not wanting to leave her warm bed. "But if I'd woken Ann, we'd have had a fight."

In her bathroom, Mireya had hissed, 'Gypsy, where are you?'

"Open your eyes, Beau," the cinnamon-skinned woman ordered. "I'm telling you stuff. So, into my cell, I said, 'In the *village*?' I asked Gypsy where were *you*? I assumed he had been out with your band."

Throwing an arm over his face, Beau rasped, "Infusion worked last night." He peeked at Mireya. "*That's* why I'm tired."

She sounded sympathetic, "I know sweet tea, but Gypsy said he told Pops—you—not to wait. He said you were drench because you gave a kick-ass show. He said everybody else was taking the train. Manhattanites." Mireya shook her head. "Gypsy said you offered to send a car for him, but he must have refused, pulling *me* out of *my* bed."

"So, *you* turned around and did the same to *me*."

Ignoring the jibe, Mireya revealed, "Now I might wind up fighting with Ann, if she thinks I went to him, to get a piece."

From the sofa, Beau asked if Mireya picked up the bald man's drums.

"I did." She sipped hot coffee. "When he got in my car with his book bag, I told him what I told you the other day; no more coming to the house, dragging stuff. I'm tired—"

"*You*, tired?" Beau croaked, "*I* worked last night; 'n it's a backpack."

"I'm talking about me, here, friend. B, I'm tired of…all this." Mireya explained that she really wanted her life in order. She wanted her own place. She didn't want to use or hurt stout Ann anymore. Mireya definitely didn't want Ann feeling like she'd become a babysitter, "While I enjoy late-night assignations, when that's not the case."

Beau wondered why hadn't Mireya waited to have her revelation?

"I just want the two of us to sort our business dealings, legally. I want to continue in *that* vein because there, we're good." Shaking her head, Mireya plaintively announced, "It's time for us to untangle, Beau."

With her eyes on the fireplace that made the hearth room great in inclement weather, Mireya didn't say that after collecting Gypsy, she'd wanted to ride him. That's how it was whenever he and she were in proximity. Nevertheless, Mireya did say that she'd been about to take Gypsy to his mother's house when he said he had no heat.

Beau looked over from the sofa. "What does that mean, no heat?"

"He forgot to pay." Mireya said Gypsy also took a call from a groupie. "I said he could forget me taking him to some *woman's* house. I said if that's what he wanted, he should've called that woman."

Knowing how his friend felt about his drummer, Beau could guess how angry she'd been. Staring into her coffee, Mireya didn't divulge that she'd hastily pulled onto a deserted street. There, she'd torn off her leather jacket and fought to get her sexy little nightgown up. Remaining silent, she remembered straddling the thick-bodied man, while with hands between them, she'd sought to open his pants. Wanting to take him in, she'd hastily positioned herself over his standing member, and ever ready for a romp, Gypsy had thumbed her thong aside.

Mireya sank down and shuddered when Gypsy's rod glided into her slick sheath. With hands clenching his shoulders, and her knees uncomfortably outside his, she'd leveraged herself. Then on his pole, she'd erotically slid up, and down, repeatedly, pleasuring them both.

Although she hadn't said it, to Gypsy, or to Beau, she had done so while inwardly vowing to make the drummer forget any woman with whom he might spend the rest of the night. With thoughts of being

Gypsy's only woman, she'd put her breasts in his face and told him to suck. Obeying, he'd clasped Mireya's buttocks and had driven deeper.

It had been as though neither of them could get enough, and Mireya wondered. What was it about Gypsy, Ainsley Fielding, that crazed her?

He'd pulled on her hair, kissed the column of her neck, and the scent of their frenzied activity had filled her car. Eagerly she'd received all of him. She had silently vowed to take his very essence so that he would have nothing left for anyone else. Pouring herself into a kiss, she'd refused to cry. She'd simply hugged him to her because she truly loved him. She wanted to be with him as much as she found herself with Ann.

Falling onto her seat, with her back against the driver's door and her legs splayed, she'd whispered, "Tongue me Gypsy." Raising a knee, she'd offered herself. She recalled that she hadn't needed his mouth on her as much as she'd needed her scent *on him*. She wanted her territory marked. As he lapped and pleasured her—like Ann never had—Mireya lay open, wanting more than Gypsy could ever give. She'd ached, just thinking that soon she would take him home, where he probably wouldn't stay, because of the cold; likely he'd go to another. Yet she consoled herself by saying they'd had 'this.'

Not bothering to button her little gown that was enigmatically prim as well as provocative, she wanted whoever might see her, to know. Ainsley Fielding had loved *her*.

In the hearth room, Mireya glanced at Beau, lying on the sofa. Unwilling to allow him to fall asleep, she mentioned screwing in the car, then pulling up to Gypsy's house. "Another car pulled up alongside us."

A woman peered into Mireya's car, and loudly, Gypsy groaned.

"It was that girl, *Mary*," Mireya announced, "the one who wears white to all your gigs. She looked sleepy, with a rag on her head."

Beau no longer felt dog-tired as he shifted to ask, "You mean that roundish girl-woman who dresses like a nun?"

"That's the one."

Beau sat up. "She was at the club last night."

Mireya rolled her eyes. "Well, I asked Gypsy what she was doing at his house. He said he didn't know. He said in the past, she had driven him home from church a few times. He said now he can't shake her."

"I'll bet," Beau nodded, knowing exactly what had happened.

"I know he slept with her, so I asked if he *told* that woman he doesn't want anything more. He said yes, but she's hell-bent on marrying him."

Beau nearly laughed. He also knew that upon hearing that, Mireya had promptly decided the woman had to go.

Mireya scowled and said she'd exited her car. "That Mary person got out of her hatchback too. She had on a slouchy tee. It was dingy, but white, of course. In her coat, she just stood there, staring at me."

Beau asked, "Did you look like that?"

Mireya nodded, "Mostly. I had my jacket around my shoulders."

Mireya recalled that upon seeing her, Mary's dark eyes had mirrored shards of jet. Slightly amused, Mireya had watched the woman's face go from stunned to angry, as Mary's eyes traversed Mireya's topography.

With disgust, Mary noted shapely Mireya's sex-tousled mane, the short, open gown, the enticing full breasts and pert nipples, all visible through thin cotton. And Mary felt volatile, like Mount Vesuvius. When her eyes scorched downward, over Mireya's silhouetted curvy body, Mary saw red. She despised that Mireya's bare legs were artfully showcased in high-heeled booties. Noticing the dark triangle between Mireya's thighs, enraged, Mary sprang forward, to scratch out that *Jezebel's* eyes!

Mireya flicked her ever-present switchblade, the one she'd used all those years ago in middle school, on Mr. McCuddy, and others. Aware that something otherworldly drove Mary, Mireya softly advised, "Back it up bitch, or I'ma become your exorcist."

With her mouth tight, round Mary stepped back and wondered. Didn't Ainsley know? It was a *sin* to hang out with a harlot! Wasn't he aware? Expending his seed in the belly of a whore was *not* acceptable!

Mary, the newest member at Gypsy's church, decided then, with narrowed eyes, that the man needed a call to holiness. Sadly, he had been beguiled, like Adam had been in the garden, when Eve sidled up using her wiles. Mary nodded because 'Brother Ainsley' needed to re-learn a few Sunday school lessons. As a child of the Most High, and as a steward of the light, he had no business with a daughter of darkness.

Feeling near gleeful, Mireya knew the exact moment when the woman in the oversized tee realized just what Gypsy had been into. Then Mireya teasingly fondled her own breast. She did so while Gypsy carried his drums into the house left to him by his recently deceased mother.

"I was *not* going to leave her there with him," Mireya told Beau. She didn't say that she'd locked her car before catching Gypsy in his open doorway. There she'd placed her arms around him, and heat flared.

In the night, Mary, who thought of herself as heaven's handmaiden, turned away. Mary recalled something she had seen in the bible.

Vengeance is mine...

Knowing some, but not all, Beau surmised, "So that's why you wanted to come here, Reya. So you could half 'truthfully' tell Ann that *you and I* hung out."

Mireya nodded, "I don't want to fight with her, not about Gypsy."

Beau smirked. "I thought she was okay with you getting some."

"She is, but she'd prefer it if I saw different people. She doesn't want me repeatedly enjoying the same person. It then becomes too much like a relationship." And Mireya had enjoyed Gypsy numerous times, in his cold house.

"Ah, I see," Beau smirked. He unfolded himself to get more coffee. "Ann probably doesn't want you seeing the same man because you might become attached to him. And where would that leave her?"

Mireya hated that Beau no longer appeared sleepy or sullen.

Going into his kitchen, he noticed the tote beside her chair, "Yours?"

"Yep, it stays in my car," Mireya announced, picking it up. "Remember back in the day when we used to go clubbing and needed a change of clothes the next morning?"

"I do." Beau chuckled. "I suppose you need a shower now, too. Right? For evidence and DNA removal before work."

"You don't have to be blunt." Mireya looked sheepish. "But, please?"

"Okay," Beau said, enjoying the exchange as much as he did his coffee. "You know where the towels are, but now you owe me."

Pecking her longtime friend and sometimes-savior on the cheek, Mireya sounded relieved. "Thank you." She started up the back steps, carrying her tote. "Oh. Can you get that houseman of yours to make me some breakfast?" She called back down, "Eggs and bacon, please."

Seated, Beau shook his head. His friend sure was nervy. She always had been.

Chapter 27

AFTER Mireya left, JeRell appeared. He complained that with 'that woman' driving back 'n forth, past his home above the immaculate multi-car garage, she'd awakened him. Twice. "I've got a good mind to use her head as a speedball," he growled, "the next time I see her."

Choking with laughter, Beau imagined Mireya's face on the boxing instrument. "Man, you've got one wicked sense of humor."

Hiding a smirk, JeRell asked, "What makes you think I'm funning?"

After coffee, when the sun had become a peach sphere rising, JeRell said he'd sat long enough. He left to shower and shave, but not before he gruffly spoke. "Guess I'd better get my butt in gear because the boss would disapprove of me sitting 'round all morning. Even though," he called, "it's because of *him* that I'm up before dawn, every day now..."

As his wisecracking houseman disappeared, Beau nearly smiled. Glad he didn't need to be anywhere until early afternoon, Beau guessed he would go work out. As he headed for his home gym, again, he thought back to when he'd been a very young man.

After his aunt had moved, and before his big break, he had done various odd jobs. He had even been an escort. He would never forget having accompanied a short, rotund man to The Met...

AN hour before time, Beau showed up. He looked around. This was the Upper East Side address he had been given. In the well-appointed lobby, he was informed that Mr. DelNabio would soon be down.

It had not been long before a limo eased into a parking space; while passing the front desk, a round tuxedoed man appeared.

That man and Beau spent a glittering evening at the New York Metropolitan Opera. Afterward, the limo driver seemed to take a different route back to Mr. DelNabio's place. Before an unbelievable home, the driver slowed. High on a grassy knoll, golden light spilled out over the Hudson.

Peering from his window, Beau wondered where they were. The structure before him was not where they'd journeyed from. Inconspicuously, Beau felt through his clothing for his dog tags. Gazing up, he wondered, why hadn't they returned to the posh apartment on Manhattan's east side?

"Well," Mr. DelNabio spoke, "we're here. Home."

Okay, Beau surmised, the man had a house, too. Beau gaped at all, as the limo wound its way upward so that its occupants might alight. Curious, he followed the man who reminded him of a penguin, in black and white. Inside the tastefully decorated, quiet abode, Beau was led to a room. There he was given a wooden stick. Holding it, he watched as the homeowner turned from closing the door. Casually, the man removed his satin-trimmed jacket and his cuffed shirt. As he did, he gave clear instructions. "Beau, I want you to use that...to beat me."

Beau stared and did not want to. His free hand again crept up to find his dog tags, because what had the man ever done to him? Still, after a bit of prodding and several of DelNabio's gestures, Beau managed to hit the heavy man on his hairy back.

"Not like that." The man turned, and Beau saw that his neck and shoulders were pale. "You have to do it harder."

Following a shrug, Beau raised the stick and landed it with a thud.

"Yeah, that's the spirit," Mr. DelNabio directed. He had his back to Beau as he knelt on a harlequin patterned rug. Glancing around, Beau saw that the room housed only a velvet settee, a bar, and a chandelier.

"Okay, again. Bring that stick down with force," the round man bellowed, "because I have been a naughty boy!"

Beau felt foolish doing so, but he raised and lowered the stick. He hit Mr. DelNabio considerably harder. Beau cringed afterward. He felt, oddly, too much like Ophelia. Often she'd hit him; she had done so with a broom handle, a stick, and a ruler; anything she'd gotten her hands on. Reminded of those things, Beau really did not want to do to another person what had been done to him. "Okay, all done," he announced and dropped the stick. He sincerely hoped that would be the end.

"Again!" the man ordered. DelNabio raised a hand. He removed his pants, then his boxer shorts. "Got to get comfortable," he proclaimed.

Beau felt things were getting stranger by the moment. He also thought, as an escort, he had gone way beyond the call of duty. Therefore, he suggested, "The agency might not approve..."

However, Mr. DelNabio, who now only wore socks, dismissed the notion. He promised there would be no touching or anything of the kind.

April Alisa Marquette
119

For that, Beau was glad, because he didn't know if he could stand to have that man put those fingers, thick like cigars, on him. Still, he really didn't want to do as the man wished. However, he continued.

"This time," DelNabio advised, "try it with gusto!"

Beau felt sickened. The thought and sound of what he was doing didn't sit right with him. He hated that each time he hit Humpty Dumpty, the man quivered and raised his posterior—that had angrily pinked up. But that didn't stop DelNabio from calling for more. "Hit my back, too."

Young Beau felt embarrassed. He knew there was staff around. They probably knew better than to intrude, though. It was how rich people and their help operated. After a hellish half hour, there were welts all over Mr. DelNabio's hairy back and buttocks. Beau was nearly traumatized, and his arms had begun to hurt like he had been hitting a most uncooperative piñata.

Tossing the stupid stick, he finally said what he was thinking. He had to go. This time he was firm. He called out, "Enough." He said he needed a ride back. "I need to get back to where we started."

Lying on the patterned rug, Mr. DelNabio groaned. Breathing hard, with those chunky cigar fingers, he massaged his exposed, extended male organ. He also managed to suggest that Beau should allow him to finish. "Then we'll have the car brought around, and get you home."

Turning away, Beau felt as though he'd stepped into some weird virtual reality. However, after gasping out his release, and tissuing off his hands, DelNabio gave the youngster, five crisp one hundred dollar bills. These were paid in addition to the check that Beau would receive from the escort agency. Therefore, Beau didn't feel quite so bad after all.

On subsequent days, Beau didn't feel too bad either when the short round man continued to call the agency to get him, alone. Then the other escorts began to whisper. Jealous, some claimed Beau had turned the man out, yet he never told them the truth. Beau let those haters think what they wanted. Only he knew. The businessman didn't want sex.

Although he tried not to think about it when he was away from Mr. DelNabio, Beau recalled that after every sparkling society event they attended, there would be a beating session. Really, it was too easy, because whenever he hit Mr. DelNabio hard enough, the rotund man got tears in his eyes, along with an obvious erection. He would also invariably cry out, "I'll be good, daddy!"

Stepping off his elliptical machine, Beau grabbed a towel and recalled something. Patron of the arts, Mr. Joseph DelNabio had been dealing with unresolved parental issues, in his own peculiar way.

It was something Beau needed to do too, at long last. He honestly needed to forgive his parents. He needed to forgive his father for working so hard, and for dying. Beau needed to let go because it was simple. His father had not been there for him. The man had had to work.

And Ophelia had left Beau, her kid, behind. She'd done so in the attempt to outrun his father by hopping from one city to the next.

Beau also needed to pardon drug-addicted, abusive, Ophelia for all the evil she had dispensed, not only to him but to his brother as well.

Aware of this, Beau finally whispered, "*I am willing to forgive...* I release all the old hurts from my past. I release anger too. I release resentment and all the things that no longer serve me well. I release myself from the past. I move on. I receive joy, because...I forgive. "

He knew that was the beginning. Beau knew too that now the universe would aid him. It would take care of the rest, simply because he was willing.

Then Beau went a step further. He did what his A'nt Nell would have. He prayed. "Father in Heaven, help me to forgive. I want to be free from the hatred I feel for people who wronged me; especially *her*. Help me, *please*, because I can't do this alone. I've tried."

Beau remembered to say, "In the name of Jesus Christ," as his Aunt had taught him so long ago, because, said she, that was from whence came the power to do anything.

Amen.

Chapter 28

KISMET was fed up. Lyle often shrugged her off or snapped at her. He came home from work late, a lot. Once, he didn't come home at all. He claimed he'd slept at his office. Whatever. Kismet had never known Lyle to cheat. That was the only reason she hadn't gone ballistic. *Besides,* she hadn't found any supporting evidence or witnesses, and she hadn't smelled pussy on him. If she had, she'd have kicked Lyle to the curb, because to keep her children's lives intact, she would only take so much. There was another reason she hadn't acted rash. She was giving Lyle a minute to get his act together. However, she had announced she was sick of her husband's drinking. Kismet said she wouldn't tolerate any more consternation with the children. She didn't want her boys believing it was okay to be mean and disrespectful to women. She didn't want them becoming men who copped attitudes because things didn't go their way, or when a woman did something with which they disagreed. The Momma also announced she didn't want her girls believing their father's antics were acceptable. They had been told otherwise. Heck, Kismet rationalized, how could she convince her girls that males were to treat *them* with respect if *she* didn't receive any?

"Another thing," Kismet announced, "I want no more moaning about the baby." She was *into* this pregnancy, at last. The fetus was growing. "Therefore," she stated, "it doesn't matter how angry you are or how much you disagree with my decision. It's done. We need to move on."

She turned, continuing with dinner preparations, and Lyle blew up.

Aware that upstairs, her children could hear, Kismet took plates from a glass-front cupboard. Despite Lyle's yelling, The Momma threw down the gauntlet. "Lyle, we have *got* to move *on*...one way or another."

He eyed his wife. "So what are you saying, Kismet Staar?"

"I'm saying," she softly retorted, "I'm tired of your mess. You're stressing the baby and me." She was in her friggin' forties, she reminded him, and after all she had been through to get this baby, she was *going to* carry it to term, God willing.

"I'm stressing you?" Lyle retorted. "Incredible. You've got all sorts of people here, doing everything, and you claim I'm stressing you."

"Yes, Lyle, you are, and you know it." Kismet acknowledged that she had household help, courtesy of her cousin. She even had her accommodating assistant from work, "But none of that negates the fact that my *husband* causes me undue stress, *on purpose.*" Kismet raised a hand as she approached the broad wooden stairs. "No more." She called her children for dinner and kept watch over a shoulder. It was a shame that she had to, but she no longer knew Lyle, or of what he was capable.

THAT had been the previous night. Now on the following evening, Kismet sat in her study, its door ajar. Raising her eyes to the red-clad women over the mantel, she realized. She again felt a kinship with them, perhaps because she was taking her power back. She knew it would be unpleasant, but more than likely, she would have to tell her man to scram. Attempting not to think about him or his antics earlier in the evening, she was just glad the kids' things were ready for the next day. She was glad she'd gotten them bathed and settled in, with no help from their father. The truth was: she had almost been grateful that he had not been around to be a menacing presence, lurking in the background.

Although she forgot last night, Kismet pondered the drama that Lyle had again stirred, earlier the current evening...

DRIVING beneath an inky sky, Lyle realized something. In his SUV, he did not know how or when it had happened, but *he* had become a drunk. So what, he wasn't like others who couldn't function when they imbibed? He still drank too much. It had become his coping mechanism.

Now, his kids were wary and slowly learning to despise him.

Heck, all he needed was a dirty wife-beater—a filthy cotton tank top—and perhaps a head of smelly hair beneath his arms. Then he could complete the picture of the proverbial alcoholic.

ENSCONCED in her recently set up home office, Kismet did not want to recall what had transpired earlier. Out, and driving aimlessly, neither did Lyle. Yet both remembered.

Earlier, Kismet cooked; she did so twice a week because her family needed *her* meals. Those prepared by the service were good, but Beau's people didn't know precisely what the Manfred family liked. Therefore, while watching 'The Barefoot Contessa,' The Momma fixed dinner. A while later, she heard footsteps.

In the kitchen that had pendant lighting and a large island, Lyle smelled food. He also noticed, the room had been cleaned. He glanced at the clock. Seven-forty, so dinner was done. Déja had most likely loaded the dishwasher, while the other children had cleared the table that Kismet was leaning over. She explained some homework bit to nine-year-old Chance. Glancing at Lyle, she mentioned having cooked.

If that had been her way of acknowledging him, Lyle didn't like it.

Both adults realized. Not many moons ago, they would have met halfway to kiss. Now, they just seemed to put up with one another.

Lyle couldn't blame Kismet for feeling ambivalent because even he knew. He had been a real donkey, one who was irrationally jealous of his wife's cousin. Lyle didn't know when the feelings had unfurled, but he really hated that his woman and Beau shared a bond, one that he and his wife would perhaps never share.

Whenever Lyle pondered it, he became angry. It was the reason he'd sneered, "So you cooked." Before this baby business, his wife had done so all the time. Now she thought she was doing him a favor? Well, bunk that. "What is it Kiss," Lyle heard himself snort, "you want a medal for doing something you're supposed to?"

That had been when nine-year-old Chance spoke up, with balled fists. "Don't speak to Momma that way. It's not nice. Furthermore, Dad," the little Brainiac had informed Lyle, "*I* don't like it."

Five-year-old Bonaire, one of the twins, had screwed up his small face. He'd chanted, "Daddy's not nice. Daddy's not nice..."

Intervening, Kismet eyed little Bonaire. "That's enough, Nar." She observed her other children. "None of you are to disrespect your father. Understood?" Following half-hearted murmurs, she spoke to the oldest. "Déja, sweet, I need you to run Belize's bath." Kismet addressed the twins, "Leez and Nar, go brush your teeth. I'll be up in a sec."

With knotted lips, The Momma turned. Her voice had been level, but to Lyle, she'd sounded like she attempted to be patient with one of the kids. "Lyle, I was just letting you know I made your favorite."

On the page before their son, she placed a finger. Lyle knew he was being dismissed. He became enraged. He also thought, damn, was Kiss luscious! Despite jumbled emotions, Lyle ached to take his wife in his arms. But he would have to apologize, for a bevy of things. Therefore, anger replaced lust. Hell, the way he saw it, some of how he'd behaved was due to how she'd caused him to feel. Unwanted and unloved.

In his SUV, aimlessly roaming, Lyle recalled mentioning such things, a while back. Seated in her study, Kismet recalled telling her husband that those were his demons, *his* insecurities. Both recalled the long ago kiss, a sweet gesture, initiated by Kismet before she said Lyle was vital to her and their family. Driving, Lyle wondered. Was he vital, now? His wife was to him, although lately, his actions had said otherwise.

When he had been home, he'd watched his wife. He'd wished they could start again, because to him, she was the ultimate, the empress. Standing there, he'd wondered, where was her come-get-me-big-boy look, the one he had always loved. He hadn't seen it lately, *but* he had seen her undergo a ton of medical procedures—to give Beau a baby. Kismet was selfless. She had bravely stuck herself with needles, and she hated them. She didn't know her husband watched, and winced with her, every time. The first few times, he'd even wanted to kiss away her tears.

If he hadn't been so pot-stubborn, Lyle realized while driving, between lanes, he could have monitored her temperature. He could have jotted down changes, the ones she thought he hadn't noticed. *And* he could have said that despite everything, yet she glowed, his empress.

Nearly swerving off the road, Lyle wondered if he and Kiss would make it. Maybe she would trade up, for one of the scores of men who noticed her. He had seen them, many times, trying to get their eyes off her. They did so due to fearing a confrontation with him. Yet he saw those same men take chances, as they eyed cookie 'n cream. That's what she called her breasts. He knew the moment a man wondered about their weight, he knew the second a man imagined himself tasting her big sexy tits. He knew those bastards thought of jerking-off in the softness.

He knew that when men glimpsed her bubblicious bottom or saw his wife's hips, they hardened, and Lyle hated it, just like he'd hated that he hadn't been able to send his son upstairs. In the kitchen, Lyle had wanted everyone to forget homework, so he could tear off his wife's clothing.

However, he'd realized, he couldn't release his dark hard rod, to please both adults because wifey was angry with him. Well, he had been upset too. Lyle had also been unable to do anything with Kismet because he remembered. She'd started *another Negro's baby*.

If she had been carrying Beau's baby, Beau's seed, and a donor's fertilized egg, Lyle would not have been as upset. But the way things had been done, Lyle felt like his wife had been sexually passed around, although that was nowhere near the case. But the truth was: she wasn't carrying her cousin's baby; she was carrying her cousin's *man's* baby! What was worse was that it was *her* baby too. Every time Lyle thought about it, he almost felt like Kiss had crept on him. He felt betrayed. Lyle sometimes also felt as though Kiss had been used. That further angered him. As her husband, all he wanted to do was protect her, his family, and their way of life. But she wouldn't let him.

Lyle had tried to forget all of it, again. He had even taken his eyes off Kismet. Then he'd noticed pots on the stove. When he heard himself say, "I ate," he wondered, *where'd that come from?* Heck, he was hungry, and just days ago, he'd berated her for not cooking more often. Lyle had done so because Beau, whom Lyle had once liked, had placed himself and others between a husband and his wife.

Kismet said to their son, "Books in your bag kiddo, shower time."

Despite a groan, the youngster obeyed, and his mother turned. "What did you eat, Lyle?" Her eyebrow winged up, "a hamburger, and greasy stale fries leftover from lunch?" About to go up too, Kismet tossed over a shoulder, "Remember tonight, next time you 'order' me to cook."

"What?" Lyle threw up his hands and kept on with the lie. "You think I ate to spite you? How was I to know you'd act on a whim?"

As her son clamored up the stairs, Kismet shrugged. "I don't wanna fight. Wash your hands—okay, and put the food away. Will you?"

Lyle grumbled, "Oh, I will. Just watch me."

Not wanting to, Kismet turned. Descending the few steps she'd climbed, she watched Lyle grab a spatula and her shining sauté pan. He pushed tender meat into the garbage. She gaped as he dropped stainless steel into her skink. If he chipped the porcelain, she thought, she'd have to replace the whole friggin' thing! However, Kismet said nothing, just watched aghast as Lyle did the same thing with the starch.

And she couldn't help but think, *stupid...mutha freakin' coconut.*

Remembering the baby and what she had been through to get it helped her keep her mouth shut. Still, she'd wanted to scream, *fool*—her! She'd thought her labor of love would be well received. Well, so much for that. Appearing nonchalant, when she wasn't, she disappeared.

Feeling like *he* hadn't received the right reaction, no yelling or astonishment, Lyle dropped Kismet's saucepan into the trash. Feeling unbelievably angry, he also proceeded to strew vegetables everywhere.

Recalling that she and the kids had cleaned the kitchen earlier, *and* that she had beaten men bigger and badder than her husband, Kismet willed herself to breathe. Upstairs, she had also wanted to call her mother, or her cousin. Yet she'd refused; to do so would escalate things, and despite the shitty way Lyle was acting, she really would not want to watch him get his butt kicked by her cousin. So slowly, Kismet had walked from room to room. She'd helped little Belize into her pj's. She'd called for twin Bonaire to come get clean. The Momma had instructed Chance to finish his shower. Shaken and angry, she'd softly told Déja, who smelled of raspberry shower gel, "No more texting tonight, baby." And The Momma knew. She could take no more.

Seated in her study, she again realized. She could not afford to act rashly. There was too much at stake. Foremost was her children's well-being. Yet she wondered, *when* had her husband had become this clown? With hand-heels to her eyes, she knew she wouldn't sleep. She would think. Then she would act.

Downstairs, and angry with his wife, but more furious with himself for acting so foul, Lyle snagged a liquor bottle. He drank half the contents before he realized the kids or his wife could come in and see him. Standing in the kitchen, he drank more. Belligerently, he told himself he didn't care; he was a grown-ass man. He feared no one.

Then why did he feel so bad? He stumbled to the den and dropped to the sofa. Why'd he feel he owed his wife a heartfelt apology?

He fell asleep and woke later with a headache, a crick in his neck, and a yuck mouth. Sitting up, he *remembered* and felt ashamed. He'd treated his wife insanely, just because she'd exercised her right—any woman's right—to do with her body as she chose.

That was when he dragged himself up and noticed. His bottle lay on the sofa, amid a liquor stain. Damn. Feeling nauseous, Lyle stumbled from the room that seemed to spin. He wound up in his SUV.

Outside in the dark of night, now he had a secret. It was one he hoped Carl, his neighbor, would never tell. A little while ago, Officer Carl had pulled him over. A breathalyzer had also been administered. "Lyle man," Carl had sighed, "I'm letting you go, although I shouldn't, but I know you and your wife. You're good people." Officer Carl handed over a ticket. "Go home, man. Get it together, and replace that headlight." The man's voice had become stern. "Next time I catch you out here like this, no warning buddy, I take you to jail."

Lyle resolved not to tell Kiss, but he would do as blond Carl had said. He *would* get it together. That Lyle promised himself.

He also wondered, as did his wife, what would their lives be like, this time next year? Would they even still be together?

Chapter 29

GINA wondered, why'd she keep finding odd jobs for Thomas to do? Why did he keep appearing? Thomas worked five days a week with a home renovation service. Why did he readily agree to weekends? Maybe, she thought, as he replaced her kitchen baseboard, he did so because he didn't have anybody—a *woman*— with whom to spend time. "Thomas, do you have a—" she found herself asking, "a woman friend?"

"I have lots of women friends," he said in his no-nonsense manner.

Oh. Gina felt like a sacked quarterback. Yet she asked, "Then why do you work weekends? Don't you spend time with them? Your women."

"I spend time with them. They cook for me."

That meant she could stop pondering inviting him over for dinner. Still, Gina wanted to know, "What do these women cook?"

"Well…" Thomas pondered it. "An't Nell cooks pot roast. She makes meatloaf too—yum! Kiss cooks everything. She's the best in the world. Brother says so, but he can't say it around JeRell because Rell will get mad. *He* cooks for Brother every day." Thomas shrugged, "But that's because Brother pays him. JeRell's food is good, but he can be a meany."

Gina nearly laughed, "But what about your *other* women Thomas?"

On his haunches, he appeared puzzled. "What other women?"

"The ones who like you; the ones who kiss you…"

"No women kiss me. Not the right way."

Gina's eyes widened because they might have been onto something here. "What would be the right way?"

"On the mouth, of course. But that wouldn't be right."

"Why not?"

"Are you crazy?" Thomas appeared shocked. "Kiss and An't Nell are my family! They're married, too. You know what, Gina? Even though I wanted to kiss *you* the right way, I think you're weird—but not in a bad way. The bad way would be if you had a kid, and you kissed him on the mouth and put your tongue in there and then took off your clothes and got on top of your kid who was a boy."

Oh my. Gina didn't know what to think, then again, she did. Thomas was telling her something, in his way. Therefore, she spoke softly, using her nurse/bedside voice. "Did that happen to someone you know?"

"Happened to me," Thomas admitted. "It was wrong. Maybe it's why you don't want to kiss me, but I still want to kiss you. I want you to take off your clothes and get on top of me. That wouldn't be wrong because you're not a mother. You're my lady-boss. A cute one."

Quickly Gina turned away because Thomas was all wrong, and then again, he was right. She *was* a mother, sort of. The nurse wanted to kiss him too and do all the things he'd said, even though nothing could come of it. Heck, when Thomas was finished with her odd jobs, and when she could find no more work for him, he would move on. He would probably become a big ol' beefy plaything for some rich woman. Mrs. Rich would love him and his near-innocence. She would love his big body, and those lips and that tongue that he wanted to push into someone's mouth.

Gina shook herself. She had to stop thinking about things that would never happen. She had to remember. She was doing penance, for life.

UAWARE that the nurse was doing what *he* would consider 'getting her hooks into Thomas,' Beau, looking his usual, casual chic, rode from one meeting in Manhattan to another. This one was a late power lunch with his longtime agent. Riding along, he recalled a different man, another that he had escorted. At the time, Beau was no older than twenty. The thick-bodied, tanned Hollywood type had explicitly asked for him.

Beau recalled the man's hair. It looked like it had sprung from a doll head. Plugs. He also recalled the ridiculously orange tan that Hill Ingham had sported. Vastly different from the ruthless ship's commander he'd played in a renowned space flick, Hill, who was anything but a ladies man, called the escort service. The older actor did so whenever he was in town, and his wife was not. Back then, he'd taken Beau to lovely places. Afterward, he'd wanted his own brand of excess.

Hill had often ordered Beau to pee on him.

A large-boned man, Hill had sometimes languidly stretched out on the tiled floor out by his pool. Other times, he'd lounged beneath a life-sized statue of mythological Venus emerging from a large shell in that pool. With eyes on Beau, Hill had deliciously shivered, as repeatedly he had intoned, "I love the golden showers, the golden showers..."

However, when he decided he wanted his young escort to go *further*, Beau proclaimed, no more body functions! What Hill's problem had been, Beau would never know. What he did know, though, was that he had to get out of his own head! As they neared 57th, he told himself to also forget the older actress with alabaster skin and kohl-lined green eyes. She, too, had called the exclusive New York escort agency just to get him. Back then, the fifties and sixties' on-screen goddess had often referred to Beau as her 'costume jewelry.' She'd explained why. She admitted she didn't particularly care for men, her little secret; however, she loved to parade young Beau around on her arm. She liked that people thought they were doing it, although sex no longer interested her.

"You're so young, and beeyooteeful," she purred. She trailed a pointy, blood-red fingernail down his chest, "like a powerful jungle cat." That passive-aggressive racist shit he'd ignored because she paid well, but what Beau did mind was when the actress had gotten out of hand.

One evening, wearing a white peignoir, the actress swept into her all-white living room. She'd shocked Beau by waving a huge scarlet dildo. "My love," Kitty Galina had chirruped, "let me do you."

Staring, Beau wondered if she was crazy. Not blinking, in her penthouse, on her white sofa, he'd sat motionless. Beau continued to stare as Kitty commanded him to lose his clothing. "Ah, yes, and turn over dahling." With her ever-present Stoli on the rocks nearby, she raised her glass. "Bottoms up!" She'd cheered like Beau would oblige.

He'd left. Yet he and Kitty had again appeared together at New York society events, but only after he'd told her, no more shenanigans. In her white stretch limo, she'd worn huge tortoiseshell shades. Staring away, she'd kitty-growled, "Sorry, dahling, you bring something out of me."

Beau, the formidable man, didn't know why he recalled such things, but he did know one thing. He would teach his kid a few life lessons. One was that there were perils and pitfalls. However, a person could rebound from most things. That, Uncle Brantley had taught him.

Beau told himself to forget memories as he exited the car door that was opened for him. He was ushered into the magnificent lobby of The Four Seasons. In The Garden Restaurant, so like an enchanted forest, he bent. At a table for two, he spoke with a silver-haired male. Chuckling, Beau bid Mr. Silver adieu.

Beau realized he loved the incredible buzz of the place. Vibrant electricity seemed to invisibly crackle in the air, despite the seemingly relaxed ambiance. As he strode on, he could nearly feel the sizzle of deals being brokered and alliances forged. Beneath a towering African acacia tree and flattering lighting, he leaned to kiss the powdered cheek of the ancient iconic actress he'd just thought of while riding over! Go figure. Moments later, managing to detangle himself from her claws and the cloud of strong fragrance ever about her, Beau gently squeezed red-tipped fingers. "Looking good, Kitten," he nodded and made her day.

In passing another table Beau shared a chinwag with a Manhattan real estate mogul. He'd met her twenty years back, long before she'd become the one to see. Leaving her and her guests, Beau realized. He had known the woman before she'd taken the helm of her family business, before she'd expanded that business exponentially, by selling New York.

Discreetly, Beau signed an autograph that had been quietly requested. Finally, at his own table, he kissed *her* cheek and noted the short glossy coif. "So Jah-YAY," he said, seating himself, "what's the word?"

Settling in across from his longtime agent, who wore a timeless taupe pantsuit and eye-catching jewelry, Beau listened. He also noted the time, just before two. That meant, after a Lyonnaise salad, seared Maine scallops, and sparkling water, he just might catch his first cousin.

Sure, he and the brown, petite powerhouse would speak of his career. He and his agent would speak of revising his artistic direction. However, Beau would not actually concentrate because he had heard 'rumblings.'

As the dynamo Jayé continued her spiel, Beau wondered. Had Kismet Staar's husband with the long locs come around? Or had the man totally about-faced? Word was: Lyle, his cousin's husband, was losing his marbles.

Chapter 30

BEAU navigated the Long Island Expressway and found himself wanting to call Jervais. Traversing the L.I.E., Beau recalled being able to talk about anything with the young dancer. Then all of that changed. Sadly, now, Beau and Jervais would never speak again. Knowing it made Beau sad. He was also cognizant of the need for someone with whom he could share. Beau wanted a relationship similar to the one he'd had with his dancer friend, although Beau and Jervais had never been involved. See? Beau thought as he drove; with *his* someone, he could share his last recollection of Jervais.

Beau had never mentioned it to a soul, not even Brett, but Beau had seen his dancer friend in the transportation hub at 42nd street. There, a person could catch any number of trains. There, he who had once been the most magnificent dancer had quickly moved. Jervais did so, despite the use of a walking stick.

A train had approached, drowning out Beau's calls with its screeching brakes. Yet Beau forced his way through disembarking passengers. He hurried past people pushing into crowded subway cars. Taller than most, Beau tried to glimpse his friend. There! Loping along, Jervais had switched directions. Dodging commuters, Beau strove to catch up. Racing down a dirty, much-used concrete path, he looked over the metal rail. Quickly Beau skirted a woman who held on so as not to tumble downward. With no such fear, Beau rushed along, recognizing Jervais' gait on the concrete below.

Sprinting downward, Beau hoped a train wouldn't come and sweep his friend away. When he reached the ramp's bottom, the tall young man saw other people, but no Jervais. So Beau dashed toward the lowest level. As he did, in the distance, he heard voices.

Leaning over the rail, Beau's heart raced because there was Jervais! Beau couldn't wait until they could talk and laugh—just catch up—since they hadn't seen one another in who knew when.

Treading further downward, Beau squinted. In the near dark, another man stood, with his back against a sooty tiled wall. He appeared scruffy, with gray stubble dotting his florid face. But where was Jervais? Beau looked. It seemed like most of those who'd been on the ramps, now waited on other platforms. Beau wondered if he'd missed his friend.

About to pivot, Beau stopped, and his heart pounded as he again eyed Scruffy. Average height, he did not appear clean. Beau watched as near-begrudgingly, Scruffy tossed money at someone. Then with horror tiptoeing up his spine, Beau saw Scruffy quickly undo his fly. No! Something within Beau yelled, as Jervais stepped out of the dimness. Somehow, Beau had known he would.

Beau watched Jervais drop down. Long and tall didn't want to see anymore. Still, he stared as Scruffy held his empurpled erection. Beau wanted to yell as Scruffy guided the bulbous head toward Jervais' mouth! Beau thought he would gag because Scruffy had no *business* with someone as gregarious, fun, and someone who had as much going for him as Jervais!

Beau could only gape as his friend worked Scruffy's throbbing member. The ex-dancer must have had a reason for what he was doing, this Beau told himself. Perhaps Jervais was in need, Beau mused—but that didn't make sense because Jervais *knew* he could come to Beau for anything. Beau wondered. Was his friend homeless now, or did he need cash? It hurt Beau to think about the countless reasons why Jervais could have been on his knees before that dirty man. One reason Beau didn't want to face. Perhaps, blowing men was Jervais' new gig.

Feeling sorely deflated, Beau didn't want to know why, but then again, he did. Stepping from the shadows, he authoritatively barked, "Alright, break it up!" He pulled his wallet, quickly flicked it open, then shut. "Vice!" he bellowed. "Looks like somebody's going to jail today."

It was some of the best spur-of-the-moment acting he'd done, Beau mused, as Scruffy yowled. "What for, officer?"

Beau spoke as the other man hastily zipped his pants, "For indecent exposure, first off." Beau caught Jervais' scowl and forgot Scruffy, who raced off, yelling, "Ya gotta catch me, first!"

Beau forgot Scruffy's stiff soles clattering on concrete. Beau only wanted to shake his friend, who wanted to shake him too.

Sounding petulant, Jervais pointed. "Look what you did!"

"What *I* did?" Beau retorted, "I saved you! That was revolting."

"Well, who asked yo' ass to stand around gawking at shit that don't concern you?"

"I know you're not upset—with *me*," Beau huffed and began to walk. Jervais hobbled along behind, having picked up his walking stick. "Vay, was that stupid stuff about money?" Beau asked, "because if you need something, you *know* I got you. I've told you. Y'ain't gotta do *this* shit."

"Bodacious," Jervais huffed and wiped his mouth, yet hobbling to keep up. "It's not about the money. Then again…it always is."

Beau turned before exiting the turnstile. "Then what is it—your high-profile sponsors not working out?"

"They're doing what they do," Jervais shot back. "And *I* was doing what *I* do—until *you*, Officer Petty Phony, broke up the party."

When they'd climbed concrete steps to blink in the warm afternoon sunlight, Beau pivoted. Over blaring Manhattan traffic, he asked, "*Why?*" Both people circumvented hordes headed for the train station stairs.

Attempting to keep up, Jervais answered, "Because I'll never go back. You remember when I got out of the hospital, what that was like."

Beau recalled the injury that had sidelined Jervais. He recalled that back then, Jervais found out he no longer had a home. Wanting to forget that rough patch, Beau suggested something to eat, "My treat."

As he and Jervais walked along in silence, Beau glanced over and noticed. In the late afternoon sunshine, Jervais appeared… *ill*. Dodging people, Beau noticed; Jervais' lips were swollen and unattractively wet. Jervais' skin lacked luster and appeared scaly. He had sores that oozed, even on his scalp, and the texture of his hair was different. Where it had once been thick and wavy, now it was super fine and sparse.

Beau experienced a type of *knowing* then, and inconspicuously, he eyed his friend. True, the dancer had never been a big man, but he was no longer diminutive, he was full-out frail. Then Beau inwardly acknowledged, Jervais was suffering from the disease he had long dreaded. AIDS. Jervais had always believed he would wind up with it.

Seated in a quiet corner of the elegant restaurant that Beau had chosen, the young actor ignored those who peered at his longtime friend. He did so, just like he'd faded others who had tried to ogle Jervais while they'd been on the street.

Beau listened then, with such disillusionment and hurt as his friend listed all he was suffering from. Beau remained quiet as Jervais detailed the loss of most of his sponsors. "They all turned tail and ran when I became visibly ill. I guess they fear for their lives now too," the shorter man quipped.

"Do you need help with anything?" Beau couldn't help but ask.

"No, Bodacious." Jervais shook his head. "You know I've always stacked my chips. By the way," the former dancer plainly stated, "what you saw earlier was me padding my coffers, so to speak."

As he drove the expressway, Beau recalled going to an ATM... He'd reimbursed Jervais for the lost 'tip' because Scruffy had dashed.

As he drove, the man, Beau, would never forget his friend's request.

"There *is* one thing I'm going to need, Bo-Dacious. If you'd just check on mom every now and again for me, I'd be eternally grateful."

These days, Beau still honored his friend's request. Every two weeks, he spoke with Ms. Lillie, whose hair had turned a beatific white. Beau liked that she was doing fine. He was also proud of the fact that Jervis had kept his end of their pinky swear. He had indeed set his mother up for life. Jervais had made it so that Ms. Lillie could send Barbara, who had once been little Bibi, to college. Beau was proud of Bibi, nearly as proud as both Ms. Lillie and his Aunt. Barbara had studied hard and she had become a pharmacist.

Still, Beau couldn't help but feel hurt. *His friend was gone.* Every so often, it hit him. It stung, especially when Beau simply needed to talk.

Actually, Beau realized while driving, he should have been on the phone with his cousin. However, he'd reached her earlier and she'd said it wasn't a good time. She'd promised to call later. She had also advised him not to worry. But she hadn't sounded right, so how was he not to worry or feel anxious? Hell, he wanted to know! What was going on in that house of hers? If Lyle was putting his hands on her...God help him.

As he drove, Beau strove for calm. He remembered that in years past, he would have had a cigarette, but he'd quit. When feeling anxious, in the past, he'd have done drugs. Sure, Beau often thought about doing so, because once an addict, always an addict, so said his twelve-step program. However, he had been clean for years, through sheer force of will. Therefore, Beau wasn't about to blow it now. Still, the truth was: today, he needed to speak with someone, somebody close, someone he liked, and trusted, as much or more than he'd liked and trusted Jervais.

Therefore, the actor called Saavion, the optician.

Chapter 31

BEFORE readying her children for school, Kismet knew she had to enter her large maple and cream kitchen. If for no other reason, she had to get her saucepan out of the trash, where Lyle had dumped it. Dreading what she might see, but knowing she wouldn't run into him because he had come and gone, she showered and dressed. Then while descending the stairs, she despised the churning emotions she felt.

Surveying her usually clean kitchen, she placed a hand over her mouth. What a mess! Kismet turned quickly, knowing that were she to remain any longer, her blood pressure would spike. Choosing to forgo running sudsy water, she forgot making sense of Lyle's mess. Angrily, with her fingertips, she dusted a hundred dollar bill from her kitchen countertop. She knew Lyle had left it when he'd scratched out the note that she crumpled. She didn't care to see anything he'd written. Yet one word jumped out. *Sorry*.

Yes, she thought as her boy twin bounded into the room where shafts of sunlight streamed. Lyle was sorry, a sorry excuse lately for a husband and father. Receiving the bill from her son, who retrieved it from the floor, Kismet poured him a glass of juice. Then despite the child's questions, she shooed him back upstairs. "Finish getting ready for school," she directed, on hold with the housekeeping service.

It wouldn't be sweet Gita with the accent, the man replied, but he would send someone. Back upstairs, Kismet offered the twins a surprise, "Only if you finish dressing quickly, with no fighting." Because she wouldn't fix breakfast that day, she found her older children. To Déja and Chance's palms, she pressed bills. "Today, my treat," she told them. They'd get the breakfast of their choosing at school.

Kismet's little male bookworm grinned. "Thanks, Momma!"

Lifting her daughter's face so that the slender girl could meet her eyes, Kismet noted the long hair pulled into a sleek, side ponytail. "You did a nice job," she said and unnecessarily smoothed the crown.

The brown girl smiled, something she didn't do a lot lately. Then Déja frowned. "Um, Mom, I saw the mess. I know Daddy did it after we cleaned the kitchen." The teenager appeared perplexed. "Why?"

"Because he's mean," Chance quickly put in, ever ready to defend his mother. "Momma was showing me homework, and Dad got mad because she cooked. He started pushing all our food into the garbage."

Déja's eyes were wide, and Kismet felt stunned. She thought she'd sent her son upstairs *before* Lyle had gotten stupid. She turned. "Chance, what makes you think that?"

"I don't think, I know. I was up here, peeking. To protect you."

"Oh, my precious boy…" Kismet held her son to her bosom. "Daddy wouldn't hurt me," she hoped, not as sure as she had once been.

From the glances that her son and daughter traded, neither were they.

"Well, we gotta go," Déja announced, heading downward.

"Love you," The Momma called. "Learn something. And no cussing."

The girl stopped on the bottom step. "Yep. Oh." She turned, "Soccer practice, Mom. Don't let Ms. Fannie forget. I need a ride home."

Kismet watched her son clunk down the wide hallway. In the twins' room, she aided sunny-faced Belize to put on her sweater. The Momma glanced through the second-floor window. She whispered a prayer for her boy and the changing girl who would ride separate buses.

Kismet spoke to Belize. "Okay, lil mama. Run downstairs. Drink your juice—it's on the table. Then get your backpack. Bonaire," The Momma addressed the boy. "Backpack. Then we'll have our surprise."

In her study, Kismet quickly dialed Beau, her eyes caressing her beloved Elizabeth Catlett painting. She didn't reach him. Grabbing her purse, Kismet checked the kid's rooms and turned out a light. Descending the stairs, she felt her baby—*Beau's* baby—stir within her. Absently, she rubbed her tummy and called, "In the car…"

Despite everything, the two who raced through the kitchen and into the garage made her smile. Backing onto their wide, tree-lined street, jubilantly, Kismet announced, "Babies, we're going to…McD's!"

"Yay-yay!" The children were ecstatic, "Ooh wee!" "Can I have French Fries?" "Before school?"

The Momma put her vehicle in drive, unaware that inside, her office phone rang. However, on her hands-free, she called Beau's assistant. "Hey Tatum, is Diddley around?"

"No, Ms. Kiss," the youngster from the Midwest replied. "I see that boss has a few meetings today—but I can have him call you…"

"Would you? Thanks, Tate." Disconnected, The Momma laughed because the twins were doing little upper body jigs within their seatbelts.

Loving their exuberance, Kismet suddenly vowed to allow no one to steal their joy, or hers. Not even their father, her husband.

She pulled up to golden arches and assisted the cute kids, smartly dressed, from her car. Crossing the busy parking lot, she caught small hands in her own. She slowed little legs down, yet she couldn't wait to drop them off at school. Passing shrubbery, she pulled on the door. Then the lighted menu, glossy food photos, and the inviting smell of coffee tantalized. Yet Kismet was aware, the moment the twins were fed, and in class, she would call her mother. While on her way to the doctor, she would again try her cousin, and Kismet would contact Valeria René—her other longtime confidante.

But most importantly, Kismet vowed, handling a laden tray as she got her kids seated, she would call her husband. Seating herself, she passed out food. As she did, she imagined speaking to Lyle about the mess he'd made, in the kitchen, and in their life.

Sipping tea, when she really wanted coffee, while the twins chattered happily away, Kismet knew she needed to initiate a challenging conversation. She would mention how ugly Lyle had acted because that, she could not let go.

Handing one of the twins a napkin and telling the other, "No baby, playtime will be later," Kismet knew something more. When she had said her piece to the man she'd married, she would wind up doing what she had since this ordeal began.

She would deal with the fallout.

Chapter 32

GINA wondered why she couldn't get Thomas Flint off her mind. Probably because she saw evidence of his handiwork everywhere in her home, her most private space.

She'd called and had hung up, twice. The third time, she'd left a message. She said she would allow Thomas to continue working for her, provided he kept doing a good job. She felt stupid afterward because why had she spoken like the snooty rich lady of the manor? What a joke. She should have kept her chunky self off the phone.

However, when Thomas called back, Gina felt ridiculously happy. When he appeared, she offered him hot tea. She'd waited a bit, though, because she hadn't wanted to appear to be hovering, although she was.

When Thomas entered her small kitchen for his break, she noticed him looking around. Then she blurted out—something she had to stop doing—that she wouldn't tolerate stealing. She said she'd make sure he wound up back in prison if he so much as took one of her CD's.

Unperturbed, Thomas chuckled. "I play music on my phone. But I've got tons of CD's, sweet, so I don't need yours. My b-brother bought my first ones. Hey," he said as an aside, "you can b-borrow some of mine."

Feeling stupid, Gina apologized. She really liked the big man and couldn't remember the last time she'd wanted a man in a man-woman way. Sure, men tried to push up; sure, they asked for her number. Some offered to take her out, probably because she had a round booty, round boobs, and an okay-looking round face. Her roundness was why her last name fit, *but* Regina Rounds did not want to be unfaithful...

As she took Thomas' empty cup, his gaze lingered. That made her *feel*. "Gina, you're a pretty a woman," he said after a while. "And that's good because I don't like girls. They're for boys, and I'm a man."

He sure was, Regina noted, as her eyes slowly slid over him. Quickly, she turned though because she didn't need big Thomas awakening things within her. They had long lain dormant, but he sure was a man.

IT arrived! It was fully assembled and had been dropped off by UPS that morning. Yet Mireya had to shower and head for The Kitten Heel Incorporated. She loved her job, and she loved the new offices too. The mail-order business that she'd co-founded with her partner Ann gave her such a sense of pride. Mireya loved discreetly supplying women with sex toys, G-spot finders, instructional videos, mood music, and other things.

Quickly, she ran her fingers over the box that sat in the small front hallway. The contents had become The Kitten Heel's newest offering. Mireya only wished she had time to drag the brown cardboard to her bedroom. There she would punch it open. Mireya wished there was time to get naked and try out The Sex Machine for herself, but that would have to wait. In her cheery new office, she had several meetings scheduled. Their current business suite was better than the first, the space that she and stout Ann had found back when Arlise had been a toddler.

In the shower, Mireya forgot the big, nearly unmarked box. Using a gel that her company carried, one that smelled of freesia and rain, Mireya thought of all she had to do before noon. However, tonight, or tomorrow, she would squirt Luv Liquid, another of The Kitten Heel's offerings, over her nether region and over the bulbous head of the Sex Machine's powerful penis. Then with Gypsy on her mind, she would lie back. Following the experience that would be pleasurable, Mireya knew; she would go online and rate the machine, for all their kitties and bigger pussies, The Kitten Heel's customers, to see.

Whoo-hoo! Being in business for one's self was so much fun!

RETURNED from her doctor's appointment, Kismet plodded through one work-related issue after another. She also vacillated between calling a locksmith and not. Seated beneath her women in red painting, she did not answer her cell as she worked. She glanced at it, though. Lyle, again.

Sometime later, Kismet's stomach growled, and she couldn't believe that soon, the day lady would appear. Then not long after, so would the twins, via their school bus. Since she wanted to be home when they arrived, Kismet ordered from the deli on Main, but not before noticing. Her husband had left a message. Again. She didn't want to deal with him just yet, so as she awaited her lunch delivery, she dialed her mother.

"Hey KissGirl," round, buxom Nell answered

"Hey, Mama. I called you this morning. Then I remembered you went to prayer. Anyway, you won't believe this…" The younger woman spoke of the prior evening's events. Careful not to embellish her story, she concluded by saying, "That's why, when I got back, I gave the cleaning lady Lyle's money as a tip."

"I'm sure she appreciated that. But hon, what will you do now?"

"I honestly don't know." Although she didn't say it, Kismet really wanted to have a rational, adult conversation with her husband. She wanted to get an understanding, even if they had to begin by going to counseling. Oh, and she wanted sex. Yet, she was embarrassed to admit those things, so she said, "Gotta go, Ma. The twins'll be here soon."

Nell clucked, "I'll be praying that you adults make right decisions."

The younger mother swallowed sudden tears. "Thanks, I need that."

Hopefully, one day soon, Kismet thought as she rang off, she could offer news that wasn't fraught with tension and dismay.

By the time her lunch was delivered, the twins were home. Full of chatter about their day, the kids tossed down backpacks, pulled off sweaters, and kicked-off shoes.

Seeing Kismet's full hands, Ms. Fannie herded the children up to change clothes. By the time The Momma had unpacked, Ms. Fannie and the little ones had returned for their snack. Yet they wanted to taste their mother's soup. They wanted a bit of buttered roll and a sip of her hot tea with lemon. Bonaire showed her a drawing, and Belize showed her a boo-boo—a paper cut. With them all over her, and Chance, the bigger boy joining the fray, Kismet nearly forgot the messages on her cell, those left by the children's father. Figuring he could wait, she assembled pots, olive oil, garlic, oregano, ground beef, tomatoes, and a baguette.

As she quickly prepared dinner, something she knew her kids would enjoy, again she asked herself. Did she really want her locks changed? She would then need new keys, a set for herself, one for Ms. Fannie, and a set for her mother. Would *Lyle* get a set? No. That would defeat the whole purpose of the change.

Kismet turned on the TV as Ms. Fannie popped up the street to retrieve the soccer girl, Déja. Again, Kismet's cell rang, but later, The Momma vowed, that was when she would deal with Lyle. Right now, she concentrated on her kids and their favorite, spaghetti & meatballs.

HER knotted stomach let her know she really didn't want to speak with him; not after that last message he'd left. Yet since the kids were down, she called. Seated in her clean kitchen, she sounded tense. "If you want to destroy things, you don't want to be here, Lyle. If you want to act like you did the other night," she advised, "then keep staying away."

Kismet didn't listen to the stream of obscenities. She simply inhaled and exhaled. She made up her mind, too, because he was scaring her.

She *would* have the locks changed because she no longer knew Lyle. If he pushed, she would take *other* measures, like barring him from the kid's schools. She didn't want to go as far as involving the police though. She would never call them if there was another option. When she heard nothing but angry breathing, she made herself sound calm, although she was far from it. "I won't change my mind, Lyle. We need this break. *You* need it most of all; maybe it'll help clear your head."

She found that she could listen to him too, and Kismet felt surprisingly calm as she ran a hand over her rounded belly. In response, she offered the truth. "I really don't want things this way. I want you home. The kids do too, but you're different, now..." She spoke softly, as images of what they had once been, what they had once shared, flashed through her mind. "I want you, but I want the you that you used to be."

She couldn't tell Lyle that just hearing his voice, when he wasn't yelling, made her want. Kismet couldn't say that her nipples were pearling because Lyle had agreed to hear her out. Although she wanted to say that she was starting to feel normal in this pregnancy, and like she needed him, pushing in and pulling out of her, Kismet could not. They both knew she was sexually ravenous when she carried, but to *say* so would give Lyle too much power, when he needed to straighten up. So Kismet forgot getting naked and freaky with her husband. She forgot open-mouth kisses before he sucked on her tits and tongued her *there*.

Instead, she answered his cantankerous question. "I don't know where you'll go Lyle, but you've obviously been going somewhere. I mean, you keep leaving the kids and me—so go wherever you been going..."

She hoped it wasn't to another woman; Kismet hoped he wasn't pleasuring someone else, but she had to remain firm. And she remembered, with his drinking, firm he was not. Flaccid was more like it.

"Yo," Lyle yelled, again, when Kismet had thought they'd been making progress. "Who the fuck are *you*, Kiss, to make all the rules?!"

Calmly she retorted, powerful in her role, the one for which she had been born. "*I – am – The Momma.*" It was that simple.

"Well, I'm the daddy!"

Kismet sounded unfazed. "Then start acting like it."

"How can I, when you're telling me not to come home?"

"I didn't tell you not to come home," the mother of four retorted. Unwilling to get into a war of words, she simply stated, "I said let's take a break. I said it because as *The Momma*, I don't want my babies privy to our shit. Whatever bad feelings you harbor, are between you and me. The kids shouldn't have to suffer because of us, because of our mess."

"You started this!" Lyle accusatorily yelled, "Ever since you got pregnant, you've acted like you don't need a man. Yeah, like when we first met! Make me sick; with your cousin and his money backing you, you're big momma—and I'm what?" Lyle audibly frothed, "the errant child?"

"Does that shoe fit?" Kismet softly inquired. Then before her blood pressure could spike, she said, "This won't work. Just stay away, Lyle."

Over his ranting, she called, "I'm hanging up now…"

Hours later, with him yet blowing up her cell, Kismet used the house phone to call Ms. Fannie. "I just wanted you to know. I've had the locks changed." It had cost a pretty penny, with it being late and all. Forgetting money, Kismet advised, "Tomorrow before you come, call the house, and I'll let you in. Then please, Ms. Fannie, remind me to give you your new keys."

In the quiet, Kismet Staar sat. She rubbed her swollen belly. When she finally exited her lovely maple and cream kitchen with its splashes of Granny Smith Apple-green, she had one wish. Entering her bedroom, she sincerely wished she yet shared that room, and the rest, in all ways, with her husband—the man she'd once thought she knew.

Chapter 33

DAYS later, Beau was on a return flight from California. He, Gypsy—the man that Mireya was crushing on—and backup drummer, Kendu, had checked out hot new tracks. The music would be used for Infusion's upcoming EP. Having been thusly occupied, Beau had no idea what his cousin was going through. He only knew they were missing each other, and he didn't like it. Heck, she was late into her fifth month. That meant, at her week 22 checkup, which he planned to attend, there would be an anatomy scan. They could learn the baby's gender –if they desired. Together, the cousins would get to hear the baby's *heartbeat*. Kismet had heard it before, but for Beau, it would be the first time!

The producer had read that his little one had begun to grow hair, brows, and white eyelashes at this stage. Now a protective coating, called the vernix, covered the fetus. Therefore, Beau decided. He wasn't going to wait until exiting The Ten, considered the Bentley of Cessna aircraft, with its black leather seats and multi-media gallery. He wouldn't wait until his feet hit the tarmac. He would call his cousin now.

But he could hardly speak with her these days because of her husband, even though the cousins had so much to discuss. Beau felt jumbled. Sure, Kismet was married, but *he*, her first cousin, was family. Heck, Beau was the one who had indirectly hooked up Kismet and Lyle. Lyle needed to remember that and be grateful and quit being a prick.

Holding his phone, Beau pondered something. He'd liked it better when Kismet had an outside office. Beau didn't much care for her new set-up. Sure, the IT company allowed her to work from home. However, for Beau, it wasn't panning out. When Kiss had the other office, they'd spoken freely. Nowadays, though, it seemed Lyle infringed on the cousin's time. To Beau, it felt like Lyle spent fewer hours in his own leased space and way too much time hanging about, hounding his wife.

It wasn't like Beau often called his cousin after dark, Beau further mused. The truth was, Kismet had different time constraints now due to her husband and family. Beau realized that he nor Kiss were the same carefree young people they had once been. It was the same for nearly everyone he knew. That was the reason Beau didn't call his aunt at all hours. Nell was married. Sure, she *said* it was okay, and the Deacon was nice enough, but what man wanted another man monopolizing his wife, even if she was seventy-something? For that reason, Beau didn't often ring Farai. Firstly, Uncle Brantley's daughter, the publishing titan, could be in Fiji on any given day. If not, she rendezvoused with her diplomat husband or chased her grown son Brosnan, or the younger Entebbe.

Beau thought as his plane taxied down the runway; all those were reasons why *he* needed somebody. He needed someone with whom *he* could speak, whenever. *He* needed to be *the most important person* in someone's life and vice versa. He wanted a life partner.

Unbuckling himself, Beau realized those things and more were why he had been pondering marriage for a while now… He had someone in mind, but he didn't want to be a pest. Beau also had so much going on that he had to wonder, if he truly was ready to commit.

All those things the actor pondered as he descended the Cessna's short flight of steps. With wind crazily blowing and his super-soft leather jacket ballooning, he turned. With an embrace for each young brotha, he told Gypsy and Kendu he would see them soon. Then accompanied by Boulder, his bodyguard, Beau strode toward one of two waiting cars.

Carrying his designer duffle, the piece he never let anyone else handle, Beau wished he could call Jervais, the tiny dancer. Man, did Beau miss the slim dark-skinned man who'd progressed to walking with two canes. Beau missed Jervais terribly because nothing he could have told the dancer would have shocked Jervais. All that was going on, Beau could have discussed with Jervais, thereby unburdening himself. Beau would not have feared either, ever hearing his words again from anyone else. Superb Vay had been Beau's vault, and vice versa.

Just thinking about the dancer brought a smile to Beau's face and tears to his heart. So he pushed Vay, his first friend, from mind.

"Diego." Beau nodded as his longtime chauffeur opened a rear automobile door. "How's Melinda? And Diego Jr., and Juan? Good."

When Beau slid into the plush warm interior, he called. The mocha-brown IndiAfricAmerican woman answered. Without preamble, he said, "It finally looks like Lyle's come between us."

"Hello to you too, Diddley," Valeria René chirped. With her youngest on her hip, she announced, "Giada says hey."

Beau cooed at the one-year-old, "Hey Gigi. How's uncle's baby?"

"She's fine," Beau's onetime roommate replied.

Aware that within weeks she would become a mother again, for the fourth and last time—so she said—Beau asked, "How're you feeling?"

"Okay, just ready to go in. Now, what's happening with you 'n Kiss?"

Beau sighed and admitted he hadn't spoken with his cousin. "Not since last week. I called the office, but she was finalizing some deal—"

"Yeah," Valeria interjected. "I heard about that."

"Her assistant said Kiss would call me, but I ain't heard a thing."

Ignoring toddler chatter, Valeria suggested, "Call the house."

"*He* answers," Beau dryly stated.

"Oh. Okay. Well, I don't think her hubby will, not this week…"

When Beau remained silent, his long-ago roommate asked a question. "Diddley, you don't think Lyle is putting undue stress on Kiss, do you?"

"I do," Beau spoke plainly. "He's never liked the idea of her carrying another man's baby. Dude won't even speak to me now. He acts like I twisted Kiss' arm and forced her to do this—when *she* suggested it. Kiss made the first appointment. She made demands and counter demands."

"To which you agreed. Mostly," Valeria interpolated.

"I did." Beau acknowledged, "But that's how we flow because Kiss is never unreasonable." In the moving car, with Boulder beside him, Beau leaned back. "Val, you spoke to her lately?"

"No. Not for a few days, but in time," Valeria predicted,

"No doubt," Beau acknowledged before revealing, "I just want to have a real, honest conversation with her, like we used to. You know?"

"I know, honey, and you will, maybe at her doctor's appointment."

Beau sighed because, for as long as he could remember, Valeria René had been soothing and encouraging. She was a jewel. Switching topics, Beau admitted, "I'm amazed I caught you."

Miz More Family than Friend chuckled. "I'm always around."

"You're always around *Fabian*," Beau pointed out.

"Well, he *is* my husband."

"Matter of fact, I'm surprised you're not beneath or on top of him."

"Oh, I'll get onto sexy chocolate, but right now, I'm fixing dinner."

Beau laughed. "Too much information, mama, but I guess I'll be the same way—when I'm married because you know my appetite…"

Valeria sounded stunned. "So, you're thinking about doing it!" Her grin was audible. "Diddley, you'll love the old ball & chain. I promise you—sex 'n all things considered. Just make sure you and your mate want similar things. Go in like you mean to be in, so you can stay in."

Beau said he would take Valeria's late grandmother's advice, if he got to jump the broom. "Hang on, Val, you just gave me an idea." Beau pressed a button which allowed him to quickly speak to his driver. "Diego…" Beau muted his call. Moments later, he said, "Val, gotta go."

Dialing another, Beau confirmed an unscheduled stop. Again leaning comfortably back, he pondered his friend's words. *He would love the old ball & chain.* Beau sure hoped so because the truth was: he really wanted someone for himself, someone with whom he was compatible in many ways. In the last decade, that had become paramount, as his sexual voracity had waned. Well, rather, it had changed. That change, Beau believed, had something to do with *Sandal*, the red-haired greed-monger.

AT a circle jerk, Beau met a slender, freckled-faced male…Beau had been sprawled in a friend's basement in the early nineties at an all-male puff-puff party. Feeling relaxed, late that Friday evening, Beau noticed someone starting the VCR. When the hot horny guys on the TV screen commenced their screw session, the real party began.

Audibly, the young man on Beau's left breathed. That man also unzipped his jeans and began to fondle himself. Before Beau knew it, Unzipped wound up nude, writhing, and erotically moaning as he manipulated his genitalia.

Fondling his own self, Beau noticed the room's other occupants, all in varying degrees of undress. Then one slim young male with blazing red hair stood. This light-skinned, freckle-faced tenderoni began to dance. While gyrating and pivoting, Red discarded clothing, and those watching began to cheer. "Yeeeah!" someone shouted. "Do that thang!"

Watching red hair, who was nude, Beau became ravenous. Thus, he stood and danced with Red, whose name he later found out was Sandal.

While yet in the rear of the comfortably warm touring sedan, Beau recalled that evening, and others like it. He also realized, Sandal should have more aptly been called *Scandal*. Beau had thought it the first time Sandal dropped to his knees to take Beau's hardened member into his pouty mouth. Beau hadn't even known the boy-man then. Beau had thought the same thing ever afterward. Beau forgot that before Sandal, he had never had anyone draw the actual cum from his dick. Beau forgot that while he'd shivered with pleasure, a big fellow elbowed him aside. Big then worked his way into Sandal's 'good graces.' Feeling delectably drained, Beau slumped and realized he was hooked. Back then, though,

Beau had not comprehended that he hadn't been hooked on Sandal, per sé, but on the feel-good that red-haired Sandal provided.

However, Sandal became clingy because Red wanted a life different from the one shared with his man, a forklift driver. The new life, Sandal wanted Beau, the hot young actor, to give him. Therefore, considering himself a power bottom, his greatest asset, Sandal forgot what he had once been told; that he should have had a vagina for all the use his penis got. Sandal focused on the fact that receiving was what he did best. Thus, he allowed Beau to give it to him in any orifice that Beau chose...until things between them got hairy.

Then Beau learned a hard two-fold lesson. One, he had to avoid circle jerks or any activity that offered the propensity for him to lose his mind. And two, he, the rising star, could not afford to become involved with anyone who did not have as much to lose as he did.

That was the reason for the unscheduled detour today. Beau wanted a quick in-person word with Dan. The lawyer knew all there was to know about pre-nups and the like.

Grateful that he was no longer in the past where he'd had the hardest time ridding himself of Sandal, the red-headed queen, Beau exited his hired car, but not before informing his driver that he would spend perhaps an hour inside the glass and steel building.

Striding fast, due to icy air, Beau fathomed that due to long-ago experiences, now, he often preferred to pump himself, by himself.

In the mirrored elevator, as he and Boulder ascended, Beau realized something more. Self-gratification was something he would still practice even when he was married. That was, Beau mused as he strode into the art deco lobby of his lawyer's office, *if* he ever really did take the plunge.

Chapter 34

SHE wondered if she was stupid for letting him back in. If he hadn't sounded calm, saying he needed her and the kids, she'd have refused. No, that was a lie. He was her husband, and he *had been* the best, back before this little ordeal, the tangle *she'd* gotten them into. When she took an honest look at their lives, she saw that she was the one who'd started this downward spiral. However, had she to do it all over again, she wouldn't change a thing because something within compelled her to carry this baby for Beau. Therefore, armed with that knowledge, Kismet attempted to be more sensitive, to see things from Lyle's point of view. Kismet saw that he wasn't entirely wrong. As the man of the house, Lyle had a right to feel as though her cousin had usurped his power. Truthfully, what man wanted another man paying for things in his household, when he was capable, and when he'd been happy to do so?

As an island man, Lyle was proud. He had strict beliefs about what a man was supposed to be and do. Therefore, feeling stripped, he'd lashed out. He had even said he felt less like the man —Kismet Staar's man. When she remembered that, Kismet had called and asked if Lyle still wanted in. He'd replied by grumbling that he wasn't the one who'd changed. Then ignoring the jibe, Kismet told her husband come home.

When Lyle was in their bedroom, removing clothing from the gym bag he kept at work, his wife saw the ticket. Forgetting it, she remembered that after putting the kids to bed, she'd showered. Watching Lyle walk, nude, into the master bath, Kismet noticed stirrings within herself. Leaning against the arched doorframe, she watched Lyle lather up. Hungrily her eyes traipsed over his dark, muscular body. Even as a little voice in her head said they needed to talk about Lyle's drinking, she anticipated having him. The voice of her conscience said Lyle needed enrollment in some program. It would offer the help he could not get on his own. Conscience said the man needed to speak with his kids, too, to ease their break-up fears. Yeah, yeah, all of that would have to wait; Kismet clapped back as she ran a hand over her nearly transparent gown. First, she needed her fill of what she hadn't had in far too long.

When Lyle exited the shower, like magnets, he and Kismet were swiftly drawn together. Looking down at her breasts, so large and heavy, he slipped her nightgown up and over her head. Lyle suckled, running his hands over and over his wife. She was carrying high, he noticed, but *that* he didn't touch. When Lyle kissed her lips, Kismet tasted mouthwash, but no liquor underlying. That fact alone made her want more, and so she said. Opening her mouth beneath his, she guided her husband's hands down her open body.

Without words, Lyle dropped to his knees. Moist and warm, she wanted him. Aware, within seconds, the man had his wife staggering. He used large fingers and his tongue to bring her up. Then, laying her down, he repeatedly filled her, sure to hit her sweet spot. He bent her over too and showed her how much he wanted her that way. Lyle pulled Kismet atop him at one point and allowed her, slick and swollen, to set the pace. In the moonlight, she was beautiful, passionately riding him with her lips parted, his curvaceous and large-hearted empress. Using his rod, with each thrust and parry, and with kisses and caresses, Lyle tried to tell Kismet how he felt because words were less his forte.

It became a night to remember.

IN the morning, Lyle told Kismet to sleep a while longer; he would get the munchkins up and ready. Snuggling back into warmth and softness, she smiled. That was some of what she missed when Lyle wasn't himself nor present. Lyle made coffee for Kismet. Then he left, taking his gym bag.

Noticing, she wondered if he'd re-packed it and was taking it back to the office, probably for the next episode. Remembering they hadn't talked, she sipped tea, no coffee until after delivery. Pensive, she was glad, in a way, that she hadn't handed over new keys. Still, she let herself reminisce on their night together, on the way Lyle had touched her, and how he had known just how to please. He had been so gentle, so careful of her pregnancy, yet when asked, he had given her so much more.

In the quiet house, Kismet began the routine of her day and noticed the ticket. She had seen it the night before, but at the time, she hadn't realized. It was a DUI. Kismet stared at the *drunk* driving issue. The date was *that* night; when he'd ruined dinner. Thinking back, she remembered, Lyle had left the house. What Kismet had not known at the time was that her man had done so while inebriated. Therefore, she surmised, when she'd gone upstairs after his little food stunt, Lyle had drank, excessively. Then he'd gotten into one of their vehicles.

What if he had gotten into an accident, or God forbid, what if he'd hit someone and wound up charged with vehicular manslaughter? What if it hadn't been just a ticket? What if he'd wrapped himself around a tree, a pole, or worse? Pondering numerous scenarios, Kismet became angry, when moments before, she'd been floating. Now reality was back, and it was a bitch. She couldn't stop herself. She called his office.

Lyle sounded happy to hear from his wife, for a change, until she started in. "Kiss, you sound like a shrew," he said, adding he didn't need her mess early in the morning.

"Lyle, you could have been killed, or maybe maimed somebody else."

"But I wasn't Kiss, and I didn't."

She asked was that all he had to say for himself.

He reminded her, "Although you are, as you so readily say, The Momma, you ain't *mine*. Quit talking to me like I'm one of your kids."

"I should hope I'm not ya mama," she retorted, "Not with the way you screwed me last night. You bent me over, opened me, and—"

"I *screwed* you?" Lyle growled, his island accent apparent. "I take offense to that," the man retorted. "Kiss, you wanted me—your husband, your man, or so you caused me to think. I *made love* to you—even though I kept thinking about that other man's baby in your belly!"

Kismet felt like Lyle had struck her. Without a word, she disconnected. This was what she got, she told herself, for caring.

Later he texted. *M sorry*.

Tears rolled down as she replied, *Me 2*. As she worked, she wondered how had they gotten *here*? Never before had either of them been so testy. Yet nowadays, everything one of them said or did got on the other's nerves. Was it her fault? Could they get past this? Kismet wondered. Would things change, she also wondered, when she had the baby and gave it to Beau?

When Lyle no longer had to see evidence of her 'betrayal' each time he looked at her, would he again become okay?

Suddenly Kismet realized, the big question was: would *she*?

Chapter 35

HE sat in a booth in the Long Island trattoria that he, Kiss, Val, Mireya, and Brett frequented. Smelling espresso and other delicious offerings, Beau pondered his drummer and the doughy woman who wore glasses. The band leader wondered why she, an obvious church girl, showed up to the band's gigs, alone. Doughy Mary should have been in service, not out stompin' wit da hellions. She should never have been seen in any of the clubs at which Infusion played.

Beau forgot the dough girl and that later in the evening, he and his band would meet to rehearse and discuss a series of upcoming events. Yet Beau recalled what Gypsy had told him.

The woman, whose face was closed-looking—as though she was hiding something—was dogmatic and pushy. Gypsy, whom Beau often thought of as a younger brother, had also said the dough girl quoted the bible whenever she spoke.

Well, if she was so much holier than others, Beau mused, why did she follow the band around, tenaciously chasing Infusion's super-bad drummer? Was Mary trying to convert Gypsy? Beau scowled because, more likely, the woman was trying to scare up a husband. She probably thought it necessary, since, in the little church at which Gypsy played, there were only a handful of men. Most were old, married, or gay.

As he sat waiting for Mireya, Beau thought about the younger man with the thickly toned arms, stupendous stamina, and a massive following. Brown, laid-back, bald, and good-looking, women thought Gypsy was a catch. Lord knew he could carry the beat all night long. Beau didn't know how Gypsy did it. Still, to save his drummer from burn out, Beau had hired a kid from his old gym, Sal & Lu's. Now, streetwise Kendu was Gypsy's backup, and Kendu was good too.

Noticing jeans-clad Mireya, Beau promised himself that at the next band rehearsal, he would ask young Kendu for a favor...

"Hey, Reya," Beau said, glad she had finally appeared. Looking wind-blown, glossy-haired, and healthy, in a burgundy cardigan with a satin bow beneath her formidable bazooms, Beau's friend turned heads.

Forgetting that and that there were very few things he kept from Mireya, Beau nixed the pleasantries. Jumping right in, he announced, "I don't like Gypsy's white-wearing groupie being around so much."

"I don't either," shapely, cinnamon-skinned Mireya acknowledged. "I told you she followed my car the night Gypsy had no heat."

"Yeah. The night you used *me* as an alibi. How'd that work out?"

Mireya ordered her favorite, a drink comprised of vanilla-infused vodka, coffee liqueur, and Frangelico. When their server left, she hissed. "We're not to speak of that, ever. But," she added, "you puzzle me."

Beau appeared quizzical. "Me? Why?"

"Yes, *you*. You usually don't have a problem with hangers-on."

"Actually, I do," Beau admitted. "I just don't show it, but with this woman, there's more." He squinted, "There's something about her..."

"You can't quite put your finger on," Mireya supplied. "I know."

Beau divulged that he'd mentioned it to his drummer friend. "Actually, I've warned Gyp several times, but you know how he is—"

"Too easy-going," Mireya interjected. "I said something, too."

As he sampled crispy, aged Provolone with tomato, cracked pepper, and oregano, Beau barked with laughter. "What did Gyp say?"

"Oh, B, Gypsy said that girl goes to his church. He sees her every week; blah, blah, but since he slept with her, he can't get rid of her."

Beau forgot the woman who gave him the creeps to say, "Reya, I know you wanted to discuss ideas you have for your business—"

She nodded, enjoying Gnocchi. "Thanks for ordering this," fluffy potato pillows, tomato cream, and fresh gooey mozzarella. "Ann and I have meetings soon with potential new investors." The Kitten Heel was expanding at an alarming rate, in part due to their newest offering, the unparalleled Sex Machine, which busy Mireya had yet to try out.

"Well, before you *interrupted* me," Beau stated, "I was about to say I want you to speak with someone I consult. This brotha's an MBA. He knows his stuff, and his time don't come cheap, but I'll hook you up."

Mireya nearly fell off her high-heeled boots trying to get at Beau. With her arms about him, she kissed him. "Ann will be so thrilled!"

"Yeah, and I'll be thrilled too," Beau stated, pretending to hold his friend off, "if you'd stop trying to get that lip goo all over my face."

"That's exactly what it's called! The Kitten Heel carries it."

"Yeah? Well, I don't want any."

As Beau ate, Mireya again mentioned the woman in white. "I hate to keep on with this, but I feel like this Mary is just waiting or planning."

"I feel that that way about the *nurse* that's attempting to get her hooks into my *brother*." Although he didn't say it aloud, Beau felt more strongly about the Gina situation than he did about the Mary mess.

"Have Nurse Ratchet checked out then," Mireya suggested, "but back to Gypsy. I reminded him that he can't lavish attention on every woman. Still, with his and my history, he probably ignored that advice, from me."

"Well, a few weeks ago, he couldn't too easily ignore me."

Beau divulged that after the first set at a club down in The Village, he had seen Gypsy, tracked by Mary. Beau pulled his drummer aside. "I warned Gyp that his mojo just might make some women crazy."

Viewing Beau as a wise, concerned, older family member, Gypsy had nodded and said, "Thanks, Pops. Good lookin' out."

"Even though Gyp was grateful for the advice," Beau told Mireya, "I can't keep lecturing him. He's a grown man. Still..." Beau mentioned the other night, at a different club. "I know I came off a bit stern, but we were in *Florida*, The Keys, for crying out loud, and who shows up?"

Mireya felt a flash of anger. "Mary?"

"Yes, and seeing her backstage, I lost it. I had to tell Gyp that although she looks like a woman, with that puffy body, she's proving she's still a girl, in her head, and an unstable one. I told Gyp that infatuated girls can be dangerous when they believe there's more."

Beau explained to Mireya that Gypsy had admitted he didn't know what to do. Beau did *not* mention that Gypsy also revealed he'd banged Mary. The man swore it was one time. However, Gypsy said, since he had no car, the woman often offered him a ride home after church. "Reya, Gyp said that woman's not his style."

Mireya offered what Beau was thinking, "But he stuck her."

"I know." Beau nodded. "It's done, so I told Gyp to move on, and don't do it again."

Although Beau was unaware, Gypsy had been stunned because Beau seemed affable with nearly everyone. Sure, Beau was a big star, and people thronged him everywhere he went, but Beau wasn't just another pretty face and buff bod. Beau could sing his behind off, and he was huge on many levels. Still, Beau wasn't full of himself like other celebrities for whom Gypsy had worked. Beau didn't march around wielding 'the ax,' threatening to fire people at will. Gypsy guessed all of those were the reasons he'd been surprised to hear Beau say he didn't like someone. Mary. "But she *is* sickening," Gypsy had admitted.

"I'll bet she is," the older Beau had nodded, "and I'll bet she keeps a big ole bible beside her bed. Bet she read it right after you banged the shit outta her. She probably held it while repenting for getting laid." Disgusted, Beau had shaken his head. "Stay away from her, bruh."

Doubled over with laughter, Gypsy gasped out the truth. "Pops...you hit the nail on the head!"

Those things Beau kept to himself, but he did tell Mireya that his stage manager had nodded as crowd noises grew louder. Then Beau had said, "Come on, Gyp, two minutes till show." Backstage, in the dimness, Beau had headed into the wings. He didn't tell Mireya that Gypsy had said, "Boss, I don't know how you knew about the all the hollering out and praying, after the deed."

Beau knew because he knew people. He had lived long enough that he had seen a few things. With an exaggerated shudder, Beau dabbed his perspiring face with a towel. "Forget it, *and* her." Beau allowed Tatum, his assistant, to take the terrycloth. Then the tall, buff, beautiful bandleader and Gypsy strode back on stage where guitar licks sizzled and screamed.

Beau did tell Mireya that under swirling lights, he'd called out, over passionate cries from the audience, "Just do me one thing, Gyp; lose that chick! She's bad for the band's image!"

Hearing those things, Mireya chuckled. Afterward, in all seriousness, she asked Beau to have his people check Mary out. "Please, B," Mireya admonished, "let them check Gypsy's stalker at the same time that you have that nurse checked out. You know, the one who's turning your brother's head."

Chapter 36

IN his SUV, Lyle sat, outside his home. He recalled that perhaps fifteen minutes ago, beneath the star-pierced sky, he'd walked around the perimeter of his house. Strapped, he made sure all was well. He'd wanted to enter his home, but he couldn't. His keys didn't work. Not surprising, he thought while laying his gun aside. Lyle's wife had changed the locks. Sure, he could have called, and she'd have let him in because he had to admit, Kismet wasn't unreasonable. Still, this was not how things were supposed to be. He was supposed to come and go freely, like before.

Sure, Lyle could have been angry. He could have been outside, beating the door down. However, that would only scare his kids. It would reinforce the notions too, the ones that had already crept into their heads, that he was scary, and that they really didn't know him. It was bad enough that he could see those thoughts skittering over his wife's face, but to have his kids believing the same thing? Nah, he couldn't do it. So the dad sat outside the gabled home, with its square front and sloped roof. He counted the windows, five across on top. There were four across on the bottom, with two on either side of the door in the middle.

How Lyle longed to be inside that house. Inside, he would have ascended the broad staircase. On the second floor, in the bedroom that he and his wife had once willingly shared, he would remove his clothes. After a shower, he imagined, he and his big sexy woman would indulge in what had been a constant for them, before, skanky sex.

Just thinking about it made Lyle's hardened penis throb and crave the haven of his wife's body. Knowing he'd been barred, though, he sat and thought. If he was inside, and his wife didn't want to mess around, he could live with that. Lyle just loved being near Kismet, in the home they'd created—well, in the home that *she'd* created.

When he was in the big old comfortable house, with her stamp everywhere, Lyle liked knowing his family was near. Now the fam was near one another, and *he* was out of doors, like some mangy mutt.

Lyle sighed and realized…he wanted more. Sure, he wanted to enter the house that he helped pay for, and he wanted to enter his wife. However, Lyle didn't just want inside Kismet's body. He didn't want to simply fuck with her anymore. Lyle had grown tired of the mind games he'd employed to always make her feel she was wrong. Now he wanted inside her head and her heart, once more. Lyle wanted discussions, laughter, and planning together. He wanted life as it had been.

Sure, Kiss was upset because of the ticket, but he wasn't. Although she didn't know it, for him, receiving it had been a much-needed wake-up call. Lyle wanted to tell Kiss that, and so many other things, but all he and she could manage these days were the kids and fighting.

True, Lyle felt like Kiss had picked a fight when she'd found out about his drunk driving, and she said he'd misunderstood her. On the phone, she'd said she was concerned. Then snarky, he'd claimed her worry for those he might have killed was admirable. She'd spat, "You don't have to be sarcastic." Then she'd begun to tear up; he'd heard it in her voice. That had been when she had brokenly admitted she was tired. She said her husband was wreaking havoc with her emotions, worse than the baby inside her ever could have. Kismet also revealed something Lyle couldn't forget. She worried about *him*.

"With you out there, driving around inebriated, Lyle," she had said into the phone, "anything could have happened—to *you*. Then who would I have had?"

Those words alone had let him know she still cared; maybe not like she once had, but on some level, Kismet yet felt for him. She cared about more than just sex with him. It was why Lyle vowed to do better. Softly he'd said, "Go to sleep, Momma," even though he'd wanted to go to her, but he couldn't. Not with the scent of his mistress on him. Looking up at the five windows on the second floor, he despised drink, the one with whom he never should have flirted. Drink had changed him, but not for the better. Now all he wanted was to get the pisser off his back.

Beneath the canopy of darkness, he sat staring at his home. That was when Lyle saw his wife. She was visible through the second-floor hallway window. Above the door, she passed, looking like a sexy, white-wearing apparition. A pregnant one. Still, to him, she was so lush and lovely. Lyle noticed his hand then. He was reaching for her, involuntarily. Lowering it, he started his SUV. Again Lyle vowed. He *would* become a better man. Although his wife didn't know it, he had already set the wheels in motion, literally.

April Alisa Marquette
157

Chapter 37

AT 10 a.m., cruising along, Beau was on the phone. He explained to the retiree from juvenile corrections that he had to make an appearance in the early afternoon. "But, I want to see you," without his entourage.

Delighted, she said, "Wonderful! Come on by, sugar."

He told her not to go to any trouble. He'd said so because he knew her; she was all southern hospitality. It had been bred in her bones.

The Louisiana girl met him at the door. Seventy-something, she turned her face up, ready to receive his kiss. "Hello, Puppy."

He folded himself into her outstretched chubby arms. He inhaled the lavender, and today there was a hint of spearmint, so clean and fresh.

"We heard the baby's heartbeat!" he blurted with a grin.

Nell closed her door. "I heard about that, and about the hepatitis B testing that KissGirl had a while back. Seems to be standard, nowadays."

"Yep, if the mother is infected, her baby can be treated."

"Thankfully, we don't have that worry. So Puppy, what'd you think?"

Beau followed his Aunt past her galley kitchen and into the living room. "It was so fast—the heartbeat, I mean." He blew out a breath. "Lemme start over. In the waiting room, I was nervous. Then they called Kiss. Later, they called me. They used a Doppler, the sonogram thingy, and A'nt Nell, my baby's heartbeat was so loud and strong until I didn't know what to feel. I mean, we're really doing this! I'm gonna be a dad."

Nell patted the sofa cushion beside her. "Yes, Puppy, you are."

Beau had to ask, "Were you this excited when you expected Kiss?"

"I sure was," Nell smiled. "We didn't have today's technology, but I know how you feel. You do feel like it's real, now, right sugar?"

Beau squeezed his Aunt's hand. "I sure do."

Nell felt a burst of love for the man who appeared awestruck. Pulling herself up, she said, "I'm gonna get you something to drink."

"Didn't I say no fussing?" Beau reminded the woman who handled a tray. She ignored him, and he eyed her cute little outfit. Nell wore khaki pants and a sweater, the color of a golden sunset. Wearing whimsical socks, at her neck, she wore a scarf with fall colors as vibrant as she. Receiving a glass of apple juice, Beau heard Mahalia Jackson singing *My*

God Is Real. It sounded old-timey, softly playing in the background. Still, it made Beau feel good and took him back to his kid days– Not the bad part, but to the day he'd first walked into the family church. Beau's Aunt and brawny Uncle had been on both sides of him, holding his hands. His cousins had been there, and he'd gazed up. Sunlight had streamed through stained glass windows. Beau had marveled at the warm church and its timeless beauty. Within Mount Hebron's hallowed halls, he'd been dazed by the serenity. He'd also been transfixed by the beauty of the large African Methodist Episcopal church's ordered worship service. And for the first time in his young life, Beau had felt safe.

That memory Beau shared with his Aunt as he gazed at her rose-colored nails. Then he looked up, into her eyes. "I love that some things about you never change." That sense of stability, Beau promised, along with other family traditions, he would pass on to his child.

Nell whispered she was glad. Wiping her eyes, she admitted she'd wondered if her nephew would give his little one a spiritual foundation.

Aware that he had to get a move on, Beau set his glass on a coaster. He reached down to help his Aunt to her feet. Touching her thick graying hair, held back with tortoiseshell combs, he told her that she and his Uncle had given him such a rich heritage, one that he would never think of withholding from his child. Beau bent to hug the woman who would be his child's 'Nannie' as all her grandchildren called her. Beau remembered Uncle Brantley and that the man was gone. Still, Beau reminded himself, his child would yet have a great Paw-Paw in Deac, his Aunt's current husband. Beau felt supremely blessed.

WHILE he traveled with Boulder, Tatum, and others, Beau would have been surprised to know that his brother called Gina. The beefy man did so before he started the bathroom reno that he'd be on for a few days. Via phone, Thomas told Gina, "I'm in y-your neck of the w-woods."

"Guess I'll miss you," she smiled, "because I'm in Islip, at work."

Thomas laughed. "I know you said no w-work for m-me this Saturday, but I c-could show up S-Sunday, or even F-Friday n-night."

"Well," Gina said, feeling trepidation, "Friday night I can cook..."

"Wow," Thomas blurted, "I'll be there. I'll bring my tools."

Gina wanted to say forget the tools, just bring you. Instead, she said, "No work this time, Thomas...*and* I might even let you kiss me."

"I can only kiss you with tongue," the big man stated. "I dreamed of that." Then he asked, filled with hope, "You still want me to come?"

"Oh, yes!" Gina blurted before she could catch herself.

LATER, Beau arrived home. He'd put in a 'Make A Wish' celebrity appearance. Indeed, he enjoyed the short visits. Most children simply wanted nothing more than to see him and spend a few moments in his presence. Yet Beau felt like the kids got cheated, somehow. First off: many wouldn't live long. Secondly, although their faces lit up when he strode through the door, he felt *he* got more out of the visits than they.

Tromping through the butler's pantry, Beau noticed his brother. Outside, Thomas rolled around on the deck with Frost. "Hey Thom," Beau called. He noted the canine's teeth clamped around a tattered ball.

"Hey, Brother!" Thomas shouted as playfully Frost growled. Beau shut the heavy door, banishing cold. Scrambling up, Thomas entered the mudroom, "I came over to m-make sure my dog didn't f-feel lonely."

At the stove, JeRell braised meat. He who had been second only to an executive chef, yowled. "Yo, don't come in here smelling like dog."

"I'm w-washing up!" Thomas retorted. "Quit acting like this yo' h-house 'n k-kitchen. You pay f-for n-nothing with your own m-money."

"This is more *my* kitchen than it is your brother's," JeRell quipped, "as much cooking as I do up in here. And this'll *be* my kitchen," Beau's henchman retorted, "for as long as I'm here. You'd betta recognize."

"You'd b-better—"

"Enough!" Beau commanded, using the colloquialism, "I don't want none." He couldn't abide the bickering. "Can it, you two old ladies."

Looking like a giant child, Thomas pouted. "Why y-you gotta yell?" He pointed at the cook. "*H-he* started. He's jealous of me 'n m-my dog."

"Jealous? Of you and some dog?" JeRell glanced at the husky before he snorted, "Please. I wish you'd take 'your dog' and—"

"*JeRell...*" Beau's tone contained a warning as he left the kitchen. Beau did not allow *anyone* to mistreat his brother. Headed to change his clothes, Beau could not help but recall his exclusive neighborhood, and the spring day, he'd accompanied his brother on a power jog through it...

HAVING begun to sweat, Beau used a wrist to mop his brow. Then he noticed. His brother was enraged by a man who hit a dog with a stick.

"Hey!" Beau sprinted. He grabbed his brother, who'd shoved the man. Boy, did Beau need to teach Thom to keep his hands to himself.

Attempting to pull Thomas away, Beau noticed the malnourished creature. Down on its belly, the dog raised frightened eyes. Yet Beau again tried to pull his brother. Heavier, however, Thomas was not swayed. Therefore, Beau levelly coaxed, "Come, Thom."

"No." Thomas spat, "He beat this d-dog. Now I'm gonna beat h-him."

With widened eyes, the pasty-faced man yanked the dog's leash.

The skinny canine lowered its head, and the mean man jerked again.

Elbowing Beau aside, Thomas intended to grind the man to powder. "You're strangling him!" Thomas' fist enclosed the man's throat.

Raising his stick, the dog owner's eyes gleamed. When he could manage to speak, his foreign accent was thick. "So what? Eez *my* beast."

Thomas squeezed the man's throat. "You don't deserve a d-dog."

Beau ineffectually coaxed Thomas away, as the sight of the struggling animal, furiously pawing air, and twisting in an attempt to breathe sickened him. Addressing the man, Beau ordered, "Let the dog down."

"Or what?" the stick wielder sneered.

Slowly Thomas spoke. "*I* – will – kick – your – raggedy – ass."

Perhaps hearing the venom in the burly black's voice shocked the man. Yet he defiantly inquired, "You and vhat other niggers vill do this?"

Beau, who'd boxed since he'd been a youngster, raised a brow. He could have made easy work of the man. Yet he sensed 'this' had become his brother's battle. Still, Beau wanted to leave, and so he said.

The elder brother didn't like the gathering group of onlookers. Many openly recorded all, and Beau knew. In a matter of moments five-o would show. No good could come of that. Heck, most onlookers probably assumed Beau and Thom had accosted the white man. That was due to centuries of media conditioning and hateful propaganda. Sickened by the man's callous disregard for life, Beau offered his brother two words. "Blue uniforms." From his peripheral, Beau also noticed a petite, tan female pushing her way forward.

Her brunette bonnet of hair shined as she commanded, her Long Island accent apparent, "Stop now Mister! You let that dog down!"

Ignoring the petite brunette, Thomas warned the stick-wielder. "You got one minute, then I'ma t-take you apart, p-piece by piece."

With eyes widening, the white man's thoughts raced across his face. Big Black was crazy. The dog-owner lowered the writhing creature. He also dropped the chain. "You zzo good," the pale man snarled, clutching his stick as he placed one foot behind the other, "You take eem."

Keeping his eyes on the man who bailed, Thomas tended the shaking creature while Beau realized it was still a pup. With onlookers clapping, Thomas said, "W-we got us a d-dog, Brother."

Ms. Petite crooned as Thomas lifted the mistreated creature. Petite also raised eyes that rounded when she looked at Beau. "You! You're on TV! Many days," quickly, she digressed, "I've seen that horrid man."

Wanting to be out, Beau couldn't believe Petite. Wanting a photo, she addressed a teenage gawker. "You there, do the honors?" She handed over her phone, still talking, "But the sad part is: I couldn't give the authorities any info." Petite stroked the canine in Thomas' arms. "Now, you've got a good home, doggie."

Dang! Beau thought as a police cruiser rolled up.

"Hey, Mac." Ms. Petite made eyes at a stocky blond officer. "Do me a favor?" She gestured to retrieve her phone. "Take a photo of these good Samaritans and me. They rescued this dog."

Wishing they'd vamoosed earlier, Beau noted the older officer.

"Daisy." The silver-haired uniform called out. "Everything okay?"

"Sure, Pop." With a wink for Beau, she divulged, "My dad; been on the force for decades." Daisy angled her small self between Beau and Thomas, who only had eyes for the dog. "Get my good side, Mac."

Concerned, Thomas spoke. "Brother, our d-dog needs a d-doctor."

Beau blinked because what was Thom talking about? Thom couldn't keep a dog, not in his tiny apartment, and Beau couldn't take a canine to his house either, not with spitting 'n scratching JaMocha kitty there.

Petite Daisy piped up. "There's a good vet up on Leopold Lane." Suddenly she barked a command. "Mac, hurry! Mr. TV here's gotta go."

Following a flash, Daisy stepped forward, took her phone, and began to jog backward. "Gotta work," she called. "See ya in the funny papers!"

When Beau found himself climbing from the rear of the cruiser, he guessed he was *it* until he found the dog a real owner, but how? He thanked the officers for the short ride. On his deck, Beau called out, "Thom, you and—your dog," he nearly choked, saying it, "stay here."

Inside, getting his keys, Beau speared JeRell with a look. "Not one word. You hear me? Just shut it down."

On the way to the vet, Beau glanced at the creature, huddled between his brother's feet. "Thom, your dog's gonna need a name. Right?"

The younger man shrugged. "I d-don't know any g-good ones."

"He's yours, now," Beau cringed. That meant the dog was *his*. But hadn't Beau planned to get Thom a dog? The older brother's plan had been to teach Thomas, as Beau had been taught, to love and cherish his pet. Well, looked like that part, Beau didn't have to teach.

"W-we'll share." Thomas shrugged. "So, what's the name?"

Turning onto Leopold Lane and into the animal hospital parking lot, Beau mused aloud. "Why not Snow, or Ice? Your pet would be that color—frosty, you know—if he was clean."

Like a child, Thomas goofily grinned. "H-hear that little d-doggie? Your name is *Frosty*, and you're gonna get gr-grapefruit sh-shampoo!"

THE following morning in the breakfast nook, Beau enjoyed fresh coffee. On his lap, JaMocha kitty snoozed as her owner finished perusing the rights to a project. Beau fingered the book also before him, *April Alisa Marquette's* mysterious thriller, *Exodus*. A colleague had approached him a while back, wanting to bring the novel to the big screen. Now Beau was ecstatic because they had the green light. About to call the author, his friend, Beau reached for his phone. However, before he could, JeRell tossed down the Sunday paper.

"Page eight, boss, when you get to it." As JeRell washed his hands, Beau flipped pages. Then he stared. He glanced up at the surly bald chef. JeRell had never whistled while making egg white omelets. Beau noticed Thomas, outside with Frost –who had turned out to be a girl. Thomas and the now clean husky with the bandaged ribs slowly crossed the sun-dappled deck. "Thom," Beau called when the beefy man entered the mudroom. "You see this morning's paper?"

"He'd better see that washroom, first," JeRell spat.

"I'm w-washing up!" Thomas yelled, splashing water.

Soon Thomas reached for the paper, as JaMocha kitty offered an ominous kitty growl. How dare some dog invade her territory?

"Hey, that's me—and you, B-brother!" Thomas grinned. "There's Frosty too, and the little jogger lady!" Thom swiped bacon, "Read it."

Aloud, Beau read the article that spoke favorably of him and his brother. The piece, Beau noticed, was written by *Daisy* Shasta. The commandeering little brunette with the police dad!

Setting the paper aside, Beau pulled his laptop and typed the necessary URL to contact Daisy, whom he would thank. On second thought, Beau mused, he would send flowers, Shasta *daisies*, of course.

Chapter 38

THAT night as Beau slept, he struggled to wake. Caught in a nightmare, he tried his REM sleep trick. It didn't work, evidenced by the fact that he 'became' a teen again. Oh no! Now he would re-live the terrible hurt that he, his cousin Kismet Staar, and his other cousin Farai had suffered. In the king-sized bed, Beau, the man, flung out an arm, somehow aware that his and his cousins' pain could not compare to his aunt's...

VIGILANTLY, she watched and waited, her eyes dark ringed. Her husband's illness had taken a toll on her too. Nell was no longer the same. Gone was her bubbly, seemingly unquenchable thirst for life. As she waited and dreaded Brantley's transition, part of her, too, had all but ebbed away.

ALTHOUGH he yet slept, the adult Beau sensed the lightening, color seeping across the sky. He felt icy fingers too, those of the incoming morning breeze. They caressed his near-nude body as he tossed and turned, engulfed in the moments before *the transition...*

IN the kitchen, the teenager busied himself. Yet he heard his Aunt move about. In the den, she tidied up and desperately clung to hope.

Despite disparaging cancer diagnoses, Nell had diligently prayed. However, her sweet, Brantley was tired. Worn from the fight, with his vitals failing, on that tranquil eve, he begged his wife. "Let go, baby." Barely audible, Brantley pled, "Just release me, Arnell. *Please.*"

Sobbing, Nell could only helplessly watch as Brantley heaved up his insides—the little he had left. The gunk and liquid appeared deep red and near black. What was she to do now? Nell was so frightened because she'd given the nurse half an hour off a little while ago.

Nell's heart raced as her hands profusely shook. There was no one to turn to, she thought, so scared. Still, Nell made herself lean over Brantley's recliner. Trying to soothingly hum, although she hiccupped with the sobs that wanted to burst forth, Nell used a soft cloth. She dipped it into the water kept nearby. Gently, she washed her man's face. While trying to soothingly murmur, she patted his mouth. She even managed to ask him to take a sip of water. She told him to spit, and the emitting water was red from all the blood and innards that he had upchucked. She and he did so twice more. She knew it took every ounce of strength he had to do so. With her breath coming in short spurts, she felt as though she was going to drop away in a dead faint. Still, Nell ignored the now-spattered and soiled flannel-lined shirt meant to keep Brantley warm. Lovingly, Nell kissed every part of his face. And her tears fell everywhere her lips had been.

Although she forced herself to calmly speak, Nell could have howled at the top of her lungs because this was so unfair! No one should have to suffer so! Yet she forced words through her sobs. She promised her sugar man one thing. *She would love him forever.* "Never forget that," she beseeched him. "Don't you dare," she told him, her hand on his face. "Don't you forget," not even when he transmogrified, entered eternity. "Always remember, Brantley, that I, Arnell Aretha– love – *you...*"

Then gingerly, with her heart feeling ripped from her chest, Nell heard Brantley Udale Moore sigh. Gathering her husband close, Nell knew something spiritual took place, when all she wanted was to keep two worlds from colliding. Nell wanted to keep Brantley in The Here and Now and not let the other realm, The After, claim him. She desperately wanted to keep what was hers. Yet she gave in and whispered, "You can go, love…" *I set you free from this awful pain and suffering.*

In the kitchen, Beau heard the scream. He dropped the fat, blue, metal can from which he'd scooped coffee. Forgetting the grinds spattering the floor, he saw Grandma Lacey. She'd been staying in Kismet's room. More fearful than he had ever been, the teenager watched the older woman shuffle down the hallway.

Caught in slumber, Beau, the man, nearly sobbed aloud as wailing went up. The youngster stared, as down on her knees, keening, and rocking, his Aunt became a hollow-eyed stranger.

Then there was a flurry of footsteps as the nurse reappeared. There were phone calls and prayers. Officials appeared, noted the time, and transported what they called 'the body.' Hordes of people showed up, Jervais, Ms. Lillie, teen Mireya, and many others. Arrangements were made. Color swirled, people murmured, and night blurred into day, again and again. College-aged Kismet Staar appeared, as did her dorm mate Valeria René, minus their classmate Ronni who abhorred the emotional.

At home, Kismet, and young Valeria, whose family lived just streets away, somberly made pallets in the finished basement. When she could,

Kismet cornered her cousin, out back of their home. Closing the kitchen door, the young woman stepped into biting wind. With eyes on the hibernating lawn, she told Beau she needed to know. How did it happen?

With hands in the kangaroo pouch of his hooded sweatshirt, he stared, his eyes shining orbs of tears. *How*, he wondered, could he tell his cousin that she didn't need to hear, or have what he had seen etched into her psyche? How could he say that his silence was him protecting her?

As tears rolled unchecked down his cheeks, Beau could only think one thing. Kiss did not need to forever carry with her the image of her father's remains spattered with nearly black blood and regurgitation. Each time she closed her eyes, she did not need to see her mother, Nell, down on the floor, inconsolably weeping, rocking, and hugging herself. However, since no words would form, Beau simply waited for his first cousin to rail at him in her grief or for her to perhaps pummel him.

Nevertheless, Kismet only tearfully begged, again, to be told.

Appearing stoic, tall, gangly Beau saw the tears that ran down his cousin's cheeks. "I have a right to know," she told him, but that knowledge still did not loosen Beau's tongue.

"Diddley," Kismet wheezed, "he was my father, too, you know."

At that moment, teenaged Beau nearly lost all composure because his cousin had unwittingly given him the greatest gift. Through her unselfish statement, she allowed him to know that she had shared and was yet willing to share *her father* with him. Beau loved Kismet so much for that. Although he was unaware of it at the time, those words from Kismet became the ties that would forever bind the cousins together.

Therefore, Beau pulled Kismet into his embrace. Not surprised, because she had seen his face, the displayed hurt, and somehow, pity, Kismet acquiesced. She knew that her taller but younger cousin was attempting to protect her, and for that, she loved him more than ever.

With her face pressed to Beau's hoodie, Kismet felt his heartbeat. She felt his arms too. The sinewy, steel-like bands surrounded her. Then she began to cry, in earnest, because their daddy, their loving, protective, and fun dad—the very best in the world—was gone. Forever.

Sometime later, when the back door opened, Beau welcomed the distraction. In the new hub-bub, he and Kismet learned that Brantley's eldest daughter, Farai, had arrived with her mother.

Yet caught in the dream world, the man, Beau, saw elderly, white-haired Pa Fulton. The older gent had cared for small Beau when his mother had abandoned him. The older man dabbed rheumy eyes. Again, Pa recounted how brawny Brantley had welcomed him into the fold. "You know, boy," Pa Fulton sniffled, "Brantley and feisty, Lil Ms. Nellie both promised I'd always be part of this family. And now he's gone."

After the funeral, at the crowded house, the older man sniffled and took Beau's hand. "I know it hurts, boy, but we gotta be strong."

Beau nodded because Uncle Brant had told him the same thing, several times. It was why Beau had tried to grow up fast, to become the man his family needed. Yet the shoes to fill had been enormous.

Beau, the sleeping adult, finally managed to heave himself up. Whew! In the darkness silvered by moonlight, his eyes darted about. With his heart racing, Beau wondered, as he had on numerous occasions, were the shoes he needed to fill *still* too large?

Reaching for his tee, Beau ignored the perspiration thinly veiling his body. Then he felt the little feet and nearly smiled. He was grateful for JaMocha, the only girl he had ever willingly slept with. In the moonlight, the Siamese treated him to her blue-eyed stare, before gracefully rolling onto her back. With small brown paws raised, she waited for his caress.

Amused, despite remembered pain, Beau obliged, "I wub you girl," he cooed. "I wub spoiled little puss." Beau clucked too at Frost, who steered clear of the cat. At the foot of his bed, the husky sleepily thumped her tail. She was his other girl now, and loved just as much.

Beau stood and cogitated. Soon he would reach his fourth decade. He wondered, would his heart ache every time he dreamt of Uncle Brantley? *And* would the questions keep coming? They were questions like: *Would he, Beau, be a good father, like Uncle Brantley? Could he, Beauregard DeVeaux, become half the father that his uncle had been to him, a kid who had not even been born to Brantley?*

Beau honestly did not know because he came from such lousy stock. Sure, Aunt Nell scolded him for saying such things. Yet Beau's birth mother had been the worst. Therefore, what if he found out—too late— that he wasn't a nurturer either? Would he wind up doing foul things to his kid, similar to those that had been done to him? Lord, he prayed not.

When Beau sat in the plush lounger out of doors, it was without coffee. He had hollows beneath his eyes and emptiness in his heart. Therefore, Beau was glad to be on hiatus from the movies. He liked that he wouldn't soon have to face his makeup artist. That impeccably groomed man wouldn't get to scold him about cutting caffeine and not getting enough rest. Because, said Mr. Makeup, "The camera doesn't lie."

As Beau pondered all that lay before him, he considered the new path. The one he had chosen. Then with all his heart, Beau prayed that he wouldn't screw things up.

Hearing something, he turned. He saw JeRell. In padded nylon, the surly chef pushed a serving trolley laden with breakfast goodies.

"Rell, man," Beau sighed, not about to refuse, "I can't keep eating like this."

Offering a hot pastry oozing with raspberry compote, the chef scoffed. "You're always at Sal & Lu's," the gym. "You'll be fine." JeRell poured coffee too as he continued, his eyes averted. "Boss, I've got a question."

"What's that?" Beau smirked, aware of what was coming.

"*When* yo' nightmare-plagued ass going back to work?"

Chapter 39

ACROSS town, headed to the hospital, Gina traversed the Northern Parkway. As she drove, she felt nervous. As a matter of fact, she'd felt that way ever since she'd picked up her phone. Thomas's *brother* had been on the line. Well, it hadn't happened exactly that way. A receptionist had dialed, from a number that Gina couldn't call back. She'd tried. Then the snooty person—who could have been a guy—had the nerve to tell Gina to hold for Mr. DeVeaux; when *they* had called *her*! Gina wanted to hang up. That would have shown them. But she was nosey, so she'd hung on.

Following that call, she'd rang Thomas. Angrily, she'd asked, "Did you give your brother my number?" He'd said no, but Thomas had been happy to hear that she and Brother had spoken. Thomas obviously thought the sun rose and set on Bro, probably because his brother was a bona fide star. Hey, maybe that was how the man had gotten her number. People with money had connecx, Gina mused. They got what they wanted. But what did the man want from her? Gina wondered because someone like Thomas' brother only deigned to speak to someone like her when it was necessary.

Well, Regina Rounds was no pion for the imperial *Mr. DeVeaux* to step on! So why had she accepted his invitation to dine out? She repeatedly asked herself. Just stupid, but she had been smart enough to ask the man, "Why?"

Then like his brother, Mr. DeVeaux had plainly spoken. He'd said there were a few things they needed to iron out. As Gina drove, she wondered what things *he and she* needed to work out, and why?

Mr. DeVeaux had named a restaurant. Afterward, his assistant threw out dates and times, one of which Gina foolishly agreed upon. They'd said 'a car' would be sent for her, but Gina had said, "Hold up," because she could not be bought. Now she was in her little car, driving herself.

Attempting to not be nervous, Gina recalled being at work and checking charts. In the hospital, she'd administered meds, and then, like now, she'd felt jittery. She'd told herself to think about the previous weekend. She called to mind the way she'd donned pretty new underthings from the big girls' boutique. Darn, if she hadn't looked supersized-sexy when Thomas had entered her home. She had been wearing a navy wrap dress. Forcing herself to forget inhibitions, she'd reached up and pulled Thomas' head toward hers. When their lips met, she'd smiled. She'd laughed when Thomas licked her lips. Removing him from her door, she'd closed it and again opened her mouth under his.

When she had been bold enough to unwrap her dress, Thomas had said, "Gina, you j-jest a b-big pretty g-gingerbread g-girl, ain't you?" Gazing at her new underthings, he'd whispered, "I hope you didn't c-cook, or dinner's g-gonna get cold."

She laughed. "I didn't cook." Barefoot, she tugged Thomas to her bedroom. "I ordered." Giddy, she'd wondered, was that feeling wrong?

Then Thomas had wanted the light on, but she hadn't because she was too fat. However, he'd looked at her the way *she* looked at donuts. When Thomas called her Sugar Cookie, Gina felt courageous enough to kiss him again, which he said he liked. Then her courage failed when Thomas said he wanted to show her something. With eyes wide, she watched him hook his thumbs in both his pants and undershorts. Pushing all down, he held that something in his hand.

Gina found that she could only stare and whisper, "Oh my…"

"I got this," Thomas said, like a child with a big new toy. "If you want, I c-could use it, to make you feel g-good." Wisely, as Beau had advised, Thomas declined to mention how he'd learned to use his 'Peter.'

Gina nodded and blurted that she wanted those big skilled hands on her, the way they'd been on her back step, and on her kitchen cabinets.

"I'm going to stain those c-cabinets s-soon," Thomas reminded her. "I'm g-gonna stain you t-too." He waved his personal tool, "With this."

Afterward, she could not believe how erotic it had been. She'd climaxed; one thing, but when Thomas had been about to, he had quickly pulled out and emitted into the cleft between her buttocks. Then using his rod and big gentle hands, he'd stroked her, spreading warmth. "I'm s-staining you, Regina," he softly stated. And she had known then.

She was his, and he was hers.

Driving along, she realized. Thomas' brother might not be pleased. Well, if she and Thomas were what 'Brother' wanted to discuss, then Mr. DeVeaux was in for a surprise. Gina was *not* going to back down or bow out. Not now, or ever.

Yet, since receiving that call, she had been worried, and she had eaten. That was how she'd gained so much weight. The weight was why she mostly wore scrubs or sweats. Still, now and again, since she'd met Thomas, Gina found herself wanting to look nice.

Still driving, Gina recalled busying herself with patients. While she had, thoughts of another night and Thomas came to mind. That night she'd cooked. It was something she hadn't done for anyone in…years. She was surprised she'd remembered how. The last time had been…for *others*. Yet Thomas had enjoyed, and he'd helped with the dishes. Gina washed, and he'd dried. It had been nice, them working together, mostly in silence. When they were done, Thomas laid the towel aside and stood close. Gina had smelled his shower soap, as softly he'd asked if he could touch her.

Nearly shivering with anticipation, she'd whispered, "Yes."

Thomas did, so gently, that Regina had nearly cried. He had also rubbed her back, and she'd felt, strangely, as though he had been comforting her. Inhaling, Gina had wondered if, in his childlike way, Thomas sensed her hurt. Did he understand that she needed his touch because she hadn't been touched since…*another*? Touching, she had not wanted, for years, because truthfully, she had not felt alive.

However, as Thomas continued to stroke her back, Gina had felt something within her give. Then silently, she began to cry. The nurse didn't know when Thomas turned her into his arms. All she knew was that he held her, resting his chin atop her head, the same way he'd seen his brother do, with their Aunt Nell, pretty Mireya, and others.

Gina's shoulders sagged beneath the weight of all that she'd borne for the last three years. Yet wiping her face with both hands, she'd felt embarrassed. Still, she admitted, "Thomas, I've been carrying a secret."

"I knew," Thomas divulged, "and I knew you w-would t-tell me…when you felt r-ready."

Bless his big childlike heart, she thought and nearly smiled.

In her small living room, Gina lit candles, and she and Thomas sat on the sofa. "Thomas," she began, determined to be like him, to just spit things out. "I have a husband. I have a son, too."

The big man had appeared confused, and she raised a finger before the questions arose. "My husband and my son are *angels*, now…" Gina could not continue, as she placed her head in her hands. Taking deep breaths, she tried to block out that fateful day. The wife and mother wanted to forget that she hadn't cried or properly grieved because she'd felt guilty, for being alive. Gina forgot that all she had been able to do was eat. Many days and countless nights, she'd stood with the refrigerator door wide, as failingly, she had tried to eat her heartache, and her tremendous loss, away.

Gina didn't know when Thomas moved closer or when he took her into his arms. She only knew that she rested against his massive chest, as soothingly, he rubbed her back. Lying against him on the sofa, she became aware that she could cry some more if she wanted.

Somehow though, she no longer felt like doing so as a single tear rolled down her cheek. Gina had then become cognizant of feeling as though the man on whom she rested, with his simplistic spirit and gentle ways, had allowed her...release, at last.

In time, Thomas left Gina. In her kitchen, he wet paper towels. Upon returning, he dabbed Gina's face. He'd seen Kismet do the same to her kids, his little cousins. Thomas produced a glass of water, too. Then after Gina sipped, he again pulled her into his arms.

"Sleep, n-nice lady," he murmured. "I'll w-watch over you. I w-won't even try to kiss you, or put my tongue in your m-mouth."

Gina felt the chuckle. It bubbled up and out, light as air. She couldn't remember the last time that happened.

Afterward, she slept, something she often had trouble doing. When she woke, with sunlight streaming over both her and Thomas, she realized. The strange man, who was childlike in some ways and full-grown in others, had given her something rare.

He had offered her the gift of something she had lost.

Hope.

Chapter 40

BEAU watched Thomas, a natural-born carpenter. Beau recalled that while on lockdown, Thomas had turned that handiness into a trade. Then Thom had been transferred to the Queensboro Correctional facility where he'd served the remaining year of his term. While out on work release, Thomas had attained his current job. Now a licensed contractor, Thomas worked steadily. He also announced he was stacking his chips, "L-like you, b-brother," because Beau currently taught his brother to invest.

Beau was proud of the younger man. It was true; they'd both had a rough start in life, with Ophelia for a mother. Still, willing to move forward, Thomas didn't harbor anger. He didn't even seem to care that he had been locked up for petty drug crimes that Ophelia had coerced him into committing.

However, now, Beau was concerned. His brother had been seeing a lot of Nurse Gina lately. With her round body and short natural, she'd said she needed a few things done around her house. Beau had found out that much. Soon, he would ascertain the rest of the woman's story. At present, Beau knew that a prior client of Thomas' had recommended Thom to Gina. That client had told Gina that Thom, the carpenter, moonlighted; he picked up odd jobs on weekends or evenings.

Quickly, Beau averted his eyes. He didn't want his brother to catch him staring. Still, Beau tried to see Thom through the eyes of a woman...

His younger brother was tall, a family trait. He had a beefy body, different from Beau's. Thom had nice brown skin and soft hair that was barbered close. Thomas could appear to be mean, until he smiled. Then the sun burst forth.

Beau tilted his head. He attempted to see Thomas through a nurse's eyes, the eyes of an educated woman, with her own home...

What, Beau wondered, with eyes involuntarily narrowing, did that woman want, from Thomas? –Or from *him*, for that matter? The truth was: by now, she had to know that Thomas was related to *him*. Beau's mouth knotted because when most people made the connection, it wasn't long before they requested something. So what did Nurse Gina want?

THAT week, he called and told her that he'd dreamed. Thomas said the dream Gina had never wanted to let him go. Therefore, Thomas revealed, "I want to be with you too Gina, and have a grown-up life."

April Alisa Marquette

Thomas had said he wanted to be like his brother, who was having a baby—with their cousin. Gina blinked, whatever that meant. Gina forgot it because she knew, one day she would know.

UNBEKNOWNST to Thomas, Beau heard him murmuring into his cell phone. Then Beau mentioned to houseman JeRell and his drummer Gypsy that he didn't like the change in his brother. Beau hadn't actually said he didn't like that Thomas seemed dreamy at times and often spoke of Gina, but Beau implied it.

He mentioned the changes to Saavion, too, as they lay spent after a sexual marathon. The man with the sunlit hair asked if Beau was jealous. Beau said no, he wasn't. Although he and the optician could talk about almost anything, Beau felt like he needed to speak with Kismet Staar. She would understand more than someone who wasn't exactly family.

"Kiss," Beau began, during one of their rare conversations, "I'm having this Gina woman checked out, for real now. The other day Thom asked me how a man would know what kind of ring to buy."

Kismet sounded pleased, and not at all the way Beau wanted her to sound. Furthermore, she advised, "Diddley, don't be grouchy. Thom looks up to you. Like you, he's attempting to create a family of his own. –And I think he has real feelings for this woman."

"No," Beau repudiated. "I think she's influencing him. You and I both know that if someone is clever enough, Thom can be easily led."

Kismet felt a prickle of dread. "You don't think she's trying to get to *you*, do you? Not through him…"

"I don't know," Beau truthfully stated.

"Why would she?" Kismet asked, "If that's really what she's doing?"

"I've asked the same thing," Beau admitted. He felt like finally, Kismet sounded alarmed and more like he wanted her to, so now they were on the same page. "I promise you, though, I'ma find out what she's up to—in fact, I'm meeting with her. I might even warn her off."

"Nooo," Kismet scolded, "don't do that. Just talk with her, or have one of your minions do it. Find out where she's coming from."

"I'm doing this, Kiss because this nurse might need some fear put into her." Beau's protective instinct exerted itself. "That I can and will do."

Well, go ahead, Kismet thought and resolved not to get involved. Her plate was full enough. Anyway, Gina had appeared with Thomas the last time Kismet cooked for Beau's band. The woman seemed nice, to her.

Ringing off, Kismet realized that unlike Beau, she wasn't itching to get in other people's affairs. Her own affair needed tending. Heck, the truth was: carrying this baby for Beau had all but wrecked her marriage. The wreckage was something Kismet did not like or want.

Kismet also didn't like that in the recent past, her husband had often said mean things. Sure, now, he seemed to be trying, but at the most inopportune times, one of his picayune phrases would mentally float back to her. Then if she wasn't careful, those words would nearly sabotage her day. Before all of this, though, the wife recalled, Lyle had been the best husband. That she wanted to remember. However, once, he had maliciously said he didn't want to ruin her lil money-making scheme. Now that, she wouldn't soon forget, or that he'd called her a fag hag. He'd said she hung out with Beau 'n all them other faggot-asses.

"No, you've taken this further, Kiss," Lyle had clarified, being intentionally mean. "You've become an all-out fag *whore*—renting out your body so you can sell babies to the highest bidder."

Kismet had seen red then because that had been lowdown and dirty. Unaware that she would, she'd smacked the spit out of Lyle. "I can't believe you!" She'd hissed, "Saying shit like that—to me! Forget me being your wife; I'm the mother of your children!"

To have the last word, he'd said, "Big deal. I'm just *one* of your baby daddies." Lyle's eyes had narrowed upon realizing he'd struck a nerve. "Never thought about that, huh, Kiss? Didn't think how iniquitous you appear to the hoity-toities down at your kids' fancy schools, did you?"

"They're your kids too," she'd reminded the man who gloated. Grabbing her laptop, she'd been unable to abide him a second longer.

"Maybe two of them are mine," the twins. Lyle had spitefully laughed, "But with this new one, you'll have *three* baby daddies, and all the little classmates will taunt *your* kids about it."

So, Déja and Chance were hers, alone, now? Kismet mused, even though for years, Lyle had begged to adopt her two little adoptees.

Not willing to dwell on stupid stuff, Kismet forgot her husband's derision. The Momma forgot her first cousin, too, the man who suddenly wanted to get in Thomas and Gina's affair. In her quiet home, Kismet bent to kiss her sleeping girls. Her mind drifted back to their father.

Kismet entered her bedroom. She realized her biggest mistake to date. It was caring what Lyle thought. Turning her comforter down, Kismet recognized more. She and Lyle might never again be what they had once been. There was too much water under the bridge, now.

Nevertheless, she wondered. If she and Lyle broke up, would she be able to forgive herself—or Beau?

Oh my. Kismet's heart stuttered because, at last, she had faced facts. *She honestly blamed Cuz for the impending doom of her marriage.*

SINCE he was having nurse Gina checked out, Beau felt he might as well do the same with the other woman. Pain in the neck, Mary. Aware that she would show up at their next club date, Beau nearly wished Infusion's itinerary was not posted on their website. The bandleader almost wished his young assistant, Tatum, wasn't so efficient. Then that white-wearing woman couldn't so easily track his friend, Gypsy. However, the band's legitimate fans would then be in the dark. They wouldn't know where the band would play next. So sucking it up, Beau made a decision. In passing, too, he said he needed to speak with his backup drummer, after rehearsal.

Beau felt terrible about what he would request, since Kendu now had his life on track. But, Beau reminded himself, 'this' was necessary. Sure, a while back, Kendu had been getting into trouble. He'd been hanging with the wrong crowd. Yet the kid whom Beau had met at the Pietro Brothers gym, was now doing well. Beau recalled Joe, Sal's son, introducing Kendu, one of Sal and Luigi's protégés.

Beau had been at the gym, to which he gave healthy donations. He'd stood with big Sal and his son Joe. All three watched a stocky, caramel-brown boy-man hit the speed bag. "Beau, Dad says this kid isn't quick like you were, but he's got heart. He listens, and he's smart."

"Yeah, like you were," big Sal agreed. "That's why Joey 'n I want you to guide him. The kid's got brains, Beau —potential, ya know? Help us make something outta him, outside the ring. *Capiche*?"

Beau nodded at his mentor, who'd always reminded him of Rocky Balboa. Beau glanced at Sal's son. Back when big Sal helped Beau detox, Joe was little. Beau recalled that up at Sal's cabin, when drug-free and his appetite had returned, he and little Joe had eaten together.

Stepping to the ring, Beau beckoned Kendu over. Beau gave the southpaw a few pugilistic pointers. Seeing his younger self in the kid, Beau had warmed to the idea of taking an active interest in Kendu. Three years later, following high school graduation, the youngster told his parents no college for him. He'd then gone to trade school—on a scholarship funded by Beau. Kendu had later joined the band. Since the kid worked, he only did local gigs and toured with Infusion when he could. An HVAC tech, Kendu had gotten his job through DeVeaux Worx, Beau's foundation. It provided guidance, job training and placement, to many young men of color.

Now Beau needed something from Kendu. Therefore, following the closed rehearsal, the bandleader sighed. While vocalists and band members alike chatted and laughed, Kendu approached his benefactor.

"Mr. B, you wanted to see me?"

"Yes." Beau got right to it. "Ken, this is important. I need a favor."

"Anything, Mr. B, I got you."

Beau placed an arm about the young man's shoulders. In the rehearsal studio, he walked him slightly away from the others. "Ken, I'm aware that you don't do certain things anymore, and that's good. Still, I need something, for Gypsy. You remember that person y'all were discussing when we played The Portland Club? Well..." Beau laid everything out.

"No worries." Kendu was not shocked. "When do you want it?"

"As soon as possible. Listen, though, Ken. I feel wrong about this, but it's for Gyp," who was like a brother to them both.

"No sweat, Boss." Stocky Kendu shrugged. "I gotta tell you, Mr. B, I was gonna suggest this. I don't get down like that anymore, but this is like, important, you know? I just thought Fatal Attraction—that's what we call her; I thought she needed to be checked."

Caught between a rock and a hard place, Beau told the truth. "Kendu, I sure hope I'm not sending you back down the wrong road."

"No way, Boss. It's just this once." Before gravitating toward an attractive young woman with long braids, a backup vocalist, Kendu turned. "Afterward, Mr. B, will I need to return it –to Fatal Attraction?"

"Nah," Beau shook his head, "too risky." Let Mary reapply for ID, Beau mused. Maybe that would sideline her, for a little while, at least.

Chapter 41

BACKSTAGE, at Cat Call, a hot New York club, Beau and Gypsy walked. The band had just finished a set. Headed toward them, Mireya was all smiles. She had not yet seen the dough girl. Accepting the towel handed him by his assistant, Beau draped it over his head and shoulders. Beau wondered, why was that white-wearing girl-woman present, again? Yeah, yeah, it was a free country, and she had as much right to follow the band as anyone else. Still, that did not negate the niggling sense that Mary should have been elsewhere.

Beau shrugged, perhaps the dough girl just happened to be the one person in life that he did not like, for no particular reason.

As he absorbed instructions from Tatum, Beau raised a hand. He told his assistant to hang on a sec. He called out to Gypsy who was about to enter a dressing room with Mireya.

"I don't think they heard you, Boss," Tatum stated. He was about to sprint after the drummer and the woman in the designer heels.

Catching Tatum's arm, Beau pulled carrot-top into the shadows. Wordlessly, Beau pointed, and his young assistant gasped.

"Fatal Attraction's here, *again*?" Tatum was miffed. "Why?"

Beau appeared pensive as he said, "My thoughts exactly." From the shadows, he and Tatum watched. The woman stood just beyond the secured area. She appeared angry while eyeing Gypsy and Mireya.

"Come on." Beau stepped forward, his face near-shrouded by the towel draping his head. He intended to tell Gypsy to be careful. Tatum intended to have security move the woman along.

However, neither got the chance to do as proposed. A trio of females bum-rushed Beau. Wild and screaming, they insisted on photos and autographs. With Boulder and security restoring order, Beau obliged. When he could finally look back, Gypsy, Mireya, *and* Mary were gone.

EARLY the next morning, Mireya called. Already up and moving, Beau announced, "I tried to speak with you last night. After the show, I really wanted to speak with Gyp, too."

"That's why I'm calling." Gazing into her office mirror, Mireya blotted her face, for a matte look. "Gypsy told me something."

"Is it about the dough girl?" Beau asked.

"Who? Oh. His groupie." Mireya snorted, "Matter of fact it is. On our drive home, Gypsy said he'd seen 'doughy' at the club. Last night."

"I did too."

Deeming her face done, Mireya wondered aloud, "Why didn't I see her? Anyway, get this. Gypsy said 'dough girl' as you call her, cornered him before y'all's first set. She told him *the Lord* spoke to her, saying Gypsy was all hers. The Lord supposedly said he's her husband."

"She's still on that stupid shtick?"

"Yep, she cray, but listen," Mireya advised, "because I've got a meeting in minutes. Gypsy told that loon he's not looking for a wife. Then ol' girl said she knows the Lord don't lie. He asked if she heard voices all the time. She said yes, like that's normal." Mireya picked up her phone. "Beau I'm taking you off speaker, but I want you to know; I really don't like that woman." The business owner brushed lint from her trousers. "*And* I'm starting to believe she ain't as harmless as she looks."

Beau admitted, "You and I are on the same page."

"Well," Mireya grabbed her attaché. "I warned him about her, again. Still, as people who love him, shouldn't *we*—you and I—do more?"

"I'm working on that," Beau admitted. Disconnected, he sighed, because heck, it wasn't like he needed *more* to add to his to-do list.

DAYS later, Beau had Mireya come to the house while JeRell was out grocery shopping. Beau met her at the rear door, and ushered her straight through his palatial home to his office. "Sit," he advised.

Mireya took a seat. She felt like she had back in middle school when she'd been summoned to the principal's office. Folding her hands, she recalled the day she'd knifed cruddy McCuddy, the glee club instructor.

Behind his massive desk, Beau handled a manila envelope. "Reya, I did as you suggested and got a hold of our stalker's ID." Beau did not mention Kendu or his help, "And I've got stuff."

Mireya's eyes rounded. "You do?"

"Yep, did a bit of digging and peeped Mary's background." Beau shook his head. "Seems lil ol' church girl ain't as young, righteous, *or* as harmless as she tries to appear."

Mireya instinctively reached for the papers. "What do those say?"

"Looks like she's some kind of black widow." Beau explained that Mary was connected to a death in *South Carolina*. "The victim was someone with whom Doughy had a 'one-sided' relationship."

Mireya was shocked. "Don't say she stalked that man, too."

Rifling through documents Beau looked grim. "It appears so; here. These statements, given by others, claim she acted young, called all the time, and followed the man different places. Ol' girl cut the fool, and a restraining order was issued. Get this, she was involved in a *similar* situation in the state of *Washington*. The Federal Way Police Department now has her listed her as a person of interest."

"Then why isn't she in jail?" Mireya demanded, jumping up to pace. "Why's she on the loose here in New York?"

Seemingly implacable, Beau replied. "According to the file on the Carolina murder, there wasn't enough evidence to convict her." Beau suddenly felt like he was back on the gritty crime scene drama that had sky-rocketed his career. "The Washington State crime lab turned up no evidence, or useful leads. But…" Beau raised a hand. "My investigator found a cousin. Mary's currently staying with this woman. My guy called and informed Cuz that he wanted to discuss a matter of importance, and Cuz was willing to talk."

Mireya pivoted from the large window, her thick glossy a-symetrical curtain of hair swinging. "Really? What did this cousin say?"

"Interesting things. Sit, and see. When asked why Mary wears white, the cousin said Mary went to college to become an AA—"

On the edge of her seat Mireya asked, "What is that?"

"An anesthesiologist's assistant. Back in the day, nurses wore white."

Mireya remembered, "Yeah, when we were kids."

"Yep, so now we know she's not so young. Cousin said Mary Elizabeth, no dummy, went further. She became a *nurse anesthetist.*"

"A what?"

"An aness-thet-tist. That's the nurse that monitors the anesthesia, after it's been administered by the anesthesiologist. Mary's cousin claims Mary said she wears white because she's pure."

Mireya snorted. "Bull crap."

"I'm just relaying what's in this report," Beau offered. "You did order me to do some digging. Cuz also said her and Mary's grandparents, devout church-goers, raised Mary. They gave her everything and told Mary that her Heavenly Father would give her anything—if she prayed for it. The cousin said the one remaining grandparent hasn't yet faced that Mary's not normal, or that she has always been twisted. Cousin told my guy she wants Mary out of her Long Island home. Actually, Cuz thought Mary would be gone by now, with the way Mary's allegedly been going on about her upcoming marriage."

"That stalker's getting hitched?"

Beau locked eyes with Mireya. "Cuz said the poor schmuck's last name is *Ainsely*."

Mireya's heart skipped a beat, "But *Ainsley* Fielding is—"

"Our *Gypsy*," Beau finished for her. Watching his friend who suddenly appeared ill, Beau knew just how she felt.

The movie producer didn't inform Mireya of his latest decision involving an upcoming trip. He and his scout team were scheduled to visit two little-known islands. The ones in his friend April's book. Preliminary movie footage would be shot on those islands. Just that morning, Beau had asked Gypsy to go, too. Beau had said it would be a nice little getaway for the fellas. About the trip, Beau kept quiet. He knew Gypsy who wasn't a talker would do the same.

It was Beau's hope that the time spent away would allow Gypsy's stalker to fixate on someone else.

Beau did, however, tell Mireya that he'd staged a one-on-one intervention with her love interest. During the hour he'd spent with Gypsy, Beau had laid out simple facts.

The actor did not divulge that he'd told mister with the honey-hued eyes that he was to – *stay* – *away* – from Mary Trumbull. Sure, Beau regretted speaking harshly to his brother-friend, but the drummer needed to understand. The woman was suspect.

"You cannot be with her, ever." Beau had leaned forward. "I might sound high-handed, Gyp, but as your employer," at Infusion, "that's it. Collusion—or *any* interaction with this person is unacceptable. You need a ride to or from anywhere, call or text this number. If you need anything, I got you. Understand?"

"Understood, Boss," the drummer nodded. Gypsy was aware that Beau, who was more family than friend, only wanted the best for him.

That scenario had taken place *before* Beau received the alarming investigative report. Watching Mireya who again paced, the movie producer wondered if his mild-mannered drummer would heed.

Mireya swung back. Ignoring her, silently, Beau prayed, again. *Dear Lord, let Gyp be smart. Let him stay away from that Mary person. –Or better yet, just take HER away. Please.*

Chapter 42

KISMET went out with Beau and Saavion, the optician. Cinnamon-skinned Mireya and her partner stout gray-haired Ann also appeared. Beau and Kismet's longtime sister-friend Valeria, and her husband Fabian, had been invited. However, Valeria had given birth.

At the hospital, earlier in the day, Kismet's friend stated, "This is it."

"What you mean, Val?"

"I've finally got my boy, Kiss. Now my tubes are tied."

Kismet peered at the beautiful brown baby. With his shining cap of hair, he'd been just hours old. "Tell me his name again, Val."

"Vale. Vale Wren. Fabian named him." Mother caressed baby's sleeping face. "My boy's name is *mine*—with a male twist."

Recalling how Valeria René's husband had named their first girl the same way, Kismet revealed, "Fabian is great with names." The Momma cradled her midsection. "Maybe he can help name this one."

Seated in an upscale restaurant, surrounded by Beau and his friends, Kismet forgot the other mother who'd seemed so happy. She tried to forget how Fabian's eyes had shown only love for his wife. Would *Lyle* ever look at *her* that way again? Kismet wondered; forget him appearing at the hospital when she gave birth.

Kismet had felt depressed ever since that visit, so she allowed her mind to wander. She pondered her children. This evening they were at home, with her mother, Nell. They should have been with their father but who knew if he'd get drunk or angry or if he'd destroy something.

All present ahhhed because Kismet was finally showing. She forced a smile. Heck, she thought, she should be showing. She'd soon be going in. Those present said she looked lovely. She felt otherwise.

Sure, for the first time since she'd been a girl her healthy hair was long again. For the time being, Kismet had stopped getting it cut because it grew so fast. People said her skin glowed too. Maybe she looked prima, but she felt so unlike herself. Probably because in the past, whenever she'd been asked out, it was a given that she *and* Lyle would attend together. Now she was the odd man out. She sat with two couples, the fifth wheel. That she had never been.

Tuning back in, Kismet realized that Beau had been in a different restaurant alcove. Returned from conversing with a New York Rangers hockey player, he focused on Mireya's Ann, who asked a question.

"So you three really don't want to know your baby's sex?"

Kismet said, "Nope." She'd never tell, but she couldn't learn the baby's gender. That would only make it harder for her to give up the baby. Feeling more melancholy now, Kismet fell silent.

Beau, however, revealed that he almost wanted to know. His cousin jerked her head up as he continued, "But then I think about how much fun it'll be to find out when baby gets here." He grinned, "And just that fast, I don't want to know."

"You go back and forth." Saavion smiled indulgently at Beau.

The actor had never been happier, while his cousin was miserable.

"This process," the filmmaker said, "has been so awesome until I have to remind myself that I want our baby's sex to be a surprise."

Both Saavion and Kismet's hearts bumped as internally they wondered, *When Beau said 'our baby' was he referring to me?*

Stocky Ann raised her pilsner glass, "To your soon arriving surprise."

Kismet forced herself to sound bright. "Déja's excited too. Ever since Beau said she could baby-sit, she's been over the moon."

"Listen everybody." Beau leaned forward to recount the conversation he'd had with Kismet's thirteen-year-old. Everyone chuckled, and Beau hugged his cousin who momentarily rested her head on his shoulder.

Surprised at the tear that trickled from her eye, Kismet dabbed at it.

"Aw Kiss," Mireya squeezed Kismet's hand. "Let's go to the ladies."

Beau rose. "Thanks Reya, but I'll walk with her. Saav, I'll have whatever you order." Gently he aided his cousin to rise. "Kiss will too."

When they stood before a vestibule window, Beau took her face in his hands. "You don't have to stay. I'll have you out of here in two shakes…"

"No." Kismet refused. "I need to be here. I need to be out, you know? Even if it's only to make a statement, to Lyle or to anybody else who has shit to say. This is *my* body. This was—and still is—*my* choice." Kismet's face crinkled. "Oh you don't know, Diddley. Lyle's been terrible, not coming home, or appearing and saying mean stuff. Then he's been sweet. It all so confusing, and not what I need right now." The Momma breathed deeply, and noticed a restaurant patron.

Approaching, the woman slowed, because was that...? It *was* the handsome actor! Patron blinked because he was with a...gorgeous *woman*. Patron's eyes slid slowly over Kismet. Patron noticed lovely hair and fabulous tits—were they real?

Kismet knew the look, she'd seen it since she was twelve. Used to it, at present, Kismet really wanted to tell the gawker to keep it moving.

Yet Patron stood, nosey as could be, staring at the goddess who was so shapely, and...so *pregnant*. Shocking, Patron thought. Photos! No. Dang. She'd left her phone. Well, wait until she told her girlfriends! Patron inched closer as Beau softly spoke to the goddess.

"Excuse me," Patron interrupted. "I just have to say;" she dragged her eyes from Goddess. "Mr. Beau—I know you from all your movies and your documentaries. Anyway," Patron gave a little wave. "I love you. I see you're busy 'n all, but I must say this." The woman spoke quickly because who knew; the man could have been an impatient celebrity. "I just knew all that *gay stuff* in them supermarket rags was untrue!" Patron excitedly bent her knees. "That's why I love you. My girlfriends do too. We support you. We would, even if you were gay, but I see," her eyes dropped to Kismet's belly, "that you're not. Oooh, I'm so happy for you! Congratulations!" Why, the woman wondered hadn't TMZ reported *this*.

"Thank you." Beau smiled, as the gawker realized she'd intruded on a private moment. With another wave, she rushed away.

Unable to stop himself, Beau chortled, and his cousin smirked. "Well," he managed to say, "she was right, about the baby..."

"Somehow she knew it was yours," Kismet nodded, realizing again that she was doing the right thing. She had just needed a little reminder.

Laughing heartily, Beau hugged his cousin, and into her fragrant hair he intoned, "God love my fans!"

IN the shabby, extended stay motel, Lyle lay sulking. He had done everything Kismet Staar wanted. Flicking through TV channels, he recalled having done so, even before he and she had married. Maybe he had been too accommodating. Maybe now his wife was getting what other women got. A rude awakening. Now Kiss realized. She couldn't run all over him. He was a man.

But then again, Lyle thought, Kismet had never really tried to, not before this. It was why Lyle had set the wheels in motion, some time back, to make things right, if his wife would allow it. And just maybe,

Lyle would even get his parents back. They had taken sides, and they had not chosen him.

THE next evening, Lyle lay sprawled on his mother's couch. He thought about his father. That island man refused to speak to him.

Lyle's mother, Collette, a robustly built, handsome woman refused to speak of why her husband wanted nothing to do with their eldest son. She told Lyle not to ask her again. She said she was in the middle enough; whatever that meant.

Lyle could hear Collette, his mother, as she clashed about in her old-ish kitchen. Suddenly, he experienced a pang of longing. At *his* gabled home, in his and Kismet's huge maple and cream kitchen, Kismet would be cooking too. About now, Kiss would be sprinkling something with coarse sea salt, while placing something else on a platter. Like Mama Manfred, as Kiss called his mother, Kiss would have their home filled with inviting scents and edibles.

Ezmerelda, Lyle's black cat with the white paws would be curled up in her basket. Lyle envisioned it. His kids, each with a unique personality, would be seated at the breakfast bar. Their colorful books, and the bigger kids' laptops would be out. They'd be jostling, and tattling, while rattling on about their day. And their mother, who had grown rounder with the baby that she carried—for love—would take all in stride. Pondering the mental scene, Lyle felt his eyes sting. Those had better not be tears. He also wondered. Why wasn't *he* at home?

Then he recalled his righteous—really, his *self*-righteous— indignation. His wife had thrown him out! Yeah, and Ms. Big Stuff had changed the locks. She had even pompously threatened an order of protection. *That* was why Lyle wasn't home. He *couldn't* go home. Lyle had to stay at a lousy hotel, where people watched his every move. They did so because of his high-end SUV. One guy thought he'd spoken softly when he told another that the car said the owner had money.

So now, Lyle mused, he was being clocked by people who wanted to pick him off. He was also subsisting off the charity of his peops. If his mother didn't feed him, where would he get a good home-cooked meal?

Wearily, Lyle placed his head in his hands, because he was twisting shit again. None of that was the reason for his predicament. He had to *stop lying*, to himself, and to others. He had to face *his* part in the mess that was now his life. That had been said in the Alcoholics Anonymous meetings. Things that were happening were partially *his* fault, because he had been a fool. Lyle had challenged his wife on all the wrong issues.

Unlike what his mother had always told him and his brothers, Lyle hadn't chosen his battles. He'd just picked fights, for no reason. Now he was essentially homeless, and fatherless—as were his children. It was a sobering thought.

"Lyle," his mother's lilting island voice floated to him. "Lyle Augustus Manfred," she firmly called. "Come in my kitchen, please."

When he entered the small spice-infused cooking space, dark-skinned Collette had her sisterlocks pulled into a ponytail, like his.

"Son, have a seat."

Lyle did. He watched his mother stir something that looked suspiciously like callaloo as softly and slowly she began to speak.

"I am ashamed of you." Collette gave her son no chance to retort. "This is not how your father and I reared you, or any of your brothers. Lyle Augustus," she continued, "you say you love Kismet Staar, yet you hurt her, again and again. I have watched you do it. I have stood by, watching while *you* teer," tear "up your family, den yuh blame others."

Collette lifted a pot lid, from which sweet-smelling steam rose. "Your children come and they are sad, especially de oldest. They should be happy in this stage of life, but no, and they say things."

That Lyle had not known.

Standing at the stove, not as big as the one at home, Lyle's mother shook her head. "You thought your wife tattled, but she is not like that. Kismet Staar is much like your mother." Beautifully dark, big-boned Collette frowned. "Perhaps your wife, not you, should have been *my* child." Lyle's mother waved. "Bah! But back to your babies; they talk, and cry. They believe that one day you will neva return, to them."

Lyle watched as his mother pivoted from her old-fashioned stove. "What you are doing, son, is creating irreparable damage, not only in your marriage, but in de lives of your children."

Lyle hated to hear it, but he knew it was true.

"And you started *drinking* –excessively," Collette sounded shocked. "Why? Who are you? In this family, who does that? Weer," where "did you learn that? Lyle Augustus, let me ask yu something: Do you like who you've become?" A veritable fount of inquiries, Collette added spices to another pot. "Are you even in control of your business affairs anymore?" She peered over at him, seated at her tile-top table. "Since your father can't stand to look at you these days, it falls to me. *I must be the one to tell you.*" Collette sighed. "*You have become a disappointment. My Augustus and I truly hope you don't believe your actions are due to any example that *he*—my husband—set, for any of his sons.*"

Collette turned, and Lyle felt like dog-stuff as he admitted, "I want to get it together, Mum. And Dad never set one bad example for any of us." There was so much Lyle wanted to say. However, he realized. *Those* things he needed to tell his wife, not his mother.

Therefore, when Lyle said nothing further, large-boned Collette made an announcement, her island accent apparent. "Tonight I feed you, my son. Tomorrow, Lyle Augustus, I will send you away. It is my prayer that you will then do right. I pray you stop hurting the ones you love—including me, and your father."

Suddenly, Lyle's mother appeared choked up. Noisily setting her big spoon aside, she fled from her kitchen.

AT her big gabled colonial, Kismet kissed her mother goodnight. She waved at Deac who had driven over. He would cart his precious Nell home. It seemed the retired police officer did not want his little round wife driving in the frosty dark, although there was a hunter's moon.

Closing her terrace door, Kismet leaned against it. She rubbed her rounded belly and thought of her husband. Feeling familiar want, she wondered where he was.

Kismet suddenly despised the fact that thoughts of Lyle could arouse her. Headed to her bedroom, she had another disturbing thought. Despite all they had been through, *she loved Lyle, still.* Kismet believed the man loved her too, although right now, that appeared debatable. True, the wife didn't approve of all that had transpired between them, but her husband was not the only one at fault. This Kismet realized more each day. Therefore, she told herself, after the baby was born, if she and Lyle didn't go back to what they had once been …then she would learn to live with it.

Chapter 43

GINA hated that at the glitzy Huntington, Long Island, steak house, there were cars everywhere. She could have kicked herself too for wondering if she looked okay. The truth was no, she didn't look right. She was fat, and her natural needed a shape up. This she thought while ordering a drink, one that *she* paid for. Let Thomas's brother see her with it. Let the big star digest that she could not be bought. This Gina thought as she followed a skinny chick to a table. It was near the back, in a glassed-in section. Surely it had to be VIP, for ballers, and high rollers.

A different skinny chick, a blonde one, mentioned the wine list. "That would be in French or Italian, right?" Gina didn't read those languages, so she said, "Please bring me another one of these." She tapped her glass and waved away the wine list. Wine? Please. She couldn't afford an appetizer in this place, with its dark paneling and cozy wall sconces.

While hearing conversation and clinking glasses nearby, Gina tried to appear bored. However, through the shaded windows, she noticed black SUVs and a few people with cameras. Slowly, cold realization dawned. Those people were *paparazzi*, and they thronged Thomas' brother!

Unfolding himself from a silver Carrera GT, Brother appeared chic, sexy, and unperturbed. Gina gaped because what did that Porsche cost— a lil over a hundred grand? Uh-oh, what had she stepped into? Gina wondered as she watched the man who was even taller than on TV. Yeah, she'd tuned in until his show was canceled, after he'd moved on to bigger things. Gina squinted because Beau was so clean. All she could do was stare even though she didn't want to; she really wanted to maintain an air of indifference. But this man was Thomas's *biological* brother?

The actor moved gracefully. No. He prowled, like a beautiful jungle cat, and those in the crowded room sensed him even before they saw him, and that light. Seeming to shine right out of him, the man's light gently bathed everyone within radius. Watching him, all Gina could think was no wonder he was a star. He was radiant, and he definitely had *it*! Granny would say it was *the anointing*.

Beau shook a man's hand and heartily pumped it while chuckling with another. He then placed his arm around a woman. Beau took someone's toddler on his arm. He did similar gracious things for people with every step, things that kept him away from his invited guest.

Still, the nurse noticed the broad bi-racial male mountain. With Brother, Mount Man had a formidable dragon tattooed on his bald head. There were other men like Dragon, too. Nearby, they hovered, but if she hadn't paid attention, they'd have seemingly melded into the crowd.

Wow! Gina had to begrudgingly admit, 'Brother' really was something; at the same time, though, he seemed real, and caring. Or he was one hell of an actor. Gina pursed her lips and wanted to despise Beau, but suddenly she felt eyes. Turned on her, people wondered, *who was she? What business could she possibly have with the bronze prince?*

Finally, at his table, the one at which she sat, Beau noticed defiance. He saw it in the tilt of the woman's head, and in the lift of her slightly pointed chin. He gave her silent kudos for not being a shrinking violet. So she had a spine, he thought. She was going to need it.

"Regina," Beau cordially greeted her, extending a beautiful hand.

No phony polished nails, Gina thought, glancing and grasping.

Authoritatively Beau spoke. "Glad you could make it." He gestured to the dragon slayer. "This is Bo, too. He'll join us."

Grudgingly Gina spoke, knowing Bo was security. "If he must..."

Thomas's brother surprised her by laughing. Still, Gina wanted to appear nonchalant. Heck, she wasn't about to allow Beau or his dragon slayer to intimidate her. Therefore, she got the party started by inquiring, "You wanted me here for what?"

Beau removed a small clean-wipe packet from his designer jacket. Tearing it open, he asked easily, as though she had said nothing, "What are you drinking?" Using the small wet-towel, he cleaned his hands.

Gina replied while feeling annoyed because she was fat and riled up. She projected annoyance onto their server too because the blonde was cute and intimidated, evidenced when Beau asked her to bring 'the lady' another of her current libation. The server turned, but Beau asked her for sparkling water. He named his preference. The girl pivoted, and musically Beau called out, "Nesta?"

Hearing her name, the server nearly became apoplectic. She was aware that consumed with jealousy, her frenemies inconspicuously watched. They also envied the tip she was sure to receive. "Yes, Sir?"

Beau asked for a longneck beer, naming a brand, before he chose appetizers. Gazing at his guest, he said, "And Regina, for you?"

Sourly, she told the girl who nearly hyperventilated with excitement, "I'll pass."

"Right, then," Beau dismissed Gina. Unfazed, he informed the server that he would need the bill for specific other tables, when the time came.

As Nesta dashed off, like an ungainly exuberant toddler, Beau asked, "So, Ms. Gina, what are your intentions regarding my brother?"

"You don't waste time," Gina retorted, her stomach loudly growling.

"No time to waste," Beau replied, as sparkling water appeared.

"I know you asked me here," Gina haughtily began, "because you think I'd hurt Thomas. Well, you're wrong." Of their own volition, words tumbled from her lips. "I've been angry ever since y'all called me. So I'm not gonna kiss your boots or play games with you. I love your brother!" Dang! Forget finesse, even though she hadn't meant to blurt things out. Well, it was done, so she continued. "You may not know it, but Thomas is the nicest, sincerest man I've met in a while—"

"So, you *love* him…" Beau repeated, studying the round woman with the crinkled hair and unblemished brown skin. "You do know," the actor quietly stated, "you can't love my Thom today, and tomorrow decide differently. My brother's not that kind of man. He would never understand, and *I* would not take kindly to you winding him up."

"Winding him up?" Thomas was no toy, and she wasn't playing! "Look, I'm not into games. Heck, *I* can probably provide a better environment for him than you can, with your—*lifestyle*," Gina huffed. There were things she knew, things Thomas had unwittingly told her, and things she'd read. Intent to make Brother see, Gina forgot those nearby. She waved the panicked server away. "Come back later." Gina didn't give a damn about the dragon slayer either and cut her eyes at him, because she *would* have Thomas, one way or another.

Beau noted the woman's fury and coldly advised, "Agitating *me* is not the way to go, if you think you want any kind of future with my brother."

The fight eased from Gina just that fast. She realized the man was powerful, and she wasn't. "I know I'm not important to you," she began. "But to your *brother*, I am. God knows I don't want to start off wrong with you because I don't wanna be found dead like people on your show, but you've gotta know, I won't freely or easily fade away."

Beau stared at the mouthy woman, cogitating on the fact that his brother would never willingly leave his care, not without his blessing. *But*, Beau realized, Thomas shouldn't have to choose. Considering the nurse, Beau nearly saw the thoughts that flitted across her proud round face. He'd studied facial expressions; he'd had to, to exact and request them while acting and directing. Therefore watching, and hopefully unnerving Gina, the director silently waited. He knew that doing so would cause the woman to admit what she really wanted.

Beau doubted Ms. Regina sought the financial, unlike others. He was aware that she thought he knew nothing about her, but he'd dug up enough. Beau saw she had good credit and that she'd received excellent references from people she had probably forgotten. Even Mireya and Kiss, true judges of character, liked her; Brett didn't, but who did Brett really like, with all her issues? Slender Brett had said Gina was pushy, a regular ol' bossy the cow. However, Regina Rounds could actually prove to be what Thom needed. Lord knew she was what he wanted.

Sick of the staring and ready to go home, Gina spoke. "I really don't want to agitate you. I just want...your blessing, Mr. DeVeaux." Gina was surprised she hadn't choked while groveling.

"Just Beau."

"Okay, *Beau*. I want you to tell your brother it's okay for him to want me. Tell him it's okay for him to love me, too, because I love him."

"You know, if I do that," Beau levelly began, "he'll want to live with you, forever. Have you considered that?"

"I have." Gina inhaled, for courage. "I know too that Thomas is like a child, in some ways, but in others, the ones that matter to me, he's not. I can handle him. I can protect him. *I* am the best person in this world for him." Gina's voice shook. "Nobody else will love Thomas like I do."

Beau watched as the woman shallowly breathed. Dang, did he wish to capture her on camera! She was formidable! Beau would have used her footage to teach his acting students to wordlessly convey emotion because boy, was Ms. Gina a natural! She was so in touch with her feelings, she wore her heart on her sleeve. No wonder Thom loved her. She was the female Thomas!

Beau gently waved the server away. "You know what, Regina?"

The nurse felt breathless. "What?"

"I didn't think I'd like you. I found out you were married, *and* a mother." Beau let that sink in. "Your family died though, in a travel-train derailment while headed to your in-laws in Vancouver. You survived only because you worked that day."

Gina spoke with downcast eyes, as painfully, she remembered. "I was supposed to meet them, that weekend..." She never saw blond laughing Steve or her little cafe-au-lait colored boy alive again.

Ah. That Beau had not known as he said, "You seem pushy, yet you heal people when you put your hands on them. I suspect it's because you really care."

Gina's eyes filled. Caring for patients had become her way of doing so for her husband and curly haired boy, who were no longer present.

"I see too," Beau revealed, "that you have a sweet, southern cadence to your voice. You carry yourself with grace. When I'm not upsetting you, that is. And 'someone' says you can cook, so contrary to what *you* believe Ms. Regina Anita Rounds, *I* believe my Thom could not do better than *you*."

Gina blinked and audibly breathed. "Oh, wow," she marveled. *Wow*.

Taking in her stunned expression, Beau chuckled. "Now, Ms. Regina, we are going to need to order, or little Nesta, our server, is going to come apart."

Gina giggled then, just like a girl.

Beau found he liked the sound as the nurse leaned in to whisper. "I know you asked before, and I acted ugly, but if I order something now, will it still be your treat? I ask because I'm starving, but everything in this place blows my budget."

Truthful, just like Thom. Beau chortled and placed his hand over hers. "Ms. Gina, I love your honesty." Beau had also noticed his security man's smirk. Mirth had really tugged up the corners of Boulder's mouth; what a rarity.

"Um, Mr. Beau?"

Beau gazed at the menu. "Regina, I told you, it's just Beau."

"Okay, Beau." Trepidation emitted in Gina's voice. "I'm ashamed to ask... but since you're paying, may I have a club soda, too?"

Returning his gaze to her, Beau kindly informed the nurse, "Order what you like, doll; taking care of it would be my pleasure."

It sincerely would, Beau thought because suddenly, he liked the nurse and her candor. Beau liked the idea of the woman belonging to Thom too, and Thom to her.

Chapter 44

INFUSION was scheduled to play The Arena, a mammoth club in Miami. Beau had asked Saavion to accompany him. The couple arrived the day before the gig. At MIA, just beyond the airport's automatic exit doors, they were whisked into a hired car. The couple felt no heat or humidity. In their climate controlled luxury ride, they were also unaware of snarled morning traffic.

MIREYA, Gypsy, and the band had arrived the night prior. In the decadent, pastel-colored hotel, Mireya woke and glanced at her travel clock, nearly noon. She saw Gypsy. He'd showered and was moving about.

Wearing shorts and a tee, he leaned to feel her up. He also announced he needed to scram. Fondling Mireya's lush round tits, he wondered. What had he been about to say? He couldn't think, not while tasting her large inviting nipples. Oh. "I gotta make afternoon sound check."

Yet Gypsy couldn't resist snaking a hand beneath the sheet. He found Mireya moist and ready. "Got ten minutes," the drummer stated. In a flash, his shorts were aside his engorged rod was in hand.

Mireya flung back the sheet. Magnificently nude, she splayed her legs. When Gypsy surged into her she moaned. "Do me fast and hard."

Afterward, sexy and tussled, she opted for a few more minutes in bed. She recalled that back in New York, after school, her seven year-old would be with Brett. In the evening however, Arlise would be back at home with Ann, Mireya's partner. Thoughts of kissing the man whose eyes were the color of honey intruded. Mireya realized, unlike most women, *she* was fortunate enough to enjoy two worlds.

IN the penthouse suite, Beau stood in the enormous shower. With hot water pelting rippling muscles he shuddered, because Saavion knelt before him. Holding Beau's brown penis, the light-skinned man whispered, "Who's your daddy?" Then Saavion took Beau soaring.

Afterward he bent, so Beau could deliciously pound him, again and again. Squeezing Saavion's high-yella waist, Beau repeatedly drove his member as far into Saavion as he could. He did so until he was spent.

Leaning against the shower wall, Beau knew he had to lather up because soon a car would arrive. It would take him to The Arena. Yet before he knew it, he and Saavion hungered again.

Throwing on clothing, Beau knew he had to get out of the bleached modern suite. The one with the bay view, marble flooring, potted palms, and vibrant, splashy artwork. He could not continue to let Saavion do sinfully erotic things to him. Not now. Later, he could succumb.

Wearing white, paper-thin couture, Beau winked at the man who watched as he grabbed his cell phone and his wallet. "Foolin' wit' you, Nugga," Beau teased, "I could wind up having a heart attack—seeing that I'm not so young anymore. Then," the bandleader called from the *en suite* elevator; "what would my crew tell tonight's concert-goers?"

Saavion grinned. "That you went out with a bang?"

Beau chuckled. "Come to sound check, or meet me for dinner."

Saavion's grin broadened. "Will I get more of the same?"

"You might get a 'tossed salad.' Later." Beau nodded at the ever-discreet Boulder, as the elevator descended. "You get you some?" Beau asked, remembering the prior evening and women who'd longed to climb the mountain.

"Possibly," Boulder replied and exited, prepared to shield and deflect.

SHE took a leisurely shower, and in a plush spa robe, padded about the air-conditioned suite. Crossing bare feet in the chair beneath her, Mireya ate breakfast, and decided she would shop.

Later, the cinnamon-skinned woman stood before a boutique's bevy of dressing room mirrors. She did so like the plum-colored sheath.

Noticing Mireya's remarkable rack, the sales woman announced that the cowl-neck knit would cling in all the right places. "Oh, and I have just the thing..."

Mireya laughed when presented with a small box containing pasties and a matching thong. She was told, "You'll knock him dead, girl."

Back at the hotel, Mireya visited the salon. Her glorious mane was tended, her cinnamon-skin buffed, and she treated herself to a mani pedi.

With skin, hair, and nails right, Mireya reveled in appraising glances as she sashayed up the hotel's main staircase, a wide marble affair. Headed to her shared suite, she felt like a million bucks. Inside the cool glossy space, she wondered. Why didn't she treat herself more often?

ARRIVING, Saavion watched as Beau's hand-held microphone was considered because he sometimes performed old school. The optician observed Beau's walk-through, which the crew expected. All held their breath, abhorring the possibility that things might not go right.

Speaking with his stage manager, and the lighting and graphics coordinators, Beau turned. He greeted staff, and remembered the names of local union workers; all essential to establishing a rapport. He saw too, that everything was to his liking, and there were inaudible sighs of relief.

Later, riding to the hotel, beneath the waning sun and swaying palms, Saavion spoke. "Beau, I know Mireya sometimes calls you controlling, but..."

Both men chuckled, and claimed it wasn't true. Well not entirely, anyway, they laughed.

THAT night at The Arena, Beau, the nascent neo-soul star, was nothing short of sensational! With his tall buff frame, he worked every inch of the stage. He prowled. Gyrating and growling, he gave the audience everything he had and then some. At one point, he even tore off his tank top and beat his chest while moaning about bitter love.

Glistening with oil and sweat, his dog tags flickered amid his custom crafted light show. Appearing glorious, a gunner god, that most everyone in the gasping audience wanted a piece of, Beau announced his last number. As the intro began, he acknowledged his backup vocalists and his kick-ass band. Loving the cheers and the chants that built to a frenzied crescendo, he made the 'mistake' of saying he felt the love.

"Miami," he whispered into the mic, as though to a lover. "Your sweet vibe is washing over me, in waves, and I gotta tell you. I'm crazy for you, Mi-am-meee!"

The audience went wild.

Sweat-soaked, Beau's jeans clung to his sinewy legs. With his rub-board abs, toned chest, and bronze arms bare, he stood grinning, and waiting for the spasms to pass. Then with hands together, as though he would pray, he began what he did best. He connected with his audience. Speaking softly, he said he knew most had read his books, those penned by his author friend April, so they knew about his life thus far. They knew what hurt or made him laugh. His followers knew his struggles, with himself, his mother, drugs, and relationships. They knew his triumphs and his tears. Therefore, he would always keep it real with them. "I know you didn't have to come out tonight," he acknowledged.

The audience cheered.

"Not one of you had to spend your money. You don't even have to care about me and what I do...but you do! You," he pointed into the cheering throng, "and you, make it so I can do what I do." Beau spoke slowly, feeling emotional as he often did by this time in the show.

"That, I *never forget*. It's the reason I love you. Be safe my babies, and be fam—be family for somebody. Everybody needs that, especially people like us. People who've chosen to live life on our own terms!"

Audience members screamed, while others wailed as Beau belted out his last verse and chorus. Then tossing his mic, he strode from the stage.

ON the move, he caught the towel that his assistant slung his way. With head covered, Beau waved as he quickly trod past palpitating hordes blocked from thronging him. From Tatum, Beau accepted a green-glass bottle of water. With Boulder and others shielding him from screaming girls as well as guys young enough to be his children, Beau entered his dressing room, where Saavion waited.

"If I hadn't seen it..." In wonderment, the light-skinned man shook his head, "If not for my own eyes, I would never have believed it."

"What's that?" Beau asked, pulling on a clean dry tee. In reply to another he acknowledged that he would indeed go back to the hotel, because he was drained.

"If I hadn't seen that crowd clamoring and jostling—like you were the second coming, I'd never have believed it. Damn!" Saavion appeared amazed. "Every single time I see that, it's new. Is it to you?"

Subdued, because to whom much was given, much was required, Beau admitted, "Yes, it's always new...but more so, *humbling*."

Covering his boss' head and shoulders in a plush terry hooded robe, so he wouldn't take cold, Beau's young assistant spoke. "Tonight was nothing. Just wait till we go on the European Fam Tour."

"Tatum," Beau softly called, as quickly they were ushered into the hallway. "We take nothing for granted—remember?"

AT the penthouse, following a shower, Beau enjoyed honeyed herbal tea with lemon. In his private quarters, nude, he sat bedside, speaking with Kismet Staar who was at home. She assured him she was fine. "Ms. Fannie," the day lady who adored Beau, "would have called if I wasn't. So how was the show?"

Craving a cigarette, Beau was modest. "It went well."

"It went better than that," his cousin chided. "Remember, I've seen you in action; when *my* cousin does his thing, he abs-so-lutely *rips* shit!"

"Hey," Beau laughed, "that excitement can't be good for my baby."

"You're right." Tickled, The Momma rang off.

Donning dark denim, a designer tee, a scarf, and sandals, hotness entered the bleached modern living room. Above the music, Beau announced to those lounging that he felt like going out.

Turning toward him, Mireya's eyes widened, and for his ears only she said, "My darling friend for life, you look so very gay tonight."

Beau air kissed her cheeks. "My boo, I must say, you do too."

"Don't I?" Mireya preened, as Beau went to sand before the large window. Staring out over the lights of Miami to the indigo ocean, he called over a shoulder, "Tatum, what's the name of that club, the one you mentioned the other day?"

Quickly the youngster rose, his ever-present planner in hand, "The one with the rotating dance floor?"

"That's the one." Beau suddenly felt like he needed to indulge in dance and drink, among other things, because who knew? This could wind up the last time he did so before the arrival of his baby.

"It's called Neo Gomorrah, Boss, and you can be there in twenty minutes."

WHEN Beau entered the club, with security and his entourage in tow, he already had a slight buzz. On the ride over, he'd enjoyed a subtle aromatic champagne cognac, a fine dry *Ambre* with a hint of vanilla.

Inside Neo Gomorrah, packed, and vibrating with techno and house music, Sally's and Becky's, who became a delightful dilemma for security, instantly set upon Beau. Yet assured that his team would do what they did, Beau squinted through the dimly lit haze and spotted the large circular dance floor. He also noticed aloof Eliana's and sultry Shaniqua's. All coolly eyed or extended near-imperceptible invitations.

Then he saw them, in the very middle of the club's ever-turning dance floor, the enclosed glass cylinders. On differing levels, these VIP sections housed decadent button-tufted circular beds and smaller cylindrical seating. Beneath mini chandeliers, in the decidedly debauched and immoral atmosphere, those privileged enough to be in the cylinders could watch hundreds of gyrating partygoers, and they could also be watched.

Mireya screamed as in designer stilettos, she and Gypsy again readied themselves to jump between dancers on the ever-revolving floor. "When?" she yelled, to be heard over booming booty-shaking hip-hop.

"Here comes a spot!" Gypsy yelled, looking into Mireya's eyes.

She laughed as Beau, Saavion, and Boulder leapt. All barely managed to remain standing. On the revolving floor, after balancing themselves, Beau and Saavion triumphantly waved.

Returning her gaze to Gypsy, Mireya yelled, "On three?"

Without warning, Gypsy spun her and wrapped her tightly in his arms. With muscular thighs pressed to her buttocks, the drummer leapt. He and Mireya landed amid the dancing throng. Planting his feet, Gypsy held Mireya as she swayed, adjusting to what felt like the pitch and roll of a ship. Turning, she pressed her face to the man's black tee.

He felt her shaking. In her ear, his voice was soft. "Bae, you okay?"

She raised her head, and swung back her blunt-cut hair.

"You're laughing," Gypsy marveled, seeing the white of her teeth.

"I tried to gauge our turn," Mireya admitted. "Then you shocked me."

The lovable man squeezed Mireya tightly, adoring the feel of her curves beneath her sheath. "Hey," he sounded awestruck as his hands traversed her. "You've got nothing on under this..."

"Maybe," Mireya forgot her thong. "Then again, maybe not." Wriggling past many, she was aided up and onto the dais where Beau and his party, at least twenty deep, entered a glass cylinder. Around the inner perimeter, security stood while Beau, Saavion, and others plopped down on a large, sinfully scarlet circular 'bed.'

Climbing onto a smaller version, Mireya grinned and hoisted herself backward so that Gypsy might also settle in. With his shoulders between her splayed legs, and the back of his head resting on her pelvis, the drummer was in heaven. Gazing up from that vantage point, he fondled the heavy underside of a breast, its shape and nipple clearly outlined.

"Lean over," Gypsy suggested, as aside, Beau ordered champagne.

Mireya did, and felt Gypsy nip her with his teeth. Oh, the gaping cowl-neck of her dress. "Keep on," she saucily promised, feeling his lips on her cinnamon skin, "and I'll put the whole thing in your mouth."

"Yeah baby," Gypsy grinned, wrapping her in an upside down hug.

Beau leaned into his optician. "So Saav, what do you think?"

Before the other man could answer, a circle jerk and having the drapes pulled for privacy crossed Beau's mind. But no, he decided, he wanted to see, and be seen.

Squeezing Beau's hand, Saavion replied. "I think this is just how I pictured Sodom and Gomorrah when I heard about it in Sunday school."

Beau laughed, "With all this drinking and dry humping, huh?"

"Mmm, more or less."

Beau guffawed, as something on the peripheral snagged his attention. "Damn," he spat, and quickly leaned forward. He reached for Mireya, but missed, as Gypsy pulled her up.

The drummer's hands ascended her torso and stopped beneath the weighty flesh he longed to fondle. Forcing his hands to rise, Gypsy grasped Mireya's head and covered her mouth with his.

Saavion and Beau watched the handsome twosome exit. As they joined the booty-shaking mass below, Saavion asked what was wrong.

With her stunning hair, stilettos, and dress that fit like second skin, shapely Mireya was a vision, just like she had been at prom. Yet, pushing remembrances from mind, Beau spoke to Saavion. "Don't look now, but to your left is that woman. The one I told you about."

"Fatal Attraction?" Saavion asked, not moving his head. He sounded annoyed. "What would *she* be doing *here*, in Miami?"

"Hell if I know," Beau stated over Two Chainz. Then he re-canted, inconspicuously eyeing the woman who stood in the shadow of a large over-hanging speaker. "She's here stalking. She's tracking and lurking. It's what she does." Maybe, Beau thought, he should have the drapes drawn, but that wouldn't help. "She thinks Gyp is her property."

"You think he's seen her?" Saavion asked.

"No," Beau surmised, feeling like he wanted to leave, or have Mary hauled from the premises. "But when he finds out, he won't be pleased."

"Neither will Mireya."

Beau's lips wryly twisted. "That's putting it mildly."

FORGETTING Mary, about whom Boulder and security had been alerted, Beau proceeded to enjoy the wild night. Stepping from his glass enclosure, sleek and sexy, he danced near Mireya and Gypsy. Beau chuckled when Boulder shook his bald head. He and his team wound up working for real. With women all over Beau, and men lustfully eyeing and reaching for the actor, Beau wound up having the time of his life.

"You've returned, from among the masses," Saavion teased when Beau flopped onto a smaller sphere because members of his entourage lounged on the larger.

"What's up with them?" Beau asked, thumbing toward Mireya, nearly rolling around with Gypsy. "They think they're the only two here?"

"They're in heat," Saavion quipped, as Beau nudged his girlfriend. "Reya," he called out, to be heard over streaming bass and conga drums.

Nibbling on Gypsy's neck, while all around, excess reigned, the woman twisted to face Beau. "You're interrupting."

"Like I care," Beau snorted and wrapped a large hand about Mireya's wrist. "Keep your eyes on me." Beau said it as Kendu, the backup drummer, bent to speak to Gypsy. Beau enunciated, "You don't want to see who I see." He told Mireya where to look, "In a minute."

Mireya's eyes narrowed as she lay between Gypsy's thighs, her breasts pressed to his torso. Slowly she turned her head. When she saw the iniquitous brown eyes boring into hers, she could have lunged.

"What is *she* doing here?" Mireya angrily inquired, beginning to haul herself up. Then she thought better. Why not make Miss Holy jealous?

With slatted eyes, Mireya faced Mary, who'd thought she was hidden, below, in the gyrating throng. Mireya made sure the other woman knew she wasn't. Mireya also made sure Mary noticed. It was *she* who was seated between Gypsy's powerful thighs, not Mary.

Aware that he had not yet seen the dough girl, Mireya wriggled, turned, and pressed her backside to Gypsy's groin. Instinctively his hands rose, to cover the taut peaks visible through her plum knit sheath.

Raising a hand to fondle Gypsy's bald head as he bent to nuzzle her neck, Mireya used her unoccupied hand to pull Beau closer.

Pulling Saavion with him, both heard the hissed question. "B, how did her homely ass get in here?"

"Who?" Gypsy asked, engaged in charting Mireya's topography.

"Nobody," Mireya whispered, and turned to press her lips to Gypsy's gleaming forehead. With her eyes on Mary, Mireya noticed.

The woman could have spit fire.

Revved up, Gypsy whispered that he was ready to go. Agreeing, Mireya allowed herself to be pulled upward, and people shifted. Beau stood, as did Saavion. Touching his earpiece, Boulder spoke, "Moving, boys." Shoulder forward, he became a shield. Catching Saavion's hand, Beau knew. In some paper, or on TMZ, or somewhere on the internet the following day, there would be a phalanx of photos. He and those with him would be mercilessly dissected, along with his performance earlier in the evening. He could care less, because the truth was: he had chosen this life. Yet his friends had not, and they would wind up in the crossfire. Sure, most would say they didn't mind, but sometimes Beau couldn't fight the guilt. Descending the steps outside the glass cylinder, the producer/director and bandleader sighed, because such was his life.

"Car's out front," Boulder announced as he and others forced over-anxious party people from Beau's path.

Half-running, Mireya fought to keep up with Gypsy who gripped her hand as he strode before her. She also attempted to talk to Beau, who was jostled about beside her as he clutched Saavion's hand. With waves of music crashing overhead, loudly Mireya spoke. "Somebody should've stopped that floor-licking loon at the door. She can't have a laminate, so what was she doing that close to us?" Tired of the stalking, Mireya also asked, "Why's she not somewhere praying, for our sin-sick souls? How crazy is she to be in Miami, chasing a man who don't want her?"

Opting not to speak, Saavion didn't state the obvious. The woman was fixated. He realized. To someone like Mary, someone who was unhinged, preference didn't matter. A stalker wouldn't care what her prey preferred. All a stalker thought about was what *she* wanted.

Baffled, Beau remained silent while being hustled from the club. He felt Boulder's hand atop his head, easing him into their ride as people screamed and flash bulbs went off in his face.

As they rode, Beau felt uneasy. He needed to meet with his team, alert them. No more playing. Mary was officially *persona non grata*.

Mireya hissed from her position on Gypsy's lap. "Beau, I want you to do something."

"About what?" Gypsy asked, indulging in foreplay in the dark.

"It's nothing," Mireya protectively replied as she became aroused.

"I still say he," Gypsy "needs to know. Now," Saavion interjected.

"I'll tell him," Mireya announced, in protective mama mode. "Tonight."

"Tell me what," Gypsy inquired, bumping Mireya with his bulge.

"We'll talk later," she promised, and in the dark, placed his hand on her fevered flesh. Although she could hardly think straight, she managed to plead with Beau who was more concerned than he'd let on. "She can't be allowed to keep turning up, B."

In thinking aloud, Saavion asked, "What kind of money does this person have, to wind up everyplace you guys go?"

In the dark, Beau pressed a kiss to Saavion's palm, "That and other things I intend to find out." He addressed Mireya. "Did *you* do as I said?"

"I didn't get the chance." She stifled a gasp as Gypsy's fingers stroked moist hidden flesh, "But I'll mention things tonight. I promise."

"Do that," Beau ordered, sick of Mary; heck, were she not skulking about, the band would still be having fun. Yet Beau wondered, as did Saavion, if Mary was a regular working woman would she be able to follow the band from city to city, or state to state? Most likely not.

In the dimness, Beau noticed Mireya, nearly liquefying with desire. "Yo, don't get so caught up that you don't open your mouth—to speak." Beau leaned forward. "Gyp man, hol' up a minute. Mireya needs to tell you about Dough Girl. Remind her. It's stuff you really need to know."

Beau sat back, satisfied that Gypsy's curiosity had been piqued.

Unsettled, the bandleader fingered his dog tags. He felt as though icy fingers traipsed up his spine. Beau felt he had to do more, because could he ever forgive himself if something happened, on his watch?

IN the pastel-colored hotel suite, Mireya disappeared. Gypsy removed his pants, from which fluttered a gas station receipt. It was from New York. What the—? Gypsy turned the paper over, knowing he didn't drive. He squinted at scrawled girlish handwriting.

THE ROD IS FOR THE FOOL'S BACK!!

Perplexed, Gypsy remembered; Mireya was supposed to tell him something. Beau had said. Yet when she appeared, magnificently nude, everything left his mind, all but the shimmering pasties covering her nipples.

Seeing the gleam in Gypsy's eyes, all that she had been commanded to say slipped from Mireya's mind.

Chapter 45

DESPITE raging wind and rain, Kismet prepared dinner for Beau's band. It was a ritual. Band members appeared at her home, usually on the first free Friday following an out of town gig. Those times, someone would get their favorite, like Gypsy would that evening. Kismet had prepared Brunswick stew and soft buttery cornbread.

Seated before the TV in his cousin's den, Beau heard the drummer murmur, between bites, that the tender meat and savory vegetables reminded him of his mother. Allowing his mind to wander, Beau thought about his upcoming trip. He, Gypsy, his cinematographer, his DP, director of photography, and others, would head for Miraunga Isle, then Karina Cay. His friend had written about the two little-known islands.

Beau wondered if the trip would need to be postponed. It was November, and the last of hurricane season neared. Beau had copiously followed televised forecasts and the storm's latest path. He knew that sweeping along the east coast, a looming storm appeared enormous.

Actually, earlier in the evening, as he'd left home, it had been blustery out and there had been rain. The authorities advised staying indoors. They deemed conditions unsafe, which included deluges, flooding in low-lying areas, and wind damage.

While eating and watching Lyle's big screen, Beau recalled. People were evacuated in the Golden Isles where his author friend lived, while others contemplated the alternative. When he'd spoken to her earlier, April had said that due to gale-force winds and high waves, shop windows were boarded up. To combat coastal inundation, storm shutters had also been drawn and boats hauled from the marina.

Unperturbed by the weather, Kismet's eldest sat beside Beau. As he spooned up delicious mac 'n cheese, she used her sibling's derivative of Uncle Beau. "Buncle, you need help." The teenager eyed the man who called her and siblings 'the monsters.' "Yup, since my momma's baby— I mean *your* baby—is gonna be born in a minute." Boldly, Déja advised, "You need to fix the baby's room –and I've got ideas. I *am* going to be an interior decorator, you know."

"Is that so?" Beau managed not to appear amused. "I guess we should put you to work then." He said it because it was time. Beau pondered getting Saavion involved, too, since he was already involved. Eyeing his young cousin, who no longer seemed distressed over the family's addition, Beau nodded. "When you help me fix the nursery, that will be your own special part. You know that, right?"

Déja nodded and blinked back tears. Beau's words warmed her inside because, being adopted, she really did need a part that was all her own.

Beau hugged her and whispered. "I was adopted too, Monster."

Déja's eyes shimmered. "I know, by my Nannie," Beau's Aunt Nell.

Later, when Kismet passed her cousin, she whispered. "Whatever you said made my Déja happy. Seems you made Gina happy, too; look how she and Thom are cuddling."

LATE that night, Lyle crept to the terrace doors. Exhausted, Kismet opened them. Against forceful wind and rain, the husband won the fight to again close them. Wet and bedraggled, he turned. He saw his wife putting the last foil-wrapped package away.

"Smells like some good cooking went on in here tonight," he remarked. He felt ridiculously overjoyed to be in her presence.

"The band is back," Kismet said simply, and Lyle understood. He watched her, round with the baby that would be so loved. Kiss deserved much better than him, Lyle thought. No, he reminded himself, she deserved *a better him.* That was the reason he had faithfully attended his meetings. He was even working with a counselor. Hopefully, soon he would better manage his simmering anger, too.

As Kismet graciously fixed Lyle a plate, he reached for her. He'd gotten sopped while running from the car to the house, yet she allowed him to embrace her. Kismet relaxed against him, and he inhaled. Wow, did she smell nice. She felt great too, his Kismet, the empress.

IN the morning, Lyle rose early, although, on Saturdays, they used to lie in.

Groggy, Kismet woke and glanced at the clock. Nine something. Although her limbs were numb with fatigue, she needed to rise, see about the children. Oh, and her mother and the Deacon would soon come for the monsters. But Kismet wanted the kids to see their dad first. The twins would be so happy. Squinting, she asked, "Where you going, Lyle?"

He knew she deserved a straight answer, but he didn't want to tell and jinx things. He didn't want to raise her hopes, either, in case he failed.

Kismet struggled to sit up. "You're packing," again. With her heart beginning to ache, she was glad she'd been tired last night. She'd done nothing other than lie in Lyle's arms. Staring out of a window, Kismet forced herself to sound calm. "What am I supposed to tell your children? They'll ask where their father is, on a Saturday morning."

"Kiss, they don't even know I'm here. Just tell them… I don't know. Say I'm at their grandparents." Lyle thumped his overnight bag down.

"They'll want to go too. They love Gran Collette and Gramps."

Lyle sounded frustrated. "Tell them another time."

"Why?" Kismet's voice rose as she flung back cover. "Why should *I* tell your lies? Our oldest daughter is upset –with *me* most of the time—and *I'm* the one who stayed! You left! You're always leaving."

Feeling the anger that never entirely left him, Lyle pointed. "Yeah, but *you* changed the locks."

"After *you* kept staying out!" Kismet wondered if hormones caused her to yell, "You kept drinking! You became mean and unpredictable!"

Couldn't she see he was doing his best? Lyle wanted to shout because, damn it, he just wanted to get a certain number of AA meetings under his belt. Then he could prove to her that he was changing. But she kept trying to send him back. She so easily stirred up mean old Lyle. "Just tell the kids something," Lyle ordered, unable to look at Kismet as he picked up his bag. "Or say nothing." The man shrugged, "I don't care. Do what you want."

"Like you?" Kismet folded her arms and stared into the fireplace. "Lyle," she called out, her voice devoid of emotion. "Since I've put up with your shit, you probably think I'll keep on. I won't, and I won't tell the kids your lies." Kismet noticed her swollen ankles. "Now that you know," she raised her eyes; "go, but beware. This is the last time you walk out." Kismet sighed and told the truth, "I'm tired of this, and you."

Lyle's heart stuttered. Slowly, he asked, "What're you saying, Kiss?"

"You heard me." Dismissively she waved and noticed movement.

In the hallway, silent as a mouse, Déja stood, stunned. In her slender arms, she held Bonaire, one of the twins.

Following his wife's gaze, Lyle spoke. "Hey, Dé. Why don't you go to the kitchen? Give Nar some chocolate milk. Okay?" Lyle didn't understand why she carried that heavy boy around, when the boy let her.

Appearing neat in jeans and a sweater, Déja's heart pounded as she asked, "You leaving, for good this time?"

"No—" Lyle looked to Kismet for confirmation. "Right, Kiss?"

Panicked, Déja's young voice rose an octave, "Then why you got a suitcase? Why Momma looks sad?" Déja's brother slid to the floor.

"I'm taking a little trip." Lyle appeared panicked. "Ask Momma."

Kismet, all raging hormones and swollen limbs, could have slapped Lyle as her daughter's eyes flickered over and back. Déja yelled, "You're lying!" Frightened, her small pajama-clad brother's eyes filled. Instinctively, Bonaire reached up for his big sister's hand.

Wanting to comfort them, Kismet could have strangled the man who seemingly squandered her and her children's love.

Unaware of what else to do, Lyle bent and held out his arms. "Dé, come." He attempted to sound authoritative, "Nar, you too."

Usually, the children obeyed; however, the buzzer sounded, and both froze. Footsteps and voices were heard. "Yoo-hoo!" Nell called out. "Hey, hey," the Deacon woofed, "family's here." It was Nannie and Paw-Paw's usual greeting, but there were no running feet or happy squeals. Down on his haunches, Lyle peered up at his wife.

Appearing in the hallway, the grandparents saw stricken looks. Nell noticed Déja, the nearby suitcase, and Lyle down, reaching for his son.

"KissGirl, we been calling out and banging on the door," Nell stated. "Finally, I used my key. We dragged our old selves up here because nobody was around. This place was like a ghost town."

Kismet watched Déja toss herself at her grandmother. Pressing the child's head to her bosom, Nell shushed her. The grandmother beckoned Bonaire. "Come on lil mister. Help your Paw-Paw find the others."

As Deac herded the small boy and his sister away, Nell remained. From the hallway, she fixed her son-in-law with a stare. Nell glanced at her daughter. The older woman then spoke softly, her words no less commanding. "Y'all fix this—whatever—that Deac and I walked in on. Get it together. Lyle, honey, you bring that luggage on back from wherever you're going because your chirren *and* your wife need you."

The older woman turned as she called out. "Know this too, Deac and I cain't do overnight. We will be branging these kids back here. We've got *communion* in the mo'ning! Oh, and look like y'all need to get up and come to church too; let the Lord heal this rift that's between you."

Chapter 46

THAT Sunday evening while in service, Gypsy thought about Beau. When they'd been at his cousin Kismet's house, the man who was like an older brother had told Gypsy a few things. While he'd eaten that great stew, Gypsy had found it hard to believe what-all Beau's papers said about Mary. She really seemed...just a little misguided, and sad, not nuts. Still, Beau had warned him to stay away from her. Beau believed Mary would hurt Gypsy. Beau thought *she* was hurt because Gypsy wasn't interested in marrying her. Beau said hurt people hurt people.

Seated behind the drums and not really listening to the preacher, Gypsy pondered the scout. He'd agreed to go with Beau later in the week. Gypsy would see Beau's team work out locations for Beau's new movie. It would be fun, Gypsy mused. He loved going to see new things.

The preacher kept talking, and Gypsy kept thinking. It looked like a hurricane was rolling up into Florida, though. It could cause other storms along the coastline. Those, Beau said, weren't good for travel. Carrot-top, Tatum, had even called and said Beau just might postpone the trip.

After church, Gypsy methodically packed his smaller drum paraphernalia.

"Good job tonight, Brother Ainsley."

Looking up and reaching to shake hands, Gypsy beamed. "Thanks, Minister Stevie. You and Sister Angie get home safe, okay?"

"Oh," Lanky Steven clutched his bible. "Do you need a ride?"

"No, he doesn't," a female crisply stated. "*I* have already offered."

Gypsy and Steven turned to see Mary, head covered and clad in white. Looking skeptical, because he and his wife had discussed the woman who'd appeared from nowhere, Steven frowned. Sure, she'd become part of their small congregation, but Steven didn't like 'Sister Strange' or that she showed no inclination to get to know anyone other than their church drummer. Steven knew. She had the devil in her.

Lanky Steven pointedly ignored the woman who gave his wife the willies. "Ride with *us*, Brother Ainsley. We pass your house anyway."

Appearing annoyed, Mary spoke before Gypsy could. "I *said* I'll take him. So you, nor that Ms. Beulah—" Gypsy's next-door neighbor, "will have to. Anyway, she's not here tonight."

Ignoring the woman who hadn't attended for the last two weeks, the pudgy one who often attempted to force her way, Steven sounded skeptical. "Brother Ainsley, will you be okay…with *her*?"

Continuing to zip different compartments, Gypsy appeared as he often did, like he hadn't a care in the world. "Minister Stevie, you and Sister Angie have the kids, so I can ride with Sister Mary here."

Lanky Steven didn't know why that statement irked him, but what could he say? Brother Ainsley was grown. "Well, see you Wednesday."

"Yep, at bible study," with a wave, Gypsy bent to retrieve his sticks. Thus he didn't see Mary churlishly stick her tongue out at Steven. He didn't see Mary scowl at the fashionable young women nearby. They discussed Sister Strange, their name for the woman who'd attached herself to fine Brother Ainsley.

Gypsy remembered the card that Beau had given him. Beau said if he needed a ride, he should contact the number on the card. But Beau would have to pay for the service. Gypsy didn't want to be a drain. As it was, the man he often called Pops was too good to him anyway.

Following Mary outside, Gypsy greeted people who still hung about. Ferrying his belongings to her car, Gypsy recalled Beau's words, those concerning Mary, who hadn't a coat or an umbrella. Settling his snare drum, Gypsy vaguely recalled warnings issued by Beau and Mireya, but he couldn't ask anyone else for a lift, now. It'd be too much trouble.

At her hatchback, Mary inquired, "You want to get a bite to eat?"

"Nah," Gypsy only wanted to get to the house left him by his deceased mother. As he and Mary rode in silence, he peered through the foggy window at rain-slick asphalt. At home, he would put a pain patch on his back. It always ached in inclement weather. Then on the sofa, he'd relax and talk to Mireya, if Ann didn't mind. Or he'd listen to the rain.

Aware that Ainsley Fielding wasn't a chatterbox, Mary spoke. As she turned onto Gypsy's street, she sounded odd. "You know," she began, "the bible says *he that findeth a wife finds a good thing…*"

Gypsy felt the first twinge of awareness because he had heard or seen that statement somewhere other than at church.

Mary repeated it, and Gypsy told her, once more, because she was becoming a pain, too pushy for his liking, "And I don't want a wife."

Mary acted as though she hadn't heard. Again, she used that odd-sounding voice. "The bible also says: *the rod is for the fool's back…*"

Gypsy jerked to look at her. *That* had been on the note in Miami.

Chapter 47

BEULAH called Mireya. "I hate to call so late, baby," the elderly woman stated, "but I b'lieve I should tell you something." Beulah didn't know how else to say it. "I mean, since Hattie," Gypsy's mother, "told me you'd look out for her boy..."

"Go on, Ms. Beulah." In bed, Mireya sleepily glanced at the clock. One twenty a.m. A stone lodged in the pit of the younger woman's stomach. It was never good when older ladies called at ungodly hours.

"Well," Ms. Beulah sighed, "lil while ago, I heard sich screaming—coming from Hattie's house, despite all that rain."

From Gypsy's mother's house, Mireya realized. Suddenly, she was wide awake.

"Them screams sounded like they come from a woman. So at first, I didn't pay any mind. I just thought that boy might have his new TV set up too loud. A half-hour in, though, I realized; even if Hattie's boy *was* watching something, them actor people wouldn't jest *keep* screaming. Movies got music too, you know? Mean music, what scares you. And I didn't hear no music, so I got my coat on and went over there."

Careful not to wake Ann, who had an early flight, Mireya rose from the bed. Pulling jeans over socks, Mireya knew she needed to go check on Gypsy. Gently, she patted Ann, who sleepily murmured. "Shhh-shh honey, lie back down." Aware that Ann needed to be fresh for The Kitten Heel's business meeting in a few hours, Mireya grabbed a sweater.

On the carpet outside the bedroom, she made herself whisper. "Ms. Beulah, did Gypsy answer the door when you went over there?"

"No, baby, that's why I'm bothering *you*; I called Hattie's old number, but I got no answer. So I wondered if you could stop by. I remember Hattie saying, 'fore she died, that she give you a key..."

Mireya's heart sank as silently she prayed. *Please, God, don't let me have to use that key.*

"Ms. Hattie did give me a key, Ma'am," Mireya acknowledged. "I'll come over. I've just got to get somebody to watch my little girl."

"Oh. Well, do what you can." The bent, brown woman sounded confused. "Just don't take too long, okay?"

"I won't, Ms. Beulah."

When she rang off, Mireya tried Gypsy's cell. Voicemail. She got it several times. Assured that her daughter's school clothes were laid out, Mireya pinned money into Arlise's undershirt. In the kitchen, she set up breakfast in case she didn't get back in time.

Then she called *him*, her gay husband.

HE looked at his bedside clock. Nearly two a.m., and he had been sleeping well due to the pounding rain. He sounded raspy, "Yeah."

He could barely understand, but he knew who it was. Beau knew too that there was trouble. "Reya. Reya. What're you saying?" He sat up. At the foot of his bed, Frost sleepily thumped her tail. "Reya, speak slowly."

As she did, he tumbled from the bed, pulling on his clothes. "I'm on my way." He remembered that people had been advised not to drive during or immediately following the storm. They'd been told to put safety first. The advice had been: if one had to go, they should watch out for flash floods, downed power lines and tree limbs, as well as blockages on many roads, so he'd take care. This Beau vowed, flying down the back stairs.

In his car, he called *her*. "Hey lady, wake up. I need you." He became blunt. "Brett, I know the time. Meet me at Reya's. Yes, it's nasty out; I saw that about the widespread power outages, but something's up. I don't know. I *said*, I don't know. Be careful. Speak to you there."

Driving from Long Island to Queens, he dialed his aunt. While speaking with her, he was mindful that severe storms like those plaguing the east coast for days had wreaked havoc in the New York Tri-State area. Beau knew that when down, the same power lines that provided useful electricity to homes and businesses could be considered deadly.

Beau informed his aunt that he was pulling up before Mireya and Ann's. Grateful that Nell would pray, the tall man hopped from his car.

CAREFUL not to wake the deacon, Nell zipped her velour robe. In her kitchen, by the light of the stove, she made coffee. She thought about calling her daughter, but no, best to let Lil Momma sleep. Nell thought to get Farai, but Brantley's daughter was halfway around the world.

The next thing Nell knew, she was saying, "Ames, honey?"

"Nellie," Pink-cheeked Amy whispered as she blinked away sleep. "Everything okay? Shhh, Harvey. Sleep now, love. It's only Nell."

"No rain damage that I know of, Ames, but Beau just called."

Amy reached for her dressing gown. "What's that now?" she quietly asked, seated on the side of the bed that she and Dr. Foster shared.

To her lovely brunette friend Nell explained the little that Beau had told her. Nell wound down with, "Now my Puppy is out there, in the aftermath of these storms. I keep thinking about flooded roads and broken trees. Oh, Ames, I'm worried. Power lines come down when trees tumble, and everything gets tangled..."

Nell refused to speak any more about it. "I told Puppy we'd pray."

"Well, Nellie, none of this is good," Amy acknowledged, hugging herself. "Dear God." It took her back, years, to when they'd lost spirited little butter-skinned Ronni. "Nellie," Amy called. "I've got a question. If you and I are to pray, *what*, my dear, shall we pray *for*?"

HE quickly ascended Mireya's wet front steps. Turning the doorknob, he heard footsteps on the glistening pavement behind him. He pivoted and saw a woman pass beneath a street light. In the dark, slender Brett rushed up. She'd pulled on a swanky belted all-weather coat and boots. Her thin, naturally curled hair, with new honey blonde highlights, appeared wild, and her eyes were wide.

"What happened?" she asked, stepping into the small hallway.

Beau spoke under his breath. "Gypsy; something's up. I can feel it. He's not answering his cell or the house phone. Reya and I both called."

"That's not like him." Although Brett suddenly felt sick, the event planner still spoke reassuringly. "He probably just forgot to charge it."

"The old lady next door called Reya," Beau mentioned. "She was a friend of Gyp's mama. Reya said the old lady heard screaming—from a *woman*. It supposedly went on for a while. The old neighbor banged on Gyp's door but got no answer. We're going over."

"I'll keep Arlise," slender Brett immediately offered.

Beau noticed the fully dressed, cinnamon-brown woman. She was seated on the edge of a kidney-shaped sofa. Lamplight made it clear. She'd cried. Now she penned a note, possibly for Ann. Beau saw Arlise too. In a nightgown, the seven-year-old hung back, appearing frightened. Beau beckoned because he knew it wasn't every day that Arlise saw her mother cry. The little girl dashed over, hugged him, and spotted Brett.

"Arlise...honey, why are you up? And where're your slippers?" Brett hugged the child and spoke to Beau. "Call me when you get there."

"Something happened, Auntie Brett," the growing girl announced. Her slender arms snaked around the slim woman. "In the rain." The child raised her eyes to Beau. "Mummy called you, Unc. Then she cried."

Brett rubbed Arlise's back. She explained that mommy would go with Uncle Beau, "But they'll be back." Brett promised.

"May I bring my blanket and lie on the sofa?" Arlise asked.

"I don't see why not," Brett answered as Mireya approached, shrugging into a jacket.

"Brett, you might wind up taking her to school. 8:15. You know. Everything's ready, but you'll have hair duty, and make sure she brushes her teeth."

Brett spoke to the girl in her mother's arms. "You heard that, right?"

Arlise nodded. "Will you get me from school, Mummy?"

"If she doesn't," Brett spoke up, "guess where you and I will go?"

"For pizza!" Arlise crowed and was hurriedly shushed.

Stepping from the house, Beau heard Mireya mention Ann. He also recalled Brett's occasional twinges of envy because she would never bear a child. "Like a donkey," Brett had often moaned, "I can't reproduce." That was why she'd told Beau to go for it, back when he'd mentioned the chance to get his own child. "Just consider me for Godmother. Please."

Mireya hugged Brett, aware that Brett would care for Arlise. The mother knew Brett would never hurt her child. Instinctively, Brett knew Mireya's thoughts, and the sentiment meant the world to her, especially since her and Mireya's bond was fragile.

Starting his car, Beau recalled that Mireya had once asked, "Brett, why do you want to be a woman, really?" Beau had been mortified. Yet slender Brett had answered with aplomb, "But I *am* a woman."

"Yeah, you believe that," Mireya waved, dismissing Brett's history. "But really Brett, why you doing all this?" Mireya motioned. "The hair, nails, the hormones, the breast injections; why go to those lengths?"

As Mireya fell into the car beside him, Beau remembered blurting, "I can't believe you, Reya! Your capacity to be judgmental is appalling!"

Mireya had become angry, but Beau had shut her down by stating, "You compare people and what they do, to you, like *your* constitution is so together. You'd like us to believe it, but *no one* is that together."

Beau steered into a turn and realized he had to keep thinking and remembering things, or he just might believe the worst concerning Gypsy, his friend and brother. Heaven knew Beau didn't want to do that.

Riding alongside him, a whimper escaped Mireya. "Gypsy is young, B, younger than we are. I guess that makes me a cougar, right?"

Beau wanted to smile, but he didn't; he just kept driving.

"Gypsy's only thirty-three," Mireya moaned. "So that means he's got a lot of life ahead of him. He'll be okay." She whispered, "Right?"

Thinking of his uncle, who had transitioned while reasonably young, Beau glanced over at the woman with whom he had come through many things. "I sure hope so," he murmured. Beau jerked to a stop before the house that offered Mireya a terrible sense of foreboding.

In the wet, chilly night, she could not know that she was feeling reverberations, many from things that had transpired earlier...

GYPSY *wondered what she'd eaten to have her gagging and heaving like that. Mary had started when he'd removed his snare drum from her car. She'd asked to use his bathroom. He'd wanted to tell her she needed to go home if she was sick, but that would have sounded mean. Seated on a plastic-covered sofa, before his big new TV, he popped open a beverage can. Oh, he had to get his pain patch. However, that could wait. Now, his ringtone said there was a message.*

Reaching for his phone, Gypsy vaguely registered running water. In his tub, upstairs? Forgetting it, he saw that Tatum had called. Pops' redhead kid probably had info about the scout trip. Wonder what it was?

Without listening to voicemail, Gypsy called the younger man back. During their conversation, the drummer forgot his unwanted houseguest, until Mary's voice floated down to him.

Gypsy blinked. She was still around? Gypsy wondered how he could have forgotten her. Although he wanted her to leave so he could get comfy, he sure hoped she was okay. He told Tatum to hang on, that he had to check something. Not disconnecting, Gypsy laid his cell phone face-up on the cocktail table. Ascending the stairs, he called out as he went. "Mary. Mary... Girl, you okay?"

MIREYA stepped from Beau's car. Gulping damp night air, she spotted Ms. Beulah. Standing inside her chain link fence, the small woman shivered. Well, no wonder. Her ancient, little lamb's wool coat had three-quarter length sleeves. Her bony brown legs were bare, and her tiny, cute, pink terry slippers had soaked up wet from the pavement.

With her voice thin and frail, Beulah called out, "You got your key?"

Mireya had it in hand, as in the dark of the early morn, Beau headed toward Gypsy's squeaky gate. Silently, Beau prayed before he touched the metal with a boot. Thank God it wasn't electrified.

Close on his heels, Mireya noticed Ms. Beulah. Pink curlers peeked from the scarf on her head. Frail-looking, the little woman fell in step behind them.

Beau turned, gesturing for Mireya's key. "I'm gonna knock." Beau kept it light. "Gyp's probably in here with some woman." Beau knew Mireya didn't want to hear that, but it was better than the alternative.

Any other time Mireya would have despised the presence of another woman. However, this time, if that was the case, she might feel relieved.

Before Mireya, Beau banged on the door. "Gyp," he stage-whispered, aware that it was too early to wake the neighbors. "Yo, Gyp," he called out, a bit louder, "open the door."

Behind Mireya, Beulah sounded shaky. "I'on't think he gon answer." She poked Mireya with a bony finger. "Why'on't he jest use yo' key?"

Beau did, and in the quiet, the door loudly squeaked.

Mireya felt a type of strumming then, as though she were an electronic instrument, vibrating with a message. But for all that she was able to decipher, the message might as well have been in Morse code.

GYPSY *passed the small bedroom, back of the house. It was the one where his new drum set resided. That set never left the house. In the dark, he passed another bedroom, filled with his mother's things. Beckoned by a weak stream of light, he pushed at the bathroom door. Since it was ajar, he entered and noticed steam on the mirror. The man wondered why his tub was nearly full. Was Mary sick? Had she soiled herself? He turned to call her—but she stood before him, her eyes lit with an unholy glow.*

Still, in his inimitable calm fashion, Gypsy asked if Mary was okay. However, he felt uneasy.

Mary said she'd be alright, just before she bent and literally snatched the rug from beneath him!

It happened so fast. Gypsy lost his footing. He felt his feet rise as quickly he sailed backward, toward the tub. Gypsy flailed, yet he fell. He heard water, felt it slosh. He also heard...the crack—as the back of his bald head hit the curled side of the hard, cold, old porcelain tub.

The man felt pain. Now his back ached, worse than when he had been at church. Really, his spine felt strained. Gypsy felt like something began to ooze out of him as he moaned. The bone, back of his head, hurt. Aside from that he felt something ebb away. He didn't know precisely what was leaving his body; maybe it was blood. He couldn't even pinpoint the region of exit, but Gypsy knew. He was quickly losing something vital.

In the tub, Gypsy sagged. His clothes slowly sopped up water. He saw Mary bend over him, with...a syringe? He felt her prick his skin. Then before his eyes, Mary seemingly swam and quickly went blurry. Yet Gypsy's brain registered the question that the woman repeatedly asked.

"Ainsley Fielding, will you marry me?" Marry me...marry me...

BEAU spoke loudly as he stepped into the house. "Gyp, you're gonna have to forgive us, but we're doing this for your own good."

Walking further into the place that smelled of bug spray and decades' worth of fried food, Beau saw a lamp. Beside the sofa, it threw a bit of light. He saw an open soda can. Gypsy's TV was also on, its volume low.

Well, so much for Ms. Beulah's loud, movie-watching theory, Beau mused. "You ladies don't touch anything," the director advised.

He passed through the living room and on into the railroad house's small dining room. He called out. "Gyp, man, come downstairs." Aware of Mireya behind him, Beau wondered if she, too, felt the unnatural cold.

Mireya and Ms. Beulah saw Gypsy's cell phone. On the cocktail table, it lay face-up. Mireya suppressed a gasp because Gypsy always kept his phone with him. Shaking hair from her eyes, she noticed Beau. Suddenly, he took the stairs, two at a time. On the second floor, she heard him call out, as quickly his boots clunked past the small back room. His hastening footsteps said he was headed for Gypsy's bedroom, the largest, at the house front.

Upstairs, before he reached it, Beau noticed the bathroom door, ajar. Apprehensive, Beau called out to alert Gypsy that he would soon enter.

HER *man, Mary thought. Her Ainsley Fielding looked so serene. He often did, but she knew this particular look was due to the effects of the drug. It would immobilize him. She would keep him in that state until he said what he needed to, what she wanted to hear.*

He was so peaceful. He didn't even struggle, but his pulse was faint. Oh, he would be all right when she brought him back around, resuscitated him. He just needed to say he loved her. He was so sweet and gentle. The one time he had come to her bed, he had proved something. She didn't know why she hadn't realized it before, maybe because she'd been blinded by jealousy; that harlot had indeed turned his head. However, the truth was: Ainsley loved her. Mary Trumbull knew it because Ainsley had never been mean to her. Unlike other men, he had never ignored her or gotten his family to chase her off.

Mary glanced down at the bathroom rug that she'd flung aside. She hadn't expected to move like lightning, but she'd had to do something, something to get Ainsley's attention. Now she'd get his attention again, she thought, gazing at him sprawled in the tub. Later, she'd have him naked. But now she said, "Sweet man, you didn't answer my question…"

She moved closer, shuffled through the water that had sloshed onto the floor. "Don't act like you're asleep." Her voice hardened just a bit because they needed to discuss their future.

Yet he played a game, so she leaned to shake his foot. With narrowed eyes, she checked his pulse. Then her pulse leaped. That could not be! It seemed he had only minutes left! Hastily she turned for her other syringe. Hurriedly, with shaking hands, she reached for the new drug, the solution that would resuscitate her Ainsley.

When the clear plastic tumbled from her grasp, Mary panicked. Oh no! With one hand, she shook Ainsley's foot. With the other, she felt around the commode for her syringe. Its contents would bring Ainsley back. She knew. She had attended doctors who had done it many times. Yes, while patients lay on the O.R. table. But where was that second syringe? Blast the small bathroom! With wet hands, and her eyes blurring due to oncoming tears, Mary needed her second syringe! If she could just locate it, all would be well!

She shook Ainsley, feeling frantic. Wake up!

Desperate now, Mary tried to heave her man up. She'd give him mouth to mouth! Yes—but he was heavy and awkwardly sprawled. Oh no! Fighting, she thought to breathe life into him, like God had done Adam in the garden. Yet slipping in the standing water outside the tub, all Mary's planning vanished. She leaned to slap Ainsley's face. "Come on," she hissed, hoping that would do it until she found her syringe. She didn't have much time. "Come on!" she yelled, knowing she only had one minute left. Maybe.

NEXT *door, at her house, Beulah Mae Jenkins put her Sunday leftovers in the fridge. She could catch The Jeffersons or Andy Griffith in*

Mayberry, on the TV Memories channel. Then again, with these pop-up storms, Beulah thought, she just might wind up sitting in the dark. Well, if that was the case, she would hold her bible and wait until all let up.

Wearing her new, pink house shoes, Beulah left her kitchen. That was when she heard it. It was distant, but no less a scream. Then she heard another, and another, each one louder than the one prior...

MARY *yowled, for the umpteenth time, as fear magnified. Her husband-to-be had not moved, at all, for any number of minutes! Shaking him, she screamed, again and again, her throat becoming raw. This wasn't right! This wasn't how it was supposed to be! She was supposed to bring him back, resurrect him! He was supposed to answer her, love her. "Ainsssleeey!" She screamed, and screamed...*

BEAU didn't touch the open bathroom door. Yet he leaned to peer in. *Oh, God!* Gypsy's eyes were open but unseeing. He was slumped awkwardly. His legs, bent at the knee, were outside the tub, but most of his body was in it. He had his clothes on—why? They appeared wet, and his countenance was marked by the waxy pallor of death.

Glimpsing all, in just a few seconds, Beau's knees nearly buckled.

Oh, God in Heaven! No. No! No! Why? *No...*

"Beau," Mireya called, having heard him stop walking. She gained the last stair. When he didn't answer, she began to shake uncontrollably.

Behind Mireya, Ms. Beulah attempted to soothingly speak. "You just take deep breaths, baby. It's OK." Although the older woman meant to comfort, her words sounded hollow even to her in the dimly lit hallway.

Beside the bathroom door, Mireya bumped into Beau. With his back to her, Beau didn't say a word; he just quickly turned. His hands closed around Mireya's upper arms, and swiftly he pulled her to him. She felt him attempt to press her face to his chest. Needing to see, she resisted, especially when she heard Ms. Beulah, who had slipped by, gasp.

"What?" Mireya asked, as in the darkened hallway, Beau forcefully turned her. "Go," he ordered. "Downstairs." His strong hands pushed her. Yet disobeying him, she spun, and he tried to block her way.

Still, she side-stepped, telling him she needed to see, to know.

Holding tightly to her, he didn't allow her to step too far into the dimly lit bathroom that was now a small room of horror.

Inevitably, Mireya staggered back and into Beau's arms. *"Nooo!"* She wailed, nearly loud enough to wake the dead. "No, B! No! *Nooo...*" she cried and felt herself forcibly removed. "Nooo!" she howled, "No!"

April Alisa Marquette

To Beau, everything felt surreal, like he sleepwalked through one of his crime scene dramas; only there was no director to call, 'Cut!' and no showrunner to say 'That's a wrap.'

With Mireya sobbing into his shirtfront and the horrified, frail, elderly neighbor gazing up at him, Beau felt waves of disbelief, grief, *and* anger. It was anger, the likes of which he had only thought he had known in the past. Beau actually wanted to tear somebody's fuckin' head off! He felt suffocated too. Beau nearly felt sunk. A bevy of emotions viciously rose and dashed downward, like waves over his head. Still, he decided. He would *not* go down, not like this, not like a chump.

Beau heard Uncle's voice too, as he often did. *Keep ya head up, boy.*

Sure, Beau was torn up inside, he probably even wanted to throw up, but he could not because there was too much to do. Hell, he hadn't been on that televised drama all those years to now act like a friggin' fool.

Therefore, his cell phone appeared in hand. Beau knew he should call the cops, but not yet; he couldn't. He dialed the kid. Dammit! The very kid who worshipped Gypsy.

Tatum picked up, sounding wiped out. "Uh, hey Mr. B."

"Tate, listen, I don't have a lot of time. Something's happened—"

"What's that noise," the redhead dared, "that crying-like over there?"

"Tate, listen. Call Mycah," Beau's publicist, "tell him to get me somebody here, *right* now, to Gypsy's house. That girl," Beau snapped his fingers. "You know the one. I want her. What's-her-face."

"Belinda," Tatum supplied, "the blonde, she's good."

"Yeah, her." They would need the publicist to spin this because once the police were called, the newswires would pick up the story, and Beau did not want a three-ringed circus. Not for Gyp. "Tell Mycah, I need that cop too; he'll know the one. Tate, reach out to Dan, Gabriel, and Phoebe," Beau's barracuda lawyers. "Then call me back."

"Wait!" Beau's young assistant yelled. "If I gotta send the cops and get Mr. Mycah to send Belinda, I'll have to say *why*, Boss…"

Beau nearly howled then, as he fought to swallow raw emotion and speak over Mireya's loud shuddering sobs. "Tell them…" Beau hated to say it, for many reasons, one of them being: the youngster had crushed on Gypsy. "Say there's been a death. No questions, Tate. Just listen. Tell Mycah I need his cop on the scene, pronto."

Beau's young assistant sounded like he was crying, "Not Gypsy…"

"Make the calls." Beau called the kid's name, "Tate. Tatum O'Reilly."

The redhead sniffled, "Sir?"

Beau emphasized every word. "Do – *not* – show up – over – here."

Tatum blew his nose. Sounding muffled, he said, "I won't."

"Good. Make those calls and get back to me." Ringing off, Beau sighed. With his arms around Mireya, who was spasming out, he put his muscular legs outside hers. He forced her backward. Taking her weight, Beau managed another call, "Saav. No time. Listen. Huh? That's Reya. I'm at Gyp's, *and it is bad* —I just wanted you to know. Call Tatum. He'll explain." With eyes on the frail little woman from next door—what was her name? Who knew? Beau coaxed her to go back downstairs.

"That's it, Ms. Honey," Beau cooed as Ms. Beulah put her small feet in motion, one damp pink slipper before the other. "Hold on." He spoke, as he would have to a child. "Now go down. Slowly. That's it."

Yet holding to Mireya, Beau felt rotten about how he'd had to speak to his assistant, but youngsters didn't always listen. They sometimes needed direction. Heck, *he* needed guidance. Bracing himself, Beau carried limp yet sobbing Mireya down the creaking stairs. Beau suddenly felt bone-weary while knowing this was just the *beginning*.

His mind raced. He knew the press would want to have a field day with this. *That* Beau would not allow! His female friend was wilting and weeping as he all but jumped her down the last two steps.

Beau's phone rang. He couldn't get it, but he did get the little elderly neighbor to sit on the plastic-y sofa. Her testimony was needed, so he couldn't allow her to become any more spooked. "You're doing great," he told her as she stared at Gypsy's phone, lying there harboring secrets.

It hurt to see it, to wonder whom Gyp had last spoken to, but Beau would find out. "Don't touch anything," Beau again told Ms. Beulah. He had the most challenging time folding Mireya into the old-timey chair that matched the sofa. Mireya bent double, shuddering as her hair fell to hide her face. She made little hiccupping noises as Beau's phone rang.

"Mycah," wearily, Beau greeted his publicist. "I couldn't pick up. Yep. That's what it looks like. Belinda? Good. Oh, he lives around the corner? What d'you mean he's no longer a blue? Ah, investigations. Wait." Beau said it because outside a male ascended the steps.

"Knock, knock." A man, in his late thirties and wearing a windbreaker called into the open door. "NYPD; Detective Givens."

Beau beckoned the man forward, as out of doors, the wail of sirens drew closer. "In here." Back into his phone, Beau said, "Mycah, Givens is here; bald, about five-seven? Yep. Thanks." Beau was about to pocket his phone when it rang again. "Tate." While listening, Beau motioned upstairs so that the now-gloved detective could visually begin to catalog some things and hurriedly take notes regarding others.

In passing, the detective announced, "My partner should be here any minute. We'll need to speak with you." He meant Beau, but he eyed hair-hidden shuddering Mireya, as well as the elderly neighbor. "All of you."

Beau knew the drill. He advised Tatum to call Brett. Beau heard footsteps, voices, squawking brakes, and car doors slamming. Through the open door, dizzying police lights flashed, and he knew. Emergency transport would appear. The M.E.—the medical examiner would be alerted, and when the tape went up, the neighbors who'd gathered would peer and speculate. They would take photos and send them to others.

Feeling weary but knowing the end was nowhere in sight, Beau again called Tatum because, in a moment, he wouldn't be able to. With a hand on Mireya's back, Beau spoke to the kid who sounded like he'd been crying, the Irish kid who lived alone, Beau remembered. Dang! Poor son.

"Tate, go to my house. JeRell will fix you something." Beau fumbled a text to his houseman as he spoke. "Drive careful, Tate." ***Rell, Tate On way. put kid n guest rm. Feed. Kp calm. Call my Ant, she'll tk over. Thnx.*** "I'm sorry this happened, Kiddo," Beau said to Tatum after texting, "but *do not come here*. Go to Icebury Court. I'll call you." Beau was about to hang up, to speak with the officers who talked at him. However, he just had to say, softly, "Tate, if you value your job, you will…" stay away from this place, Beau thought, but said, "*behave*."

Damn, Beau mused, as he began to take questions, while all around things were poked, tagged, dusted, and photographed. He knew to Tatum he'd sounded harsh, like someone's father, but he'd had to make it clear.

Later, Beau would explain, but right now, he didn't want the kid any more hurt than he was. Seeing what Beau had seen would not do Tatum any good. The kid needn't drag a morbid memory, or the pall of death with him throughout his life. Heck, if a youngster could be shielded, like Beau's aunt and Gran had tried to shield him years ago, then why not?

It hit Beau then, as by rote he answered question after question.

He had a baby on the way. By default, he had become a father figure to Tatum, his young personal assistant. Beau had long been the stand-in dad for Arlise, Mireya's daughter. He had been and would continue to be a father figure for his younger, slower brother Thomas. Beau would be something similar for Thom's kid, too, when Thom and Gina hit that milestone. And...Beau's knees nearly buckled as he thought of *Gypsy*. Gyp had often teasingly, and not so teasingly, called him Pops.

Beau excused himself. In the tiny, first level half bath, Beau sank to his knees, ambushed by grief. Unclasping his dog tags, he rose and leaned over the sink. Beau suddenly realized. He *was* a father, already, many times over! He had to stop worrying about what it would be like, and how he would do when his baby came. He was now the responsible man that his Uncle had instructed him to be, all those years ago.

What had Unc said? Oh, yeah; that men were made, as they kept moving, as they remained firm. Real men were forged in fire. Unc said they held their center; they didn't panic or fall apart. They kept their wits about them. True men commanded respect, by the way they conducted themselves, and through how they handled their business.

You comport yourself with dignity, boy. You keep your head up, ya hear? If you cry, don't do it where it can be misconstrued as weakness. You hear me, son?"

Beau heard Unc all over again. Beau even found himself nodding as he stood in that tiny half bath. Never had he forgotten Uncle Brantley's words. Nor had Beau forgotten the man who had made him a man.

Beau suddenly had Gypsy, Ainsley Fielding, to thank for making many things crystal clear, under the worst circumstances.

Dear God; Beau *wished* to Heaven he could get Gypsy back. *Please, please, just let me have him back, Lord*, Beau prayed.

Feeling utterly ill, but wetting and wiping his face, Beau knew that particular prayer was futile. He'd prayed it many times in the past regarding his uncle. Therefore, Beau would do what needed to be done. That he promised.

Exiting the bathroom and becoming barraged by inquiries, people, and lights, Beau hated that this night had cost him his dear, dear friend.

Chapter 48

AS he often did when upset, Beau fingered his dog tags. Seated in his office, he stared out at the snowy landscape. Trying to forget the gaping hole in his heart, he knew others were hurt as well. All winter, it had been evident. Christmas had been somber, as had New Year's. Beau thought about his young assistant; Tatum had had an obvious crush on Gypsy. Therefore, the redhead was all messed up. Infusion band members and backup vocalists alike were one big devastated family. Beau's stage manager and all their road dawgs had been in pieces, too. Everyone was incapable of making heads or tails of the iniquity, the senselessness of Gypsy's death.

Oh, but the fans; they were the best. Their love kept pouring in, seemingly from every corner of the earth. Many expressed sorrow, while others tweeted that they were praying. The fans held candlelight vigils. They kissed life-sized photos of the baddest drummer Beau had ever known, Ainsley Fielding, *the wandering Gypsy.*

Beau's biological family was hurt too. Expecting, Kismet Staar felt especially bad because Gypsy had always headed straight for her home whenever Infusion came off the road. He did so with or without the band. The man loved her cooking. He and Lyle had been friendly, too. Beau remembered that Gypsy had also loved his Aunt Nell's chicken 'n dumplings and her biscuits. With his winning ways and gentle manner, the women, including nurse Gina, would have done anything for Gypsy.

Beau wanted to smile, but he couldn't as he recalled that for him too, the get-togethers at his cousin's big gabled home had been a treat, especially after ingesting catered, hotel, and restaurant food for months on end. The fellowship had always been as special as the ability to sleep in one's own bed. Sure, the average person thought a performer's life was glamorous and fun, but it could get cold, old, and tired very fast.

Stroking his dog tags, Beau recalled joking with Gypsy while riding their tour bus. Wearing a bandana, Gypsy had ribbed Beau about gaffs made while on stage. A time or two, Beau had yelled into that evening's crowd, "What's up L.A.?" or "What's happening Cleveland?" when in truth, he had been in Sacramento or Akron. In the bus lounge area, Beau, Gypsy, and others had snorted with laughter. The laid-back drummer had softly said, "Don't sweat it, Pops, you apologized." Gypsy even shrugged, "Hey, when *I* woke up, I didn't know where I was either." The drummer admitted he often turned to local news. Then he knew on what leg of the tour they were.

Thinking about his friend and the outings that he'd thought would continue indefinitely, Beau felt the breaking. Again he trembled with grief. Doubled over, he clutched his knees. Placing his head between them, he attempted to breathe through the heinous ache. Beau hated feeling like he had when the fam had lost Uncle Brantley.

"Oh, God," he managed to moan. "I want no more of this," *heartache.*

Beau knew he was sniveling. He knew death was part of life, yet he wanted to escape. And he sure as heck didn't want to think about *her.* The one person who was possibly more hurt than he. *Mireya.* Beau couldn't contemplate her pain. Seeing it so visceral and raw on the night they'd found...Gypsy's body...had been overwhelming. Beau knew that drugs like Ativan, Valium, and Percocet had been needed.

All had been worse at the the funeral. At Gypsy's church, there had been caterwauling and crying. Slender Minister Stevie had been removed while releasing gut-wrenching sobs about how he could have prevented things. "*I* should have taken him," Lanky Steven had wailed. Averting his gaze, Beau was aware that people were torn up because Gypsy had been incomparable. Somehow, the man had been simple too. He'd loved everyone and had let anyone get close. In a manner of speaking, Gypsy had been like a child. Like Thomas. *Oh God*, Beau thought again with a clarity that stung anew; he *had not protected Gypsy.*

Sure, Beau's aunt said, "Puppy, you try, but you can't protect everybody. In wanting to do that, you are so like your uncle." Beau had hugged her, for Nell had given him a gift, a sort of freeing. Yet sometimes, when Beau reminded himself that fault and blame played no part in what could not be undone, he failed to believe it. Often Beau felt as though he had allowed that woman—the one he had never liked—to steal someone precious. It had not even been a surprise to find out she was involved, or that she had committed the heinous iniquity. However, the pieces probably would not have come together as fast without Tatum. Beau's young assistant had incoherently blubbered to JeRell about 'having just spoken to Gypsy.' The youngster had said he'd heard the drummer calling out...to *Mary.* Then Detective Givens had informed Beau that Tatum's call had been Gypsy's last.

Forgetting all of it, Beau heard Tatum's young voice emit through the intercom. Tatum sounded better today as he informed Beau that sunlit Saavion would soon arrive. Beau straightened up. Handling his worn-smooth dog tags, Beau didn't want the other man to see him grief-stricken again. But really, the optician had seen Beau worse and better. Actually, Beau realized, Saavion had always been there, a steadying presence in his life. Therefore, Beau told himself, he was simply going to appear as he was, hurt and broken. Then in time, he would pack up the worst of the pain. He would even get back to 'the project' the one that he and Gypsy had discussed indefinitely. Easing thoughts of his friend from mind, Beau leaned back in his comfy desk chair. Staring at the color-saturated painting above his desk, absently, he reached for his phone.

Her voice was rich and soothing as she said, "Hi, beautiful Beau."

"Hey April," sounding worn, Beau asked, "How's it going?"

Aware that the tall brown filmmaker had been scheduled to tour the little-known sea isles she'd written about, and aware that he wanted to do so for his upcoming project, April remained silent. She knew that for Beau, many things had been delayed since his friend's passing. Aware that Beau was deeply hurt, the author exuded empathy. "Sweet Pea, the question is…how are *you*?"

Beau could barely catch his breath because she *understood*. That was one reason he loved her. Some things April just knew. Therefore, Beau didn't feel ashamed or like he would be judged when he took a few moments to quiet his rioting emotions. "I'll be fine. When I get *there*."

"So," she knowingly stated, "this place is still calling to you."

"It is," Beau admitted. Aloud, he wondered how she knew.

"I know," the author stated, "because Karina Cay calls artists."

Beau recalled what he had known while reading her book *Exodus*; it was the reason he'd decided to base a movie on it. *He and she were kindred spirits.* Years back, his publicist, who was hers also, had introduced them. They'd then begun work on the bestsellers about his life, and Beau had been comfortable. Even when April poked and prodded him for clarity. The author had been gentle. Although focused, she had never caused Beau to feel as though she'd pushed too hard. April had been thorough, and amid penning his story, it hit Beau. There was so much more they would do, together. Now they needed to get to it.

Therefore, Beau said, "I'm still flying down and taking the ferry over." He needed to get to where she was, so they could get cracking. It was what Gypsy would have wanted, Beau silently acknowledged. The younger muscular man with the laid-back manner would not have wanted 'Pops' to lie around, blaming himself and others for the heinous occurrence that had taken Gypsy to another realm.

Therefore, Beau laid out his intentions. Afterward, when he and his author friend were about to conclude, Beau felt surprisingly better. Out of habit, the actor started to say his assistant would contact April. Instead, Beau advised, "Keep an ear out for my jingle early next week."

"I will, and I'm praying for you," April offered and was gone.

Beau inhaled and realized he had so much to do! Buzzing Tatum, he said, "Tate, we 'bout to be busy." Wanting their trip rescheduled, Beau tossed out tentative dates. "I want all the same arrangements," He advised, needing a conversation with his agent and his business manager. Beau said he needed his prelim crew, a boom—the microphone placement operator; a gaffer, for the lighting plan; and a grip, who'd be responsible for the positioning of equipment on the set. Beau asked for his assistant director, cinematographer, and his director of photography. Man, Beau admitted, he needed so many things, including a chat about soundtrack ideas with über music producer, Joseph Forrester.

Leaning back in his chair, Beau realized. His creative juices were flowing again, something he hadn't felt since…before Gypsy's demise.

IN her office that no longer seemed cheery, Mireya sat, remembering. A little while back, Beau had called her over. Spring was upon them, but back in the winter, she had again felt like the bad girl summoned to the principal's office. There, she had receive the worst news of all.

Seated behind his massive desk, Beau had been blunt. "Gypsy's death *was no accident.*" Mireya recalled staring, while she'd thought no, Gypsy had slipped, fallen into the tub, and he'd hit his head. Yet Mireya remembered he'd. Gypsy had had his clothes on. Beau had persevered and she'd cried, "No Beau, those papers can't be right. Gypsy could *not* have had damage from the fall, to his spinal cord."

That Mireya hadn't wanted to accept because it meant one thing. Sweet, unsuspecting Gypsy had *suffered.* That Mireya couldn't bear, nor could she forget that while in Miami she hadn't told Gypsy about Mary.

Unaware, Beau spoke of Detective Givens, saying the man had offered condolences, then info that Givens said, "Might make all of this a bit more palatable." Like that could ever happen, Mireya thought.

Givens spoke of an out of zone phone call, not from Queens, New York. The Long Island jurisdiction intercepted and later found Mary.

As Mireya stared, Beau mentioned a depolarizing drug. Mary had used it on Gypsy. Beau spoke of a syringe, the autopsy, and a lethal dosage. Beau also mentioned a resuscitating syringe. Blinking, Mireya had been horrified as she tried to comprehend. *Mary had actually killed Gypsy.* Mireya had asked, "The first drug is called Suss-what?"

Succinylcholine. "Sus-seen-nil-ko-leen." Appearing stoic, Beau spoke. "That—woman injected a high dose into Gypsy. Since the drug is a short-acting skeletal muscle relaxant, she watched him suffocate."

Mireya heard her own voice rise, "But where did she get that shit?"

"I told you before." Beau's voice remained devoid of emotion, "The bitch worked at hospitals, as a nurse anesthetist. Givens said the drug is used as an adjunct to general anesthesia, to help with tracheal intubation." Beau handed over paper. "Says here in the case disposition, it can create an inability for patients to control their airway. This neuromuscular blocking agent can produce respiratory system paralysis." Beau scanned the sheet. "Here, it says brain or spinal cord injuries may prolong the drug's effects... So, when Gyp fell, she had him in a state of suspended animation." Beau dropped the papers, scrubbed hands over his face. Without warning Beau howled so loudly that his dog, Frost, dashed into the room furiously barking.

"Come, girl." Beau pulled the canine over. As the dog whined he patted her. When she sat on his foot, the pet parent tried again. "Says here, the drug has no effect on consciousness or pain; it says patients must be carefully monitored in case of needed resuscitation."

"So you're saying he was *conscious* when this shit happened?" Mireya felt herself begin to spiral out of control. "Are you saying Gypsy *knew* he was dying? And that bitch didn't help him?!" When Beau appeared pained, Mireya banged on his desk. Despite Frost's barking, Mireya verbally barraged Beau. Then she yelled, "Answer me, B!"

Soothing the lunging husky, Beau had one reemerging thought. He would love to take Mary's life, ever so slowly, and immensely painfully.

LYING with Ann, all Mireya could think about was Gypsy. Ainsley Fielding. She vacillated between thoughts of him and what she had been told, what Beau's detective and the authorities had pieced together...

Mary had allegedly run from Gypsy's house as furious winds, and a deluge of rain began once more. In her little car, Mary had been headed to Long Island where wind and flooding rains had wreaked havoc...

MARY *just wanted to get to her cousin's house, quickly. Panicked, she would grab a few things and flee. However, first, she had to get through water-logged roads, some littered with tree branches and debris.*

Feeling increasingly fearful, as though the very hounds of hell were on her trail, Mary took a shortcut. Sure, the rain had momentarily let up, but travel was still slow-going. News radio said there were flash-floods and downed power lines. The announcer said rubble on any road could camouflage danger, but Mary had to keep moving. Fumbling with her cell phone, she called her cousin. Mary told the near sleeping woman to look out for her, better yet, just leave the door unlocked.

Mumbling that she would, Mary's cousin clicked off.

With bits of flotsam flying before her and most roads deserted, Mary needed to place her phone in the console. For one moment, she took her eyes off the tarmac. When she looked back up, she saw...a flying lasso?

No. Mary squinted. Then she felt fear because that was a -- power line! Wildly blowing in the wind, the line furiously lashed the road before her. Seeing sparks and their upward spray, Mary became flustered. Wild-eyed, she gazed around. With her foot on the brake, she knew one thing. She could not go back! Therefore, as the power line flew up, Mary wondered. Could she push it, speed forward, before the line twisting in the wind blew back down?

She could only try. Mary thought it as she gave her car gas. She gunned the engine—and made it! No. She felt a jolt. She also saw, just barely, through her rear window that the power line had hit her car! She screamed, aware that due to the contact, her vehicle had become energized.

Mary knew she should stay inside and call for help, but she was wanted, or she soon would be, because everything with Ainsley had gone horribly wrong. Mary's eyes rounded, because was -- that -- fire? Was her car on fire? Mary told herself not to panic, but what should she do? Frantic, she tried to see out of the window. Was her car in standing water? If it was, and she stepped in that water, she would be fried alive. Yet if she stayed in the car, Mary realized while breathing hard, she might burn to a crisp. So she had to chance it, to get away.

Terrified, Mary knew the way she exited would determine whether or not she lived. Therefore, cautiously, she opened her door—and furious wind snatched it from her! Knowing she had a 50/50 chance, stay alive or die, Mary got her feet on the floorboard. It was hard, but she attempted not to hang onto any part of the sparking car. Then quickly, with feet together, she launched her heavy self from the vehicle.

She tumbled and rolled, not wanting to become an electrical conduit from the energized car. Despite pushing wind, now hurt, Mary hauled herself from the wet ground. Bruised and sore, she hobbled toward what appeared to be an industrial park. In the cold November dark, Mary saw a security fence. It blocked access from the back road. No! Dragging her skin-chaffed leg, Mary just needed a way through that fence. With wet, greasy hair blowing into her eyes and her knee bloodied, she hoped one of the buildings would offer shelter. Then she could plan her next move.

MIREYA recalled Detective Givens' investigative report. It detailed that with power lines down due to the storm, even non-conductive materials had become electrical pathways. Mireya recalled other typed words: **Metal security fence/hazard.** Givens' report also alluded to nearby trees and branches harboring danger. Wet, everything had become a ground way, an avenue for electrical currents.

Therefore when attempting to wedge herself—like a fat mouse—through a break in the security fence, Mary found herself in a death trap. Perhaps, Detective Givens had told Beau, the woman could have survived the current that electrified the fence. Highly unlikely, Givens had said while chewing gum; "With the additional current running ground wise, all of that was a recipe straight from the bowels of hell."

Electrocuted. Suspect in case, Mireya read, **deceased**.

"Toasted, *unmercifully*." The detective had said. He shook his head. "What a terrible, terrible, way to go. Suspect became a statistic." The man shrugged, "I've seen it time and again, a smarty-pants screws up. The face was charred, eyebrows were gone, and clothing was burned into the skin. The perp had to be cut out of that fence. Found out her organs were cooked. Man!" Givens shuddered, "nearly unidentifiable, that one."

WEEKS later, Mireya pushed things like poetic justice from mind to recall why she no longer lived with Ann.

The older woman had been excited to try new equipment offered by The Kitten Heel, yet Mireya felt listless. With a sigh, Mireya admitted to knowing she had to go on, to live and raise Arlise, but she couldn't find the strength. Still, she handled her aspects of the Kitten Heel's business while feeling like she slept-walked through each day. At night Mireya allowed Ann, who seemed inordinately happy, to use her body. While stout Ann did so, Mireya mentally escaped by thinking of Gypsy.

Mireya thought about Brett, too, *the Godsend*. Slender Brett knew Mireya was grieved. Brett was aware that Mireya had wanted Gypsy to be her man, not everybody's man. Brett had even helped get some of Mireya's things into Mireya's new temporary bedroom. As she did, Brett admitted, "It takes time to get over debilitating grief." That was why Brett would continue to help Mireya, now a guest in Brett's home. And slender Brett would continue to help care for Mireya's eight-year-old.

When spring arrived, Brett noticed. She had been aiding with the care of little Arlise since November. And Brett had loved every moment.

Slender Brett had even announced that when Mireya was ready, they would find mother and daughter a realtor and a sweet home of their own. Yes, Brett said, just like Mireya had done for Beau, all those years ago -- since Mireya could no longer stomach the sight of Ann.

MIREYA often mentally replayed the night she'd left. She had just known that Ann had not called her stupid! Ann was supposed to care that she was hurting, unbearably. This Mireya thought as Ann went further to say that with Gypsy's death, she had hoped things would change.

"He always came between us in life," Ann announced. "So when I heard he was dead, I thought we could start over."

Hollow-eyed, Mireya had stared at Ann across the dining table.

Feeling it was about time, Ann divulged all that she had held back. Ann concluded with, "Oh and Mireya, I didn't say anything, but I saw photos, of Miami, on different sites. There was The Arena, that club, and Beau on stage. Great light show. Then there was *after* when he and his entourage partied." Ann sounded dreamy. "*You* were there, looking so beautiful." Ann caught herself. Then her voice dripped venom. "You were with *him*. Frankly, I'm *glad* he's dead. Dude got what he deserved."

Stunned, Mireya watched Ann, who calmly continued to eat. Mireya also thought, what a horrible thing to say or feel about another person.

Suddenly Mireya realized. Ann was just like Lana, good ole mother. Like Lana, Ann had never been one to soothe or care for anything that didn't directly pertain to her. Now Ann talked re-defining their relationship. Really? Mireya waved and said she couldn't discuss 'them' right then.

Ann shrugged. Sipping wine, to Mireya the stout gray-haired woman sounded lofty and oh so judgmental. "Honestly Mireya, I don't know how you get in all these lil mix-ups. And your poor daughter; you might want her to grow up straight, but she's destined to grow up believing men are vile. She probably sees them all as deviant, due to the company her mother keeps. You surround yourself with gays, strays, and—"

Stunned, Mireya blinked as haughtily Ann continued. "Heaven knows I've tried to pull you from that filthy lifestyle, but *you* too must want out."

Out? Yes. Mireya nodded. She latched onto the word. Out. That was just what she wanted. Wearily, she rose. "I can't fight with you, Ann." In the front hall, Mireya held to Arlise with one hand, and her keys with the other. Over a shoulder, Mireya tossed, "At least my daughter will know she has choices, since she already knows her mother will back her, regardless. Oh, but what will you have, Ann, when you're all alone?"

Appearing flummoxed, Ann had not expected anything of the sort. Scrambling after her little family, stout Ann offered a half-hearted apology.

Descending the outside steps, Mireya was dismissive. As she and her child went, she said Ann's offering was too little, too late.

The older woman stood in the doorway of the small house that Mireya had brought to life with her exuberance and presence. Feeling wooden, and bereft all of a sudden, Ann wondered. Why did all her relationships with beautiful women end— precisely the same way?

Chapter 49

AFTER Gypsy's death, Beau needed to experience life. Realizing it, he took Saavion's hand. Seated before a cozy bedroom fire, Beau admitted, "I'm glad you're here, Saav." Beau kissed Saavion. "Since my screenplay is finally acceptable, I want to explain a few things."

"The screenplay for your new movie," Saavion interjected.

"Yes," Beau's eyes were on the dancing flames. "My team has polished the script, procured the money, and my casting director's doing her thing." A few technical people, Beau revealed, would soon accompany him down to where April lived, part-time.

Saavion looked askance, attempting to follow. "She's the author, right? The friend whose book you're basing this new movie on."

Beau nodded, "So while visiting the isles that she wrote about, we'll scout locations and look for rehearsal spaces. My DP," director of photography, "will set up shots and we'll discuss them." Beau explained. The man's knowledge of how professional cameras worked made it necessary to collaborate. "He knows lighting and the effect it'll have on certain scenes. The DP is the one who makes the pretty pictures you see in movies. He might even take some of the promo stills. Then when we get rolling, he'll oversee several cameramen."

Beau further explained that as The Director, *he* would be more concerned with the overall story and the acting. Beau, his assistant director, the DP, and others, would discuss how the whole project should appear. "When I get to the island, I'll check settings like the local market." Beau shrugged, "I want to see the cool, as well as the spooky places mentioned in the book. Then my peops will speak with the managers of those places; they'll apprise them of our intentions. My team might even remind them that our presence equals revenue. Then we'll get signed releases, where we can. Those will allow us to record locations or a proprietor's image. Then the team and I will plan the shoots, with an eye on minimizing days spent, equipment used, and the amount of time needed for everything."

Saavion nodded, thrilled that Beau felt free enough to discuss his work. "So does this mean you'll shoot a few scenes out of sequence?"

Beau nodded, impressed the other man knew as much. "If those scenes are set in the same location. Doing that is harder, but after screen tests, it really can save time and money."

"Sounds exciting," Saavion stated, his hand yet in Beau's.

"You know what sounds exciting to me?" Beau quietly asked.

"What?"

"You and I, us getting hitched. Become my life partner, Saav."

Saavion's heart thudded as he said, "This is sudden."

"It's not," Beau refuted the notion. "We're more than five years in. Gyp's death reminded me that life is short and unpredictable, so I want to commit—to you. Since gay marriage was legalized," in New York in 2011, "why not?" In the flame light, Beau got down on one knee. "Marry me Saav. Step fully into my world. Help me raise our baby."

In the firelight, Saavion appeared awestruck. Although he'd longed to be an integral part of Beau's life, the optician hadn't known Beau wanted the same thing. "Dude, you're serious…"

"I am," Beau acknowledged. "I know it's not the most romantic proposal, but you're already one of the biggest—and best—parts of my life. You know me better than most anyone. We throw great parties, together. The morning after, you give good head, and I give good dick."

They laughed.

"Seriously though," Beau resumed, "you love me, and God knows I love you. So what do you say?"

"It has to be done through legal channels," Saavion interrupted, sounding pensive. "I won't do it otherwise. You've got to protect you, your assets, and I've got to do the same."

Beau laughed. "That's why I love you, Saav. You get right to the point, and I'll tell you something else. I've already met with my lawyer."

"Then I'll meet with mine." Saavion dared to hope as he asked, "Will we tell people? Will we have guests, and a ceremony, someplace nice?"

"Why not?" Beau suddenly felt elated. "We can hammer out the details later. I just want you mine before I leave. Deal?"

Following an arousing kiss, Saavion nodded, "Deal, husband-to-be."

Chapter 50

ON birthing day, Beau was so jittery! Sure, Kismet was supposed to have had natural childbirth, but the placenta blocked her cervix. Therefore, Beau found himself wearing scrubs and waiting until he could see his baby. It wouldn't be long now. Within minutes, hospital staff would hold his newborn infant up over the sheet that shielded the in-progress Caesarean section.

Then Beau would learn his baby's name. With his heart beating double time, he squeezed his cousin's hand. Numb from the waist down, she again said she was glad he was right there with her.

The doctor announced that in a minute they could meet the newest member of the DeVeaux clan. Beau could hardly wait! Nor could he believe this was really happening, to him! His cousin was actually bringing his child into the world. *Wow*. He had never felt so anxious!

HE fell to his knees, not really crying or laughing but emitting a combination of the two, because…he had a *daughter*! She was tiny, perfect, and scowl-y-faced. He, Beauregard DeVeaux, was *a father*, at last! He loved his baby girl. From the moment he'd seen her, all bunched up against the cold of the outside world, he had fallen head over heels. No. Beau realized. He'd loved her when she had been nameless, faceless, and sexless, just an *idea*. He'd loved her while she grew in her mother's womb. Now he loved her in all her tiny tangible glory! Beau laughed, robust and full when his daughter began to squall.

Her name, he learned, was as beautiful as she. Beau was so glad he hadn't previously known it. Man! His baby's Momma could not have chosen better. *Gemma. Janell.*

Kismet Staar said she'd picked Gemma, because it brought to mind a precious gemstone. Kismet said they could call the baby 'Gem' for short, if Beau wanted. He did. He loved that her middle name, Janell, a derivative of Jane, meant *the Lord is gracious*, because He certainly was.

And to think, he who had once been the irregular little idiot boy, the abandoned kid who had felt so unloved, now had a daughter! Life was amazing. Beau now had a whole family, really, full of people to love, and they loved him back! As he mused on life's gifts, Kismet was wheeled from the O.R. to a post-operative recovery room.

In the hallway, Beau could hardly breathe and Saavion had to retrieve him from the shiny tiles, again. Beau felt overwhelmed. On his knees, he thanked God for everything; for his first cousin who was the best, and the fact that she'd remembered what her mother Nell had taught her, him, and Farai decades ago. Aunt Nell had opined that names were powerful. Nell said they meant something, and often influenced the wearer, whether or not the wearer knew. Thus, Kismet Staar had given Beau's daughter the perfect moniker, Gemma Janell. Each time he called her name, he would be reminded. His girl was a precious gem from the Lord.

In Saavion's arms, Beau had been unashamed to cry, and laugh. Beau had even kissed the other man, just laid a big ol' smackaroo on those lush pinkish lips, the very lips that their baby had, in miniature.

Beau held Saavion. Looking into the hazel eyes, Beau knew too that they had done well. Two weeks prior, they'd acted on impulse and drove to City Hall. They'd taken vows, and Beau had never felt more right.

For so long, Beau had pondered fatherhood, and marriage. He'd vacillated between feeling worried and not. He'd wondered what type of father and husband he would make, because of his past. Then one day something clicked, enabling him to recall the self-help books, the therapy years, the boxing, drowning in drugs, the demons, getting clean, and the affirmations. All had culminated in one realization. *He was not defined by his past.* It could only control his future if he allowed it.

Beau had decided to shut the door on worry and anxiety. Surprisingly, then his nightmares ceased. He was able to clearly ponder two of the most important people in his life; Kismet and Saavion. Beau's longtime friend and former roommate Valeria had hooked Beau up with the optician. Thinking about his first cousin, and his years-long confidant, Beau considered the wondrous gift those two given him. In many ways, both had rearranged their lives to enhance his, and Beau was elated.

When they were able, the new Dad and Saavion stood at the nursery window. Both marveled over everything about their new little baby-bird. Then taking Saavion's hand, Beau proudly strode to greet family and friends, all of whom had appeared to share their special day.

Beau didn't remember walking the tiled hallway, clutching Saavion's hand. However, he did recall the commotion, and the throng of people, some his band members, and his friend Valeria, a new mom herself. His surly chef, JeRell, was there, and sweet, pink-cheeked Amy. Beau's aunt cried, while he accepted congrats from the Deacon, his daughter's Paw-

Paw. Beau smiled as the gray haired man soothingly rubbed his wife's back, saying. "There, there, Nannie." Wow, Beau thought, now Nell was *his* daughter's grandmother, too! Uncle Brantley's daughter Farai was present, fresh from Milan. Beau's road dawgs stood around, while Boulder almost smirked, the closest he ever got to a smile. Glad to see everyone, Beau hugged drummer Kendu, Thomas his brother, and Nurse Gina. The round woman even handed Beau a beribboned gift.

Slender Brett kissed Beau, as did cinnamon-skinned Mireya, and in each other's arms the two who had been childhood friends suddenly missed Gypsy. Ainsley Fielding really should have been present. Yet determined not to feel melancholy on so momentous a day, Beau jovially accepted a cigar from Tatum, his young assistant. After hamming it up with Saavion's people, Beau turned, and noticed…Lyle.

Apart from the others, his cousin's husband stood. The dark man with the long locked hair nodded, then quickly pivoted. Yet Beau had seen Lyle's look, and Beau knew. The man was proud, of his selfless wife.

LATER, when she was able to receive visitors, Beau entered her quiet room. He bore gifts.

"Diddley," Kismet began, "you've got to stop with all the stuff."

"No," the younger cousin chided, "you've got to accept it." Beau gazed at the ceiling. "What was it you told me when we decided to do this? When I kept balking? You said I had to *allow* people to do things for me. You said I needed to allow people to love me. Well now, I'm telling you that. Allow stuff, Kiss."

Shaking her head, the woman smiled. However, she appeared sad when asked if she wanted to nurse her baby. Beaming, the hospital attendant said, "Be mindful, your milk won't fully be in for another day or so. But you two *can* bond…"

Watching all, Beau could tell. His cousin wanted that, with the baby. Then the light left Kismet's eyes. Backing away, the nurse said she'd give Mom time to decide.

Watching the exchange, Beau could not know that his daughter's mother thought of her other children. Returned from school by now, they would be attended by Ms. Fannie, the day lady. The plucky birdlike woman who said she couldn't wait to get 'that new baby' into her arms.

Recalling it, Kismet was unaware that her cousin studied her. Lost in thought, she remembered that after only a few months of nursing the twins, she'd stopped. So she had no right to want to nurse this new baby.

April Alisa Marquette
235

The infant that was no longer hers. But if she did nurse, her selfish part pointed out, she'd get more time with the baby. But no, Kismet shook her head. Gemma Janell was not hers. The infant belonged to Beau. Now.

As the one who'd given birth, Kismet knew her breasts would ache, and feel aflame. They would do so when there was no baby to suckle the nourishment that her body produced, but Kismet would deal with it.

Holding his breath, Beau watched as his baby was brought into the room. Instinctively, he directed the nurse toward Kismet.

Engrossed in staring down at the little one, for whom she had gone through so much, Kismet whispered. "Diddley, we did it."

Noting how she lovingly gazed at the tiny bundle, Beau's throat constricted. With such love in his eyes, for them both, he whispered back. "*You* did it, Momma." Then squeezing Kismet's hand Beau said, for the thousandth time, never would he be able to thank her enough.

Suddenly, "Let's change the rules," tumbled from the tall man's lips.

Puzzled, Kismet looked up. "Huh?"

"I need more, Kiss. It's really for...*her*, for Gemma Janelle."

"Anything, Diddley."

He said it quickly. "Nurse her."

Beau's cousin appeared stunned, then her eyes filled.

"I need you to," Beau pled, "and *she* needs it. We know mother's milk is the best. It'll give her antibodies and ward off infections. Ah, and it'll help return your womb to its pre-pregnancy size."

Kismet appeared amused. "Somebody's been reading."

Undeterred, Beau said, "You want to, Kiss. I see it in your eyes." The younger cousin spoke softly. "When you look at her, it's apparent. You love her." Beau took his cousin's hand free hand. "I know it was hard when you nursed the twins, but that was different. When they were born, we," The Cohorts, "were in turmoil. The whole fam was grieving," over their loved one, Ronni Brown.

Kismet recalled her longtime sister-friend as Beau continued. "This time is different, Kiss. We're more settled." Beau disclosed that he and Saavion had discussed things. "True, we're grieved over Gyp, but for you it's not the same. You weren't as close to him as you were to Ronni. So Kiss, please?" Beau stared down at the woman who cradled his baby. "Uh, and keep her—for the first few months."

Kismet's mouth dropped open, because she had not even let herself dream of such a thing. "Diddley, I can't..."

"You can. We'll work it out." Beau nodded, and felt afraid suddenly that she would say no, or that she might say yes. "We just have to figure this out," he continued. "But the biggest thing is: she needs *you* right now. And you need her. Kiss, *I* need you. You know I got my project, the one with April. It's rolling and the train can't be stopped. Saav's got his work, but you... You'll be home, recuperating. I'll get you more help. I'll send over anything or anybody you need, just as long as you say yes."

Kismet could barely think. "Diddley, stop. You've got a whole suite prepared. You and Déja worked hard on it. We had parties, and showers; you've got so much stuff that the baby—your baby, will need."

"You've got goo-gobs of stuff too, Kiss, designer mess from Farai."

"But don't you want her, in your house, at home with you?"

Beau patted his cousin's hand, like his aunt would have, because he could tell he'd frightened her. He had actually scared himself too. "Kiss, I know you think I'm reneging on our deal, but I'm not."

She did think that, and his reneging just might allow her to do what she had so desperately wanted to do. But no, Kismet told herself as Beau found the courage to tell the truth; she would simply listen, then decide.

"I do want her with me," Beau admitted, "but in time."

"Diddley," Kismet near wailed, "you've got a bassinet. You've got stuff from the event that Brett planned."

"So? I'll use it, on weekends or on the nights when you need rest, or when you go back to work. Listen, Kiss, I just need my daughter to be with *her Momma*." Beau appeared ready for battle. "*I* can't *mother* her, cuz. I ain't even gon' play like I can. I need *you* to do that. Be what you *are*, Kiss. You know I've said it before; I want you to be all you can be, all you *want* to be to her, to our—your, my, and Saavion's baby. Sure, Saav said he'll stand on the sidelines; he'll be the fun guy, but you know a child needs parents, real ones. So that's gotta be me, and you. Somehow. *Your egg*, remember?"

Kismet slumped against her pillow. Despite feeling uncomfortable due to the Caesarian surgery, she suddenly felt as though *she*—not Beau—had been given the greatest gift!

Now she didn't have to give Gemma up. Now she could mother her third daughter. Sure, there was Lyle, and her crumbling marriage to consider, but this was her child! She'd used her egg to bring this baby forth. So if the situation needed re-tweaking, she could do that.

"Beau," Kismet cried with shining eyes. "I don't know what to say."

April Alisa Marquette
237

"Just say yes." He turned quickly away, but turned back.

Beau's cousin nearly laughed because the man was such a softie, inside. Re-positioning their bundle Kismet asked, "You want to hold your daughter?"

Beau felt for his dog tags. Wow, was he nervous. "I do, but she's so tiny. I'm scared, a bit. I don't want to hurt her."

"You sound like most new dads, but you'll get it. Sit. Next to me."

"I'm a new dad," Beau proudly repeated and obeyed. When his cousin groaned, he jumped. "What? What'd I do?"

"Your moving," Kismet stated, "it makes me feel my cut."

"Oops, sorry."

"I've felt worse," Kismet admitted. "Remember, I've had natural."

"TMI," Beau whispered as gently, the tiny gem was transferred.

As he cradled her in his arms, the doors of Beau's heart flew wide open. Sure, he'd held many newborns; indeed he had a bevy of women in his life. Yet, for Beau this was supremely different. As he held his daughter, holding Mireya's Arlise for the first time briefly crossed his mind. Arlise had been a toddler, because, regrettably, he'd missed the first part of her life. However, *this* was a whole different ball game. Gemma Janell belonged *to him*. She was *his* to protect, to teach, to love, and worry over, from day one. What an exciting journey, Beau thought.

He nearly hyperventilated, until he remembered. He was not alone. this new journey Beau realized, was one that he, Saavion, *and* Kismet would take together. Caressing tiny pale fingers, the man couldn't tear his gaze away as he said, "I wouldn't want a different Momma for her…"

Involuntarily, Kismet heaved up a sob, one that she tried to choke back.

Beau laughed. Then he stifled a strange sound of his own, as he rested his head on his cousin's. "I love you, girl."

"Ditto, " Kismet managed as lovingly, she gazed down, at the proof of her love.

Chapter 51

APRIL stared at the invitation.

The honor
of your presence
is requested at the
Candlelit Love Ceremony
for
Beauregard DeVeaux
&
Saavion Delano Kennings
Saturday
February 14th
6 p.m.
The Cay Abbey Chapel
on
Karina Cay
Reception
immediately following
at
The G. Baptiste
Constellation Conservatory.

The author chuckled because Beau was really doing it. On Valentine's Day too. Go 'head brotha man!

When Beau and his crew flew down, they'd checked many things for what they called 'the project.' On Miraunga Isle, Beau met lush, lovely Aqua. He'd thought her intriguing, the woman whom his movie would be based upon. Aqua had shown him the tract of land where her real-life story had taken place, on the island where she lived. There, Beau mentioned having the outside of the spooky old homestead recreated. As he, April, Aqua, and others tromped about, the filmmaker mentioned shooting the interior scenes on a soundstage. Beau and his crew talked technical and mentioned the outlying areas to be used for actual footage.

When away from the site and back on Karina Cay, the island where April lived, Beau told her he was excited. He divulged that he couldn't remember the last time he'd felt the same type of adrenaline for any project. Again he marveled at the timeless beauty of his surroundings. Then Beau admitted, "This island feels like home, for some reason."

Saying she well knew, April invited Beau, and his crew, to share a meal at her bayou country abode.

BEFORE sunset, Beau noticed bright-faced tiger lilies. On his friend's porch, he fell in love with buttery pine floors and a plush, pine-framed sofa. He liked that in the quiet, ceiling fans whirred, while atop a trio of nesting tables, a lone mason jar held a bright pink Limonium.

"A, I know you could've used cut crystal," Beau began, "but that jar with the flower in it feels so—homey."

Appearing wistful in golden light, April revealed why she'd put it there. "Mason jars and flowers always remind me of my grandmother."

In the alluring space, Beau turned and saw a large open book on polished pine. There was also a white stoneware mug and teapot on a side table. Seeing all, Beau asked if he was too early.

"No…" April assured him. "I was just enjoying a few moments, but now you can too. Sit. Want a drink? Tell me. Are things panning out?"

Accepting a cold beverage from April's husband, Beau's gaze followed the tall man back out to the grill. There shrimp kabobs and savory meat appealingly sizzled. Beau realized, everywhere there was beauty. A butterfly bush, accented by white Queen Anne's lace, attracted bees behind the house. On the lawn, cushion-covered wicker furniture, palm trees, and a pergola were all inviting. As a breeze blew off the nearby bay, Beau became cognizant of an inexplicable yearning.

Later, when he and his crew had dined sufficiently, Beau recognized what he'd felt earlier. He had *fallen* for the island where his author friend resided for a portion of each year. He loved her Chateau-style home with its quaint keeping room and fireplace. Beau imagined her curled before flame light on chilly evenings. He loved that stately old trees, including fragrant magnolias, surrounded her house. Inside, Beau adored the sweeping staircase. Outside, he liked April's torch-lit lanai. He sat there as people began to head through the acreage in the rear, to the bay. Apparently, it was something that was done each day at dusk.

Hanging back, Beau saw that only he, the author, and a few others remained. With eyes on the large tabby cat on her lap, he swirled amber liquid. Softly Beau divulged, "It's strange, A, but suddenly I find myself yearning for a place here," on Karina Cay...

Therefore, while holding the invitation that announced the filmmaker's nuptials, April smiled. She remembered introducing Beau to the local real estate agent. She also re-lived an early morning phone call.

"A, I know we're scheduled to meet later this week," Beau began. "When we again take the ferry to Miraunga, but I wondered. Would you show me the real Karina Cay before then?"

"I'd be delighted, Beau! Is there any place special you wanna go?"

"Well, although we saw sites for the project," Beau revealed, "I want to see as much of this place as I can. You know, the places *you* go." Beau couldn't explain, he admitted, "But among other things, here, the sun's brightness, and the night creatures' song just seems to call to me."

Having adored the island from her first moment, too, April understood. "You know *I* wound up here after penning Aqua's story." The author then teased that if Beau spent any more time on the island, its inhabitants, the calm, the warm blue-green water, and the sultry nights would take hold of him. "Then you'll never want to leave."

Chuckling, Beau admitted, "I already feel that way."

MANEUVERING a golf cart beneath the azure sky, April appeared at the lovely island resort where Beau stayed. Seeing her, he swiftly exited the *Canopus Arms*. Passing trees, including stately date palms, he glanced from puffy white cumulus clouds to the brown woman who had long ago become his friend. He liked her flowy tangerine dress. Her subtle scent, amber and citrus, wafted to him as lifting her shades, she said, "Hop on board." Then they were off, with her explaining that the island was named Karina [*Eta Carinae*] for the second brightest star in the constellation, Canopus. April said islanders were called Karinians, and she mentioned why cars weren't allowed on the island. The author pointed out places, and beside her, in shorts and sunglasses, tall, buff, and brown, ingested all.

In picturesque residential areas, Beau's heart beat quickly as he viewed stately old homes, their bases hugged by lovely pink or white oleander. He loved their French doors and wide veranda steps. Beau noticed that on broad manicured streets, there were no yellow lines to delineate opposite travel lanes. Yet vivid green grass berms separated traffic. Within those berms, lovely lantana bushes, as well as lavender hydrangea, flourished, in the shade of centuries-old oaks.

April Alisa Marquette
241

In the quaint but enchanting commercial district, April turned onto Main Street. Passing the courthouse and the post office, Beau saw the bank. Its huge clock face could be seen for miles around. He saw an inviting bookstore, a coffee house—the Carlotta Café, and the gated African Methodist Episcopal church. On an avenue lined with trees dripping with Spanish moss, they rode past lovely mocha-skinned women with wrapped heads. Turning on his seat, Beau gazed at café au lait girls with beautifully cornrowed hair. Seeing people swathed in colorful sheaths and sandals, the producer/director felt like rejoicing.

Men in bandanas, tees, and torn jeans worked while others in uniform unloaded parcels before sparkly stores. Quickly, Beau and his 'tour guide' passed young, virile men. Beneath brilliant sunshine, chocolate-skinned adolescents in neon-bright gear pedaled colorful bikes.

Amazed that most everyone nodded or waved, Beau returned the gestures. He saw sweet shops and geraniums in pots on second-story balconies. He held on as April swerved around the town green, the excursion taking them past a bent old woman. With a gnarled stick, she waved and gratefully declined April's offer to ride. Bidding the woman good day, they passed the golf course. Not far from the pristine green, golden sea oats fluttered in the breeze. Moments later, Beau and April bumped over dunes while glimpsing the sugar sand beach. Extending an arm, Beau wanted to gleefully whoop as he touched aged driftwood and wire, the fencing alongside Beach Road. Back in town, they passed a gorgeous structure. With his hand on April's arm Beau yelled, "Stop!"

Startled, she stamped the brake. "What happened?" she asked, hoping no family of ducks crossed unseen before her.

Beau gazed up, pointing. "What is this place?"

April eyed Palladian windows. "Oh, that's the G. Baptiste Constellation Conservatory. Islanders just call it The Conservatory."

Beau hurriedly unfolded himself. "I need to go inside."

Giving her golf cart the go, April called, "I'll park, and—"

Beau didn't hear as purposefully he loped up the immaculate walk. He liked the white rocks lining it; behind was low creeping phlox, and the taller, more brilliantly flowering bougainvillea. Inside the cool glass and white steel structure, Beau heard the massive fountain and saw more foliage. Feeling as though he'd stepped into a tropical oasis, he heard April's bejeweled sandals clack on the flagstone floor. Turning, he peppered her with questions. "What is the function of this place? Who owns it? Can it be booked –for affairs? And how long out?"

"Oh, it's used for a host of things," the author waved, as a cocoa-skinned woman approached. The woman greeted Beau as April continued. "Hi Afeni, I was telling my friend that Karinians hold anniversary celebrations here, christenings, weddings—"

"That's it!" Beau nearly shouted. "Is there an outside?" Not awaiting an answer, he strode toward a great wall of windows. "This is it!"

Appearing amused, April didn't know what 'it' was, but she figured the filmmaker would tell her. Therefore, she followed him through enormous glass pocket doors. Outside, with the beach beautiful and far-reaching before them, Beau turned and grasped her hands. "I'm so glad you wrote *Exodus*," he announced, "because, without it, I'd not have my next movie. Without you and that book, I'd not have come to this island, nor seen this perfect spot! It's what I've long envisioned. *That's* what I call synchronicity." Beau squeezed April's arms. "You know, when the external syncs up with the internal. *This* is where I want my reception!"

With the sun breathing warmly on them, the author beamed up as Beau raised a finger. His free hand finagled his phone. "Saav," he intoned, nodding at the curator. "I've found the perfect place…"

Now, fingering the embossed envelope, April remembered Beau's next call. "Brett. Looks like you've got another event to plan…"

Continuing to smile, April sat, surrounded by scent and flowers, while her laptop stood open. Again, she fingered the lovely silver and white wedding announcement and remembered. Days later, Beau reminded her, "You introduced me to your real estate agent, so I thought it befitting that you accompany us to see a house. If you can."

Gleeful, April sang out, "I'd love to!" Before she could ask when, Beau tossed out his own inquiry.

"Didn't I see," real estate agent, "Yael in *Exodus*?"

"You did, and before you leave, you may meet others from the book."

Beau laughed and said he felt like Alice, falling into Wonderland.

Seated and yet holding Beau's wedding invitation, April pondered The Old Habersham place, *now Beau's home.* She remembered that when Yael had pulled his golf cart up before the house with the scrolled iron gates, Beau had repeatedly flipped his dog tags. As the real estate agent suggested having Beau's new house name engraved on the sign, Beau walked ahead to push one gate open. Later, Beau told April that even before being drawn to the brick walk in the back, the one that led through the grass to a horizontal boardwalk, he'd decided. Before Beau was led through the home's interior or out to the private beach, he had exhaled. Then to April and Yael, Beau had announced he didn't need to see or hear any more. The filmmaker said he knew. He had come *home*.

Gingerly re-tucking the invitation into its lovely silver-lined envelope, April figured she'd better get in some writing. Yet, she couldn't help but smile because Beau had wanted a home on the island. Although real estate was scarce, he'd gotten it. The filmmaker had desired The Conservatory too, often booked months to years in advance, that he too had obtained, for his reception. He'd wanted the priestess, whom the author had written about, several times. However, April had introduced him to another spiritual leader.

Now, Beau would get his wedding, with all the trimmings. He would do so on the lovely little island on which he now lived.

Fingering the beautiful envelope, April vowed to be at the Cay Abbey chapel. At Beau's ceremony, she would hug, kiss, and wish her friend every happiness ...because if anybody deserved that, and more, it was Beauregard DeVeaux.

Chapter 52

STANDING outside the white clapboard chapel with the cross over the door, Beau glanced over at Saavion. The wedding rehearsal was done. Wearing shorts, a designer tee, and sandals, Beau released a pent breath. Clad in faded jeans and a button-front shirt, the man with the sunlit hair gazed back. Both men burst out laughing. Doubling over with mirth, Beau realized. He and Saavion were really doing it! For some inexplicable reason, both found that funny, and clasping his partner's hand, Beau managed to croak, "Tomorrow, baby."

Rearing back, Saavion sang off-key, "Going to the chapel 'n we—"

"Gonna get mar-ah-arried," Beau joined, yet laughing. Déja sang along. Kismet's fourteen-year-old knew the song. She called it one of her Nannie's 'moldy oldies.' Déja's cousin, Brosnan, looked on. Farai's eldest and his smaller brother, an adoptee like Déja, glanced over.

Shaking his head, twenty-two-year-old Brosnan said, "Beau, man, I'm 'bout to believe you been drinking."

Grasping the college graduate's nape, Beau shook the young man. "Just wait, my boy, until it's your turn. Then we'll see what *you* do."

The young man snorted, "Marriage is *not* in my plans."

Beneath an indigo sky and towering pines, Beau tossed his golf cart key. In the balmy night, Brosnan caught it as he crossed the crushed-shell parking lot. Beau told Kismet's boys, Chance, and Bonaire, to hop aboard with Entebbe, Farai's youngest. From his peripheral, Beau saw slender Brett, the last to exit the chapel. Beau glimpsed Mireya too. She rode with Kismet, as Kiss motored her daughters away. Beau saw Deac, and Mireya's daughter. "Ya can't play with baby Gemma right now," Deac announced, before he advised Arlise to buckle up.

Loping over, Beau took little precious into his arms. "You know Auntie," he began, "my bugaboo *can* ride with me."

"Gimme my baby." Seated on the rear-facing seat, Nell reached for the ten-month-old who'd grasped the tags ever about her father's neck.

"Alright, Nannie." With a big smoocheroo for his princess, Beau pried the pudgy little hand open. He kissed it and told his daughter to be good. Then he returned the biscuit brown toddler with the corkscrew curls to her grandmother's arms. "Wait," Beau said. He adjusted the headband that kept his daughter's mane from her face. Just seeing her touched his heart, and Beau reminded the baby, "I love you, Gem…"

"Wub!" In Nell's arms, the baby joyfully flailed, "Wub, Da-da!"

"Enough *luv*," Deac called out. "Kiss left, 'n I'm hongreh! Let's go."

AT Ms. Nalonni's Fish A' Frying House, Beau sat. With a menu before him, he recalled why he'd chosen the casual eatery. For nearly three months, the actor had lived on Karina Kay. During that time, at the bar & grill, he'd discovered fantastic island fare, including catfish, grilled ahi, and a host of summer salads and drinks. Beau loved the family-friendly atmosphere. Currently, there was boogie-woogie playing, and eatery patrons yelped to it. Beau liked that Karinians hosted everything at the fish fry house; parties, showers, and business lunches.

Beau's gaze traveled the length of the deck where his family of friends sat. Beneath sago palms and twinkling lights, he knew they were in for a treat. Therefore he grinned when their server asked, "Who's ready for Ms. Nalonni's good ol' bayou cuisine?"

Raising glasses, some of which boasted cutesy umbrellas or straight liquor, Beau's peops began to call out what they would have, as his daughter climbed onto his lap. "Doose," she said and pointed. Knowing she meant juice, he allowed her a sip of pink lemonade. Beau heard people call out a muffuletta, fried chicken & waffles, gumbo, and shrimp & grits, all great choices. "Leave room for dessert, y'all," Beau called, as another group celebrated their own event. Leaning over, Beau spoke to his daughter's Paw-Paw. "Deac, you've gotta try the banana custard."

The gray-haired man nodded, eying his menu, "Thinking 'bout that, *and* the peach cobbler."

IN the morning, Beau tossed back the striped sheet. While donning a pair of cotton lounge pants, he vaguely recalled his dream. Not wanting to wake Saavion in the guestroom, Beau quietly padded through his bayou country home.

He passed his baby's room, empty because Gemma had stayed the night with her Mom and siblings. Where, Beau wondered, was his German shepherd? Usually, the big clumsy pup called Shep followed him everywhere. Passing a curio containing precious things, Beau recalled those who'd passed on. They had been in his dream. He had seen his first love, sweet southern Tony, with the chipped tooth. Also present had been Grandma Lacey and Pa Fulton. Jervais, Beau's little dancer friend, was there, along with his former roommate Ronni. Beau's beloved uncle Brantley *and* Gypsy had appeared. All were gloriously healthy and out on the beach behind his home. Garbed in white, each person had happily waved, seemingly telling Beau to go on. Not wanting to leave them but aware of their love and blessings, he had done so.

Beau woke. His heart had ached, but not as severely as it had in the past. He made coffee, and fed JaMocha kitty. Remembering his beautiful dream, Beau felt a bitter but sweet sense of joy. Passing through his living room, with a mug in hand, he glanced at photos. There was a sepia picture of his aunt and uncle as a young couple. There *he* was too, with Saavion, bent over Gemma at only days old. She had Saav's sunlit hair and skin color. Beau then eyed a candid shot of Brett, Mireya, and Arlise, and one of Ms. Fannie, the day lady, kissing six-month-old Gemma. There were photos of all his nieces and nephews, Valeria's kids included. There was even one of a sudsy Gemma being bathed by her Momma. Beau smiled at little round Nell, done up in an ecru wedding dress, her head lace-covered, just seconds after her and the Deacon's nuptials, and Beau remembered. Today was *his* day! Today, before God and others, *he* would commit to loving one man till death did them part.

Out back of DeVeaux house—which his older neighbors would always call the old Habersham place—Beau stood on the veranda. He stared at tall loblolly pines. On the damp side were swamp trees: cypress and tupelo, dripping with Spanish moss. In the morning sun, Beau eyed lovely pastel begonias and gardenia bushes. The actor felt he was doing quite well for one who had never known the names of flowers. He even had geraniums in pots, and alyssum, like back at his Long Island home.

Suddenly Beau wondered if bayou country was in his blood. His aunt and her brother Emmett, his father, and the DeVeaux clan had migrated from Louisiana. Perhaps that was why Beau loved Karina Cay from the moment he'd read about it in his friend's book. Maybe that was why he'd felt at home the second he'd stepped on the ferry and saw marsh grass and ospreys, before he became cognizant of the humidity and salty spray.

Seating himself on rustic furniture with African fabric pillows, Beau stared out at the brick walk. It led through a mile of seagrass. The bricks joined the beach's horizontal wooden boardwalk to form a T. Gazing at his gazebo-like pier, Beau realized he loved this new simple life. He loved the quiet and the private beach—upon which he saw a man loping, with two dogs. Forgetting the driftwood bonfires that he and his husband would have in the evenings, Beau blinked. The man coming from the beach was Saavion. The dog that began racing Beau's way was Shep, the big clumsy puppy. Frost, Beau's husky, trotted alongside Saavion. Beau watched as from boardwalk to bricks, the puppy outpaced the others to greet him. Grinning, Beau stood and suddenly felt overjoyed.

AT noon, sexy in linen slacks and a shirt, Beau sat in Ms. Nalonni's upscale restaurant for those with discriminating tastes. He was glad that his aunt, the deacon, his longtime friend Valeria René, her husband Fabian, and her parents Chitra and Horace, along with his aunt's beloved friends Amy and Dr. Foster, had appeared at The Constellation. Also in attendance were chef JeRell and Ms. Lillie, Jervais's mom. Thomas had begged off, but Beau didn't blame his brother. The younger man wanted to spend as much time as possible with Nurse Gina. Besides, the couple would be at the ceremony. With blazing sun behind white plantation blinds, Beau and guests sat in an exotic enclosed outdoor room. As they started with mimosas, fruit and parfaits, Beau gazed at those he had invited to brunch. Eyeing their lovely array of resort wear, he revealed what each person had meant to him, down through the years. As platters of crepes, pancakes, quiches, and breakfast meats appeared, Beau spoke to curly-locked Valeria René and pink-cheeked Amy. "I truly wish *Ronni*," his former roommate and friend, "could have been with us today."

Addressing JeRell, Beau wondered aloud if he would soon lose his chef. Indeed Beau had noticed. His oft-times dour houseman had become sweet on Ms. Nalonni, the island's brown-skinned restaurateur.

AT the *Canopus Arms*, Beau lounged. After a facial and a shower, in the late afternoon, he relaxed on an accent chair, the peachy-pink of a guava-inside. And he remembered. Back when he'd previously visited, his friend April had picked him up from the same resort. In the presidential suite, Beau eyed pristine white furniture and carpet. He saw crisp green silk throw pillows. They brought to mind the guava's rind. Gazing away from an enormous framed flower likeness gracing one wall, Beau realized he would soon need to slip into his wedding attire. However, not before he finished with his daughter. Prettily outfitted, she tottered at sliding glass doors, closed to the ocean beyond. With her curly hair a huge halo about her head, the ten-month-old dropped down.

Unwilling to allow Beau to put small diamond studs in her ears, the little one quickly crawled away.

Loud enough for the women in his wedding party to hear, Beau grumbled. "Kiss, why won't you or Mireya help me?"

Busy dressing, unseen, Kismet reminded him, "Yesterday I said 'leave the earrings with me,' but you didn't."

"So now," Mireya called out, "you're on your own, friend."

Stunning in coral, the color that the women would also wear, Déja took pity on Beau. The fourteen-year-old caught her baby sister. Holding the squirming toddler, Déja quickly affixed the tiny earrings. Releasing baby Gemma, Déja called to her other sister, a flower girl, "Come Leez."

Belize, the little girl twin, hid, but Arlise, also a flower girl, appeared. As Kismet's teenager fussed over Mireya's daughter, Kismet's girl twin reappeared. Six-year-old Belize toted Beau's kicking-mad baby.

Why did the kids insist on carrying Gemma? Beau wondered as he separated them. Thinking about Saavion in the men's suite, the handsome dad wondered. How had he gotten stuck with the ladies?

Oh. He'd wanted to be with the baby that he currently soothed.

Brett entered, lovely in a cocktail dress. With her hair fashionably slicked back, she announced, "Time for the ride to the chapel."

Having quickly donned a couture white linen tunic and matching pants, Beau re-entered the living room. He burst out laughing, just like he had the night before. Swinging his ten-month-old up onto an arm, he nuzzled her pudgy neck. "Dad has to get hold of himself. Doesn't he?"

The baby nodded as though she understood. Beau chuckled, and to think he'd wondered whether or not he'd make a loving father. Sheesh, he mused, he had nothing but love for his beautiful baby.

Grabbing her purse, Kismet patted the baby's dress down. Breezing toward the door, she called Belize, Arlise, and Déja. "Mireya, forget that lip goo. You're beautiful enough. Come on y'all, we gon get married!"

STANDING Before the altar, in the lovely, candle-lit chapel, filled with candles and scent, Beau realized. In a minute, it would all be over. No, he amended. In a moment, *the ceremony* would end, but the *next phase of his life* would begin – and he couldn't wait!

When he tuned back in, the officiant said he could salute his life partner. Realizing all present expected him and Saavion Kennings to kiss, Beau gladly obliged.

Hugging his man, Saavion whispered, "I'm so glad we did this."

April Alisa Marquette

As those congregated cheered, Beau palmed the back of Saavion's head. With their lips meeting again, Beau admitted, "Me too, baby. Me too." Turning, he reached for his daughter, and he and Saavion both kissed the baby's cheeks. However, squirming, little Ms. Busy only wanted "Down. Down!" she vehemently repeated, causing her daddies and others to chuckle.

THE sunset reception took place at the G. Baptiste Constellation Conservatory with its high Palladian windows, arched ceiling, and flagstone floor. Gazing about, Beau felt as though slender Brett had really outdone herself. Sure, his ceremony, at the clapboard chapel, had been a lovely little affair, but his reception took the cake!

As he and Saavion Kennings enjoyed the groom & groom's first dance, they floated along to Vocalist Mz Diamond's rendition of George Gershwin's *S'Wonderful.* As the songstress crooned, *"It's marvelous, that you should you should care for me...,"* Beau felt those were the very sentiments of his heart. He hummed along as the ingénue intoned, *"It's awfully nice... It's paradise..."*

The baby grand trickled and trilled, along with the soft brush of the drummer's high hat. On the song's bridge, Beau noticed his aunt and her dapper deacon. In a cocktail suit and a tuxedo, she and he joined the newlyweds. As the twosome gingerly stepped about, others came forth.

Raising Saavion's hand, Beau pressed a kiss to slender fingers. Again, Beau recalled that his friend Brett had outdone herself. She'd had perfumed hand soaps, along with scented lotion and candles, all in his wedding colors, placed in the restrooms. Brett had even had a three-tiered bandbox constructed for the live musicians. Glancing around the extended dining area, Beau saw that all was elegant, in hues of coral and warm gold. He saw ambient lighting and candles gracing each table.

With music gently wafting over him, Beau was loath to let the song go. Yet as the number began to fade, with the pianist's nimble fingers tripping lightly over the ivories, the newlyweds left the dance floor. As the band slid into the Jones' Girls *Nights Over Egypt*, Beau greeted guests. However, catching Saavion again so that they might move to the funky beat, Beau glanced at coral-hued begonia topiaries. He saw round tables covered in crinkled gold chiffon. He saw sheer ribbon ties on chairs, and he realized his event planner friend had truly gone above and beyond. She had seen to all the frippery, details with which he would not have been so bothered. When he left the dance floor, lithely moving through the room that was open to the beach on one side and the flagstone garden on the other, Beau felt as though he floated in a beautiful breezy dream. He approached guests who sipped champagne. Above the music that gently rose and fell, he fingered his platinum wedding band and said he trusted all were enjoying themselves.

Really, he couldn't believe the amount of people who'd turned out to celebrate with him and Saavion. With many of his guests, Beau shared a chuckle. Tall and buff conversed with basketball's five-time Hall of Famer. Beau discussed his nearly complete movie soundtrack with Joseph Forrester, and he kissed Abigail, the music producer's better half. Beau thanked the lovely brown actress Abrielle Moonion and her baller husband for attending. He guffawed with movie mogul Nyler Terry. And he slow danced with network owner and media titan Opal. Beau sipped a lemon-drop martini with his author friend and new neighbor, April Alisa Marquette. She, he, and real estate tycoon Yael Skylar then raised their glasses in a toast, "To having found DeVeaux House."

Then it was time for the grooms to cut the cake. Beau wasn't sure he wanted to; the five-tiered confection was so beautiful he hated to ruin it. Cutting through a lifelike coral flower, spun sugar dewdrops, and edible gold ribbon, Beau grimaced. Saavion laughed as their knife slid effortlessly through fondant. Within seconds, the grooms sampled moist cake, and one another's fingertips.

As people stood about, petite dishes of Ms. Nalonni's signature desserts and elfin cobblers were served. While guests partook and marveled, Beau offered a short speech. He thanked all for attending and for sharing his and Saavion's joy. Beau mentioned that instead of a wedding registry, he and Brett had come up with the idea of an endowment for the arts. He thanked those present who had generously donated to the fund, named after his first friend, Jervais Krig. Nodding at Jervais' mom, silver-haired Ms. Lillian, Beau announced, "Your donations will enable scores of young people to pursue their dreams of dancing, for years to come. For that, Saav and I are truly grateful."

When music rose, Beau caught his cousin's arm, "Dance with me a minute." Cuz said he had something to share. On the flagstones, Beau noticed his brother. Thom danced with nurse Gina. Boy, did she and he clean up nicely. Beau saw his drummer, Kendu too, and his assistant, red-haired Tatum. Beau noticed his head of security. Wonder why Boulder intently watched Mireya, of all people?

On his left, Beau saw others. Yet his eyes strayed back to a tall, tan physician, Gemma's doctor. Heck, if there weren't a dozen tales about the man that Karinians called Doc Dear! Come to think of it, Beau believed April had hinted that she was working on the physician's story. That, Beau couldn't wait to read! Noticing the sensuous woman in the doctor's arms, Beau remembered. The little mocha-skinned beauty was a primary school teacher. He'd heard that on Miraunga Isle, where his movie would be based, Doc Dear's interracial relationship had stirred up a hornet's nest. On that little island, African-American, Gullah, Latinx, white, and Native peoples had managed to coexist for centuries, but nowadays, folk chose sides. There, where Beau had just wrapped filming, it seemed many weren't keen on the eligible white doctor seeing the younger attractive black teacher, in this day and age!

Forgetting island drama, Beau thought back to what he wanted to tell his cousin. Oh. Yeah. He reminded her that often brides and grooms gave each other wedding gifts. "So in that tradition, I gave Saavion a gift...one that includes Gemma Janell."

The Momma's interest was piqued. "Now, how does that work?"

"Well..." Beau explained. He'd had DeVeaux House, and the surrounding property, entailed, for Gemma Janell Kennings-DeVeaux. There was also a trust created to maintain all. "Never in Gemma's lifetime, or that of her descendants, can the property be lost or sold. If Saav and I never divorce, he can live out his days there, even if I pass."

"So our Gem will always have *a home*," Kismet whispered. Touched beyond words, her eyes filled. "Diddley, you think of everything."

"Got the idea from you," Beau nodded, "when you insisted on your egg." Turning, he deposited his first cousin in the arms of the man she'd married, long ago. "I think," Beau said, noting her surprise, "it's time you and Lyle talk. Shush. Gemma will soon be a year old, and you've said her step-father has proven himself. So gi' da man a chance."

Leaving to catch up with Mireya, Beau gave Lyle an encouraging pat on the back. Then ensnaring the woman who'd lost so much weight due to grief, Beau ignored her protests. "Yo, just one dance," he coaxed, noting the way Boulder yet watched Mireya. "Please, Rey?"

As Beau determinedly swayed with his friend in his arms, she refused to move her feet, and her lower lip trembled. Softly, she began to sob.

"Stop. Stop that," Beau gently commanded, yet swaying, even though Mireya remained motionless. "I understand," the tall man softly revealed, "that you were supposed to slow dance with Gyp tonight..."

Mireya raised shimmering eyes and asked how Beau knew.

"I know," he said and swallowed emotion, "because me too."

Laughter burst out of Mireya, and she choked out, "Gypsy would never have slow danced with you."

"I know." Beau grinned, "but the man *was* fuine. And I did wonder a time or two, what it would have been like. Them big muscular arms..."

"Cut it out." Mireya pushed at Beau. "You're not telling the truth."

"I'm not." Beau no longer played. "Seriously, I never once thought of Gypsy that way. He was my brother. And knowing him like I did—"

Mireya knew what was coming.

"Reya, I know he'd want you to go on; Gyp would want you happy. Girlfriend," Beau softly called, "I'd be the last person to tell you 'it's time.' I'd never presume to know how long, or not, a person should grieve. Still, I am asking you to *come back*, to us. Gyp would not have wanted you like this, a zombie—a cute one, but nonetheless a zombie."

Mireya dropped her head, resting it on Beau's shoulder. "You smell nice. Always," she divulged. "And," she softly admitted, "I'm trying."

Chucking her beneath the chin, Beau said, "I know, babe. Just try a little harder, for Arlise. She needs her mom all the way back."

When his friend-for-life hugged him, Beau knew. Mireya would attempt to do as he had asked. Didn't she always?

Out of his arms, she looked back. "Friend," she called. When Beau turned, she smiled, her eyes shimmering with love for him. "You look so very gay tonight. I only hope you're as happy as you look."

"I really am, boo." With a wink, Beau goofily preened. He and Mireya chuckled. "Rey, you look quite gay tonight, yourself, girl."

When Mireya was tenderly intercepted by Boulder, of all people, Beau found himself standing with Dan, his attorney. Could it be that Bo was sweet on Reya? Beau wondered, as he saw Saavion sidle up, but not too close. Apparently, Dan saw too. The shorter man quickly congratulated Beau. He who had not yet stepped out of the closet called out over music. "Beau, do me something?"

"Depends on whether or not it's doable."

Attorney Dan spoke quickly. "Make mad homo love tonight."

Heartily, Beau laughed. "I will." Beau wanted to tell his lawyer to find someone worthy and do the same. However, aware that Dan wasn't yet ready for that, Beau nodded. "Speak to you soon, Danny Boy."

As the band segued into Michael Bublé's *Save the Last Dance for Me*, Beau winked at Saavion, who announced, "Beau, my sexy husband, I'm gonna allow you to dance with whomever you want, here tonight—"

"Oh, you're gonna *allow* me," Beau teasingly cut in and kissed Saavion's banded hand, "to dance with people, huh?"

"That's right," Saavion jubilantly quipped. "Long as you don't forget who's taking you home; in whose arms you're gonna wind up, later."

Noticing his daughter, asleep on her Nannie's bosom, and that content to rock her, Nell waved him away; Beau caught the sleeve of Saavion's white crepe tunic. Although he longed to hold his baby, to kiss her sweet sleeping brow, maybe even while he stood on the serene, lantern-lit brick walk out back of DeVeaux House, Beau gestured at the beach.

Stepping out into the sultry night, he asked, "Wanna go make out?"

Saavion Delano Kennings chuckled. Grasping Beauregard DeVeaux's hand, the optician nodded. He pulled Beau out onto the moonlit beach, and suddenly feeling ridiculously giddy, both men ran.

Saavion could not have been happier. After all the years of him just waiting, in the wings, Saavion and Beau were married. And they were friends, first and foremost. It was more than Saavion had ever dreamed of, and it was real, and true.

The couple found themselves just beyond the golden light of their reception. With the loll and roll of the ocean surrounding them, the newly joined stood in the surf. In the moonlight they locked lips. As the sea stole sand from beneath their bare feet, neither knew who said it first. However, both men truly meant it. "I love you, husband."

THE END

NOT...

Why not meet again in the new book?

IMPROBABLE
The Cohorts, Generation Next

Photo: Tina Dennis©

As an author, editor, and freelance writer,
April Alisa Marquette
pens fiction as well as non-fiction.
A lover of art and literature, she is committed to creating beautifully
detailed works about people of color and others.
Ever working on something,
she is currently tweaking one of the exciting novels in her series:
The Cohorts, Generation Next
Visit her at www.aprilalisamarquette.net

www.ingramcontent.com/pod-product-compliance
Lightning Source LLC
Chambersburg PA
CBHW032032240626
47154CB00003B/882